Summer
of Love

ALSO BY CARO FRASER

The Summer House Party

Summer *of* Love

Caro Fraser

HEAD *of* ZEUS

First published in the UK in 2018 by Head of Zeus Ltd
This paperback published in the UK in 2019 by Head of Zeus Ltd

Copyright © Caro Fraser, 2018

9 7 5 3 1 2 4 6 8

A catalogue record for this book is available from
the British Library.

ISBN (PB): 9781788541404
ISBN (E): 9781788541374

Typeset by Silicon Chips

Printed and bound in Great Britain by
CPI Group (UK) Ltd, Croydon CR0 4YY

Head of Zeus Ltd
First Floor East
5–8 Hardwick Street
London EC1R 4RG

WWW.HEADOFZEUS.COM

Summer
of Love

1

1949

THE AIR WAS full of the fresh, damp scents of early spring as Meg and Dan Ranscombe turned off the road and walked up the narrow path that led to the back of Woodbourne House. They made a handsome couple – Meg, in her early thirties, was vividly pretty, with dark eyes and chestnut hair curling to her shoulders; Dan, a few years older, was by contrast fair-haired and blue-eyed, his clean-cut features marked by a faint arrogance, a remnant of youthful vanity. They walked in thoughtful silence. It was four years since they had last been to Woodbourne House, the home of Sonia Haddon, Meg's aunt and Dan's godmother.

'I'm glad we took the train instead of driving,' said Dan, breaking the quiet. 'I have fond memories of this walk.'

They paused by a big, whitewashed stone barn standing at the foot of a sloping apple orchard.

'Uncle Henry's studio,' murmured Meg. 'I remember that summer, having to traipse down every morning with barley water and biscuits for him while he was painting.'

Sonia's husband, Henry Haddon, had been an acclaimed artist in his day, and in pre-war times to have one's portrait painted by him had had considerable cachet. In Britain's post-war modernist world, his name had fallen out of fashion.

Dan stood gazing at the barn, lost in his own memories: that final day of the house party twelve years ago, when he had come down to the studio to say farewell to his host. Finding Henry Haddon, his trousers round his ankles, locked in an embrace with Madeleine, the nanny, against the wall of the studio had been absurd and shocking enough, but what had then transpired had been even worse. He could remember still the sound of the ladder crashing to the floor, and the sight of five-year-old Avril peeping over the edge of the hayloft. Presumably the shock of seeing his daughter had brought on Haddon's heart attack. That, and unwonted sexual exertions. The moments afterwards were confused in his memory, although he recalled setting the ladder aright so that Avril could get down, then sending her running up to the house to get someone to fetch a doctor, while he uselessly attempted to revive Haddon. Madeleine, unsurprisingly, had made herself scarce. And the painting – he remembered that. A portrait of Madeleine in her yellow sundress, seated on a wicker chair, head half-turned as though listening to notes of unheard music, or the footfall of some awaited lover. Haddon had been working on it in the days running up to his death, and no doubt the intimacy forged between painter and sitter had led to that brief and ludicrously tragic affair. The falling ladder had knocked it from the easel, and he had picked it up and placed it with its face to the wall next to the other canvases. He didn't to this day know why he had done that. Perhaps as a way of closing off and keeping secret what he had witnessed. To this day nobody but he knew about Haddon's affair with Madeleine. Had the painting ever been discovered? No one had ever mentioned it. Perhaps it was there still, just as he had left it.

Meg glanced at his face. 'Penny for them.'

'Oh, nothing,' said Dan. 'Just thinking about that house party, when you and I first met.'

What a fateful chain of events had been set in motion in the summer of 1936. He had been a twenty-four-year-old penniless journalist, invited to spend several days at Woodbourne House with a handful of other guests. Meeting and falling in love with Meg had led to the clandestine affair they had conducted throughout the war years behind the back of her husband Paul. Its discovery had led to estrangement with much of the family. Paul, a bomber pilot, had been killed on the way back from a raid over Germany, and the possibility that his discovery of the affair might have contributed in some way, on some level, to his death, still haunted them both. They never spoke of it. Meg and Dan were married now, but the guilt of what they had done remained. Meg's mother Helen had been trying for some time to persuade her sister, Sonia, to forgive Meg and Dan, and today's invitation to Woodbourne House was a signal that she had at last relented.

They walked up through the orchard, and when they reached the flagged courtyard at the back of the house Meg said, 'I'm going to the kitchen to say hello to Effie. I don't think I can face Aunt Sonia quite yet. I'll let you go first. Cowardly of me, I know, but I can't help it.' She gave him a quick smile and a kiss, and turned in the direction of the kitchen.

Dan found Sonia at the desk in her little sitting room, answering letters. She looked up as he knocked and put his head round the door.

'There you are,' she said.

'Here I am.'

She rose and surveyed him, her expression sad and thoughtful. She was a tall, attractive woman in her late fifties, with a long, patrician face and an air of pre-war Bloomsbury elegance.

'Thank you for inviting us here today,' said Dan. 'I

know how difficult it must have been, given the way you feel about... well, everything.'

'It wasn't so difficult. Helen made me see how pointless my anger was. What you and Meg did, for whatever selfish reasons, is in the past. Nothing can change what happened, or bring Paul back.'

'We didn't mean to be selfish. We were in love.'

'Lovers are the most selfish people on earth.'

They stood looking at one another in silence for a few seconds, then Dan said, 'Can I... may I hug you?'

She accepted his embrace, then asked, 'Where is Meg?'

'She went to the kitchen to see Effie.'

'Then let's go and find her and have lunch.'

Dan sensed that although the past might be forgiven, it would not lightly be forgotten. Conversation over lunch was tentative to begin with, but when Sonia made the surprising announcement that she was in the process of selling Woodbourne House and moving to London, reserve and awkwardness quickly fell away.

'Oh, Aunt Sonia!' exclaimed Meg. 'You've lived here simply for ever. Won't it be a wrench?'

'If the truth be told, I'm quite relieved. Now we are all being taxed out of existence, the expense of a house this size is really beyond me. The heating alone costs a fortune. And I had to let most of the kitchen garden run to seed this year. We simply don't need all those vegetables. Not like during the war, when the house was full of people.' She sighed, her gaze fixed wistfully on some place in the past. 'At any rate, it will be a blessing not to have to concern myself with leaky gutters and rotting window-frames. They have building managers to look after all that in my new flat.'

'Whereabouts is it?' asked Dan.

'Mount Street, in Mayfair,' replied Sonia. 'It's an excellent location, with the park nearby and Bond Street just around the corner, and the size is perfect – a drawing room, a dining room, and three bedrooms, so Avril and Laura will each have their own room. There's a maid's room, too, but I rather think I'm done with maids. It will do as a spare for visitors. The kitchen and bathroom are all newly fitted – we even have a refrigerator.'

'What do the girls think?' asked Meg.

'They don't know yet. I'll tell them when they come home for the Easter holidays. I doubt if they'll mind very much. Avril is always grumbling about how boring the countryside is, so I'm sure she'll like living in London. I'm afraid Laura may be upset about having to leave her pony, but there are ways round that. I remember riding in Hyde Park as a girl. We'll sort something out.'

'How is Laura enjoying being at big school with Avril?' asked Meg.

'It's hard to tell. Her letters home suggest all is well, but' – Sonia sighed and put her knife and fork together – 'there's no use pretending that Avril won't always resent Laura. I suppose it's hard to share your life and your mother's affection with someone from outside the family. I only hope she isn't making Laura's life difficult.'

'As I recall from my boarding school days, the lower third and the sixth form don't have much to do with one another,' observed Meg, 'so I shouldn't worry.'

'Perhaps it was a mistake to send Laura to Avril's school. But I thought it would be nice for the girls to be there together, if only for a year. Something to look back on.'

Meg couldn't imagine Avril and Laura ever looking back fondly on anything they did together. But Sonia had always had something of a blind spot where the two girls were concerned, tending to ignore the fact that her own daughter, Avril, was a difficult and moody girl, with whom she didn't have the best of relationships, and to pretend that Laura, who wasn't part of the family, but whose temperament and charm invited affection, received no special favouritism.

'I always think it was quite heroic of you to take on Madeleine's baby. Not many people would have.'

'I have only one regret, and that is that the girls don't have a better relationship. Maybe things will improve as they get older. Anyway, on the subject of schools, how is Max looking forward to Eton?'

Meg exchanged a glance with Dan. Max was her son from her marriage to Paul Latimer, and it was something of a sore point with her that Max's education was entirely controlled by the Latimer family trust, set up by Paul to maintain and educate Max at schools of Paul's dictating, until he was twenty-five and came into his inheritance. Meg had been cut out of Paul's will almost entirely. Not that she blamed him for that. But it was hard to have Max's life controlled from beyond the grave.

'That's a couple of years away, Aunt Sonia. He won't go there till he's thirteen.'

Effie, Sonia's cook-cum-maid, arrived to take the plates away.

'Thank you, Effie,' said Sonia. She turned to Meg and Dan. 'Coffee?'

Dan glanced at his watch. 'As long as we don't miss the three-thirty train. I'm off to Berlin next week, and I have a lot to do.'

'Berlin? But it must be in a dreadful state, what with the Russians blockading everything.'

'Precisely why Reuters are sending me.'

'I want to go with him,' said Meg, 'but he won't hear of it.' She paused, and gave her aunt a tentative smile. 'The fact is, I'm expecting a baby.'

'Oh, that's wonderful news! When is it due?'

'October. Just think, you'll be in London by then.'

Effie brought coffee, and Sonia and Meg discussed the exciting prospect of the new baby. At length Dan said to Meg, 'Come on, we should be making a move. We don't want to miss the bus to the station.'

A few rays of March sunshine were struggling through the grey clouds as they stepped outside. Meg glanced wistfully around the familiar lawns and gardens.

'Aren't you the tiniest bit sorry to be leaving, Aunt Sonia? It's been such a wonderful home.'

'Oh, I'm quite over the sentimental part – my main concern is the upheaval. So much clearing out to do.'

'I couldn't help wondering,' said Dan, 'as we came up the back path, when anyone was last in Henry's old studio.'

'No one's been there since the day he died. I simply couldn't face it myself. Such horrid associations.' She paused. 'Henry never kept anything of value down there. But I suppose I shall have to take a look and see if it needs clearing out.'

So the painting of Madeleine must still be there where he had left it. Dan wondered what effect it would have on Sonia when she saw it. Might she make the connection and realise that Henry could be the father of Madeleine's child, whom she had brought up for the past twelve years? Somehow he doubted it.

Sonia watched Meg and Dan make their way through the orchard and past the barn, until they were out of sight. She was profoundly glad she had made her peace with them. Their mistakes lay in the past, and they had a future to look forward to now, and she could be a part of it.

Meg and Dan lived in Belgravia, in a house left to Dan by his father. It was too big for them, and somewhat run-down, but in the years since the war they had never got round to selling it and finding somewhere more suitable. The Saturday after their visit to Woodbourne House, Meg returned home from shopping to find Dan in the study sprawled on the battered green velvet sofa acquired in his Cambridge days, smoking and reading. She gently shoved his legs aside so that she could sit down next to him, and tapped his book. 'What's this you're reading?'

'A poem by W.H. Auden. A very long poem.' He held it up so that Meg could read the title.

'*The Age Of Anxiety*,' she read aloud. '*A Baroque Eclogue*. What's an eclogue?'

'You may well ask. I believe it's the name for a classical style of poem. It's absolutely impenetrable, but then so are most of the things Harry asks me to review.'

'Very generous of you to go on reviewing things for him, when he hardly ever pays you.'

'Well, as he's my oldest and dearest friend, it would seem churlish to refuse.'

'Has he got a title for this new magazine of his?'

'The last I heard it was going to be called *Modern Critical Review*. Anyway, now that he's come into a bit of money, I expect to be paid properly for all my pieces. It's not going to be like the old days, when he ran *Ire* on a shoestring from a cupboard in Soho.'

'Oh yes, the great inheritance. So, just how rich was this great-uncle of his?'

'Rich enough to allow Harry to buy some country pile in Kent, apparently. He telephoned to tell me about it half an hour ago. He's very excited. Says it's a bit dilapidated, but he's enjoying renovating it.'

'Harry having money – it's quite a strange notion.'

'I know. He's invited us down to see the place. I thought we could drive down on Monday. I'm off to Berlin on Tuesday, so we won't get another chance for ages.'

'Lovely. I'll go and check we've got enough petrol coupons.'

On Monday they drove to Kent to see Harry's new house.

'I wonder if this is going to be one of Harry's sudden enthusiasms that he'll tire of once the novelty has worn off,' mused Meg, frowning at the map in her hand.

'I doubt it,' replied Dan. 'Taking on a property is a big thing. I don't know how much he's inherited, but if he's spending money on the place he'll see it through. Besides, I know he's hungry for some kind of stability. His world rather fell apart when he lost Laurence, and he's been trying to rebuild it ever since.'

'Who's Laurence? I've never heard Harry mention him.'

'He was before your time. He was Harry's lover, much younger than Harry. When he went to fight in

Spain Harry went through hell, terrified he wouldn't come back. He survived, though. Then when the war came, Harry wanted Laurence to get out of conscription – which he could have, of course. They both could have, if they'd been prepared to be classed as suffering from sexual perversion.' Dan smiled. 'Harry always maintained he revelled rather than suffered. But neither of them wanted to take that way out. Laurence was killed in Burma, just before the war ended, and Harry was heartbroken. I think perhaps buying this place and making it a proper home is his way of trying to find some peace of mind.'

'How sad. Poor Harry.' Meg glanced out of the window. 'That was a sign for Adisham, so I think we've come too far. The map says the turning is before that. Honestly, this place is like a rabbit warren.'

Dan sighed and turned the car around in a gateway. 'I'll stop talking so that you can pay attention to the map.'

Fifteen minutes later they found the house, down a narrow road overhung with trees just coming into leaf. A faded wooden sign bearing the word 'Chalcombe' was attached to the pillar of a stone gateway, whose rusted gates were thrown back against tangles of nettles. Dan turned the car up a curving driveway bordered by sprawling shrubs. The house, when it came into view, was compact, built of pinkish-grey brick, and consisted of two storeys, with dormer attic windows in the slate roof adding a third level. Though not dilapidated, it had an unmistakable air of desolation. The grounds were overgrown, and among the tangle of nettles and brambles the remnants of a garden could be discerned, with a stone urn at the centre of what had once been a lawn. A semicircle of trees framed both the house and garden.

As they got out of the car, Dan and Meg could hear the sound of hammering. The front door stood open, and they stepped inside into a stone-flagged central hallway, with doors leading to adjoining rooms, and a staircase curving up to the next floor. Through the doorways they could see evidence of neglect, patches of crumbling plaster, stained ceilings and dusty floors. A passageway led from the hall to back of the house, from where the hammering was coming, and Dan and Meg ventured down this, emerging into a large, light room, at the end of which workmen were working on what appeared to be the construction of a conservatory. Harry, who was standing with a tweed-suited man poring over plans spread out on a trestle table, greeted them. He was a tall, barrel-chested bear of a man, with thick, dark hair, a short beard, and a rich, drawling voice. He was a notorious member of London's homosexual fraternity, and in the early days of their friendship Dan had suspected Harry nursed hopes of something less platonic, but after twelve years the relationship had found a satisfactory level of mutual fondness. Meg, too, had come to know and love Harry, although she hoped that his latest stroke of good fortune, the inheritance from his great-uncle, would put an end to his regular applications to Dan for loans of a few pounds 'to see him through'.

Harry introduced them to his builder, then said, 'Come, I'll give you a grand tour. This' – he gestured around the room – 'is a sort of main reception room, and I'm adding a conservatory at the end. Somewhere light and airy with big doors giving on to the garden so that one can eat breakfast outside in summer.'

He showed them around the house, enthusiastically conjuring from the neglected spaces visions of beautiful rooms, then led them outside and explained his plans for the restoration of the garden. While Harry and Dan wandered to the edges of the garden for a smoke, Meg sat down on a stone bench and gazed around. She recognised the ring of trees encircling the garden as mulberries. There had been a mulberry tree outside the back door of Hazelhurst, the home she and Paul had shared after their marriage, when they were still happy – before the war, before Dan and all that had ensued. She sighed, shaking off the memories. She could see why Harry had fallen in love with Chalcombe. Nestling in its little valley, it possessed a wonderful tranquillity. It was rather mournful in its present state of neglect, but it wasn't hard to imagine it coming alive, the garden tamed, the rooms bright and tastefully furnished, filled with life. She felt she knew what Harry wanted to bring about, the kind of home he wanted it to be.

Dan and Harry strolled back, and Harry pointed out a dilapidated barn that stood to one side of the house.

'As far as I can tell, someone used it for hatching pheasants. I'm thinking of knocking it down and putting a hothouse there. It would be amusing to cultivate something exotic, like orchids, don't you think?'

'You sound like you're going to be a tremendous man of leisure,' said Meg. 'What about the magazine?'

'Oh, I'll run it in London. I don't intend to spend all my time down here. Besides, once Chalcombe has been restored to its former glory I'll have blown most of Great-Uncle Cedric's money. I still need to earn a crust. Can't imagine not working, really.'

'I never had you down as a man who hankered after a country retreat,' said Dan, 'but I have to say it's a topping place.'

'I want you and Meg to promise you'll come and stay this summer. I'm determined it will be utterly perfect by then.'

'We promise.'

'Splendid! Now, let's jump in the motor and see if we can find a pub for a spot of lunch.'

2

Sonia told Avril and Laura about the move to London when they came home for the Easter holidays.

'I didn't write to tell you,' Sonia told them, 'in case it made you upset.'

'I'm not upset,' said Avril. 'I'd rather live in London than be stuck away in the boring old countryside.'

'But what about Socks?' asked Laura anxiously.

'Well, darling, I rather think it will be difficult to find stables for Socks in the middle of London.'

Avril glanced at Laura. 'Oh, for heaven's sake, don't start blubbing. It's only a pony.'

The two girls were markedly different in looks. Avril, seventeen years old, had brown hair cut in a straight bob, and although not pretty in any conventional sense, her full mouth and sulky dark eyes gave her a certain compelling, intense attraction. Laura was slender, tall for her age, and delicately pretty, with unusual grey eyes, high cheekbones, and dark brows and lashes that contrasted with her blonde hair.

'Don't be unkind, Avril. Laura dear, you can always ride in the park in London, and besides, you'll soon be outgrowing Socks. We must just make the best of the changes. We shall be moving in a month's time, so you must both start sorting out your belongings.'

Over the next few days, with Effie's help, Sonia turned out all the rooms in the house, deciding what would be kept, what discarded, and what, if anything, put into storage. Wardrobes, drawers and cupboards were emptied, boxes filled, and labels stuck on furniture earmarked for the Mayfair flat. While Laura was busy sorting out nursery toys for the local orphanage, Sonia and Avril made a tour of the library to see which books should be kept.

'There isn't room for one fifth of them in Mayfair,' said Sonia, surveying the shelves. 'We must decide what we want to take with us, and then I shall have someone come up from London to value the rest.' She sighed. 'What a labour it all is. I despair at the thought of the attics. We had a good clear-out up there for your Aunt Helen's rummage sales during the war, but there's still no end of junk to be gone through.'

'Why go through it?' asked Avril. 'If it's junk why not just chuck it all?'

'Because one never knows. Oh, that reminds me. We

must go and see what's in the barn. We might as well do it today. It's forecast to rain tomorrow.'

Together they walked down through the orchard to the barn. At the sight of it a kind of shutter seemed to slide back in Avril's mind. Revealing... what? Not so much a memory as an unsettling feeling. She had no clear recollection of ever having been in it. When she was a child her father's studio had been very much out of bounds, and since his death it had remained locked, a forbidding place she had no wish to visit.

The barn door had become swollen with the damp of a dozen winters, and they had to push hard to get it open. Mother and daughter stepped inside. A faint scent of turpentine hung in the air, strangely evocative. Paint-splashed trestle tables stood beneath the window, and the floor was littered with tubes of paint and unswept shards of broken jars. A few canvases were stacked against one wall, and in the middle of the studio stood a wicker chair. The light that slanted through the big windows, once full and bright, was dappled now with shadows from the bushes and young trees that had grown up outside. A pigeon flapped from a high beam with a whirring clatter of wings, startling them, and circled the space in the hayloft.

'There must be some broken slates up there,' murmured Sonia.

Avril bent down and picked up some tubes of paint

from the floor, and put them on a table. She walked over to the big ladder leading up to the hayloft, and stared up into the darkness. Again she experienced that sense of some shadow in her mind. Something frightening, elusive. She walked over to the canvases stacked against the wall and began to turn them over. They were mostly blank and untouched, though a couple were daubed with sketchy, preparatory brushstrokes. The last she turned over was a portrait, complete and perfect, of Madeleine, her old nanny, sitting on a wicker chair in a yellow sundress, head half-turned in a listening attitude. Avril stared at it, wondering why the picture seemed to strike some strange chord of recollection.

She brought it over to her mother. 'Look at this.'

Sonia turned to look, and put her hand to her mouth. 'Oh, my goodness! How extraordinary. How absolutely extraordinary!' She stretched out her hand to touch the canvas. 'It's the painting your father was working on before he died. Madeleine sat for him for a few days. I had quite forgotten. To think it's been sitting here all this time.'

Avril studied the painting with detachment. She was already developing a good eye, and she knew that this portrait, among the many of her father's that she had seen, possessed a special quality.

'I remember complaining about the time she spent here,' Sonia went on, 'when she was meant to be looking after you.' She took the painting from Avril and gazed at it for a long moment. 'I should give it to Laura. I really feel it belongs to her.'

The rapidity with which Avril's mind dealt with this suggestion was belied by the reflective, calm tone of her response. 'Don't you think perhaps Laura's a little young to be given something so valuable? Besides, it might upset her. Why don't you keep it for her and give it to her when she's older, when she's ready to appreciate it?'

Sonia considered this. 'You're right. I could have it framed and give it to her when she's twenty-one. I shall put it away until then.'

Sonia found a piece of canvas to wrap the painting in, and then, once she and Avril had searched the studio and satisfied themselves there was nothing else of interest or value, they went back to the house.

After the girls had returned to school, Sonia moved to Mayfair. Avril and Laura saw their new home for the first time in the summer half-term. Laura, who was still grieving over the loss of her beloved pony, was far from impressed with London. In the wake of the war the city was still run-down and dilapidated, with unrepaired blocks of flats, shored-up buildings and shabby shops, and bomb sites full of weeds and scavenging urchins. The grey streets and mansion blocks of Mayfair seemed dreary and unfriendly. Avril, on the other hand, was well content. She was nearly eighteen, in her final term of school, and was looking forward to going to Italy in the autumn to study fine art. She had always enjoyed expeditions to London art galleries, and spent much of that week wandering around the prestigious little Mayfair galleries, and visiting the Wallace Collection and the Tate, investigating and learning. The bustle of city life had a special savour for her; on the cusp of being grown-up, it seemed to her to hold an underlying sense of excitement and promise, a far cry from the inertia and seclusion of Surrey.

Meg's son, Max, was spending a day at his grandmother's house in Chelsea during the half-term break. Helen, who at fifty-six was a prettier, more compact and fashionable version of her older sister, whisked into the drawing room in search of Max and found him lying on his stomach reading a copy of *The Hotspur*.

'There you are! We need to get ready to go out,' said Helen. 'I've organised an expedition to the zoo with Laura and your great-aunt Sonia. You remember Laura, don't you?'

Ten-year-old Max looked up at his grandmother. He had his late father's handsome, grave features and Meg's dark, waving hair and brown eyes. 'Yes. But I haven't seen her for ages. Or Great-Aunt Sonia. Why haven't I?'

'Well...' Helen hesitated. She had no idea what explanation, if any, Meg had ever given her son for the estrangement from her aunt. 'I suppose it's been difficult, with Great-Aunt Sonia living so far away. But now she's moved to London, maybe you and Laura will see more of one another. Now, off you go and get ready. And be sure to brush your hair.'

Sonia and Laura were waiting for them outside the gates of the zoo. Laura gave Max a wary smile. He'd been seven when she'd last seen him, just after his father had died. Apart from playing together in the woods at Woodbourne House in the den Dan had built for them, and with the gardener's little dog, Star, she didn't remember much of their time together.

'Well, say hello, you two,' said Helen.

The children murmured greetings, and fell into step behind Helen and Sonia as they approached the ticket booth.

'Have you been to the zoo before?' Max asked Laura.

'No. We only moved to London a few weeks ago.'

This gave Max, who had been to London Zoo often, a certain confidence.

'The boa constrictor's the best thing. All the snakes are good. Some of them are so poisonous that if they bit you, you'd be dead in seconds.' Laura looked suitably impressed, and Max went on, 'When the war started they had to destroy them all, in case they escaped in a bombing raid and killed people.'

'Aunt Sonia says there's a bear that's just had cubs.'

'They might be fun. The chimps' tea party is jolly good, too. And I want to see the elephants.'

They spent two hours going round the zoo. Max had a gruesome fascination for the snakes and tropical spiders, Laura was enchanted by the three new brown bear cubs frolicking in their enclosure, and both children screamed and laughed delightedly when an elephant tried to pluck Max's school cap from his head with his trunk. By the time Helen and Sonia sat down in the café for a cup of tea and a bun, Laura and Max had rekindled their friendship and were perfectly at ease with one another. Helen gave them money for ice creams, and permission to wander over to the reptile house, while she and Sonia drank their tea and talked.

'They seem to get on as well as they ever did,' remarked Helen.

'It's nice for Laura to get out of the house. She's still mourning her pony. I'm going to arrange for her to go riding in the park, but at the moment she rather mopes around. Avril spends all her time revising for her exams. Not,' sighed Sonia, 'that she'd be much company for Laura even if she wasn't. They'll never be close in the way I'd hoped.'

Helen had to bite her tongue and refrain from reminding Sonia that she'd more or less predicted this when Laura was still an infant. Instead she said, 'Max was asking me earlier why he hadn't seen Laura or you for so long. I didn't know what to say. Obviously he hasn't the least idea about Meg and Dan – I mean, about their affair.'

'And long may it stay that way. Think of the damage it would do.'

'Quite. Max positively dotes on Dan, but at the same time he worships his father's memory. If he were ever to find out that while his father was fighting for his country, his mother and Dan—'

'It will never come to that,' said Sonia firmly. 'The past is the past. It's just as well that I've made up with Meg and Dan. One less thing for the boy to wonder about.'

Max and Laura licked their ice cream cones and watched the terrapins slip slowly in and out of the water.

'Do you remember the tortoise at Woodbourne House?' asked Laura.

Max nodded. 'I took him inside once and he did a wee on Great-Aunt Sonia's rug.'

Laura giggled. 'We've got a tortoise at my school. He belongs to the gardener. He hibernated all winter in a box filled with straw.'

'What's your school like?'

'It's fun. Though it was a bit horrid last term when people found out about my mother. Avril told them.'

Max broke the bottom off his cone and scooped ice cream into it. He held it up to Laura. 'Look, two ice creams!' She smiled, and he asked, 'What about your mother?' He had never troubled to think about Laura's place in the world. All he knew was that she wasn't Avril's sister. His mother had never said anything more, but then, he'd never asked.

After the events of last term, Laura had learned that the best way to deal with her illegitimacy was to confront it head on, before people had a chance to judge and denigrate.

'She wasn't married. She had me and she left me with Aunt Sonia.'

Max had a hazy notion that having a baby when you weren't married was a pretty low thing. He felt sorry for Laura. 'Do you miss her?'

'My mother? No. I never knew her, so how could I?' This wasn't true; Laura had often felt an ache of loss, but she couldn't admit it to Max.

'I suppose.' Max finished his ice cream, then said, 'I miss my father, but that's because I remember him. He was a war hero, you know. He got the VC.'

'Aunt Sonia told me. He must have been jolly brave.'

'He was. Dan was, too. He used to blow stuff up, bridges and trains and things. But a lot of the things he did were secret, so they couldn't give him a medal.'

'He's your stepfather now, isn't he?'

Max nodded. 'He's a lot of fun. And he was at school with my father, so he tells me things about him, how brainy he was and good at cricket, and I like that.'

'Dan's nice,' agreed Laura. 'I think he's very handsome.'

Max had no views on this. 'Have you got any good games at your house? Grandma's only got dominoes and draughts.'

'We've got a whole games compendium, and

Monopoly. But I've no one to play with, because Avril's always got her nose stuck in a book. She's got exams next term. Why don't you ask your grandmother if you can come over to ours tomorrow?'

The following week, when Max had gone back to school, Meg invited her mother and aunt for tea.

'How is Dan getting on in Germany?' asked Helen.

'Oh, he's fine, but he says Berlin is terribly grim. The airlift kept people from starving, but the city's still desperately short of food. Apparently the Tiergarten has been turned into one vast potato field, and the Russians have put up a monument in it to their dead soldiers.'

'Imagine!' exclaimed Helen. 'A Red Army monument in the middle of the German capital – Hitler must be spinning in his grave.'

'Dan says the rebuilding of the city is painfully slow. Poor people.' Meg handed round the cake plate.

'I wouldn't feel too much sympathy for them if I were you,' remarked Sonia, helping herself to a piece of seed cake. 'I shouldn't think they'd have had much for us, if they'd won the war. They deserve to feel humiliated and defeated.'

'That attitude isn't going to help them rebuild the country, is it?' replied Meg. 'And that's important, if we want to avoid another war. Dan says the airlift has done a lot to foster good feeling for the West. The Russians would have starved Berlin out, if they'd had their way.

He called it the greatest battle ever fought without a shot being fired.'

Helen gave a little smile; Dan's every word seemed to be gospel. 'Well, I'm very glad you're here and not there, at any rate,' she remarked.

'Yes, but it's lonely now Max is back at school. Still, Dan will be home for a couple of days next week. That's something.'

But Dan's brief return to London merely reinforced Meg's sense of isolation.

'It's ridiculous – instead of enjoying having you here, I can think of nothing but how miserable it's going to be when you go.' Meg was stretched out on the sofa while Dan leafed through the post that had arrived in his absence. He ripped open an envelope.

'Ah, a letter from Harry.' He lifted the hem of Meg's skirt and gently stroked her thigh as he scanned the first page. 'He says he's had the devil of a time with the builders at Chalcombe, but they're done now and he's pleased with the result. Says the garden is taking shape.' He turned the page over and read aloud. '"I have to say I'm at a loss as to how to decorate and furnish the place. I'm not much of a hand at that kind of thing and don't entirely trust my own taste. Until I do that, of course, I can't have people to stay, which is what I want above all. My whole vision for Chalcombe is to have guests to bring the place alive. I want the sound of chatter and laughter, the clink of glasses, long, lazy dinners on summer evenings with plenty of wine and good conversation. But at this rate I think it's going to be a dull, empty summer."' Dan read on for a moment or two, then folded the letter up. He bent and kissed Meg softly on the lips. 'What he needs is someone like you. Didn't you design the whole interior of Hazelhurst?'

Meg returned his kiss lingeringly. 'Every last detail. It was my great project. I utterly adored doing it.'

Dan sat back, regarding her. 'Why don't I write to Harry and suggest you take up residence at Chalcombe for the summer, Max as well?'

Meg shifted restlessly. 'It seems rather an imposition on poor Harry.'

He bent and kissed her again, deftly unbuttoning her dress and slipping his hand inside to caress her breast. 'Not if you're offering your services free of charge to help him decorate. Think how much better it would be for you and Max if you could be in the Kent countryside, arranging Harry's house for him, rather than moping around in Belgravia all summer.'

Dan kissed her again, his hands straying downwards, and she felt her body respond to his touch, the way it always did. Always had. Then his hand was between her legs, and she let out a little gasp of longing as his fingers did their work. She heard him unfasten the buckle of his belt and kept her eyes closed, relishing the anticipation that rose to an ache of desire until the moment when he was inside her, and the weight of her anxieties fell away, leaving only this tender, urgent reality.

Afterwards she murmured, 'You can write to Harry, if you like. I'll go to Chalcombe and help him with the house, if he'll have me. But you must promise to come as often as you can.'

'I promise.'

3

ON HER FIRST morning at Chalcombe, Meg was woken by early sunlight filtering through the makeshift muslin curtain. She lay for a few minutes absorbing her surroundings. The room in which she'd slept contained nothing more than a bed and a bedside cabinet. She knew from her brief tour of the house the night before that, beyond basic bedroom furniture and the necessaries of the kitchen, Harry had so far made no other decorating or furnishing inroads. The plaster-pale walls of the house, the bare boards of its floors and its naked windows, all awaited her inspiration. The thought that Harry was willing to trust her with the project made her both excited and nervous.

She went to the adjoining bathroom to wash. It was a clever idea of Harry's to have arranged a bathroom for each bedroom, but she wondered how much it must have cost. She wondered, too, what the budget would be for furnishing Chalcombe. When she and Paul had bought Hazelhurst, money had been no object. It was, she reflected, the only way she knew of doing things – extravagantly.

By the time she had finished dressing it was still only half past seven, and when she went downstairs the house was silent. She stood for a moment gazing around the empty hallway, then wandered in and out of the main reception rooms, trying to visualise colours for the walls and woodwork, already planning and assessing.

Hearing feet on the staircase, she returned to the hall and saw Harry coming downstairs, dressed in sandals, flannels and a capacious white linen shirt, with Hamlet, the young springer spaniel he had acquired a few months ago, at his heels.

'Good morning!' he exclaimed. 'Hope you slept well?'

'Yes, thanks. I was just having a look around, trying to work out where to make a start.'

'Time enough for that after breakfast. Come on.'

Harry led the way to the kitchen, Hamlet pattering behind him. What had previously been a small, rather awkward area, with a separate scullery and larder, had been transformed into an open, airy space, with light spilling in through a large window overlooking the sink. The wooden floor had been relaid with warm terracotta tiles. The walk-in pantry had been retained, the oven, hob and refrigerator were all brand new, and a large wooden table and chairs stood in the middle of the room.

'You should find bread in the crock in the pantry,' said Harry. 'And butter and marmalade. I'll make us some coffee.'

When the bread was toasted and the percolated coffee piping hot, Harry put together a tray with plates, knives, cups and napkins and took it through to the adjoining conservatory. He folded back the doors to let the morning air spill in, fresh with the scent of overnight rain and filled with the promise of sunshine.

'Still too damp to sit outside,' he said, 'but this is the next best thing.'

They breakfasted at a table looking out on to the terrace and the garden beyond. The overgrown shrubs and tangles of bramble and nettle had been cleared away to reveal the neglected borders and an area of lawn, which had been reseeded and was now a carpet of tender green, shimmering with dew. The stonework of the sundial had been newly cleaned and its brass dial gleamed. Young shrubs, rose bushes and bedding plants sat stark in the freshly dug black earth of the flower beds, and at the edge of the garden the mulberry trees spread their branches in graceful, leafy splendour. Hamlet sat on the terrace keeping a keen eye on the birds as they came and went on the grass.

'It's already so pretty – just think how glorious

it will look in a couple of years' time,' said Meg. 'I remember how impatient I was for the kitchen garden at Hazelhurst to get going. It took three years to become properly productive.'

'I'm not sure about a kitchen garden,' replied Harry, scratching his beard. 'Isn't it a lot of work?'

'That's what a gardener is for. It's just one more bit of planning, and it will be worth it, trust me. There's nothing quite like a freshly snapped stick of your own rhubarb, or a basket of raspberries picked warm after a day's sunshine.' She pointed at a couple of trees at the edge of the terrace. 'You already have a plum tree. And the damsons will be wonderful in autumn. And you see those espaliers against the wall? I have an idea they're peaches. With a little love and careful pruning they might fruit again.'

Harry smiled at Meg. 'You're just what this place needs. I can tell you're going to help me bring it to life.'

'It's a wonderful house. Thank you for letting me stay here.'

'I'm the one who should be grateful.' He poured more coffee. 'Let's finish breakfast and get started on some plans.'

Harry's budget for decorating and furnishing Chalcombe was large enough for Meg to manage comfortably, and she was able to make efficient savings here and there. Over the ensuing weeks the interior of the house gradually began to take shape. Meg and Harry pored over brochures and catalogues, and made trips to London to choose furniture, carpets and curtain fabrics. The influences of that first morning – the light through the muslin curtain, and the airy charm of breakfast in the conservatory – had inspired Meg to keep the colour schemes fresh and clean to ensure that there was nothing dark or heavy about any of the rooms. Since the house was in a dale, surrounded by woodland, she knew it was important that the interiors should be bright to ward off the gloom in winter. Harry had his own ideas about artworks, and spent happy times in galleries and shops acquiring pictures, sculptures, screens and vases that combined with Meg's interior designs and colour schemes to produce a stylish and quixotic effect.

Max arrived for the summer holidays at the beginning of July. He didn't know Harry well, and felt awkward at first in the big man's hearty presence, unsure of his place in the half-decorated house with its echoing floors and whistling painters, and with little to occupy him. He took himself off to explore the nearby lanes and fields, and by the end of the week he had met a boy, James Treeves, who was also home for the school holidays. By this means Meg got to know James's mother, marking the beginning of Harry's tentative entry into local society.

Thereafter, Max spent most of his days with James, scouting the woods, climbing trees, fishing and building dens, although occasionally James was required by his family for various social excursions, leaving Max to his own devices. On the first day that Max found himself companionless, he wandered around the house, intrigued by the states of decoration and development of the various rooms. As he was passing Harry's study he heard music and paused in the corridor. Harry, clacking away at his typewriter, caught sight of Max hovering and called him in.

'Not out with your chum today?' he asked.

Hamlet was lying next to Harry's desk, his nose between his paws, and Max bent to tickle his ears. 'He's gone to visit his grandmother.' He shyly indicated the gramophone. 'I like that music. What is it?' Lazy trumpet notes drifted through the air, then faded as the song drew to a close.

Harry smiled, and reached out and lifted the needle from the record. 'That's jazz. Humphrey Lyttelton. Like to hear some more?'

Max nodded. Harry turned the record over and set the needle into the grooves. After an initial crackle, the first wistful notes of 'Trouble In Mind' filled the room. Harry turned back to his typewriter and continued to tap out his editorial. Max, content to be ignored, sat down on the sofa by the window and listened, his mind idly transported to some place that felt both happy and sad. When the record came to an end, and the needle was grinding round and round in the empty grooves,

Harry remarked mildly, 'Well, change the record, can't you?'

Max got to his feet and lifted the arm from the turntable, and carefully removed the record. He slipped it back into its paper sleeve and fished through the other records in the case by the desk until he found one he liked the title of: 'When It's Sleepy Time Down South'. He put it on, and went back to the sofa to listen. Harry sat at his typewriter, paying him no attention.

So the morning went by. Harry worked, Max played records, at first giving his full attention to the music, then eventually, still enjoying the jazz but mildly bored, picking up a copy of a magazine from a nearby table and leafing through it.

Max broke forty minutes of peaceable silence by asking Harry, 'What's the Iron Curtain? Is it a real thing?'

Harry sat back in his chair. 'It's a metaphor. You know what a metaphor is? It's when you use an expression to describe something, and the expression isn't literally right, but it describes the thing well. So the boundary that's existed between Western Europe and the Soviet Union since the end of the war is called the Iron Curtain because it's a good way of describing it not just geographically, but intellectually, too.'

For the next ten minutes Harry explained to Max the war of ideas between East and West, and Max listened with interest.

'The Russians can try to ban their people from reading

foreign books and newspapers, but there are other ways of transmitting ideas. Radio, for instance. There are a lot of people in Russia who listen to the BBC, or Voice Of America. Technology helps people to understand the freedoms they're being denied. Now,' said Harry, 'put on another record and let me finish my work.'

After that, whenever Max was at a loose end he would wander to Harry's study and make himself at home. Sometimes Harry was there, sometimes he wasn't. Max would play records and browse back copies of *Horizon*, *Poetry Review*, *Venture*, anything that came to hand, and pluck interesting-looking books from Harry's shelves. When Harry was there they would converse idly on any manner of subjects, from cricket – a discussion of the remarkable abilities of the two left-handers in the visiting New Zealand cricket team, Donnelly and Sutcliffe, prompting Harry to explain to Max the origins of the word 'sinister' – and the Bible – a rumination on the David and Goliath story leading to speculation as to whether you could actually kill a man with a home-made catapult. Max liked the matter-of-fact way that Harry talked to him, treating him like an equal, with none of the usual, patronising indulgence of grown-ups. Harry, who had hitherto had limited contact with children, found Max's company, and his candid curiosity about life, refreshing, and an easy camaraderie developed between them.

*

By mid-August work on the house was virtually complete. Dan, back in England for a short holiday, was impressed by the transformation. Harry prepared a cold lunch for his arrival, which they ate outside in the shade of an apple tree growing next to the terrace.

'Excellent lunch, old man,' said Dan. 'Nice to have some decent ham for a change. The food in Berlin is still lousy.'

'Meg's been teaching me to cook, but my efforts so far are rather hit and miss. Can't go wrong with a ham salad.'

'You're coming along very well,' said Meg. 'It's all a matter of practical necessity. I didn't know how to boil an egg until the war made it impossible to find servants. Which reminds me, Harry – I've found you a daily woman who'll come in from the village three times a week to clean and do the washing.'

'Marvellous. I don't know how I'd manage this place without you. Dan, can she stay for ever?'

Max, clad in a short-sleeved shirt, shorts, sandals and no socks, appeared on the other side of the lawn. He came towards the terrace, dragging a stick, Hamlet trotting next to him. When he saw Dan he broke into a run, and gave him a happy hug.

'Max, lunch was half an hour ago,' said Meg. 'Where have you been?'

'Sorry. I think my watch is busted.' He took it off and held it to his ear, giving it a shake.

'Here, let me have a look,' said Dan, taking it from him.

'Well, come and have some food,' said Meg. 'There's a bit of ham and salad left, and some bread and butter. And strawberries for after. Though I think you should wash your hands first.'

Max went inside, stroking the filmy curtains by the open French windows, enjoying their gauzy feel. He kicked off his sandals so that he could feel the nubbly rush matting on the conservatory floor beneath his bare feet. The air smelt of fresh paint and new things, and everything was light and summery. He was proud of the house, feeling that he was somehow part of its renovation. He vastly preferred living here to Belgravia, with the woods and fields and streams at his disposal, and wished he could come here every holiday. He washed his hands at the basin in the downstairs lavatory, then went back outside, where his mother had set out a plate of ham and salad.

Dan laid Max's wristwatch on the table. 'I think you must have over-wound it, old fellow.'

'Oh, Max!' exclaimed his mother. 'Dan just gave it to you for your birthday.'

'Sorry. I didn't *mean* to.'

'I'll see if I can get it fixed,' said Dan, and put the watch in his pocket. He turned to Harry. 'So, when are you going to have your first batch of proper house guests? We don't count, obviously.'

'Meg has put so much effort into the house that I was going to ask if the two of you would like to invite friends to stay next weekend, before you go back to Germany.'

'That's awfully nice of you,' said Meg. She thought for a moment. 'You've met my Aunt Sonia, haven't you?'

'Dan's godmother? Yes, I have. She's a wonderful character. Why not ask her?'

'I shall, but be warned, she'll have a couple of schoolgirls in tow. Avril and Laura are home for the holidays.'

Max's face lit up. 'Yes, let's have Laura to stay!'

The grown-ups laughed. 'So Laura's a special favourite, eh?' asked Harry genially.

Max blushed. It was hateful when grown-ups ragged you like this, and it wasn't the way Harry usually treated him. To change the subject, he asked, 'Mummy, can I have some strawberries now, please?'

Meg spooned strawberries into a dish and handed it to him.

'If Sonia's girls will be company for Max, all the better,' said Harry.

'I'll write to her this afternoon. I'm sure she'd be happy to get out of London for a few days.'

Sonia was more than glad of the invitation to Chalcombe. She had been feeling mildly out of sorts for a month or two, though the doctor could find nothing wrong with her. Most of her friends were out of London for August, and Helen had taken herself off to the Riviera with a group of friends that included a Frenchman, Serge, with whom Sonia thought her sister might be developing a romance.

She opened Meg's letter at breakfast. 'How nice. We've been invited to spend a few days in Kent next weekend.' She scanned the letter. 'A place called Chalcombe. It belongs to Harry Denholm, a friend of Dan's. I've met him a few times. A very' – she searched for an apt description – 'a very colourful individual.'

'Well, I haven't met him,' remarked Avril. 'I don't want to go and stay in the country with people I don't know.'

'You will know people. Meg and Max are staying for the summer, and Dan will be there, too.'

'I want to go,' said Laura quickly. She would be pleased to see Max again, and to be in the countryside. 'Are there horses?'

'I'm not sure, dear. Mr Denholm didn't strike me as a very horsey sort of person.'

'I can't think of anything more boring,' sighed Avril. 'Can't you two go, while I stay in London?'

'Certainly not,' said Sonia firmly, folding up Meg's letter.

'Oh, Mother, for heaven's sake – I am eighteen.'

'You're not staying here on your own, and that's final. Now, both of you clear up the breakfast things, please. I'm going to go and answer Mr Denholm's letter and tell him that the three of us are very much looking forward to the weekend.'

4

THE SUMMER OF 1949 was proving to be an exceptionally dry one, and by breakfast time on Saturday a listless heat was already settling over the Kent countryside. Harry's idea of putting together a picnic lunch and making an excursion into the coolness of the surrounding greenwood appealed to everyone.

'At least it's something to do,' said Avril to her mother, as they went upstairs. 'I'd forgotten how boring it is, being in the country.'

'Don't be so ungracious,' replied Sonia. 'Anyway, it's nice to be spending time with Meg and Dan. How long is it since you last saw them?'

'Oh, years.' Avril's clearest memory of Dan was when he'd built the air-raid shelter at Woodbourne House one summer during the war. She must have been ten or eleven, old enough to have developed an intense crush on him, thinking him the handsomest man ever. Seeing him this weekend had brought those feelings flooding back. She added, 'Not since you sent them both to Coventry, obviously.'

'I was well within my rights to be deeply disappointed in them both. Conducting an affair like that, for all those years. And Paul such a good man.'

'At least he never found out about it.'

'But that's just it,' replied Sonia. 'Paul did know. He found out not long before he flew that last mission. That was the appalling thing.'

Avril absorbed this information. She had been fourteen when the scandal concerning Meg and Dan had erupted – old enough to pick up what was going on, but too young to have been vouchsafed details – and hadn't been aware of this aspect to the tragedy of Paul's death.

'Anyway,' added Sonia, as they paused outside Avril's room, 'it's all in the past now. One must learn to forgive and forget. We have to get on with our lives, and I am glad Meg and Dan are back in mine. Now, are you going to wear your nice new sundress for the picnic?'

'Maybe. I'll see.'

Avril went into her room and closed the door, leaning her back against it for a moment. Thinking about Dan sexually, about him conducting a passionate affair with Meg – or anyone, for that matter – excited her. She moved to the cheval glass that stood next to her dressing table and examined her reflection dispassionately. She wasn't beautiful, she knew that much, but she was aware she had a good figure, and that although her features lacked delicacy, her full mouth and dark eyes were definitely attractive. Men looked at her. One of her reasons for longing to escape her mother's home and get to Italy was so that she would be able to have a love affair. And when she did, it would be with someone like Dan. In the meantime, fantasies about him would have to do.

'There.' Meg packed the last of the picnic fare into a basket and covered it with a gingham cloth. 'We have cold chicken, sandwiches, strawberries and a ginger cake. Oh, and lemonade.'

'And for those who *don't* fancy potted meat and cucumber sandwiches, I'm taking along a loaf of crusty bread and some decent cheese,' said Harry. 'And a bottle of wine.'

'Well, don't forget glasses, in that case. How are we going to carry all this, as well as the rugs?'

Harry caught sight of Max and Laura outside the kitchen door. 'That's what strapping young people are for. Here, you two, come and take charge of the picnic hamper.'

Sonia and Avril appeared in the kitchen, Avril wearing her new yellow sundress, sprigged with little red flowers, her dark hair tied up with a red ribbon.

'That's a pretty frock, Avril,' said Meg. 'Would you mind taking the rugs? They're on a chair in the hall. I'll just go and find Dan, and then we can get going.'

The picnic spot was a ten-minute walk through the woods from the house. The party made their way along the shady, musty-smelling path, Harry leading the way, Hamlet scampering in and out of the undergrowth, until eventually the path dipped down to a grassy grotto, dappled with sunlight, and surrounded by gently sloping banks of fern. One of the banks gave way to a kind of gully on the other side, fringed with tall trees, where someone had slung a piece of rope over a tree branch, knotted at the end to make a crude swing.

'Can I have a go?' asked Max excitedly, when he saw the swing.

'After lunch,' said Meg. 'Come and help me spread these rugs. Laura and Avril, you can get things out of the basket. What a lovely spot, Harry.'

They sat around chatting, eating and drinking, enjoying being in the cool, quiet depths of the wood. The only sounds apart from their own voices were the drowsy cooing of the wood pigeons and the occasional scurrying of squirrels. Harry gestured towards a tree with the knife he had been using to cut off hunks of cheese.

'Look, a red squirrel. You don't see so many of them these days.'

'Why not?' asked Max.

'The American grey squirrels are taking over. Our native squirrels can't compete with them. They're bigger and greedier.'

'Just like Americans themselves,' sighed Sonia. 'We're all made to believe that everything that comes out of America is perfectly marvellous. They'll be taking us over soon.'

Dan held out his glass to let Harry pour more wine. 'A sort of reverse colonialism.'

'The mistake was letting them become independent,' said Harry. 'They've got ideas above their station now.'

Max knew enough about the War of Independence to pick up on this. 'But we couldn't have gone on governing America,' he protested. 'It wouldn't have worked.'

Harry ruffled his hair. 'It was a joke.'

Max responded to this by announcing that he was going to play on the swing, and Laura got up to join him.

Dan watched as Max ineffectually tried to clamber on to the knotted rope, but it was too high from the ground. Laura, though slightly taller, met with similar lack of success.

'Here,' said Dan, getting to his feet, 'I'll see if I can sort it out for you.'

He gazed up at the tree, assessing the situation. Then he got a foothold at the base and swung himself up, first to one branch, then the next. The foliage shook and young acorns pattered to the earth. Avril, her eyes fixed on Dan's flexing muscles as he scaled the tree, felt a delicious sense of excitement in the pit of her stomach.

'Dan, for heaven's sake be careful!' called out Meg, murmuring to the others, 'He thinks he's still a boy.'

Sonia watched as Dan reached the high, thick branch where the rope was fastened. She remembered the war wound that had shattered his thighbone just five years ago, and marvelled that he was still so limber.

Dan sat astride the branch and inched himself along until he reached the spot where the rope was tied around it. He called down to Max to slacken it by lifting the knot, and Max did so, holding it aloft while Dan began, with difficulty, to unfasten the coils of rope. Eventually he worked them loose and let out a foot or two.

'How's that?' he called down.

'Perfect!' Max shouted back.

Dan refastened the rope, reaching down and tugging to make sure it was secure, then made his way back along the branch and down the tree. He jumped to the ground, dusting off his hands and pushing a lock of blond hair out of his eyes. Max was about to try the swing when Dan said, 'Hold on a second.'

He searched around the grove until he found a thick length of wood. He loosened the knot, inserted the piece of wood, then tightened it again. 'There. That should make it easier.'

Max jumped astride the wood, and Dan gave him a gentle shove so that he took off from the lip of the shallow gully and swung out over it, whooping with delight, while Hamlet barked with excitement. Everyone applauded. Max swung back and forth, and at last came in to land, his sandalled feet scuffing the earth. He held the rope out to Laura.

'You have a try! It's ripping!'

Laura clambered astride the swing, but just as Dan was about to shove her off she gave a little scream. 'Don't! I'm scared! What if I fall off?'

'You won't,' said Dan. 'Here, I'll take you with me. Watch your legs.' He took hold of the rope and stepped on to the length of wood, his feet on either side of Laura. Avril, watching, felt an unexpected smart of anger and jealousy at the sight of Dan's body close against Laura's. She was sure Laura was pretending to be scared, just to get Dan's attention. 'Now, hold tight to my legs. Max, give us a shove.'

Max stepped forward and pushed. Laura wrapped her arms around Dan's legs and suddenly they were swinging out together. Laura gave a scream of laughter. Holding on to Dan she felt safe and secure. Nothing could happen to her. The rushing air and the giddy sense of flight was delicious. She threw her head back as they swung, gazing up at the kaleidoscope of sunlight shimmering through the translucent green of the summer trees, aware of an immense and powerful thrill of happiness. She wanted to swing for ever, marvellously detached from the earth but anchored to Dan, the panorama of the woods spinning around her.

Eventually the momentum slowed and they crested the lip of the gully for the last time. Dan jumped down and held the swing so that Laura could climb off. 'Golly, I'm quite giddy!' She stood waiting for the dizziness to subside.

Dan glanced around. 'Anyone else fancy a shot? Avril?'

For an enticing moment she longed to do as Laura had done, to hold on to Dan as they swung out together over the dip, grasping the strong muscles of his legs. But that simply wouldn't happen. She wasn't a child. The idea was unthinkable. She shook her head. 'No thanks.'

Dan sat down on the rug and helped himself to wine and ginger cake, and browsed a copy of *The Times* while the children took turns on the rope swing. Harry dozed on his back with his hat over his eyes. Avril, whose gaze had been surreptitiously fastened on Dan, now settled on her back on the rug and stared up at the trees, listening to Max and Laura's excited shouts of laughter, feeling remote from everyone, neither child nor adult.

Eventually Max and Laura tired of the swing and returned to the picnic rug, foraging for scraps of cake and feeding sandwich crusts to Hamlet. Max said to Laura, 'D'you want to see the pond where James and I go fishing? It's not far.'

'Yes, all right.'

'I'll come with you,' said Avril.

With Hamlet trotting at their heels, the three of them set off along the gully, following its upward path until they emerged from the shade of the trees into bright sunshine. From the edge of the wood a meadow sloped down to a large pond in an old quarry, long disused and fringed by bushes. The air around them fizzed with the sound of insects. Butterflies swarmed giddily among the wildflowers.

'Come on!' shouted Max, and he set off down the slope at a run, Hamlet at his heels. Laura ran after him, and Avril followed, hopping carefully among the scrubby tussocks of grass. By the time she caught up with them Max was seated at the water's edge with Laura, pointing across the expanse of glinting water.

'James's father says there's a monster pike out there somewhere.'

'It's probably just a myth,' said Avril, tucking her skirts beneath her and sitting on the grass.

'No, James's father has seen it. Anyway, Dan said he's going to come fishing with me and bring a proper rod, to see if we can catch it.'

Avril sat back on her elbows, plucking a sappy stem of grass and chewing it. 'Dan's quite your hero, isn't he?'

Max frowned, sensing he was being lightly mocked, then shrugged. 'He's pretty good at most things.' He picked up a pebble and threw it into the still waters, watching the ripples subside. Then he turned to Avril and said, 'He was in Special Operations during the war, you know. Mummy thinks he was a commando, but she's not sure. He doesn't talk about it.'

Avril said nothing.

After a moment's silence Laura murmured to Max, 'You're so lucky being in the country for the whole summer. It's deadly dull in London.'

'I really like it here. I keep thinking about the autumn term and wishing it was months away instead of weeks.'

'No more school for me,' said Avril, stretching her arms above her head. 'I'm off to Italy in September. I can't wait.'

Max turned to look at her. 'What are you going to do there?'

'I'm going to study fine art in Rome. Italy's famous for its Renaissance art.' She gave Max a glance. 'Though I don't expect you know what that is.'

'Yes, I do,' replied Max hotly. He hated Avril's air of superiority. He remembered not liking her when he was little, the way she bossed everyone around, and she wasn't much better now. 'I know a lot of the statues.' In fact, his knowledge was confined to a few arresting pictures he'd come across in a book of Harry's about classical sculpture.

'Oh, really? Name me some.'

Max blushed and racked his brains. 'There's that one of Hercules killing a horse.'

Avril gave a snort of laughter. 'It's a centaur, not a horse. By Giambologna.' She stretched the Italian vowels affectedly. 'Is that all you know?'

He remembered the one of those chaps wrestling with the snakes and looking like they were coming off worst. 'Those men being attacked by snakes. Cocoon and his sons.'

Avril gave another hoot of laughter. 'Laocoön, you complete ass!'

Max sat with fury in his heart, wishing he'd never said he knew anything. Laura probably thought he was a prize idiot. But Laura merely gave him a smile and said, 'Don't worry. You know more than I do.'

'My father was an artist, so I know quite a lot,' said Avril. 'He was very famous, you know.' Even at eighteen, Avril wasn't beyond a bit of childish bragging.

Max stood up and flung another pebble in the lake. 'He didn't win a VC in the war, though, did he?'

'Of course he didn't. He wasn't alive then.' A kind of darkness touched her mind, as it always did when she thought or spoke about her father's death.

'My father flew a plane on a bombing raid all the way to Dusseldorf and back, even though he was badly wounded,' said Max. 'He died saving his crew from a crash landing.'

'Bully for him,' replied Avril. What a smug little tick Max was. In a rush of spite she added, 'I suppose he didn't have a lot to live for, after what your mother did.'

Max stared at her, puzzled and afraid. 'What d'you mean? My mother didn't do anything.'

Avril smirked. 'That's all you know. She and your precious Dan were having a love affair for ages, and your father found out all about it—'

'Avril, stop it!' exclaimed Laura, horrified. It was the first time she had ever heard this, and she was sure Avril was making it up. 'That's a terrible thing to say!'

'It's only the truth.' Looking at Max's pinched, white face, Avril's momentary misgiving was eclipsed by the satisfaction of having wounded him. Teach him to be so full of himself.

'That's not right.' Max felt shaken. 'The war was all over when my mother and Dan got married.'

'Simpleton. Doesn't mean they weren't already carrying on behind your father's back.'

Max suddenly flew at Avril and pushed her hard, shouting, 'Liar!' It was a clumsy, ineffectual lunge, but the shock of it angered Avril.

'Stop it, you brat!' She shoved him back. 'Don't take it out on me! Time you stopped hero-worshipping everyone, particularly your stepfather who you think is so wonderful. He made a fool of you both, you and your precious father.' Tears sprang into Max's eyes, then he turned and raced back up the path away from the quarry. 'That's right – run away!' taunted Avril as he fled.

Laura jumped up, intending to go after him, then thought better of it. She stared at Avril in anguish. 'That was a horrid thing to do. How could you?'

'Oh, don't you start. It's time everyone around here grew up a bit. What difference does it make whether he knows? He was bound to find out sooner or later. I've probably done him a favour.' Her eyes followed Max's running figure, then she looked away, her heart beating hard.

5

WHEN HE REACHED the edge of the wood Max slowed down, pushing his way through the low shrubs until he reached a small clearing, where he sat down, panting, wiping the tears from his face. He didn't want those beastly things Avril had said to be true. His mother and Dan weren't like that. He snapped off a stalk of bracken and picked the fronds off one by one, laying them over one another in a criss-cross pattern, trying to assemble his confused and frightened thoughts. He knew about sex, about the things people did in bed. He remembered the excited, whispered discussions about it in the dorm after lights out the term before last. He hadn't wanted to hear, but he had, and once you knew these things, you couldn't un-know them. An affair was when married people did the sex thing with someone who wasn't their husband or wife. It was a terrible thing to do, the worst kind of betrayal. He knew that from the whispered rumours that had flown about when Hector Grigsby's parents got divorced.

He thought back to the day when he and his mother had left Woodbourne House, not long after his father had died. They'd had to run to catch the bus, and when they were on it, his mother tried to hide that she was crying. He'd been seven. They'd taken the train to London, and then another bus. That was the first time he'd been to the house in Belgravia, Dan's house. They'd stayed there a few days, and then they'd gone to Grandma's, where they'd lived for what seemed like a long time, maybe a year. Then his mother and Dan had got married.

A cold feeling settled in his stomach. He had never given any thought before to the timescale of these events, but now everything Avril had said made sense. His mother hadn't been crying on the bus about his father. She'd been crying about what she'd done.

His thoughts shifted to the picture of his father that stood on his bedside locker at school, the familiar features of the handsome, smiling man in RAF uniform. He had always loved that smile, but suddenly he was filled with a sense of its pathos. His developing empathy with the feelings of adults allowed him to glimpse, in an immature way, the terrible hurt and desolation his father must have felt when he found out what his friend and his wife had been doing. An awful thought struck Max, like a knife to his heart. What if finding out had made his father want to die? What if it was *why* he'd died?

His mother had been pretending all along. Pretending that she was sad about his father, when all the time she must have been glad, because he was out of the way and she could marry Dan. Pretending was the worst part. A lie happened on its own, but pretending – pretending went on and on. And if she'd pretended to love his father, she could pretend to love anyone, himself included. The new baby brother or sister he would have in a few months would be the one she really loved. He'd be shut out. Feelings of misery and rage seemed to thicken in his chest, swelled by a sense of protective love for his father which was all the more powerful for being a sacred memory rather than a live, present emotion. His mother and Dan were beastly, beastly bastards! All the bad words he knew crowded his brain. He wanted to do something, to hurt someone, strangle and choke them, but all he could do was tear at the ferns and weep. He hated his mother. He would never love her again. Or Dan. They had done that to his father and then lied about everything to him. They were both damned cheats and cowards. They would both go to hell, the bastards, the bloody, bloody bastards.

He got up and walked back to the picnic, unsure of what he would say or do, aware only that he, and everything in the world about him, was changed. The bright summer day had turned dark.

At the picnic site Meg and Sonia were clearing up the remains of the food, while Harry folded up the rugs. Dan had strolled off into the woods. As Max approached, it was clear to the grown-ups that he had been crying. Meg got up and went to him, saying, 'Darling what on earth's the matter? Have you hurt yourself?'

Harry couldn't hear the boy's reply. He saw Meg put her arms anxiously around him, and Max's body stiffen in rejection. He was talking, half-crying, in a low, angry voice, and after a moment Harry heard Meg say incredulously, 'What? Who told you that?' Again Max's reply was inaudible, but he was resisting ever more fiercely Meg's physical attempts to hold and soothe him. He was struggling in her grasp, then he began to shout.

'Stop *pretending*! That's all you do – you just *pretend*!'

Meg said something inaudible in a low, urgent voice, to which Max retorted, 'Stop *lying*! I *know* it's true, and I hate you! I hate you both!' He wriggled out of Meg's grasp and backed away from her, crying, wiping his face with the back of his hand and shouting, 'You're bloody bastards!' And with that he turned and stormed off the way he had come.

Meg shouted after him to come back, her mind in turmoil. He had never been meant to find out. She had long ago decided it would be pointless and dangerous, that he would be happier never knowing. *But this is what happens when you lie. You thought you had braved the world with the truth when you left Woodbourne House to be with Dan. You were prepared to forfeit everyone's love and respect. But the one person you couldn't tell was your son. You were never brave enough for that. And look what's happened, you fool, you fool. You have to explain. You have to make it all right.* She hurried after him, walking as swiftly as her seven months pregnancy would allow. How was she ever going to make this right? It had come right with Sonia, she could make it right with Max. But who earth had told him? It had to be Avril. That malicious girl. She reached the edge of the wood, where the shade of the trees gave way to sunshine, and saw Max trotting down a flat, grassy slope. She hurried after him, calling his name.

At the sound of his mother's voice Max broke into a run, determined to get away, not wanting to hear what she had to say. It would just be more pretending, more lies to try to make everything right. Nothing would ever be right again. Then when he realised he was heading back to where he and Avril and Laura had been sitting by the gravel pit lake he veered away along the narrow path at the pond's edge in the other direction. He could still hear his mother behind him, shouting his name.

Meg watched helplessly as Max ran off, feeling a stitch in her side. She realised she probably shouldn't be hurrying in her condition. She staggered to a halt on the path, her hand to her stomach, and as she did so her foot slipped on the loose gravel edge and she tumbled sideways, grabbing at air as she fell, skidding down the loose shale of the bank towards the water, landing on her back, her head striking a boulder by the water's edge with a dull crack that was the last thing she heard, and the last pain she felt, before blackness descended. Blood began to seep among the pebbles and into the water.

Max kept on running. He could no longer hear his mother's voice, and the momentary anxiety this caused him was quickly swept away by an exultant gladness that he had escaped her, as though outrunning her was her first punishment, a way of showing her how weak and bad she was, bound to fail now in every way where he was concerned.

He ran until he could run no more. He sank down on the ground on the other side of the pond, panting, and stared across the stretch of water. His mother was nowhere. He could see Laura trekking back up the meadow towards the wood with Hamlet at her heels. Misery clutched at his chest, and he began to sob again.

Dan strolled back through the woods to the clearing, and found only Sonia and Harry there, packing the remains of the picnic away.

'Where's Meg?' he asked.

'Max was upset about something and ran off, and she went after him,' replied Sonia. 'I expect they'll be back presently.'

'What was he upset about?'

'I haven't the faintest idea. Perhaps he quarrelled with Laura and Avril.'

'Which way did they go?'

Harry pointed. 'That way.'

Dan set off along the path, and met Laura and Hamlet coming back. 'Hello,' he said, 'you haven't seen Meg and Max, have you?'

'No.'

He regarded her troubled face. 'I say, did you and Max have a quarrel?'

Laura shook her head, then after a moment's hesitation said, 'Avril was a bit mean to him.'

'Ah. Well, everyone else is heading back to the house. I'll see you later.'

Avril sat alone by the lake, telling herself she had nothing to feel bad about. It wasn't her fault Meg and Dan had tried to cover up what they'd done, and let Max think everything was wonderful. He would have found out eventually. If Max chose to make a fuss about it, no doubt they would all blame her for him being upset, even though they were responsible.

She got up and dusted down her dress. No point in going back just yet. Give it a bit of time. Maybe Max wouldn't say anything to anyone. She set off to walk around the pond. The sun glimmered on the water. Dragonflies darted and skimmed. The heat seemed to hang heavy over everything. Apart from the low hum of insects, the only sound to break the stillness was the crunch of her sandals on the gravel. When she caught sight of Meg lying at the water's edge at the foot of the bank, it took her a few seconds to make sense of what she was seeing. She gasped in horror and scrambled down to the water's edge, the loose shale rattling dustily under her feet. She crouched next to Meg, taking in the white, still face, the hair matted with blood. She reached out trembling hands, uncertain whether to try to lift her head up, not wanting to touch her at all. A fly landed on Meg's cheek, and in horror Avril swatted it away. She cupped her hand beneath Meg's neck with unwilling fingers and tried to raise her head. She could feel the stickiness of Meg's blood, and her head was strangely heavy and inert. With her other hand she patted Meg's cheek gently, hoping to rouse her, but her face was slack and unresponsive. Realising that something awful had happened and that she must get help, Avril stood up, wiping her bloodied hand on her dress and looking frantically around. The heat of the day had suddenly become menacing. She climbed up the bank, her breath coming in frightened little moans, and as she reached the top she saw Dan coming along the path.

Dan saw Avril's wide-eyed, stricken face.

'What's wrong?'

'It's Meg,' panted Avril. 'She's had an accident.' She pointed to where Meg lay on the stones, and in an instant Dan had descended the gravel slope in three bounding strides and was at her side. He lifted her head, speaking her name over and over. Then he turned and shouted to Avril, 'Run and fetch help! *Run!*'

Avril hesitated. Dan turning and shouting at her to fetch help had disturbed some dark memory, something buried and forgotten. She struggled to retrieve it. Then Dan shouted at her again, and she ran back as fast as she could.

Dan stroked the bloodied hair away from Meg's forehead and kissed her cheek, speaking her name softly, waiting for her to stir. But beneath the caress of his fingers he could feel no pulse beating in her neck. The numb dread that filled him threatened to squeeze the very breath from his throat. He had seen death many times before, and knew he was looking at it now.

Avril sat on the edge of her bed, staring at the tops of the trees beyond the window. Somewhere below she heard a telephone ring, then a door open and close, and the murmur of her mother's voice in the hall. She knew what was going on, but felt utterly detached from it all. In the hours following the picnic Meg's body had been brought back to the house. A telegram had been sent to Helen in France. The doctor had been and gone. The cause of death, he had concluded, was a fracture of the cervical vertebrae caused by the impact of striking her head on the rock. In other words, Meg had broken her neck. The police had been informed, but an inquest was unlikely. Everyone accepted that it was a tragic accident, that she had slipped and fallen while pursuing Max. The wild, horrible scenes with Max shouting and crying and refusing to be pacified by anyone, least of all Dan, had driven Avril to her room to consider her part in all this.

Guilt lay like a painful weight in her chest. Meg's death had just been an awful accident, but she knew that if she hadn't said what she had to Max, none of it would have happened. Yet surely she couldn't be blamed. Could she? Glancing down, she was startled to see a reddish-brown streak on her dress, where she had wiped her hand after putting it to Meg's head. She stared at the mark, telling herself over and over that she wasn't to blame. She was sorry for what had occurred, but it wasn't her fault. She rose from her bed and went to change her dress.

Harry sat at his desk in his study. Max sat in an armchair opposite, head bowed, hands gripping the arm rests. The pose was implacable. Harry felt weary. The boy was beyond reasoning with. He tried again.

'Max, you have to go back to London with Dan.'

'I won't. I hate him.'

'Look, this terrible thing has happened – terrible for both of you. But your mother loved you and she wouldn't want you to make it all worse.' Was this the right thing to say? Harry wasn't sure there were any right things to say. He could only do his clumsy best.

'I hate her, too!' shouted Max, and burst into sobs yet again, hiding his face on his arm.

Harry sighed. Every time Max declared that he hated his mother he meant something quite different, of course. He couldn't imagine what the boy must be feeling. The devastation of loss, guilt, anger – emotions hardly within his childish capabilities.

Harry rose from his chair. 'Stay here a moment, Max.'

He went downstairs and found Dan in the garden, smoking, pacing beneath the trees. He looked up as Harry approached. His face was grim, as though the events of the past hours had aged him by ten years.

'How is he now?' asked Dan.

Harry shook his head. 'He's still refusing to go back to London with you. It's hard to say what's going on in his head, but I think it's going to take him a long time to come to terms with... well, whatever he learned today.'

Dan nodded. He flung the remains of his cigarette away. 'Christ,' he muttered, 'I can't cope with any of this. Harry, I don't know what to do. I can't think.'

At that moment Sonia emerged from the house and crossed the lawn. In her customary way she was coping with a terrible situation and mitigating the suffering of others by taking charge of practical details.

'The arrangements are all in hand,' she told Dan. 'I've spoken to the local undertaker, and Meg's— Meg can be taken back to London tomorrow. You can go with her, if you wish.'

Dan nodded. 'Thank you.' After a pause he added, 'Max is refusing to come with me. He won't even speak to me.'

Sonia laid a hand on his arm. 'With everything that's happened, it's natural that he's confused and upset.'

'That's putting it mildly.' He sighed. 'What am I going to do, Sonia? What the hell am I going to do?'

'Perhaps,' said Harry tentatively, 'Max could stay here. For a while, you know. I'm happy to have him.'

'What about the funeral?' said Dan.

'At his age,' ventured Sonia, 'I'm not sure attending the funeral would be a good—'

'She's his mother, for God's sake!' exclaimed Dan angrily.

Harry said quickly, 'I'll bring him with me. Perhaps after a couple of days he'll have calmed down.'

Dan turned to Sonia. 'I'm sorry. I'm just… I'm just at the end of my tether.' He paused, then said to Harry, 'If you're willing to let Max stay here for the time being, perhaps that would best. I'd be very grateful.'

'It's no trouble.'

'Helen will be home tomorrow,' said Sonia. 'I'm sure she would have him to stay with her for a while, if things are still difficult.' Though she wasn't sure how her sister was going to cope with the terrible tragedy of losing her only daughter.

'How long will they go on being difficult, though?' asked Dan. 'He's got it into his head that I wronged his father. Which I did, of course. Meg and I both did. We were fools to hope Max would never find out. I just didn't think...'

'Avril was responsible for that,' said Sonia. 'She admitted as much to me.'

'No point in blaming her,' sighed Dan. 'But now that he knows, I don't see how I can make amends. If Meg were still here, perhaps we could set things right. But on my own...' He closed his eyes briefly, going through one of those moments – and there had been several, over the past few hours – when all this seemed unreal, ridiculous. That Meg should be gone, dead, no longer part of the world, was preposterous. It made no sense. His existence without her made no sense. It was something he would have to come to terms with. And Max, too. But as things stood, they were utterly unable to help one another.

That evening, after Sonia and the girls had gone to bed, Harry and Dan sat up late, talking and drinking, the whisky bottle on the table between them. The conservatory doors were wide open to the summer night. They talked for a long time, not of Meg or of the day's terrible events, but of random events from their years of friendship, as though this was necessary therapy. Eventually, though, on the third glass of Scotch, the talk came home to the present, and to Meg.

'It hasn't sunk in yet,' said Dan. 'It seems utterly unreal. She's part of me. Of all the women in my life, she is the only one I've ever loved.' He took a gulp of whisky and said with a catch in his voice, 'Christ, Harry, I don't want to wake up tomorrow.'

Harry grunted. 'You will, though. And the day after that, and the day after that. There is no cure, but with time it gets better. I learned that after Laurence died.'

There was a long silence, then Dan said, 'The strange thing is, when she told me about the baby, she was so happy, you know. And I was, too. It was just that I somehow didn't believe it. Maybe it was just the years passing, and her wanting it so much, and nothing happening – whatever it was, it feels now as though I had some sort of premonition. Which is ridiculous, of course. I didn't. I could just never imagine us having a child. And now they're both gone. Everything's gone.' Without warning, and for the first time that day, Dan wept, his hand over his eyes, his body shaking. Harry laid a gentle hand on his friend's shoulder, waiting. At length Dan drew a long breath and spoke. 'God, you start a day in one way, never dreaming that – that it will end in quite another.' He picked up his glass and drained it. 'I should go to bed now. I need to face tomorrow.'

6

THE FUNERAL TOOK place in London a few days later. Harry brought Max, who stood on the other side of the grave from Dan, his face blank and stern, his eyes never meeting his stepfather's.

After the burial was over, as the mourners stood talking in small groups, Dan noticed an elegant blonde woman conversing with Sonia. Her face was partially obscured by the dark veil of her hat, and it took Dan a few seconds to realise it was Diana, Paul's sister. In the wake of the discovery of Meg and Dan's affair five years ago she had cut off all contact. Communications regarding the administration of the trust that Paul had established to pay for Max's education, and of which Diana was a trustee, came via solicitors. He hadn't expected to see her here today, but he thought he knew why she had come. Social convention might have dictated that she could have nothing to do with the woman who had betrayed and dishonoured her brother, but she had loved Meg once and must have been as horrified and saddened as anyone to hear she had died.

He went over to speak to her.

'Hello, Di,' he said.

She put out her gloved hand to shake his, but her gaze held no warmth. 'I'm sorry for you. And for Max.'

There was an awkward silence, then Dan said, 'I take it Sonia told you what happened. I mean, about Max finding out everything.'

'Yes.' That he and Meg had only themselves to blame was a truth that hung unspoken in the air.

'He wants nothing to do with me now. Can't say I blame him. Can't say I ever blamed you, either. I'm hoping he'll come round in the end, but life is going to be difficult for the foreseeable future.'

'I'm sorry to hear that. If I can be of help regarding Max, please let me know.' Her tone was stiff. She was doing what she perceived as the right and necessary thing, no more. She added, 'Perhaps he could come to us for half-term now and then. It's been difficult, only having contact with my nephew through presents at birthdays and Christmas.'

'It couldn't have been otherwise, I suppose.'

Diana lifted her chin a little. 'No. I hated you both. I still hate what you did.' She glanced away to hide her tears. 'But it's useless, really.' With these words something seemed to relent a little between the two of them, as though Meg's death had revealed the pointlessness of feuding and hatred.

Dan took his cigarette case from his pocket and proffered it. 'How's Roddy?'

She took a cigarette and tucked up the veil of her hat as Dan lit it for her. He could see now that her lovely face was tired and strained. 'He's… he's not so good these days. Hard to explain. But we get along.'

Another brief silence ensued. 'We're having a small gathering back at the house,' said Dan. 'You're welcome to—'

Diana shook her head. 'No. No, thank you. As I say, please let me know if we can help where Max is concerned.'

'I will. Thank you.' He watched her go. The rift would never heal entirely, he knew. He wondered what the problems with her husband were. He hadn't seen Roddy MacLennan since the war.

It wasn't until the funeral gathering in Belgravia that Dan had a chance to talk to Harry about Max. 'How has he been?' Dan asked.

'Withdrawn. He spends most of his time in my study, listening to music, reading, staring out of the window. He doesn't want to see James Treeves. He won't even take the dog for a walk. I've done what I can on your behalf, tried to explain to him that marriages aren't always straightforward, and that sometimes people can't help their feelings. I told him you and Meg never meant to hurt his father. But he doesn't want to listen. He just shuts himself off.' Harry's big shoulders heaved in a sigh. 'Yesterday he asked if he could come and live with me. But I explained it was impossible. It's a miserable situation, old boy.'

Later, when the mourners had left, Dan went over to Max. 'I must speak to you, Max.'

Max, standing close to Harry with his eyes fixed on the carpet, shook his head.

'Max, you have to talk to Dan,' said Harry.

Gently, Dan grasped Max's shoulder. At first he thought Max would resist, but his stepson accompanied him silently upstairs.

Dan closed the door of Max's bedroom and regarded him. 'Max, look at me.'

The boy lifted his eyes and stared expressionlessly at him.

'We have to sort this out. You're coming back here to live. It's your home. I know it can never be the same without your mother, but this is where you belong.' After a pause he added, 'I love you, you know.'

Max looked away. 'No, you don't.' He spat the words coldly. There was a silence, and then he went on, 'If you make me come back here, I'll still hate you. I'll always hate you.'

Dan sighed. 'Max, that's childish.'

Again the boy's eyes met his. Their chilling expression seemed far from childish.

'I know Harry's tried to explain things to you,' said Dan. 'Maybe it's too soon. You need... we both need time to come to terms with what has happened. Then we can talk, and perhaps you'll understand. But in the meantime, you have to do as you're told. Harry can't have you for ever.' He regarded Max's sullen, closed face with impatience. The funeral, and his own grief, had sapped him of compassion. 'Do you understand?'

'Yes.' Max understood his limitations only too well. He was a child, powerless in the world of adults. Dan might compel him to return to Belgravia, but he could expect nothing beyond that.

The next fortnight was a trial to them both. Max spent his days in his room, avoiding Dan, refusing to talk to him beyond the most necessary of exchanges. Nor would he leave the house. His stubbornness wore down Dan's patience almost to breaking point. Every time he met Max's implacable gaze he was reminded of Paul. The same dogged single-mindedness which had made Paul so unknowable, and in the end so heroic, had found fresh embodiment in his eleven-year-old son.

Dan had agreed with his employers that he would work in the London office and return to Berlin when Max went back to school. That would be in two weeks, during which time Dan knew he couldn't leave the boy to fend for himself throughout the day.

'The situation's dreadful,' he told Sonia in a phone call. 'We're both unhappy as hell, wandering around in this space that Meg has left. He won't let me begin to talk to him. I have to go back to the office on Monday, and I can't leave him here alone.' He hesitated. 'I know you said Helen might have him to stay, but I don't like to ask her directly. She was in such a terrible state at the funeral, she might not be up to it. I wondered if perhaps you would gently sound her out?'

'Of course. Having Max around might help her. It would help Max, too. You and he are doing one another no good, that much is obvious.'

Helen greeted the idea of having Max to stay with more enthusiasm than Sonia had expected, even when Sonia warned her how badly Max had been affected not just by his mother's death, but by what he had learned about Meg and Dan.

'He's going to struggle to come to terms with it all,' said Helen. 'Dan is the last person to help him. Perhaps I can.'

That night Dan informed Max over one of their otherwise silent meals together that he would be going to his grandmother's that weekend.

Max considered this, then asked, 'Can I go straight back to school from Grandma's?'

Dan gazed at him. The boy had just lost his mother,

yet he could face the prospect of returning to school life with perfect equanimity. Perhaps lessons and routine and the company of his friends were the distraction he craved. 'If you like.'

'Good,' said Max. 'Then I won't have to see you again.' He put his knife and fork together and left the table.

Dan returned to Berlin, and it was late December before he and Harry met up again. They went for a drink one evening in their old Soho haunt, the Wheatsheaf.

'By the way, thanks for that excellent piece you sent over,' said Harry, as Dan brought pints of beer to the table. 'I'm aiming to run it in the November edition of the magazine.'

'Glad you liked it. Though I doubt if the treatment of British journalists in communist countries is going to change just because of my article.'

'Maybe someone will get the powers-that-be to sit up and take notice. Ronald Russell, for instance.'

'If he gets elected. Though he seems to think that if we make life difficult for Communist journalists here, that's going to help in some way. I don't see it. It's not likely to make it any easier for me to get a visa for Czechoslovakia if Britain kicks out some reporter for the *Soviet Weekly.*'

'True.' Harry took a pull of his pint, then tapped two cigarettes from a packet and handed one to Dan. 'How long are you back for?'

'Only a few days. There wasn't much point in coming back for Max's half-term. He didn't answer any of my letters. Probably didn't even read them.' He leaned into the flame of Harry's lighter. 'Anyway, he made it pretty clear to Helen that he wouldn't spend the half-term with me, and apparently Helen herself has decided to move to France. So I took Diana at her word and asked if Max could go to her, and she was good enough to agree.' Dan sighed. 'Max has effectively cut me out of his life, with a single-minded obstinacy that he seems to have inherited from his father.' He dipped into the inner breast pocket of his jacket and drew out an envelope, which he pushed towards Harry. Harry picked it up and saw it was addressed to Dan in childish round handwriting. 'Have a look inside.'

Harry drew out a boy's wristwatch.

'I had it mended and sent it to him at school. He sent it straight back.'

Harry returned the watch to the envelope and handed it to Dan. 'Surely you have some right to maintain contact?'

'Being a stepfather doesn't appear to mean very much, legally. It's not as though he needs anything from me. Di pays his school fees – well, the trust does – and if he doesn't want anything to do with me, no one can force him.' Dan stroked the tip of his cigarette against the ashtray.

'Give it time.'

'I don't think time is on my side, Harry. The more of it goes by, the longer Max is able to nurse his wrath against me, the less likely he is get over what I did. What we did.' He paused. 'He can hate me all he likes, that's my punishment. I may get the chance in the future to put things right. But Meg will never have that chance. And for him to feel that way about his mother…'

'It's a damned shame,' said Harry, with feeling. 'What about holidays, all that kind of thing?'

'He's not short of offers. Diana and Sonia have both invited him for Christmas.'

'You know, I'm pretty fond of the little chap myself. I've told him he's welcome to come to Chalcombe in the holidays. Maybe I can talk to him. Make your case, as it were.'

Dan smiled sadly. 'I doubt if he'll let you do that. But it's a kind thought. I'll put you in touch with Diana. It looks like she'll be running Max's life from now on.' There was a pause, and Dan added, 'Sonia feels that Helen is somehow abandoning her grandson by starting a new life in France, but I can't say I blame her for not wanting to stay here. Meg was her life. She was my life, too. Without her there's no reason for me to make a home in England either. Not if Max doesn't want or need me.'

'So what will you do?'

'I'll carry on working abroad. Go where the news takes me. I feel quite' – he searched for the word

– 'untethered. "The wandering outlaw of my own dark mind." Who was it said that?'

'Byron?' Harry scratched his beard. 'Yes, I think it was Byron.'

Max chose to spend the Christmas holidays at Diana's. He liked his aunt. Her cool, unfussy manner let him feel he wasn't the constant object of pity and concern, and he could keep himself to himself whenever he chose. Which was most of the time. His Uncle Roddy was all right, too, though he seemed to drink a lot, and his cousin Morven, who was four years younger than him, was a decent enough kid.

He didn't allow himself to think about last Christmas, when the world had been simple and kind. There was nothing to do but set the past apart and concentrate on the here and now.

The day after Boxing Day Diana invited Sonia and Laura to lunch. She was concerned that Max was spending too much time on his own and thought that perhaps Laura might bring him out of himself.

'You'll find him in his room,' she told Laura. She turned to Sonia. 'Come to the drawing room and we'll have a sherry. Lunch isn't for another half-hour.'

'How has Max been?' asked Sonia, settling herself in an armchair.

'It's hard to tell.' Diana poured two sherries, handed one to Sonia, and sat down. 'He's so very self-contained.

He's polite, and he talks well enough – that is, as long as no one mentions his mother or Dan. If they do he just leaves the room.' She sipped her drink. 'He's not what I'd call cheerful – that's hardly surprising – but he seems to be coping.' She shrugged. 'Though of course one hasn't a clue what's going on in his mind.' She gestured to the Christmas tree, beneath which a couple of presents lay untouched. 'He didn't open the presents Dan sent. Didn't say anything about it, just left them there.'

'Oh dear. What a sad business. Poor Dan.'

'I rather think Dan brought it on himself.'

'Must people go on suffering for their mistakes for ever?'

'Just because you forgave them both, Sonia, doesn't mean everyone should.'

'Perhaps not. But surely you'd rather things hadn't turned out this way? The idea that Max goes around thinking… well, whatever it is he thinks about his mother. It must be harmful to a boy of his age. No matter how well he may appear to be coping on the outside.'

Upstairs, Laura was sitting with Max at the table in his room, where he was building an Airfix model of a Lancaster bomber that Roddy had given him for Christmas. Diana had been doubtful about the appropriateness of the gift, since Paul had flown Lancasters in the war, but Roddy had astutely understood that this was why Max would like it.

'That glue stinks,' said Laura, peering as Max affixed a tiny propeller to one of the engines.

'I like the smell. There, I'll let that dry and do the rest later.' He set the model down and gazed at it with satisfaction. Then he glanced at Laura. 'What did you get for Christmas?'

'Aunt Sonia gave me a locket.' Laura held up the gold oval locket on a thin chain around her neck. 'And Avril gave me a book called *The Otterbury Incident*. It's really good. I can lend it to you. It's all about some boys tracking down a thief who steals their money. Oh, and I got a good new murder game called Cluedo. It's got real little weapons, a rope and a gun and other things. You could come over and we could play it, if you like.' Max said nothing, picking up with a pair of tweezers some small decals that were soaking in a saucer of water. Laura studied his face for a few seconds, then intuition prompted her to add, 'Avril won't be there. She's going back to Italy tomorrow.'

Max looked up. Laura had understood that the last person in the world he wanted to see was Avril. 'All right. Thanks.'

Downstairs, Sonia and Diana were still talking and drinking their sherry when Roddy came into the drawing room. Sonia, who hadn't seen Roddy since the war, was startled by the change in him. She remembered him as a tall young fighter pilot with dashing good looks and a thatch of red hair. At thirty-nine he was good-looking still, but his face was faintly blotched with tiny networks of broken red veins, and the red hair was thinning.

He greeted Sonia with keen pleasure and a firm handshake, then headed straight to the drinks tray, where he poured himself a large whisky and soda.

'I'd better just check on lunch,' said Diana, and left Sonia and Roddy together.

As they talked over old times, Sonia reminisced, 'I remember you used to drive racing cars before the war. I don't suppose you do that now?'

Roddy shook his head. 'It's a young man's game. I did try to take it up again after the war, but it didn't work out. There I'd been, going up in the old Spitfire day after day to take on Jerry and thinking nothing of it, but then when I got out on the circuit I found I'd quite lost my nerve. Funny, eh?' The slight, charming stammer with which he had always spoken now had a nervy, awkward quality. He knocked back the remains of his whisky. 'Can I interest you in another sherry?'

'No, thank you.'

He went to the drinks tray and poured himself another whisky. 'I've had a couple of business ventures here and there. You know, just the odd thing to keep me busy, keep the finances ticking over. Nothing much to speak of, though.'

These words revealed to Sonia that the post-war years had not been kind to Roddy, perhaps even hinting at failure. Hence the drinking? Presumably they were living on Diana's money.

He sat down again, gulping his whisky, and at that moment Diana reappeared and announced that lunch was ready. As Sonia left the drawing room she was aware of Roddy, behind her, furtively topping up his drink.

Roddy drank whisky and water all the way through lunch, and although his conversation was lucid, if a little animated, his tipsiness was evident to all. Diana, though she tried to conceal it with her usual cool, smiling demeanour, was clearly embarrassed. Sonia guessed that for Roddy to be drunk during the day was a common occurrence, and she felt sorry for her. It was something of a relief when the meal was over and she and Laura could take their leave.

'Can Max come over to play?' Laura asked Sonia, as they were putting on their coats.

'Of course, if that's all right with Diana.'

'By all means.' Diana was relieved at the prospect of Max doing something more than hiding away in his room with his Meccano and model aircraft for hours on end. She knew, too, that things were far from well with him, and that someone should talk to him to try to dissipate the anger and resentment he was nursing behind the mask of good behaviour, but she had harboured those same feelings for too long to be the person to help him. Perhaps Sonia, or even Laura, would find a way.

But on his visits to Mount Street Max resisted all attempts by his great-aunt to coax him to talk about his mother and stepfather. His obstinacy wore her down and in the end she let the subject alone. Laura, in her childish wisdom, never broached it.

'He's quite determined not to have anything more to do with Dan,' Sonia told Diana. 'That much is obvious. And it's more than just a phase.'

'He can't simply be passed from pillar to post. He needs somewhere to call home. I think he should come and live with us in Kensington. I'm going to propose it to Dan.'

Dan realised he had no choice but to agree. So Max's belongings were moved out of the Belgravia house and he went to live permanently with his aunt and uncle. Dan knew now there was nothing left for him in England. The people who mattered most to him had been ripped from his life, and his existence there made no sense any more. He would live and work abroad from now on, and leave behind the memory of everything he had lost.

7

1953

During the three years that Avril spent studying in Rome, she wrote infrequently to her mother and came home only briefly at Christmas and in the summer months. The result of this was that Sonia turned her affection increasingly to Laura, something that was evident to Avril every time she returned to Mount Street. Even though she herself was responsible for distancing herself from her mother, she blamed Laura, fuelling the cycle of resentment that had begun in Laura's infancy. For Avril, Laura would always be the intruder, the usurper of love and attention that should rightfully have been hers.

Sonia had hoped that at the end of her studies Avril would return to London to live, but with characteristic resourcefulness Avril found a job and told her mother she would be staying in Italy for the time being to work in one of the city's prestigious commercial galleries. Although the work was largely clerical, labelling and cataloguing works of art, Avril knew it would help to extend her network of contacts in the art world, so that one day she could fulfil her ambition of running her own gallery.

In the late spring of 1953, a month after Laura's sixteenth birthday, Sonia began to feel unwell. She had lost her appetite and even found her daily walk in the park fatiguing. She put it down to her age and tried to ignore it, but when she began to experience stomach pains, too, she felt obliged to consult her Harley Street doctor. He conducted various tests, and three weeks later, on a sunny morning in late June, Sonia returned to his surgery to receive the results.

When she stepped out of the consulting rooms into the sunshine, the bright softness of the day seemed to have hardened into something glaring and hostile. She walked with unseeing eyes down Harley Street and crossed the road to Cavendish Square, and sat down on a bench. Nearby, a small girl was feeding crumbs to the sparrows and pigeons. Sonia watched them, thinking of the birds that used to come to the bird table at Woodbourne House, remembering the garden, and herself on a day such as this, wandering in the sunshine among the flower beds with her trug and secateurs, snipping fresh blooms for the house. It had been one of her greatest pleasures. Random thoughts filled her mind, a stream of memories, like the shadows of clouds drifting over a familiar landscape. All this was to end: her memories, her sentiments, her cares and pleasures, her very existence. Liver cancer, which had spread beyond the bounds of curability. She tried to summon back the numb shock with which she had received the diagnosis, but she could no longer make herself feel it. The shock had flattened out into fact. She sat there on the bench trying to accept the prognosis and her new reality. Her end. Two months, the doctor had said, perhaps less. How strange to think what different things two months might mean to different people. To that little girl, for instance, it might be the amount of time till her next birthday, and feel like an eternity. To Sonia it felt like nothing, no time at all. Why, just a fortnight ago, on the day of the Coronation, she had been wondering how many years of the new young queen's reign she might see, and now she had the laughable answer. And only the other day she had been speculating on taking a trip to Nice at the end of July to visit Helen, who had recently married her nice Frenchman and intended to live permanently in the South of France. No trip now. No holiday. No time.

She sat in the park for a while, directing her mind to practicalities, trying to subdue her sense of panic at the thought of all that needed to be done in so little time. She had rejected the idea of hospital – what point, since there was no treatment? – and the doctor had told her she must, in that case, have a nurse. She might feel well enough to get around at the moment, but it had been made clear to her that things would change rapidly. A sudden shaft of pain in her abdomen was a reminder of that. Engaging a nurse would be the first thing. And the girls must be told, and Helen, though that would have to wait until she and Serge returned from their honeymoon in America. What a cruel irony, that her sister should be beginning a new and happy phase of her life, while in a matter of weeks, her own would be over. For the first time since she had left the consulting rooms, she wept.

The doctor had provided a list of recommended and available nurses, and Sonia conducted interviews until she found one who met with her approval. Nurse Cardew was a large, middle-aged woman, cheerful without being garrulous, efficient, kindly and discreet, and it was arranged that she should come in twice a day, until such time as Sonia required lengthier spells of care.

Sonia wrote to Avril straight away. The lack of closeness between them somehow made it easier to tell her frankly about her condition, and the prognosis. Avril replied that she would be home within the week.

She took a little longer to write to Laura, and when she did she was careful to say nothing of how grave her condition was.

The doctor says I am rather ill and will need looking after for a while, but you mustn't distress yourself. I

have an excellent nurse to look after me, and Avril will
be back from Italy in a day or two. I am counting the
days till you come home for the summer holidays.

Literally, thought Sonia, as she folded the letter and
put it in an envelope.

When Laura came home from school she was alarmed
by what she found. At half-term Aunt Sonia had been
much her usual self, but now it was as though some
inner spring had wound down. She was listless and
tired, and although she still dressed with her customary
elegance, she had lost weight, and her beautiful rings
were loose on her thin fingers. On the first night of
Laura's return she joined the girls at the dinner table,
but ate hardly anything, and shortly afterwards she
went to bed.

'I hadn't realised she was so ill,' Laura said to Avril.
'How long do you think it's going to take her to get
better?'

Avril said nothing. Her eyes followed Laura as she got
up and went to the sideboard to fetch a dish of grapes.
At sixteen, Laura was heart-stoppingly lovely. Even the
unflattering blue gingham school dress couldn't disguise
her shapely figure, with its narrow waist and high, small
breasts. Her ash-blonde hair seemed to glow with silky
light. Her skin was milky, her cheekbones flawless, and
her grave grey eyes with their thick, dark lashes shone

with youthful lustre. Her graceful unselfconsciousness only added to the effect.

'She's not going to get better,' said Avril. 'She's terminally ill. Maybe she thinks she's being kind, not telling you, but it's better that you know.'

Laura put the fruit on the table and sat down, aghast. 'She's going to die?'

'Yes.' Tears welled in Avril's dark eyes.

Laura put her hands over her face and burst into sobs, her shoulders shaking.

'Stop it,' said Avril quietly. 'She might hear you.'

Laura fished a crumpled hanky from her dress pocket and mopped her eyes. 'Sorry.'

'We have to do our best to make things normal for as long as we can.'

Laura nodded. 'All right.'

Avril gazed at Laura's tear-stained face. She was going to be useless, that much was obvious. She'd always been a mawkish kid, crying over ponies and dead rabbits. Putting up a brave front was probably beyond her. On the other hand, her mother might prefer that, being on the emotional side herself. Avril, much as she hated the thought of her mother dying, knew herself to be incapable of sentimental displays. Laura was demonstrative in a way that she never could be. Blinking back her own unshed tears, she lit a cigarette.

Laura sat with her crumpled hanky in her fist, stricken and miserable. The idea of Aunt Sonia dying was so scaring that she could hardly comprehend it. She tried to imagine the future without her. No one to write to her at school, no one to offer a loving welcome at the end of term. No one in the flat. No home. Just emptiness. Where would she go? Who would look after her? Aunt Sonia was her entire world, and she had taken for granted that she would always be there. She looked at Avril. She had been struck, when she came back, by how grown-up she seemed now. She wore lipstick and had gold studs in her ears, and was dressed in a full-skirted, tight-waisted dress and Italian shoes with low heels, her dark hair fastened in a neat chignon. Laura's sudden sense of insecurity filled her with an impulse to get up and go to the older girl to seek some comfort, a kiss, a kind and reassuring embrace. But she resisted the urge, knowing Avril would hate it. She watched Avril smoke, her eyes fixed on the crimson nails and white fingers, the square silver bracelet that slid up and down her wrist each time she tapped the ash from her cigarette.

'How long will it be?' she asked at last.

Avril shifted her gaze to meet Laura's. 'Possibly only a few weeks.'

What would happen after that? Laura wondered. She had never felt so unprotected, so unsure of the future.

*

Sonia tried to conduct her life as normally as possible, for the girls' sake. But the illness had begun to take its toll, as though it were consuming her day by day. She could see the time when she would be confined to bed permanently rapidly approaching, but she was not yet ready to succumb. As long as she could manage, she would maintain a rough semblance of her normal routine.

One day, when Nurse Cardew was there and both girls were out on various errands, Sonia said she was going for a walk.

Nurse Cardew looked apprehensive. 'Would you like me to come with you?'

'Whatever for?'

'Just in case. It's a very hot day.'

'No, thank you. I can manage. Would you mind fetching my hat?'

Sonia got into the lift. The sense of being unwell had been with her for so many weeks now that it registered only as a kind of unearthliness, a feeling of exhausted detachment. She exchanged a few words with Sidney, the doorman, and stepped out into the sunshine. She had intended to go round the corner to Mount Street Gardens, but as she stood there on the pavement it seemed a very long way. Absurdly far. Suddenly her vision seemed to tunnel, the pavement rising up to meet her as the sky spun, then darkness.

A passer-by stopped to assist, Sidney was summoned from the building, and Sonia was helped back to the flat. Nurse Cardew undressed her, put her to bed, gave her a cup of tea and some tablets, then drew down the green blind against the brightness of the outside world, into which Sonia would never venture again.

A week later Laura was sitting in Sonia's bedroom, reading her snippets from the morning paper, gently stroking her hand as she read, the skin like silky tissue beneath her fingers, close to the bone. Avril came in and surveyed the scene, wrinkling her nose against the mingled smell of Nurse Cardew's lily-of-the-valley toilet water and the ethyl alcohol that was part of Sonia's pain-relieving medication.

She approached the bed and dropped a kiss on Sonia's forehead. 'How are you today, Mama?' Sonia, lying with her eyes closed, merely nodded. 'Aunt Helen telephoned. She's back from America and she got your letter. She says she'll be here at the weekend.'

Sonia nodded. 'We must make up the bed in the spare room.' Then she added weakly, 'Someone should tell Dan. I haven't wanted to worry him. He's covering the war in Korea, you know. Such a long way away.'

Avril was aware that Dan came to visit Sonia when he was back in England, which was infrequently, but she herself hadn't seen him in years. Of course he should be told. In fact, she could hardly believe her mother hadn't written to him at the outset.

'Have you an address for him?' As she regarded her mother, Avril found herself wondering if, by the time a letter reached Dan, it might not be too late.

'He wrote not long ago. I keep his letters in my desk in the drawing room.'

Avril nodded to Laura, indicating that she should go and check. Laura folded up the newspaper and went to look. Sonia's gaze followed her as she left the room. She lifted her hand and clutched Avril's fingers. How fierce the grip of a dying person was, thought Avril. As though desperate to hold on tight to life.

'We must have a talk about Laura. I need to make sure about certain things.'

'Yes. But not now. You're tired.'

Nurse Cardew came in. 'Time for your medication, Mrs Haddon,' she said gently.

Avril left the bedroom and went through to the drawing room. Laura was sitting in the chair by Sonia's desk, her back to the room. As Avril approached she saw that Laura was absorbed in reading Dan's letter, chewing the end of a lock of hair. She looked up at Avril with a start.

'You're only meant to be looking for an address, not reading private correspondence,' remarked Avril.

'Aunt Sonia always lets me read Dan's letters. He

writes so awfully well. This is his most recent one. It's got an address.'

Avril took the letter from Laura. 'Fine. I'll try to put something together.' It wasn't going to be an easy letter to write. 'You go and make a start on supper.'

Helen arrived and took up residence in the spare room. She had come determined to assume charge of the domestic situation, but Nurse Cardew's efficient presence meant there was little for her to do, and she spent her time talking and reading to her sister. The girls came and went, trying to maintain cheerful demeanours, but the atmosphere in the flat was one of looming sadness.

Early one afternoon, when Avril was in the drawing room, Nurse Cardew put her head round the door.

'Miss Haddon, your mother's asking for you.'

Avril followed the nurse through to her mother's room. Helen was at Sonia's bedside, and the two of them were reading through a document.

'That seems fine,' said Sonia. She stretched out a thin hand to pick up a pen from the bedside table, and laboriously signed the document.

'What's that?' asked Avril.

'It's a codicil to my will,' murmured Sonia. She was by now painfully gaunt, her skin yellowing and lightly flecked with greyish freckles. 'I've decided I would like to leave Laura a few things. You will have all the money and this place, and so on, so I want her to have some pieces of my jewellery. And the portrait of her mother, of course.'

'May I see?' asked Avril.

'Of course,' said Sonia. 'You will be the one who has to deal with everything when I'm gone. Just let Nurse Cardew and your aunt put their signatures to it.'

Avril waited until the document had been witnessed, then took it and read it through in stunned silence. As well as the painting, her mother was leaving Laura her most precious items of jewellery, including pieces her father had bought for their wedding. The Fabergé earrings and necklace alone were worth a small fortune. That her mother wanted Laura, and not her, to have these most treasured possessions left her wounded, angry beyond words.

At that moment the doorbell buzzed in the hall. 'I'll go and see who that is,' said Helen.

'The solicitor says it's most important that this is put with my will,' Sonia said to Avril. 'You know where to find it, in the compartment in my desk.'

Laura came in, her eyes shining. 'Guess who's here? Dan!'

Sonia's face lit up. 'Oh, how wonderful!' She turned to Nurse Cardew. 'That's my godson. He's come all the way from Korea.'

'Korea, goodness! Well, don't let him tire you out. Now, I'd best be getting off. I'll see you this evening.'

A moment later Dan came into the room. He looked

tired from the flight and his chin was rough with stubble. He approached Sonia's bedside with a smile and bent to kiss her. If he was shocked at the change in his godmother, he was careful not to show it.

'I can't believe you've come all this way,' murmured Sonia. 'How perfectly lovely.'

'I booked a flight as soon as I got Avril's letter. Some things are more important than Chinese and Korean peace negotiations.'

'Have you come straight from the airport?' Helen asked. 'You must be exhausted. I'll make us all some tea, shall I?'

'Thanks. I could rather do with a cup.'

Helen went off to the kitchen. Dan drew up a chair next to Sonia's bed. Avril left and went to the drawing room. She could hear the clinking of crockery from the kitchen. She went to the desk and slid open the compartment containing her mother's will, and stood there, the codicil in her hand, her heart beating hard. Her aunt's voice from the hallway startled her. 'Now, where did I leave my spectacles?' she heard her say.

Swiftly closing the desk, she bent down and opened a drawer, and stuffed the codicil amongst some old letters. She straightened up as Helen came in.

'Ah! Here they are.' Helen picked up her glasses from a table. 'Would you give me a hand with the tea things, Avril, dear? Then we can go and hear all Dan's news.'

In Sonia's room the atmosphere was quiet but cheerful.

Laura had poured out tea, and Helen had helped Sonia to sit up among her pillows to take a cup. It had been difficult for Dan to grasp the change in his godmother. The elegant, vital woman he had always known had been reduced to a spectral figure, ravaged by illness, and at first he had hardly known how to greet her or what to say. But delight in seeing him shone from her tired eyes, and although her voice was weak, the enthusiasm with which she asked him questions about his flight, and Korea, and his work, was so familiar that his distress melted away, and they conversed happily, lovingly.

'I find it hard to keep up with all the changes in the world,' said Sonia, 'though Laura reads me important things from the newspaper every day. You say the war in Korea is almost over? Well, that's a blessing. The fewer wars the better. No, I don't think I could manage a biscuit, my dear,' she said, as Laura handed round a plate of shortbread. She gave Dan a weak, fond smile. 'So will you be home for good after Korea?'

Dan hesitated. 'I'm not sure I count England as home any more. Things have changed so very much. In my own life, I mean. I'm thinking of going to work in America.'

'Oh.' Sonia nodded. 'One hears great things about America.'

'Too many, for my liking,' observed Helen. 'I like the *place* well enough, but I'm afraid the people are far from ideal.'

'You never did like the Americans, did you?'

murmured Sonia. 'I must say I thought the GIs who were stationed near us in the war very dashing.'

'So I recall. You insisted on inviting several of them to tea, and they ate a week's rations in one sitting.'

'I think you were just a teeny bit jealous that that nice air force general was so attentive to me,' said Sonia.

'Far from it. He was too brash for my liking. Very fond of the sound of his own voice. Frankly, I found most of the GIs very vulgar. They stuck chewing gum to the bottoms of the cinema seats. Still, each to his own. They say it's the country of progress, at any rate.'

Dan smiled. It was reassuring to hear Helen and Sonia conversing as they had always done, as though nothing were amiss, as though death was not a shadow waiting at their elbows.

After another quarter of an hour it was evident Sonia was exhausted, though she was reluctant for Dan to go.

'You'll come back tomorrow?' she asked.

'Of course.' He dropped a kiss on her forehead. 'Forgive my unshaven state. I'll be more the thing tomorrow morning.'

'Where are you staying?' asked Avril, as they left Sonia's room.

'My club. The Belgravia house is rented out.' Dan picked up his suitcase and jacket. 'I'll see you all tomorrow.' He glanced over Avril's shoulder and gave Laura a special smile, one that was not lost on Avril.

Sonia lay among her pillows, drowsy from the pain relief that Nurse Cardew had administered a few moments ago. How lovely it had been to see Dan, how good of him to come so far. As she closed her eyes, she suddenly remembered what it was she'd meant to say to him. What had stopped her? Oh yes, Helen coming in with the tea tray. And Laura and Avril had been there, so she couldn't... She'd meant to ask him to look out for Laura. Not that she didn't trust Avril to care for her, it was just – oh, it was all so difficult... She felt she was leaving Laura all alone in the world. Why should that be, when Avril was there to look after her? Because Avril was... she was... oh, how hard it was to think. The pain pulled one's mind this way and that. But she would say it to Dan when he came tomorrow. Yes, tomorrow. She would put it all right tomorrow.

Nurse Cardew's night duties involved making three-hourly checks on her patient to see if she needed more pain relief or other attention. When she went in at seven o'clock the next morning she knew as soon as she saw Sonia's frail, sunken face, the thin mouth agape, that she was gone. The doctor had murmured to her just the previous afternoon that he thought the end could not be far away. It was odd, she thought, as she made a few brisk checks to confirm what she already knew, no matter how many times you encountered death, its presence always gave you that funny shrivelling feeling inside. Still, it was a mercy Mrs Haddon had gone as peacefully as she had. The poor woman would have endured painful agonies if she had held on much longer. She'd seen it before. Nurse Cardew folded Sonia's withered hands and tidied her so that she would look serene when the girls came in, then went to put the kettle on and prepare herself to deliver the news to the rest of the household when they awoke.

8

SONIA WAS BURIED in Brompton cemetery on an afternoon in early August. A sizeable crowd of mourners attended, friends from London and the country, and her close family. Max came with Diana. He had been at Eton for two years now, and his life out of school had settled into a regular pattern. In the holidays he lived with the MacLennans in Kensington, going to Torquay with them for two weeks in August, then staying with his grandmother in France for another fortnight. Whenever Harry Denholm issued an invitation to Chalcombe, which he did regularly, Diana always found reasons why it was not convenient for Max to go. Her disapproval of Dan extended to Harry, and knowing what she did of Harry's sexual proclivities, the idea of Max going to stay with him made her apprehensive.

Though protective, there was nothing maternal in her relationship with the fifteen-year-old. She treated Max with a kind of distant affection, which suited him very well. His school life was everything to him, the weeks spent in Kensington mere humdrum interludes. Since his mother's death he had developed an aversion to close relationships with adults, though he was fond of his grandmother, and his holidays at the Villa Clémence were the ones he enjoyed most. He loved being on the Riviera, with its elegance and perpetual sunshine. There he was granted a freedom he experienced nowhere else. He liked being solitary, and would spend hours lounging in his favourite spot in a hammock beneath a fig tree in the villa garden, reading, daydreaming, and watching the little lizards scutter among the dusty undergrowth. Sometimes he would stroll down to the harbour in Antibes and wander along the marina, admiring the yachts, or take the bus into the hills to St Paul-de-Vence. He loved the pretty village with its colony of artists, and was especially fascinated by the film stars who frequented the Colombe d'Or. He would buy an ice cream and hang around on the dusty pavement outside the hotel gate, occasionally rewarded by a glimpse of Alain Delon or Simone Signoret whisking through the gateway into the restaurant. He had a half-formed dream that one day he would lead his own louche, exciting life on the Côte d'Azur, but quite what that life would consist of wasn't yet clear. He just knew that being there was the closest thing to happiness in his life.

He stood now between Diana and his grandmother, watching the coffin being lowered into the grave. Over the past two years he had grown from a schoolboy into a tall, handsome young man. He glanced around at the grieving faces and felt utterly detached and unemotional. All of this seemed to have no connection to the kindly woman who had been such a solid part of his early life. Great-Aunt Sonia might be in that box, but in his heart and mind she would always be living at Woodbourne House, tending her pigs and chickens and vegetables.

He cast a covert glance at Laura, who was standing on the other side of the grave. He kept trying not to look at her, and the harder he tried the worse it got. He had always thought of her as pretty, but it had never mattered much before. Now he found something so entirely compelling about the translucence of her skin and the touchable softness of her blonde hair, the way it spilled onto the shoulders of her black dress, that he simply had to stare. Oh Lord, she'd looked over and seen him staring. He glanced away. In the last two years he had seen her only once last summer, when she had come over to Kensington and they had gone out together to the park to eat a packed lunch and feed the ducks. But somehow things hadn't been quite right. Max had felt tongue-tied and unable to respond intelligently or easily to anything she said. The conversations about anything and everything that had once flowed so easily between them seemed to have dried to stilted exchanges about school. Only afterwards did Max kick himself for not telling her about his holidays in the south of France. He visualised himself talking animatedly about the glass blowers in Biot, about the fun of going out in Serge's speedboat to Golfe Juan and having a picnic lunch of shrimp and cheese and bread, and swimming off the boat, and Laura listening with attentive awe. He would have looked interesting and sophisticated, instead of awkward and schoolboyish. Maybe he'd get a chance to talk to her later, and make a better effort than last time.

Avril had arranged for tea and sandwiches to be served at the flat in Mount Street after the funeral. She issued the invitation in her usual negligent manner, as though it was a matter of indifference to her who chose to come. Which in many ways it was.

'I need to get back,' Diana told Max. 'You go if you want, though.'

Roddy had lately been ordered by the doctor to give up drinking, and she was anxious to get home and make sure he didn't have the kind of lapse he'd had last week, when she had gone shopping and he'd drunk half a bottle of Scotch by lunchtime.

As he walked back with the others to Mount Street, Max was so busy planning what he would say to Laura that it took him by surprise to find she had fallen into step next to him. She gave him a smile, and every carefully prepared utterance fled from his mind.

'I notice you're still not speaking to Dan,' she observed.

He hadn't expected this. 'Nothing's changed,' he replied, 'so why would I?'

'He's terribly fond of you. He was asking all about you the other day.'

'I frankly don't care.'

They walked in silence for a moment. Ahead of them they could see Dan talking to Harry and Helen.

'You can't stay angry at someone for ever,' persisted Laura.

'Please, can you drop it?' He ignored the reproachful expression in her grave, grey eyes. 'He did something I can't forgive, so that's the end of it. All right?'

They had reached the mansion block. She shrugged and walked in ahead of him, leaving him on the pavement. He wasn't sure what he felt. All he knew was that the candid, grown-up nature of the exchange had imperceptibly moved their relationship to a different plane, and he was glad of it. They wouldn't have to pretend to be children any more.

The mourners made their way into the drawing room.

'Sorry I haven't been able to give you more news of Max while you've been away,' Harry said to Dan over their cups of coffee. 'I don't think his aunt is terribly keen on him coming to Chalcombe. She's blocked every invitation I've issued.'

'Probably because she has such a down on me,' said Dan. 'Anyway, old chap, it doesn't much matter. I'm entirely persona non grata where Max is concerned, and I don't expect it to change.' He glanced at his watch. 'I should get going. Got a meeting. Bill Shirer introduced me to a chap called Alastair Cooke last time I was in the States, and he's over in London for a few days – could lead to a job, if I'm lucky. How about a drink tomorrow evening?'

'Certainly. Seven o'clock, usual place.'

Avril had put Laura in charge of serving sandwiches and making tea and coffee, while she dispensed drinks.

As Laura passed her she said in an aside, 'Laura, it doesn't do to have all these dirty ashtrays. Can you empty them, please?'

Max saw Laura collecting ashtrays and helped her take them to the kitchen.

'Thanks,' said Laura, as they emptied the fag ends into a bin. 'I'll give them a wipe and you can take them back. Ugh! What a beastly smell.'

'I'm sorry I was a bit short earlier,' said Max.

'It doesn't matter. You had every right. I always think I can make things better for people, which Avril says just annoys them. She calls me Pollyanna, and I don't think she means it as a compliment.'

At that moment Harry came into the kitchen, cigarette in hand. 'I've come to retrieve an ashtray. I can't go strewing ash on the Aubusson rugs.' He glanced at Max. 'How are you, young man? It's been a while, hasn't it? You must come and spend some time at Chalcombe soon. The gramophone's been missing you. In fact, unless your aunt has other plans for you, why don't you try to find time to come down? Maybe next week?'

Max hesitated, then said, 'Thanks – I'd love to.'

Harry turned to Laura. 'And what about you, young lady? I imagine your summer is rather at sixes and sevens with all this sad business. Why don't you come as well?'

At that moment Avril came into the kitchen. Harry and Max were momentarily hidden by the door, and she could see only Laura at the sink, wiping the ashtrays. 'For heaven's sake, hurry up. There are plates that need—' The door swung back and she caught sight of the other two.

'Hello, Avril.' Harry smiled to cover her discomfiture. 'I was just asking these two if they'd like to come and spend a few days in Kent. The place is in need of some young faces. You'd be most welcome, too.'

'That's kind of you, Harry, but I don't think I can spare the time. My mother's death has left a lot to be done.' She paused. Sonia's illness had forced her to leave Italy abruptly, and she needed to go back to sort things out. She had recently been calculating that if her mother had left enough money, she might be able to set up her own business in London, as she had always wanted. If

Laura were to go to Chalcombe for a while she could make the trip to Rome without leaving her alone in the flat, which she knew Laura wouldn't like, especially in the wake of Sonia's death. She turned to Laura. 'But why don't you go? It might be good for you. It's been such a miserable time lately.'

'I'd love to come,' said Laura, and Max's heart rose at the thought of being with her for a week at Chalcombe.

As he got off the bus in Kensington and walked home, Max wondered what state Uncle Roddy would be in. The doctor's prohibition didn't seem to have made much difference. A month ago the drinks trolley had been cleared of sherry, gin, whisky – anything that could be regarded as alcoholic, including the Angostura bitters. For a while it had worked, and his uncle had been sober, if miserable, for days at a stretch. But lately he had relapsed, and was clearly obtaining alcohol on the sly. Twice recently he'd been drunk by midday, and on both occasions it had happened when Diana was out of the house. This morning his uncle had made excuses for not attending Sonia's funeral, and Max thought he knew why. He suspected his aunt did, too.

When he let himself into the house he met Diana coming downstairs, her blonde hair awry, her face weary and stricken, an empty Scotch bottle in her hand. When she caught sight of Max she tucked the bottle behind her skirt.

'You OK?' asked Max.

'You uncle's not very well.'

The household euphemism for Uncle Roddy being tight as a tick exasperated Max. He gave a dismissive shrug. 'Harry Denholm asked if I might like to go to Chalcombe the week after next. I told him yes.'

Diana frowned. 'I'm not really sure—'

'I want to go. Laura's going, too.'

'Oh. Oh well, in that case... And if you really are keen—'

'Thanks,' said Max abruptly, and went upstairs to his room.

Three days after the funeral Laura came back to the flat to find Avril unwrapping a parcel on the floor of the drawing room.

'What's that?' she asked, watching Avril pulling off brown paper and corrugated cardboard.

'One of my father's paintings,' said Avril. 'I thought it was time I had it framed.'

She drew out the painting in its slim gilt frame and propped it against the sofa. Laura gazed at it.

'It's beautiful. Who is she?'

'Someone who stayed at Woodbourne House one summer, I believe. Mother and I found it in the barn when we were selling up.' She glanced around the room. 'Now, where best to hang it?' She picked up the painting, which wasn't large, measuring no more than twenty-four by eighteen inches, and took it to the end of the room. 'Here, above the bureau, don't you think?'

Laura considered. 'Yes. It'll look perfect there. And it will catch the morning light.'

'So it will.' Avril propped the picture on the bureau. 'I'll fetch the stepladder and do it now.'

Ten minutes later they stood back and admired the painting.

'It has a sad quality somehow,' said Laura. 'As though whoever she's waiting for isn't going to come.'

Without a word Avril folded up the stepladder and took it back to the hall cupboard.

9

THE DOORBELL BUZZED in the flat at Mount Street. 'My taxi's here!' shouted Laura.

Avril emerged from her bedroom, putting on her hat.

'I'll share it with you. I have to go to Clement's Inn to see the lawyer.' There was something gratifying about appropriating her mother's solicitor, along with everything else. It gave her a feeling of substance. The flat, the money in the bank, her late father's paintings – the fickle art world might not presently put a very high value on Henry Haddon's work, but the wheel of fashion would turn eventually – and whatever shares and investments her mother had held. She would find out today the total value of the estate.

As they went down in the lift Laura asked, 'When do you get back from Rome?'

'The same day you come back from Kent.' She surveyed Laura critically, noting her breasts taut against the bodice of her blue linen dress. 'We should have got you some new summer dresses. You've grown out of everything.'

'The ones I have are fine. Well, for this summer at least. Though I think I need a new school blazer.'

Avril made no reply. She had her own ideas about whether or not Laura would be returning to Abbeyfield in September. The fees were absurd, and she wasn't sure another two years at boarding school would do Laura much good, since she wasn't exactly academic.

When Avril had dropped her off at Charing Cross, Laura bought her ticket and met Max at the platform as arranged. He was dressed in navy slacks and a blazer over an open-neck shirt, his unruly dark hair had been fiercely combed down, and he was doing his level best to appear casual and matter-of-fact, and not to betray his heart-thumping pleasure at seeing Laura. They walked down the train till they found an empty compartment, put their cases on the luggage rack and settled into their seats.

'This is the first time I've been on holiday on my own,' remarked Laura, pulling off her cardigan and folding it on the seat next to her. 'You'll laugh at me, but I feel fearfully grown-up.'

It was the opening Max had been hoping for. 'Really? I'm quite used to it. I go to my grandmother's place in the south of France on my own every year.'

And as the train pulled out of the station he began

to tell Laura all about the Riviera and its glories. She listened, impressed and wistful.

'I've never been abroad,' she said. 'I sort of hoped Avril might invite me to go and stay with her in Rome. But I suppose she didn't want to be bothered having a schoolgirl hanging around.'

'Why would you want to stay with her? She's not even that nice to you half the time.'

'She isn't so bad. Anyway,' Laura glanced out of the carriage window, 'she looks after me now. She's the closest thing I have to family.'

Max made no reply. At least he had his grandmother and aunt and uncle, and his cousin. He tried to imagine what it was like to feel so utterly bereft of relations, and to have to rely on someone like Avril to look out for you.

His thoughts shifted tack when a moment later Laura asked him, 'What are you going to do when you leave school?'

'I don't know. Maybe become a lawyer.' During the Easter holidays he had gone with a friend to the Old Bailey to watch his friend's father defend a man accused of murder. The pomp and drama of the courtroom had excited and moved him, and he had since thought that a career at the bar might be interesting. He knew that he would come into his money when he was twenty-five – quite a great deal, he gathered from his aunt – but the idea of leading a purposeless life did not appeal. 'What will you do?'

'Oh, I don't know. I never think about the future. I just let things happen.' She closed her eyes. At that moment the sun burst from behind a cloud, and a shaft of sunlight struck her face, burnishing her hair and lighting the contours of her cheek and brow. She looked so ethereally, obliviously lovely that Max's infatuated heart felt as though it would burst, and he realised in that moment that beauty such as Laura possessed had a purpose all of its own. Somehow she must innately, complacently know that it would take her anywhere she wanted. No wonder she gave no thought to the future. The world rushing past the carriage window as she sat with her eyes closed seemed expressive of all this. He found himself suddenly saying, 'You look very pretty like that. In the sunshine, I mean.' He wished the words back as soon as he had uttered them, they sounded so feeble.

Laura opened her eyes. 'Do I? I think I look like a duck most of the time,' she said it without affectation, and he realised she meant it. Maybe beautiful people really didn't have any proper idea of the way they appeared to the world. Maybe what they saw in the mirror each morning was something utterly different. Max pondered this for the remainder of the journey.

Harry was waiting with the car at the station and hailed them from the end of the platform as they disembarked.

'Stow your cases in the boot and hop in.'

As they drove along the leafy, winding roads Harry remarked, 'You'll be pleased to know there's another young person about the premises – my godson, Philip Carteret. You probably know him, Max. He's just left Eton.'

The truth was, in inviting Max and Laura, Harry had been motivated not only by hospitality but also by the need to provide company for Philip, who was staying at Chalcombe while his wealthy parents went through an acrimonious divorce. The visit had so far not been an unqualified success. Philip was amusing and clever, but Harry's various weekend guests seemed to find the eighteen-year-old's precocity and candour a little too much, and Harry hoped that Max and Laura's presence might have the effect of damping down Philip's extravagant personality.

When they reached the house Max and Laura climbed from the car and surveyed the gardens. The herbaceous borders had matured, peonies and cyclamens glowing against a backdrop of blue and white campanula mingling with drifts of phlox, and roses blooming around the base of the sundial in the centre of the square lawn. The circle of mulberry trees made a majestic framework for it all.

'It's so beautiful,' said Laura. 'I mean, it always was, but now it's even better.'

'Not bad, eh?' agreed Harry. 'Hard to remember what

a tumbledown wilderness it was just a few years ago. Anyway, come and I'll show you where your rooms are. You can unpack and freshen up, and then we'll have lunch. I've left Philip preparing it.'

Max chucked his case on the bed and went to the open window, leaning out and gazing across the woodland in the direction of the gravel pond. He took a melancholy pleasure in being at Chalcombe again. It somehow helped to make sense of his feelings. His anger towards his mother had dwindled in the years since her death. By convincing himself that everything had been Dan's fault he had absolved her – almost – from blame, and could now remember her as he wanted to. He could come to Chalcombe and look at the beautiful rooms she had helped to decorate and furnish and to know that she was a part of it, and that he was, too. It was a healing, comforting thought.

When she had finished unpacking, Laura went downstairs and wandered through to the conservatory, whose wide doors were open to the terrace, where a table had been prepared for lunch. Four places were laid with Harry's best silver and new Fornasetti plates, and cornflower blue linen napkins, each with a sprig of lavender next to it.

Laura was admiring the perfection of it all when a voice behind her said, 'If you're thinking that the napkins don't sit at all well with the plates, you're absolutely right.'

She turned to see a young man regarding her. He was very tall, dark-haired and strikingly good-looking, with high cheekbones and narrow blue eyes beneath dark brows, and was dressed in a white shirt with a dark blue silk cravat, and high-waisted linen trousers that made his legs look immensely long.

'I'm Philip.' He put out his hand and she shook it.

'I'm Laura. And no, I think the table looks perfect.'

'Kind of you to say, but I really believe Harry's wonderful Italian flatware is crying out for something more rustic. Still, it's the best I could do.' He strolled around the table, gazing at it critically, and Laura couldn't help thinking how elegantly self-assured he was, and how handsome, with his intense, dark blue eyes. When he glanced at her and smiled, as he did now, it made his face even more compellingly attractive.

'Would you like to help fetch the food?' he asked.

Laura followed him to the kitchen. On the table sat a jointed cold roast chicken, crayfish arranged around a dish of sorrel sauce, a Spanish omelette and a bowl of rice mixed with chopped tomatoes.

'Golly, did you do all this yourself?' Laura asked Philip. She was unused to the idea of any young Englishman having the faintest notion of how to prepare food.

'I did. I even caught the crayfish.'

They took the dishes to the terrace, and Harry

arrived, then Max with Hamlet at his heels. Laura knelt down to cuddle the little dog, who rolled over and put an ecstatic tummy in the air to be tickled.

'Latimer – good to see you.' Philip extended a hand.

Max shook his hand and murmured a diffident greeting, a little put-out by the presence of the older boy. Over lunch he watched Philip's admiring and attentive behaviour towards Laura, and listened to him regale her with amusing stories, realising with a sinking heart that he had a formidable rival on his hands.

As the days passed, Laura fell entirely under Philip's spell. He made her laugh, and on the occasions when they were alone together he listened attentively to her girlish talk, evincing utter fascination with everything she had to say. The truth was, while he thought Laura extraordinarily pretty, Philip was these days simply trying out his charms on every woman he encountered, of whatever age. Max watched it all with a savagely unhappy heart, aware that he was utterly eclipsed by Philip.

On the final day of Max and Laura's visit Harry's business partner Edgar Lightfoot, who was also a moderately well-known poet, came to Chalcombe for the day to discuss the future of *The Modern Critical Review*. The magazine was struggling, and Harry was anxious to revitalise it. It was a rainy day, and he and Edgar settled themselves with whisky and sodas in armchairs in the conservatory while Max and Laura and Philip played three-handed bridge at a table on the other side of the room. Hamlet lay under the card table with his nose between his paws, gazing mournfully through the French windows at the rain falling on the terrace flagstones.

'What the magazine requires is more original writing and less rigid critical analysis,' grumbled Edgar. 'We're losing readership.'

'The problem is finding interesting new home-grown contributors,' said Harry. 'All the good writing seems to come from America these days.'

'Frankly,' sighed Edgar, 'the whole literary culture in Britain seems to be in decline. Everything seems to have retreated into banality and conservatism.'

Harry chuckled. 'What, is it closing time in the gardens of the west already?'

Edgar shook his head. 'You may laugh, but literature is the test of a civilisation. When *Horizon* folded I began to despair. I seriously wonder if *MRC* has any future. I wonder if western culture has any future. When I think of the writing that was produced before the war – Thomas, Auden, Isherwood, Spender… Are we ever going to see any new talent emerge?'

Harry poured more whisky and reached for the soda siphon, only to find it empty.

Laura was aware that Philip kept glancing across at the older men, his attention caught by their discussion. Now, in the interval of silence, he laid down his cards and said, 'Forgive me, but I couldn't help overhearing. Perhaps the problem lies with your generation. You remember the world the way it was before the war, before it changed you – and everything – for ever. You hanker after that. You hanker after your lost selves. That's what you want to recreate. But I don't see how you can.'

The two men turned to him in surprise, and Edgar replied with mildly suppressed irritation, 'And yours is the generation to show us the way forward?'

Philip shrugged. 'I don't know about that. I don't think we have anything original to say, not yet. The world is still frightened and confused. There's no sense of future joy. Maybe ten years from now we shall see a golden dawn of new things, of art and thinking and expression that we can't imagine. But recreating the way things were fifteen years ago – I don't think that's any good.' He picked up his cards.

Harry, after a moment's discomfiture, said mildly, 'Well, we still need voices to fill the silence until that happy day. And I need to inject some new lifeblood into *Modern Critical Review*. Perhaps, dear boy, you wouldn't mind fetching some more soda water from the pantry?'

Philip rose and crossed the room, picked up the soda siphon, and went to the kitchen to refill it. He returned moments later, and as he set the siphon down Edgar said to him, 'You know, one of the most attractive characteristics of young British people before the war was their fierce desire to change things, to overthrow governments, to bring about new movements in art and literature. But what have the young offered us since 1945? Moribund ideas, a total lack of originality or idealism. Where is the pioneering fervour? Small wonder we hark back to a better time.'

'To obsolescence, you mean,' replied Philip. There was a faint edge of anger to his voice. 'That's the problem with getting old. You look back, instead of ahead. But don't worry – we don't need you to trust us. We just need you to get out of our way.'

With that, he left the room.

Harry began a flustered apology, and Laura glanced at Max, who met her eyes with an embarrassed shrug and gathered up the cards. Without a word she got up from the table. Instinct took her through the kitchen to the small porch at the back door. Sure enough, there was Philip, leaning against the porch door jamb, smoking a cigarette.

'You sounded really angry,' said Laura.

'I am.' He flicked ash from the tip of his cigarette. 'Old fool.'

'That's not kind.'

'What has kindness to do with it? We won't get anywhere if we defer to that lot all the time, with their mournful complacency about the decline of everything. As though the future's in their hands.'

Laura said nothing. It had never occurred to her to question the way grown-ups ran the world, and it had surprised her to hear Philip challenge them so eloquently.

He glanced at the sky. 'Rain's beginning to clear. Shall we take a walk?'

'If you like.' She had no wish to return to the uncomfortable atmosphere of the conservatory.

They crossed the wet lawn and took a path into the woods. When Philip began to talk about his exchange with Edgar, Laura assumed he must now be regretting his rudeness. Far from it. Philip was scathing of the older man, dismissing his views as outdated and his poetry as facile and derivative.

'But he's famous!' protested Laura.

Philip regarded her with a smile. 'What a child you are.'

'Don't be patronising,' replied Laura in irritation. 'At least I don't go around pretending to know everything, the way you do. You know, it makes you look just a bit ridiculous. Especially when you get into arguments with your elders and betters.' She said this, but in fact she'd listened to what Philip said to Edgar with a thrill of admiration.

'Elders and betters?' Philip raised a sardonic eyebrow. 'In this day and age, no one knows anything, least of all *that* generation. The old certainties have gone. It's up to us to shape the new ones.' He gazed at her for a moment, and then quite unexpectedly he leaned forward and kissed her. She was about to pull away, but the touch of his lips awoke in her a delicious thrill of desire that was intense and entirely new. No one had ever kissed her before, and she gave herself up to it with amazement and pleasure. He carried on kissing her for a long time, gently manoeuvring her against a tree and pressing his body close against hers, enjoying feeling how utterly submissive she was. He had kissed quite a number of girls and regarded himself as fairly experienced.

When the kiss ended they walked on through the woods, talking and arguing, stopping occasionally to kiss again. By the time they returned to the house an hour later Laura had decided she was in love with Philip Carteret.

The next morning the skies had cleared and sunshine had returned. Laura laid the table for breakfast on the terrace while Max made toast and coffee. Philip arrived and settled himself in a chair with lanky grace.

'Shame you have to leave,' he remarked to the other two as he helped himself to toast. 'What time's your train?'

'Ten forty,' replied Laura. The desolation she felt was a new emotion to her. She could hardly bear to look at Philip. Today she would leave and might never see him again.

Harry appeared at that moment, bearing the morning post, and laid a buff envelope next to Philip's plate; Philip's post was being forwarded to Chalcombe for the duration of his stay.

'Well, this is a sad day for us all with you two

departing,' remarked Harry, as he took his seat. 'The week has gone all too quickly. Hamlet will be bereft.' He glanced at his godson, who was ripping open his letter with a lazy finger. 'And Philip, too, I dare say?' Philip made no reply. 'Not bad news, I hope?' asked Harry, without any apparent consternation.

'It's my call-up. My National Service.' Philip's voice was hollow.

'Oh, my dear boy,' Harry murmured sympathetically. He'd had an inkling of what the buff envelope might contain.

'It says I have to report to a place in Croydon for a medical on Monday.' He looked up, trying to smile. 'How utterly appalling!' But this attempt at insouciance failed.

'Well, I imagine you knew it had to come,' said Harry, spreading his toast with a generous helping of marmalade.

'Not this soon. I thought I'd still have time to enrol at the Slade and see if I could get it deferred.' He shot Harry an anxious look, as though hoping he might be able to help in some way.

'You've left it a little late for that.'

Harry genuinely felt sorry for Philip. He remembered all too well getting his own call-up in the war, the freezing barracks, the sadistic sergeants, the sheer misery of hours of basic training, the blistered feet and the loneliness. Added to which Philip would have to endure the hostility and derision of his fellow conscripts, most of whom would be from backgrounds very different from his, and who would soon let him know what they thought of his urbane demeanour.

'Best to get it out of the way now,' Harry went on. 'Don't look so glum. I believe those who have been to public school, or borstal, survive it best. You'll be fine.'

Philip folded up the letter. Laura laid a sympathetic hand on his arm, but he didn't even look at her. He rose without a word and left the breakfast table. An hour later, when Harry was preparing to drive Max and Laura to the station, he was nowhere to be found.

On the train back to London Max was keen to make up for the ground he felt he had lost that week, but Laura met his attempts at conversation with monosyllabic replies. As they sat in silence, the countryside rattling past in a haze of steam, he grew miserably convinced that she was thinking about Philip. He picked at the wound as he would a fresh scab, knowing the pain it would give but unable to help himself.

'What did you think of Philip, then?' he asked.

Her answer wasn't what he'd expected. Laura merely shrugged and said, 'Not much.'

Max, unversed in the subtleties of the female mind, was delighted at this unexpected reply and was quick to offer his own enthusiastic criticism. 'I agree. He's such a show-off, always thinking he knows better than anyone else. Yesterday afternoon was too embarrassing for words.'

Laura gave him a bleak glance. 'I don't think so. He was saying what he believes. I admire that.'

This was perplexing and annoying, but he wasn't about to concede anything. 'You should see the crowd he goes about with at school. They think they're artistic and intellectual and superior to everyone else, but it's all a huge pose.'

'I think he's very clever.'

Max gave a snort of derision. 'That's what he wants you to think.'

Laura studied Max. 'I don't understand what you've got against him.'

'Don't you? The way he was coming on to you the whole week was quite sickening.'

'What's that to you?'

He studied her face, and suddenly understood that despite what she'd said it was exactly as he'd suspected. Unable to curb his jealousy he said bitterly, 'I suppose you think you're in love with him.'

Laura's eyes blazed with anger. 'You know, you can be quite juvenile sometimes.' She got up and opened the door of the compartment and walked off down the corridor, where she stayed for the remaining twenty minutes of the journey. As the train pulled into Charing Cross Max got her case down from the rack and gave it to her.

'I'm sorry about what I said—'

'It doesn't matter,' replied Laura coldly. 'I don't want to talk about it.' She got off the train, throwing a quick 'goodbye' to Max over her shoulder, and headed to the taxi rank.

He stared after her. To think that at the beginning of the journey he'd been planning an easy, intimate conversation, at the end of which she would ask him to write to her next term, and he would promise to. She seemed further from him now than she'd ever been.

10

WHILE SHE WAS in Rome Avril came to the firm conclusion that there was no point in throwing away good money on school fees for Laura. She had never distinguished herself academically, and Avril could see little benefit in her frittering away another two years at Abbeyfield. When she got back from Italy, and without bothering to discuss it with Laura first, Avril rang the headmistress to inform her that Laura would not be returning in the autumn term. She delivered the news casually to Laura at dinner that same evening. Laura, still miserable at having left Chalcombe without having spoken to Philip, was unprepared for this fresh blow.

'But what will I be doing if I'm not at school?' she asked.

'Saving me money, for a start. My mother may have been content to pay your way through life, but I'm not. Plenty of girls are earning their own living at your age.' She glanced at Laura. 'For heaven's sake, don't look at me like that. I'm not turning you out. I just can't afford the fees. I'm starting my own business, and I need to put every penny I can spare into it.'

'You want me to get a job?'

Avril regarded her dispassionately. 'You could do secretarial training. Go to college, or something. Maybe you can help me in my gallery once it's up and running.' She helped herself to more salad. 'Unless there's something else you'd rather do.'

But as Laura had told Max, beyond another two years of school, she'd given no thought to her future. She'd always relied on Sonia for guidance, and had assumed she would find some path for her in the world. Laura realised how exposed she was without her. How alone. Sonia hadn't even mentioned her in her will. The sense of having been cast aside, left to fend for herself, had hurt. And now this. She felt slightly panicky at the idea of being plucked from the warm, safe realm of school and joining the adult world. She thought of protesting against the decision, but Avril's impassive expression told her there was little point. Avril had never been open and sympathetic to any of Laura's concerns, and Laura didn't think that was about to change now.

That night she wrote a long and tearful letter to her

best friend at school, telling her the news, and imploring her to stay in touch. Afterwards, in bed, she put out the light and thought about Philip, realising with a throb of romantic sympathy that they were both sharing the fate of being thrust into new and unknown worlds. If only he had asked for her address to write to her. If only she could believe he had any interest in her beyond a few stolen kisses. But she knew deep down that Philip was probably not really interested in anyone besides himself.

Over the next few weeks Avril was too preoccupied with setting up her new business to give much thought to Laura. Sonia's investment portfolio was healthy, and there was a decent sum in the bank, so she could afford to do it in decent style. There was the jewellery, too, but Avril had no intention of parting with any of that. She began to look around for suitable premises. Not, she decided, in the vicinity of New Bond Street – her gallery was going to be very different from those respectable and rather tame establishments. She found a defunct draper's shop in Alfred Place near Goodge Street station that she thought would do pretty well, once the space had been opened up and the frontage redesigned. Her next task was to find work to sell. She had no intention of filling her gallery with tranquil rural scenes, or the work of St Ives watercolourists. Her instinct was to concentrate on new trends and future markets. She began to cultivate young painters from St Martin's and the Royal College of Art, whose expressionist work was daring and innovative, but who had yet to find a market. Avril calculated that she had little to lose by taking them on – if the worst came to the worst, and if London evinced no interest in the works of Frank Auerbach and Leon Kossoff, she could always revert to safer themes.

The gallery was to open at the end of September, and as Avril was busy every day and spent many of her evenings away from the flat, Laura was left to her own devices. A charlady came in twice a week to clean the flat, but Laura did the shopping, tidying and cooking, and performed chores that Avril was too busy to attend to. She bought a sewing machine and started designing and making some of her own clothes, studying the pages of Avril's magazines, and beginning to wonder if she might not make a career in dressmaking or fashion. She suggested to Avril one morning over breakfast that perhaps she could go on some kind of course.

'Maybe I could go to art school.'

Avril, who had a headache from a party the night before, wasn't feeling indulgent.

'What, and hang around with a load of beatniks? I don't think so. Besides, the rag trade's hardly respectable. I told you, you're much better off getting some secretarial skills – they're always in demand.' She drained her coffee. 'I'll have a look and find something suitable.'

Avril investigated a few establishments and eventually found a college in Kensington that wasn't too expensive, catering for suburban girls and equipping them for a year or two of working life until such time as a husband might be found. Avril estimated that Laura's looks would soon attract some suitable man, who would take Laura off her hands so that she needn't be troubled with her any more.

'I've registered you as Fenton,' she told Laura. 'I thought it was time we dropped the Haddon thing. I don't know why my mother started it, to be honest.'

Laura realised she didn't mind at all. She had got used to Haddon, but there was something good about having her own name, her real name.

Every day for the next six months she caught the bus to Kensington and spent the morning learning shorthand and how to take dictation, and in the afternoon she and twenty-nine other girls clattered away on typewriters. Twice a week she had lessons in book-keeping and duplicating. After the novelty had worn off, she began to find the course extremely boring, but she stuck it out, for want of anything better to do. She got on well with the other girls, and made particular friends with two, Gloria and Pamela. They infected Laura with their love of going out and having a good time, and soon coffee bars, Guy Mitchell records, and cinemas and bowling alleys were taking the place of hockey sticks, pet rabbits and midnight feasts. The world of school grew dwindlingly remote.

When the course ended Laura duly began work at the

Haddon Gallery in Alfred Place. After six months the business was doing well. Avril's instinct for developing trends had attracted discerning customers, and she needed the extra pair of hands. Laura found working in the gallery more enjoyable than she had expected. The secretarial work was undemanding, and as Avril had quickly recognised that Laura's looks made her a valuable front-of-house asset she found herself at the reception desk much of the time, greeting customers and showing them around. Avril regarded the dress allowance with which she supplemented Laura's modest wages as an investment, and it meant Laura could spend happy hours browsing the fashion departments of Fenwicks and Selfridges and indulging her love of clothes.

All in all, for the next year Laura was content with her existence. Her sense of subordination to Avril was so familiar that she never questioned it, and she had no desire to strike out on her own. Life in the flat was comfortable. Avril was busy most of the time, caught up in what seemed to be a somewhat fraught love affair, and outside the gallery they didn't see much of one another. Her social life consisted of going out with Pamela and Gloria at the weekends, and the occasional trip to the cinema. She wasn't remotely interested in any of the boys she met. None of them measured up to Philip in any way.

A couple of months after Laura's eighteenth birthday, Avril's love affair came to an unhappy end and she decided to escape on a month's holiday to Corsica. She was willing to leave Laura in charge of the flat, but not the gallery, and brought in a friend to run it in her absence. Norman Burgess was in his early thirties, handsome, effeminate and efficient, and Laura disliked him intensely. His treatment of her was remote and unfriendly, and he left her to do most of the work in the gallery while he spent his time talking on the telephone to men friends or swanning off for long lunches.

With Avril away, Laura decided to invite Pamela and Gloria to supper. They were wonderfully impressed, both by the flat and the meal Laura cooked for them. After the success of supper Laura, feeling bold, sophisticated and in possession of her territory, mixed them all drinks. They sat around, listening to some of Avril's jazz records, the windows open to the summer air.

'I like this song,' said Gloria. 'Who's singing it?'

Laura picked up the album sleeve. 'Someone called Chet Baker.'

They listened as the lazy, sweet sounds of '*My Funny Valentine*' drifted from the radiogram, then Pamela said, 'Why don't we go to a jazz club some night? There's one in Soho that my sister Alice is always talking about.'

'I've never been to Soho,' said Laura. 'Isn't it a bit

sleazy? I thought it was all strip clubs and horrible pubs.'

'Well, if my sister survives it, I'm sure we would. Gloria?'

Gloria drained the remnants of her drink and nodded. 'Sounds like fun.'

'All right,' said Laura. 'Let's.' And she mixed them all another drink.

The Three Jays jazz club was in a basement below a coffee bar in Dean Street. As the girls descended the narrow staircase, they could hear the notes of a saxophone tuning up, then the sudden riff of a snare drum. The club was smoky and cramped, buzzing with conversation. Pamela caught sight of her sister Alice sitting with her friends at a corner table, and the three girls joined them and ordered drinks. Alice was an art student, and Pamela always spoke of her with some reverence, so Laura was expecting to meet someone poised and sophisticated, but Alice was unremarkable, with brown hair scraped back under a hairband, no make-up, and wearing slacks and a big sloppy sweater. In fact all the girls looked scruffy to Laura, who had dressed for the evening in heels, a pretty, narrow-waisted blue dress with a flared skirt, and a thin cardigan draped over her shoulders. Alice's men friends weren't much better. Most wore jeans and the same large sweaters or duffel coats, and some had beards and hair over their collars. Despite their unkempt appearance they seemed confident and at ease in their surroundings, and Laura began to feel self-conscious and overdressed. People were drinking beers and coffees and chatting in low voices, as though waiting for something. Then there came the snare drum riff again, a light cymbal crash, and someone with a microphone at the back of the room made an announcement that Laura couldn't make out. The talk died away, and after a moment the music began. It was a kind of jazz that Laura had never heard before. It was insistent and discordant, instruments running off in different directions over a thrumming bass note. At the end of the set everyone clapped enthusiastically. The musicians started another piece, and a single saxophone began to dribble out slow, low notes. The sound grew from a rippling lament, then lifted into an aching crescendo, the notes slipping off the edge of the rhythm, pure and sad and ecstatic. Laura was thrilled, exhilarated; the music churned feelings within her that she couldn't name. She smiled unawares, lost in the smoky sound, and was still smiling at the end of the set. The audience let off a burst of applause, and the musicians nodded and smiled in acknowledgement, then dispersed for a break.

Laura saw one of the musicians coming towards their table, and recognised him as the saxophonist. He was young, black, tall and broad-shouldered.

He sat down with Alice and her friends, shrugging off their congratulations, accepting a drink. Laura watched him with interest. When he threw his head back and laughed the sound did something to her that the saxophone had done, too. It captivated her. He glanced in her direction and she couldn't help smiling. Someone returned to the table with a drink, and he stood up to make room, moved his chair, and suddenly he was sitting next to her.

'You smile like you know me,' he said. His voice was American, dark and loose, like him.

Laura laughed, confused. 'No – it was just I thought your playing was wonderful. I've never heard anything like it.' He glanced with speculative interest at her pretty dress and her pinned-up blonde hair. 'Your first time here?' She nodded. He put out a large, bony hand and Laura shook it. 'My name's Ellis Candy.'

'I'm Laura Fenton.'

'You like jazz, Laura?'

'It's fine,' she replied uncertainly. 'I haven't... I mean, I don't ever hear much. So it's—' But she was interrupted; someone tapped Ellis on the shoulder. He knocked back his drink. 'Gotta go,' he said. 'See you later.' And he gave her a smile, rose and left.

Laura watched him as he returned to the stage. She had never spoken to a black man before. She'd seen a few coloured people around London, and one of the conductors on the bus she caught every day was

Jamaican, she thought, but she'd never spoken to a black person up close like that. There had been something so vivid, so different about his eyes and his smile. She moved her chair so that she could see him properly. She watched as he played his saxophone, long, black fingers pressing down the keys, his mouth tight, blowing out the notes. She watched barely anything or anyone else all night, and once, just once, she thought he looked up and caught her eye.

'Laura? *Laura!*' The sound of Pamela's voice broke her concentration. She was leaning over and tapping her watch and Gloria was picking up her handbag. 'It's nearly half ten. I have to get my bus.'

The music died away, and a spatter of applause broke out. Laura rose from her seat. Everyone was saying their goodbyes, and she realised that she'd barely spoken to anyone all evening. Conversations had been going on, people had been making friends and getting to know one another, and she'd been entirely detached. Ellis Candy had stayed on stage all night; he hadn't come back to their table as she'd hoped he would.

She picked up her coat, and as she reached the stairs, Pamela and Gloria ahead of her, she felt a hand on her arm. She turned and saw him standing next to her.

'I'm sorry I didn't get to talk to you more,' he said. 'Drop in again sometime.'

Laura gave a nod, flustered because he looked serious – or not smiling, at any rate. Then he grinned, and she felt a curious relief. Pamela called down the staircase to her. Ellis Candy lifted his hand, and Laura smiled, then turned and went upstairs.

The three girls walked down to Charing Cross Road together. Laura said very little. Pamela and Gloria talked most of the way about some man called Gordon, with whom Gloria had agreed to go to the cinema next week.

Pamela turned to Laura. 'Did you like it?' she asked. 'You were awfully quiet.'

'Oh, yes. I loved it. The music sort of grows on you, doesn't it?'

'I thought it was smashing. Let's go again next week.'

Laura thought about what Ellis Candy had said. He wanted her to go back to the club so he could see her again, and that thought produced a little knot of excitement in her stomach.

11

A WEEK LATER Ellis was sitting in the empty club
waiting for the evening to begin, wondering,
as he did every night, if she'd be in. He had a hard
time recalling how she'd looked exactly. Blonde and
beautiful was all he could recall. It was like trying to
remember something so dazzling you couldn't see past
the brightness. He watched the waiter lift the ashtrays,
wipe the table, set them down again. On stage the guys
were setting up their instruments. He stubbed out his
cigarette and got to his feet. Half eight. The club began
to fill with customers, feet on the staircase, the scrape of
chairs, the rising murmur of conversation. He wondered
whether he should skip the evening set and come back
and play after midnight, when the hipper people were in,
and the mood was cool. The sound of girls' voices made
him glance in the direction of the stairs, and there she
was, dressed in a checked skirt and a tight sweater, hair

loose on her shoulders – oh God, she looked good. His heart felt like it had leapt from his chest to his throat. She raised a shy hand when she saw him, in the hardly-moving-the-fingers little wave that English girls did. He lifted his hand in reply, then he went over.

'Hello,' said Laura.

'Hi. Good to see you. Wasn't sure if you'd come back.'

'Of course. I liked the music.'

'You liked the music.' Ellis chuckled. 'I'm glad you liked the music. You here for the night?'

'Oh, yes. Well, till about half past ten.'

'That ain't the *night*! We hardly get going till around then. Oh, well.' He paused. 'I have to go set up. I'll come and see you later on.'

Laura nodded and watched him walk to the back of the club with that loose, rangy walk of his. How strange, she'd only ever had one conversation with him – not a proper conversation, either – and tonight they spoke as though they knew one another. As though something was taken for granted.

At the end of the first set she waited with nervous anticipation, but to her disappointment he didn't come over to their table. He went to the bar for a drink, and just stood there talking and laughing with some man. He never looked in her direction once. Oh well, she had probably made more out of it than she should have. She sipped her drink and tried to concentrate on what Pamela was saying, determined not to look his way, but when the break ended and the musicians were assembling, she couldn't help glancing towards the stage. He was looking in her direction, and when he caught her eye he smiled and raised one finger and pointed it right at her. The bass player brought in a low beat, and as soon as Ellis closed his eyes and the first sweet, troubled notes drifted from his saxophone, Laura could tell this was for her. Whatever he was playing, she knew it was for her. The honeyed sound rose and fell over several moments, struck a minor key, swooped, slowed, turned into a low fever of yearning that stretched out seemingly for ever, and went murmuring into nothing. A pause, and the other instruments came in. She felt touched in some nameless, wonderful way.

They played three more pieces, and in between each one he smiled at her, and she at him. At the end of the set he bought himself a drink and came to the table. He gave Pamela and Gloria a nod and a smile, and they said 'hello' to him in an uncertain way, glancing from him to Laura.

'I don't need to play any more tonight,' he said to Laura in a low voice. 'Well, not till later. What say we go somewhere and get a coffee?'

Laura wasn't sure what to say. She had come here with Pamela and Gloria. She couldn't just leave them and go off with this coloured man that she hardly knew.

What would they think? She looked at Ellis Candy, and decided she didn't care. Let them think what they liked. She nodded and picked up her handbag. She could feel her friends' eyes fixed on her. She turned to them and said, 'I'm just going for a coffee with Ellis. I might see you later.'

They walked through the streets of Soho to a café off Leicester Square, where they bought coffee and doughnuts. They sat at a formica table next to the steamy window, away from everyone else, and talked. She asked him how he came to be in London and he told her about his home in Memphis, about his brother who had been in England in the war, and who had liked England and said to Ellis he should go there some time. He told her how he'd been playing sax for eight years now, since he was fifteen, and how hard it was to get work in clubs in the States. Told her how he and his friend Lester had come to London a year ago, looking for work. That was his story. What about her?

'Oh, well – there's not much to tell, really. I'm eighteen, I work in an art gallery, and I live in London.'

'Where in London?'

'I suppose you'd call it a posh part of town – in Mayfair.'

'Posh?' He tried to imitate her accent, and Laura laughed.

'It means expensive, sort of.'

'Ah, so you're a little rich girl.'

She shook her head. 'I don't have any money.' She told Ellis her whole story, and said at the end, 'So now I live with Avril and work in her gallery.'

'Well, well, that's some set-up.' There was a silence, and then he said, 'It beats me why you're sitting here with me.'

'I know,' said Laura. 'It's funny, isn't it?'

The earnest way she said it made him laugh.

'What?' asked Laura, smiling, but puzzled.

'Why do you think you're here, having coffee with me?'

Laura hesitated. 'I – I don't know. I like you, I suppose. I saw the way you played the saxophone that first night, and I thought *that* was wonderful. And then' – she laughed and shrugged – 'well, you seemed very nice. So, here we are.'

'Nice. I like that. I like that you think I'm nice.'

He gave a slow smile, and it felt to Laura as though his eyes were burning into her. A little confused, she said, 'Tell me more about your music. I don't really know a great deal about jazz.'

Ellis talked about jazz, and about himself, and all the time he talked she was busy etching every part of him on her heart – the lively, liquid beauty of his eyes, the sheen of his dark skin, the way he shrugged his shoulders beneath his turned-up collar, the sudden, cracked sound of his laugh, his long fingers, and the strange, handsome pinkness of his palms. She was used to the pallor of London faces, people who lived drab lives and ate bad food and lived in the aftermath of a stunting, terrible war, and Ellis Candy, the size, the colour, the energy, the difference of him, was like a man from another planet.

Eventually the talk slowed, and Ellis became conscious that their coffee cups had been empty for a while.

'I'd buy you another,' said Ellis, 'but I haven't the money. Sorry.'

'I'll buy them,' said Laura, and opened her bag to dig for change. He gazed at her as she did so, loving the way her hair grazed the soft bloom of her cheek, and wished he could put out a hand to touch her. She was so dazzling, so fresh. It wasn't just the way she looked. Plenty of good-looking girls came into the club, and he'd had his share. She had some special quality, something he'd recognised the moment he'd looked across the table that first night and seen her smiling at him, at the fact of him, before she even knew who he was.

She bought them another coffee each, and they talked some more, and then Laura looked at her watch. 'Golly, look at the time! It's nearly eleven. I have to catch my bus.'

'You want to go back to the club and pick up your friends?'

Laura shook her head. 'They'll have gone already.' She felt a pang, wondering what Pamela and Gloria were thinking of her right now.

'Can I see you next week? Maybe for lunch, say? I don't do much in the day, just bum around.'

Laura hesitated, thinking of Norman, then said, 'Yes, I'd like that.' She gave him the name and address of the gallery. 'I get off around one.'

'Come on,' he said, 'I'll walk with you to your bus.'

They walked down to Charing Cross Road, still talking. Laura's bus came almost immediately. 'Goodnight,' she called to Ellis as she stepped aboard.

The conductor, standing on the platform, glanced from her to Ellis, but Laura didn't see his look. Ellis ignored it. 'Night,' he called, and waved as the bus pulled away.

On Monday Ellis came to Alfred Place at ten to one. Norman, sitting importantly doing nothing at the gallery's reception desk, noticed the black man strolling back and forth on the pavement. He didn't much like the look of the fellow. After watching him for a while he opened the door and called out in his cold, high voice, 'Can I help you?'

Ellis glanced at him in surprise, and was about to reply when Laura appeared. She smiled at Ellis, then said to Norman, 'I'm just off for lunch.'

Norman shot Ellis another suspicious glance. 'Make sure you're back at two o'clock sharp.' He watched Laura and Ellis walk off together. What on earth was the girl thinking of, going about with a black man? He would have to say something to Avril when she came back from holiday.

'Who's that guy?' asked Ellis.

'Norman. He's in charge of the gallery while Avril's away.'

'I hate his type.'

Laura looked at him in surprise. 'What type?'

'He's a faggot. I can tell. I hate the way they talk, the way they walk, the way they laugh, and most of all I hate what they do.'

'What do they do?' Her idea of people like Norman was that they were just a bit feminine and silly compared to most men. She knew no more than this.

'You don't want to know. But it's right they lock them up. Goddam perverts.'

Laura sighed. 'Forget Norman. Let's find somewhere for lunch.'

When Laura returned at two, Norman said waspishly to her, 'Please ask your friend not to hang about in front of the gallery like that in future. It doesn't look good. Most off-putting for the customers.'

'Why? Because he's black?'

'I didn't say anything about that.'

After a pause Laura asked, 'Norman, do you like jazz?'

He raised a surprised eyebrow and replied crossly, 'I do, as a matter of fact. What has that to do with anything?'

'Nothing. Just asking.' And she returned to the little back office, wondering why Ellis felt the way he did about Norman, and Norman felt the way he did about Ellis. It seemed such a stupid waste of time.

After that, Laura made sure that Ellis picked her up from the gallery every day, just to annoy Norman. She didn't care that what she was doing went against nice social conventions. She loved being with Ellis. He made her laugh, and he was utterly unlike any man she knew. Compared to him, everyone else seemed drab and boring.

As for Ellis, he felt both easy and strange with Laura – easy because she was sweet and beautiful, and strange because he'd never met a girl who acted like she didn't expect him to touch her, not even so much as hold her hand. Ellis was used to quite a different type of girl, and although he kind of liked the change, it puzzled him, too.

At the end of lunch on Friday he asked, 'Can I see you tomorrow night?'

'Aren't you playing at the club?'

'Not till ten. I could take you someplace before that. Maybe we could see a movie?'

'Yes, I'd like that.' Laura looked at her watch. 'I have to get back. Norman will be hopping mad if I'm late.'

'I'll walk back with you,' said Ellis, and he took her arm and slipped it through his. It was the first time he'd touched her. It gave Laura a tight, happy feeling around her heart to be walking with him this way, feeling the warmth of his arm through hers.

On Saturday evening it was raining. They met at six and went to a Western double feature. They sat together in the smoky darkness, deeply conscious of one another's proximity, eyes fixed on the screen. Laura found she couldn't concentrate properly on the first film, which had to do with people trying to run a railroad, and some swindling property owner; her thoughts were running all over the place in a strange confusion. He hadn't touched her or taken her arm on the way here, as he had yesterday. Ellis sat wondering what it was she did to him, why the smooth moves he usually put into operation when he was out with a girl just wouldn't come to him. It was like there was some tiny electric force field around her, attracting him and yet pushing him away.

'You like an ice cream?' he asked her when the lights came up in the interval.

'Yes, please,' said Laura. She watched him as he moved, head and shoulders above everyone else, to the front of the auditorium where the girl stood with her tray. On the way back to his seat, Ellis decided he had to stop pussyfooting around. A whole week, and they were getting nowhere.

Laura ate her ice cream and sat with the empty cup in her lap as the lights went down for the second film. Ellis shifted a little, then lifted his arm and put it around her. She couldn't look at him. She had no idea what to do, or whether anything was expected of her. His other hand crept out, feeling for hers. Startled, she moved and sent the empty ice cream tub rattling to the floor. She leaned forward to rescue it, but he stopped her, slipping his hand over hers, smooth as a glove. Laura sat back, her hand in his, feeling enveloped, protected, and dizzily happy. After a while he began to stroke the inside of her palm with his thumb, sending little waves of soft pleasure through her. He continued to do this throughout the film, and when the lights came up, Laura had only the vaguest idea what it had been about.

'You want to get something to eat?' asked Ellis as they left the cinema.

'Yes,' said Laura. She didn't care where they went or what they did. She was simply happy. And when he clasped his fingers between hers, she felt happier still.

They went to a greasy spoon in Brewer Street. 'Cheapest place I know,' he said, 'but the food is good.'

'Let me pay,' said Laura, when the bill came. 'You bought the cinema tickets, after all.'

'I can't let you.'

'I don't have to pay rent like you,' insisted Laura. 'I can spend all the money I earn. Please, I'd like to.'

He shrugged. 'OK, then.'

They ate and talked, and afterwards, finding the rain had stopped, they wandered round the damp, seedy streets, past the striptease clubs and pubs and cafés, utterly absorbed in one another, until it was nearly ten and time for Ellis to do his set. They stopped by a doorway a little way up from the Three Jays.

'Thank you for a lovely time,' said Laura. It sounded absurdly polite and formal, but she didn't know how else to begin the goodbye she didn't want to utter.

He took both her hands in his and drew her into the shadows of the doorway. He held her against him; she felt light and fair as a moth, she smelled of something fragrant and faint that wasn't quite perfume, more just the scent of her. Laura sank against his body, and it felt like coming home. Her head rested on his chest, and he stroked her hair. She lifted her head to look at him, and for a moment he just gazed at her, then moved his mouth towards hers. He sensed her hesitation.

'What?' he breathed. She was so close, he could almost taste her. He tried to read the look in her eyes. 'Don't tell me you never been kissed before?' His smile was faintly teasing.

She smiled and thought of Philip. How could she ever have cared about him? It was like looking back at herself as a child. 'No, it isn't that.'

He drew her towards him once more. 'No white man will ever kiss you like this. *That* I promise.'

They kissed in the shadow of the doorway. 'Don't go home,' said Ellis, exhaling the words on a shuddering breath of desire. 'Don't go home yet. Come to the club. Just sit there while I play.'

She felt breathless, trembling with the powerful feelings of being kissed in such a way. She could hardly speak. At last she managed to murmur, 'I'd feel strange on my own.'

'You wouldn't be on your own. You'd be with me.'

They went to the club and Ellis bought Laura a drink, and found her a seat at a table not far from the stage. She sat there while he played, bound up entirely with the man making music a few feet away from her.

An hour later he walked her to the bus stop. Because it was a Saturday night there were more people about than usual. Although she held his hand tight, Laura was aware, as they approached the bus stop, of a change in his demeanour. A crowd of teddy boys moved towards them.

'Oi, monkey-boy!' one of them suddenly shouted. 'Why don't you go and find one of your own kind? Leave our girls alone!'

One of them sniggered at Laura, 'Yeah, darlin', what you want to hang around with that black cunt for? Has he got a big one, then?' The other teds laughed.

Laura was shocked; no one had ever used language like that to her in her life. Ellis let go of her hand and turned on the boys. There were four of them, but despite their big drape jackets and carefully combed quiffs, they were young and scrawny. Ellis looked large and threatening next to them, and they moved away, still jeering and swearing.

Laura felt shaken. The other people at the bus stop, a middle-aged man and two women, looked away, embarrassed. One of the women whispered something to the other and shot a glance at Ellis, and then at Laura.

Ellis said nothing, didn't look at her, just stared fiercely into the distance as though looking for the bus. Laura felt unhappy and afraid; she couldn't think of anything to say. She put her hand tentatively into his, trying to ignore the women glancing in her direction, and eventually was relieved to feel the pressure of his fingers tightening round hers.

The bus approached. Ellis looked down at her at last. He smiled, but said nothing.

'Will I see you next week?' asked Laura. She felt almost panicky at the thought of leaving him.

'If you like,' he said, then added in a lower voice, 'But you may begin to think this ain't such a good thing, you know.'

Laura found the sadness in his eyes unbearable; until this moment, she had never seen him anything but full of life and laughter and confidence. He seemed angry and altered, diminished by the events of a few moments ago. She raised herself on tiptoe and kissed him quickly on the mouth, not caring about the other people at the bus stop.

'Come to the gallery at one as usual.'

12

AVRIL WAS IN a good mood when she got back from holiday. She had brought Laura a couple of small gifts, and Laura had cooked sardines on toast for supper, which she knew Avril liked. She listened as Avril talked about Corsica, the quaint villages and the marvellous food, glad that Avril was back and she would no longer be on her own. The unusual pleasantness of the conversation and her own good mood prompted Avril to say, 'You should take a holiday. I don't mind paying. You could go away for a few days with your friends.'

'That might be nice, thanks.'

'Anyway, I'll just go and ring Norman and check how sales have gone while I've been away. Did he give you the keys?'

'They're on the hall table.'

Laura cleared away the plates while Avril went to make her phone call. A few moments later she returned to the kitchen and said to Laura, 'Come through. Leave the dishes. I want to speak to you.' Laura followed Avril to the drawing room. 'Sit down.' Avril's face was stony. 'I won't beat about the bush. Norman tells me that some black man has been picking you up from the gallery while I've been away.'

'Yes.'

'Who is he?'

'He's a musician. He plays the saxophone in a jazz club.'

'A *jazz* club? Where?'

'Soho. I met him when I was out with Pamela and Gloria.'

'Honestly, I go away for three weeks, and you go off to sleazy clubs and make all kinds of unsuitable acquaintances. I can't believe it.'

'He's not unsuitable.'

'He most certainly is. You'll have to stop seeing him.'

'Why?' demanded Laura.

'I promised my mother I would see to your welfare. How can I be said to be doing that if I let you get a reputation for yourself? Be sensible for once in your life.'

The reference to Sonia stung. Laura knew deep down that Aunt Sonia would never have approved of Ellis Candy. The thought that she was in some way letting her down upset and confused her.

'But you don't even know Ellis. If you met him you'd realise he's really nice—'

'That isn't the issue,' interrupted Avril. 'You simply can't go running around Soho with black men. The very idea. You'll have nothing more to do with him.'

'I'll do as I please. I like him, and I'll see him if I want to.'

Avril stared at Laura. Defiance was a new article in their relationship. Laura's deference was something they were both accustomed to.

'As long as you live under my roof, you will do as I say. And that means not behaving like a slut.'

'Don't call me that!'

'Why not? If you behave like one, that's what I'll call you. What will people think of you?'

'I don't care what they think!'

'Of course you don't.' Avril's notoriously short temper was now thoroughly up. 'You're just like your mother. She was a slut, too.'

'Don't you dare say that!'

'I'm only glad my mother's not alive to see this. I repeat, you will not behave in this fashion while you're living here.'

'Then I won't live here! Why should I? You've no business telling me how to live my life!'

'Get out then!' replied Avril contemptuously. 'Go on! See how easy you find it to survive on your own. See how easy life is without all the things I give you, that you simply take for granted – a home, a job, clothes, money. See if your negro can give you those!'

Laura went to her room in a fury and began to pull clothes from drawers. What to put them in? She opened the closet and stared at her school trunk in despair. Then she took a small suitcase from an upper shelf and started to cram things in. She wanted nothing more than to be out of the flat, away from Avril, and to be with Ellis. She had a sudden image of him in the club, in the smoky, warm basement, playing his saxophone, and felt a surge of certainty and longing.

Avril unstoppered the sherry decanter and poured herself a drink as the front door slammed. Stupid girl. She probably had little more than her bus fare. It wouldn't be long before she was back.

Ellis was on stage when Laura came down the basement steps and into the club. She stood in the shadows at the back, still in her coat, her suitcase at her feet, and watched him. He had his eyes closed, playing a slow section, the sorrowful sound sliding out, winding itself around the minds of the people in the room. He looked so separate, lost in himself and what he was doing. A hopeless space hollowed itself out in her heart. Here she was, bringing herself to a man she hardly knew, asking him to love and protect her. Her sense of isolation was acute.

The set came to an end, the applause rippled, and the musicians left the stage. Laura stood at the back, watching Ellis talking to friends at the bar, unable to bring herself to go to him. Then he came towards the back of the room. He didn't see her, walked straight past her, and into the gents.

He isn't even thinking about me, thought Laura. *He's in his world, and he doesn't need me in it. This is a mistake. I shouldn't have come here.*

She picked up her case and was turning towards the stairs when Ellis came out again. He saw her, and suddenly it was all right, because the gladness that shone in his face was unmistakable.

'I didn't think I'd see you this soon,' he said, and kissed her. 'Get your coat off, come and sit down.' He saw the suitcase. He looked from it to her. 'You going somewhere?'

'I've left the flat,' said Laura. 'I had a row with Avril. About you.'

'Oh, man.' He should have seen this coming.

'She said I couldn't stay if I was going to go on seeing you.' She blinked back tears. 'What right has she to say something like that, when she doesn't even know you?'

'Baby, she doesn't have to know me. I'm black, and for most white folks, that'll do. Sit down. I'll get you a drink.' He came back a few moments later with a small glass of brandy. 'There. Hit that back. Make you feel better. Listen, I got to go play, but I'll be back in a bit.'

He came back an hour later. 'Lester, the guy I share the room with upstairs, he's gonna sleep somewhere else so you can stay tonight.'

'And then?'

'And then? Oh, baby, I don't know what.' He felt touched with despair. She would have to go home sooner or later. He couldn't keep her here. He spread his hands. 'What do *you* want?'

'I don't know. To live with you. For us to be together.'

He shook his head. Nothing like this had come into his computations. He hadn't *had* any computations. The Ellis Candy philosophy of life did not involve looking too far ahead. 'Look, let's talk about that kind of stuff later. Come and I'll take you upstairs.'

The room that Ellis shared on the top floor of the building was lit by a naked bulb, and contained two iron bedsteads, a chest of drawers, a low table and a dilapidated armchair. The music and noise of late-night Soho seeped through the rickety window, which was covered by a single, thin curtain. Ellis set down Laura's case.

'You be OK here?' he asked. He pointed to the bed nearest the window. 'That's my bed.'

She glanced around uncertainly. 'Should I sleep in Lester's bed?'

He put his arms around her. 'That's up to you.'

She gazed into his eyes. This, she supposed, was the night when she grew up properly.

When he had gone she put her case on a chair. She lifted the curtain and looked down at the dirty back alley, hearing distant traffic sounds and the odd, raucous shout from a nearby pub. She opened her case and realised she hadn't brought a nightdress. She hung her coat on the back of the door, then unzipped her skirt and tugged off her jumper. She felt so tired. She looked around. There wasn't even anywhere to wash her face. Ellis had pointed out a dingy bathroom on the way up, but she couldn't face it. She peeled off her underpants, stockings and suspender belt, and left just her slip on. She glanced across the room at the other bed, then pulled back the covers on Ellis's bed and lay down on the thin mattress. It was his bed, so it was good. She pulled up the covers, turned her face to the pillow and breathed the faint smell of him. She was here now, with Ellis. He would keep her safe. She put one hand beneath her cheek, as she had done since childhood, lay thinking for some minutes, and then fell asleep.

It was gone two when Ellis came back to the room. He glanced at his bed and saw, by the ghostly light from beyond the window, Laura sleeping there. So she had made a choice. He leaned over and looked down at her. Her hair looked like a cloud of gold against the pillow. He hung his clothes over the back of a chair and got in next to her, settling himself so that he was lying against her back, his breath against her neck. She stirred and he moved his body against hers, sliding his arms around her, enfolding her. He ran a hand gently over the curve of her hip, feeling his erection swell and stiffen, stroking her upper arm with one hand, cupping her breast with the other. Carefully he slipped on the rubber he had taken from its packet a moment ago. She turned over sleepily and murmured his name, and he kissed her. He had thought this was going to be difficult, that she would be hesitant and fearful, but she responded to him as though it was the most natural thing in the world, arching her body against his and welcoming him. As he entered her she gave a gasp, her body locked against his, then she relaxed and kissed him, and a few seconds later he came before he could stop himself.

'It won't be so bad the next time,' he whispered.

'It wasn't bad, honestly,' she whispered in reply, but he knew she was lying.

Dawn was grazing the sky when they made love again, and this time it was slower and better, and he could look at her and talk to her, and they were entirely aware of the intensity of what they were doing, the intimacy and power of it. Afterwards she nestled against him and murmured happily, 'I love you, Ellis.'

'I love you, too, baby.' And he supposed he did. Though where this went from here, he had no idea.

They went to a café for breakfast, and Laura told him about her fight with Avril.

'I couldn't stay there, not if it meant not seeing you.'

'But have you any idea of what you're throwing away?'

'Don't! You sound like her. I'm not going back. I'd rather be anywhere with you, than in Mount Street with Avril.' Laura mopped up the remains of her fried egg with a piece of bread. 'We love each other, and that's all that matters.'

He didn't know whether to laugh or cry – she looked so beautiful, her faith in their love so earnest and touching.

'What happens now?' she asked.

He took her hands in his, saying nothing for a moment. Then he smiled. 'Baby, what happens now is up to you.'

The gesture and his words seemed to light something inside her. Until this moment she had thought of herself as passive, a girl to whom things happened. But she had brought this about. She had taken a stand against Avril, she had put her love for this man above everything else, and that was the reason they were sitting here now, contemplating a future together. It filled her with a sense of power and purpose that she hadn't known before. What happened now was up to her.

'We have to find a place to live,' she said.

He nodded. Lester would find some other musician

to shack up in the room above the club. But how and where were he and Laura going to find a place to live? He'd ask Vince. Vince generally had answers to most problems.

Vince came into the club just before lunchtime, as he did every day. He was a stocky, sharply dressed cockney in his forties who owned the Three Jays, managed a handful of acts that played in the clubs around Soho, and ran a couple of record shops. Ellis talked to him at the bar while Laura sat at one of the tables, reading a magazine.

'I ain't got no more rooms above the club, if that's what you mean. Sorry.' Vince glanced across at Laura. 'You can look around the area, but you won't find it easy to get a decent place, my son. Not the two of you. If it was her on her own – no problem. You on your own' – Vince made a little so-so gesture with his hand – 'limited choices, but you'd get a gaff. Better than that room upstairs, too, if you had the money. Problem is, you've got no money to speak of, have you? What about her? She got a job?'

'Uh-uh. She had one. I guess she could get another.'

'Thing is… no offence, son, but you know the score. A black man and a white girl, landlords don't like it. Not if they ain't married. Even *if* they're married.' He took a drag of his cigarette. 'Some might say, *especially* if they're married.' He tapped Ellis on the lapel. 'Like I said, no offence. You know I like you. It's just the way it is.' He eyed Laura. 'She's certainly worth the trouble.

She doesn't strip, does she, by any chance? No? Pity. Anyhow, best of luck, son.'

Laura was optimistic when they started walking round the area looking for a place. There were plenty of 'Rooms To Let' signs. Some of them carried the words 'No coloureds' as well, and Laura took this to mean that where the signs didn't say this, they might have a chance. She was wrong. Every single one of the landladies took one look at Ellis and shook their heads. 'Sorry, dear, nothing at the moment.'

'But your sign says—'

And the door would slam.

Door after door. One woman even leaned into Laura's face and hissed, 'You ought to be ashamed of yourself, taking up with a nigger! Dirty little cow!'

Ellis's response was stoical. Laura's was indignant and eventually tearful.

'This is how it is, baby,' he told her.

'Why do you say that as though it's all right? As though people are entitled to treat us this way?'

For the first time in her life, she saw him angry. 'I don't say that! I don't say it's all right! I just see it like it is!'

It was almost seven o'clock and dusk was falling when they knocked on the door of number eighteen Luscombe Street in Somers Town. The house was a narrow, four-storey building, set in a dingy little terrace backing on to the railway sidings by Euston station, with the usual 'Rooms To Let' notice in the downstairs window, which had filled Laura with such hope five hours ago, and now promised nothing.

The door was opened by a scrawny, middle-aged man in shirtsleeves and baggy trousers and braces, with a cigarette between his lips. His sallow cheeks were pitted with smallpox scars. He glanced from Laura to Ellis. 'Yeah?'

'We've come about a room,' said Ellis.

The man's glance shifted between them once more. 'What, just the one?' He gave a wheezing cough.

'Yes,' said Ellis.

The man gestured them in. 'Come on up,' he said, and they followed him, exchanging glances. The house was filled with the rank smell of old cooking, and the wallpaper on the narrow staircase was faded, the stair-runner shabby and worn. When they reached the third floor the wallpaper gave way to whitewashed plaster, and the stair-runner gave out entirely. They trod the bare wooden stairs up to the top floor and the man opened the only door on the landing.

'Attic room. You got your electric...' He switched on the light to reveal a long, low-ceilinged room, sloping down at the far end with the pitch of the roof. It contained a rickety iron double bedstead, a table and two chairs, a little stove and a sink, and a chest of drawers that stood beneath the gable window, an open rail with a handful of wire coat-hangers next to it. A basin and jug and an age-stained mirror sat on the chest of drawers, and the dim central light bulb hung beneath a fly-spotted parchment shade. The fireplace was tiny, the floor covered with cracked lino. 'And your gas.' He pointed to the fireplace and then to the little cooker. 'Meters are out on the landing.'

He turned and looked expectantly at them both. There was nothing for Ellis and Laura to discuss; it was enough that they had found anywhere at all.

'How much?' asked Ellis.

The man took his cigarette from between his lips. 'Three bob a week, two weeks' rent in advance.'

Ellis nodded. The matter was concluded. He searched in his pockets for the money, but while he was putting together what loose change he could find, Laura took a ten shilling note from her handbag.

'Let's say three weeks in advance,' she said.

The man nodded again and pocketed the note. 'I've got a bob here somewhere.' He fished around and produced two sixpences and pressed them into Laura's palm. 'Bathroom's on the floor below. I'll get you a couple of latchkeys.' As he turned to go he said to Ellis, 'I got nothing against you black people, personally.' He spoke in what he obviously considered generosity of spirit. 'My missus isn't too keen, but I knew some very decent blacks in the war. But I don't want no racket, mind.' And he went downstairs to get them their keys.

Laura put her arms round Ellis. 'At least it's somewhere.'

Ellis looked around. 'Yeah, it's somewhere, all right.' It was no worse, he supposed, than the place he'd shared with Lester, but at least the room above the club had a good feel to it, sitting over a kind, warm world where people laughed and made music. This was a mean place, a sad place. He'd lived in such places before from time to time, but he wondered how Laura would cope away from her nice flat in Mayfair, and all the things she took for granted. It was going to be some test of her love.

The man returned with keys, and then they were left alone in the room.

'Tell you what,' said Ellis. 'You stay here and get a rest. I'll go to the club and get your case and my things, see if I can pick us up some food on the way back. OK?'

Laura nodded. She listened to his feet descending the stair, then went to the window and watched his tall figure until he was out of sight.

A few days later Avril came home from the gallery to find that Laura had been to the flat while she was out, and had collected more of her belongings. So she had found somewhere to stay. Avril reckoned it could hardly be anywhere comfortable, and she fully expected Laura to return home within the month, chastened, her lesson learned. She'd never known anything beyond the comforts of home and school, after all. The real world would be too much of a shock for her to cope with. But days went by, and Laura didn't come back.

Avril spoke to Pamela, and persuaded her that she was

concerned about Laura and asked her to try and obtain Laura's address from the club. A part of her needed to know where she was. Pamela, who was still shocked at what Laura had done and hoped Avril would persuade her to go home, obtained the address in Somers Town and passed it on to Avril. But Avril had no intention of doing anything with it. A few letters had come for Laura since she'd left, but she didn't see why she should go to the trouble of forwarding them. Laura had made her bed, and she must lie in it. It helped, though, to know where that bed was and just how uncomfortable it must be. When the worst happened, she would have the satisfaction of saying 'I told you so.' But if Laura thought she would be able to return to Mount Street and resume life in its comforts, she'd be in for a shock. She must live with the consequences of her actions.

The weeks passed, and autumn turned to winter. Laura had found a job in a book-keeper's in King's Cross, Matthew & Son, and on her wage and what Ellis earned, they scraped by. She bought another portable sewing machine, and spent the evenings when Ellis was at the club listening to the radio and running up clothes for herself. It was cheaper than buying them, and it helped to fill the time. Occasionally she would go to the club, but it was a lonely experience. Ellis had friends among the other musicians and various punters, but Laura didn't feel she fitted in with their world, and often she had no one to talk to, although now and then she would go and chat to Vince in his office. He treated her with friendly detachment. Occasionally Alice and her friends came to the club, but they greeted her with half-hearted embarrassment and she knew they wouldn't welcome her company. She had put herself beyond the pale. She understood this, and hating the injustice of it didn't help.

She lived for the end of every day, when she and Ellis could be in bed, in their warm, private world. Beneath the blankets and eiderdown they could forget about the cares of their daily existence and immerse themselves in one another, talking and making love. The one part of her life with Ellis that dazed and amazed her and convinced her she could be nowhere else, was their lovemaking. She had come to sex with nothing except her instincts, but she had learned from Ellis, and now, through luck and love, each time seemed better than the last. The gratification of every orgasm and the satisfaction of bringing Ellis equal pleasure were overwhelming to the point where they made everything bearable. However dreary and mundane the working day, she only had to think about the prospect of being in his arms at the end of it, and nothing else mattered. She loved Ellis, body and soul. The only thing that fettered the spontaneity of their lovemaking was Ellis's insistence that they always take precautions. One night, when he had run out of condoms, he refused steadfastly to make love to her.

'Things are bad enough, baby,' he told her, 'without you getting pregnant.'

'Bad – don't say they're bad, Ellis.'

'OK, that's not what I meant, but there's no way I'm going to take any chances. You wouldn't thank me, trust me.'

They had argued for over an hour, but in the end she'd given up, and fallen tearfully asleep.

She lived in this suspended state, with no wish to address the future, or discuss with Ellis where their life together was heading. She wanted only to be in the here and now of being in love, trusting to fate, and he found her refusal to face up to present, let alone future difficulties, frustrating. Right now she made him happy – happier than he could remember being since childhood – but he knew too well that reality had a way of taking happiness and wringing the life out of it, and occasionally he would withdraw into moods and silences where Laura couldn't reach him. Sometimes he would wake in the night and, unable to find sleep again, would get up and wrap himself in his coat, and stand by the window, smoking and gazing out at the rooftops of the cold city and wondering where he would be if he hadn't met Laura. Not here in London, he didn't think.

When spring came and the days began to lengthen, Laura vowed to herself that whatever happened, they wouldn't spend another winter in Luscombe Street. A few days after her nineteenth birthday, when she was walking home from work, she saw a card in the local newsagent's window advertising a one-bedroom furnished flat to rent at twenty-one and six a week. It was only a few streets away. Ellis was bringing home roughly three pounds a week, including tips, and Laura's wage was two pounds and ten shillings, so she calculated that they could afford it and still have enough over for living expenses. She jotted down the address and went home in excitement to tell Ellis. He was at the little stove, frying bacon.

'We could take a look at it before you go to work,' said Laura. 'Just think how good it would be to have somewhere bigger with decent furniture. And the houses in Tate Street are much nicer.'

'No point,' said Ellis shortly. 'No one's going to rent to you and me.' The gas ring gave a little pop. 'Damn, the gas is out.'

Laura took her purse from her beg and fished for a shilling, which Ellis took to feed the meter on the landing. When he came back he relit the ring and resumed his bacon frying.

Laura watched him in silence for a moment, then went on, 'We're renting this place, aren't we? Why do you always have to assume the worst about people?'

'Because I know people.' Ellis slid the bacon out of the frying pan on to a plate, took two slices of white bread from a packet and began to spread them with margarine.

'Oh, Ellis, please – just for once, can't we try? You never know, they might—'

Ellis slammed down the knife in anger, and Laura flinched. 'Goddammit, Laura! Why do you want to put us through that kind of humiliation again? Wasn't it bad enough the first time?'

Laura got up and splashed water from the tap into a glass and sat down wordlessly at the table.

'Face it,' went on Ellis. 'It was a miracle we got this place.'

He slapped the sandwich together and cut it in two, then brought the plate over to the table. He offered it to Laura. 'You want one?'

She shook her head. 'No thanks. I'm not hungry.' She rubbed her forehead wearily with the heel of her hand and said, 'There are areas in London where there are more coloured people. Notting Hill, for instance. Why don't we move there? Then we wouldn't have a problem.'

He put his sandwich down and gazed at her incredulously.

'Are you out of your mind? They wouldn't welcome you and me there any more than people round here do. You don't get to belong just 'cause you're with a black guy.' He shook his head. 'You live in a dream world, Laura.' She made no reply, but got to her feet and went to wash the frying pan. He sensed her deflation, and went over and put his arms round her, kissing the side of her face. 'You coming to the club?'

She shook her head. 'I'm going to take a bath. If

there's any hot water, that is.' She thought of the stained bathtub in the chilly bathroom on the floor below, and hoped there was a clean towel somewhere. 'Then I have to take the washing to the launderette.' She closed her eyes, Ellis's arms still around her, remembering the bathroom at Mount Street, the scented Cussons soaps and talcum powder, the fluffy towels in the airing cupboard, the way the laundry used to be collected every Tuesday, coming back clean in a crisp brown paper bale three days later. Why even think about it? It wasn't as though she wished herself back there. She was just feeling a bit low. The pathetic dream of the one-bedroom flat in Tate Street had evaporated. Nothing to dream for, except maybe earning some more money, but where was that going to take them if there was nowhere for them to go? She turned to Ellis and kissed him sadly.

'Come to bed,' he murmured. 'We got time.' It was their way of making things better, for a while at least.

An hour later Ellis walked to Soho. He didn't have to be at the club until nine, but he needed to get away from the attic room, away from Laura. It wasn't that he didn't love her – he loved as much as ever, if not more. But he could see the change in her, and it seemed like a reproach. When she'd walked into the Three Jays that night last summer she'd been golden and fresh, just a girl. It was like she had a light inside her, one that made her skin and eyes glow. That light had grown dim over the past months, and he was to blame. She might be happy with him – she said she was – but how long could that last when the life they were leading wasn't about to get better any time soon? He mulled over the problem all the way to the club, finding no answers, eager for the hour when he would be on stage and could lose himself in the music.

13

1956

O N THE FINAL day of his last term at Eton, Max
boarded the early afternoon train to London.
Now nearly eighteen, he was a little over six feet tall,
and two years of rowing had developed in him the
athletic, muscular build of his late father. After seeing
his trunk and other belongings safely stowed in the
guard's van, he settled himself opposite his friend, Alec
Orr-Lowndes.

'Goodbye to all that, eh?' said Max with a grin.

'And amen.' Alec pulled out his cigarette case, lit
two cigarettes, and gave one to Max. Alec was shorter
than his friend, slender, with sandy hair and glasses,
and a personality that more than made up for his lack
of height. Their friendship had been fuelled by shared
interests, and by the fact they both felt themselves to
be in the ranks of outsiders at school. Alec's father was
a self-made man whose modest wealth came from the

manufacture of glassware, and was therefore regarded by the other boys as being in 'trade'. Max, having no parents and no family name of any particular distinction, fell into a similar kind of social limbo. He had achieved acceptance and popularity by excelling at sport, while Alec's status was maintained through his wit, and his reputation as a rebel. Their personalities complemented one another – Max's steadiness and easy good humour seemed to ground the more volatile aspects of Alec's character, while Max admired and enjoyed Alec's showmanship and flights of eccentricity. It was a strange friendship, but it worked.

Outside on the platform the guard shrilled his whistle, and with a hiss of steam the train lurched out of Windsor and Eton Central. To mark the end of their schooldays, the boys had gone to the extravagance of buying first class tickets, and had the carriage to themselves. Max now produced a hip flask and a small cylindrical leather case that contained four little silver cups stacked into one another. He handed one of the cups to Alec and filled it with whisky, then filled his own, raised it aloft, and gave a toast.

'To the future.'

'The future,' echoed Alec. They drank. Alec indicated the little leather case. 'That's nifty. Where did you get it?'

'A present from my uncle,' replied Max, playing with the little press stud on the leather lip of the case, thinking how the gift reflected Roddy's chief preoccupation in life – drinking. He wondered what scenario awaited him in Kensington. Diana had abandoned attempts to make Roddy give up alcohol altogether, and to his credit Roddy did his best not to drink to excess. But last half-term had been the usual dismal charade, his uncle rarely sober, his aunt gamely trying to carry on as though everything was normal.

Alec's voice interrupted his thoughts, asking him what plans he had for summer.

'Nothing much. I'll spend a couple of weeks with my grandmother in the south of France,' said Max, 'and maybe visit a friend in Kent in August.' Harry had already extended an invitation to Chalcombe, but had made no mention of whether Laura would be there. That was all over and done with, anyhow, Max reckoned – he'd written three times, and not once had she replied. It would probably be just as well if she wasn't there.

'I propose we go out on the town,' said Alec. 'Go to some jazz clubs, have a good time.'

'I'm all for that.'

'Oh, and my cousin in Manchester has offered me a couple of tickets for the test match at Old Trafford at the end of the month. If you're interested, that is.'

'I'll say I am.' Alec held out his empty cup, and Max obligingly refilled it. 'The Aussies look like giving us a run for our money.'

'Not with Laker's bowling.'

They talked of cricket until the ticket inspector appeared, and then ambled along to the dining car to have lunch, feeling very much, now they were free of the constraints of school and elevated by a couple of shots of whisky, young men of the world.

At Paddington Max found a porter to take his luggage, and caught a taxi to Kensington. As he brought his trunk and suitcase inside, Morven was coming downstairs. At fourteen she was tall for her age, like her mother, but her schoolgirl lankiness had yet to transform itself into Diana's grace and elegance. She had her father's reddish hair and a pretty face with a pointed chin and slanting blue eyes. The potential for unusual beauty was there, but it was marred today by an expression of injured sullenness.

'Hello there,' said Max. 'Anyone about?'

'Mother's out,' replied Morven. 'Father's somewhere around.'

Max handed the cabbie a sixpence and thanked him. Closing the door he noticed Morven's expression and asked, 'Why the long face?'

'Olivia invited me to her parents' place in Shropshire, but Mother says I can't go. She says it's when we're going to Torquay. I hate beastly Torquay. There's nothing to do there.'

'You always liked the beach well enough, making sandcastles, and things,' replied Max, with a mental note to ensure that he got himself out of the family holiday somehow.

'I'm not a baby now. I'd much rather be with my friends.' She relented in her peevishness and gave him a kiss. 'Anyway, I'm glad you're back. That makes things less boring.'

'Thanks. Care to help me heave this thing up to my room?' He pointed to his trunk.

Morven gave a sigh. 'Come on then.' She lifted the handle at one end. 'It's terribly heavy.'

'Don't worry – I'll take most of the weight. You just hold on to the other end and steer. When did you break up?' asked Max, as they carried the trunk upstairs.

'Last week.'

'Everything OK round here?'

They bumped the trunk into Max's room and set it down.

'I suppose you're talking about Daddy,' replied Morven. 'Actually, he seems all right at the moment. Just one drink in the afternoon, then a glass of wine with dinner. Anyway, I'll leave you to unpack. I'm going off for a game of tennis. See you later.'

Max unpacked, changed and went downstairs. In the kitchen he made himself a cup of tea while the daily that Diana employed prepared the evening meal, then took himself off to the morning room with *The Times*. To his dismay, he found Roddy already ensconced there, sitting by the French windows with a book. It was too late to withdraw, but when Roddy spoke Max realised with relief that his uncle was sober. He seemed delighted to see Max.

'Hello, my boy! I didn't know you were coming back today.' He set the book aside and shook Max's hand. 'So, all done with school now. Suppose you must be feeling a bit sad, eh?'

'Not really. I'm quite elated, in a way.'

'You wait. One day you'll look back and realise just how golden your school days were.' His watery eye, glimmering with recollections of the lost happiness of his own youth, strayed to the drinks trolley on the far side of the room. Max followed his gaze, and saw that it was well-stocked with gin, whisky and sherry. That his uncle hadn't so far helped himself to any of it was impressive testimony to his willpower.

Roddy caught his eye and winked. 'How about a little afternoon snifter to celebrate your return?' He glanced at his watch. 'Soon be five o'clock. I normally have something around now. Just the one, mind. On best behaviour these days.'

Max hesitated. He didn't want a drink – the couple of shots on the train had been more for swagger than anything else – but he could see his uncle did. It seemed like an unkindness to refuse. He went over to the trolley and poured himself the barest amount of whisky and topped it up with water, then poured Roddy a slightly more generous measure.

'No water for me. Criminal to pollute a good Scotch like that,' said Roddy, his eyes fixed greedily on the glass as Max handed it to him. 'Here's to you, my boy.' He drank, then asked, 'So, what are your plans? Your aunt said something about reading law at Cambridge.'

'Yes. I've managed to defer my National Service till after university,' replied Max, settling himself in an armchair. 'The longer I can put it off the better.'

'You might enjoy it more than you think. Being in the RAF was one of the best times in my life. I loved flying Spitfires. Wickedly beautiful planes they were, built to win. You didn't fly them – they flew you. I remember my first time, hooking up my parachute and climbing in. It was magical.'

'I doubt if square-bashing measures up to being a fighter pilot.'

'True,' replied Roddy, swallowing the remains of his drink. 'We were like duellists. There was respect for the enemy, even a sort of fellow-feeling. I remember this Messerschmitt I shot down. We were so close I could see the fella's face, his plane was on fire and all I could think was, "Jump, you silly German bastard! Use your parachute, why don't you?" But he didn't. I felt sorry for him. It could just as easily have been me.' He eyed his empty glass reflectively. 'When I told your father about that, he said I was lucky to be able to fight fair. Said he had no chance to think twice or feel sorry for the people he dropped bombs on.' He held out his glass.

'These days I usually just have the one, but I don't think another will hurt. Fill her up again, would you?' Max hesitated, thinking of what Morven had said, but felt he had to oblige. Roddy watched him beadily as he poured. 'Don't be stingy, now, old chap.'

Max handed the refreshed glass to his uncle, who said, settling further into his chair, 'Did I ever tell you about the time I had to bail out over the channel? This ruddy great fleet of German bombers came out of nowhere and knocked out my sump and set me on fire. I was out of my seat like a cork out of a bottle, I can tell you.'

Max listened, trying to see his uncle as a young man, calculating how much courage he must have had to take to the skies day after day, in the knowledge that each one might be his last. When he finished the story his glass was empty. His face had taken on a light flush, highlighting the broken veins in his cheeks. 'You know what, old fellow – I think I could do with just a splash more.' He held out his whisky glass.

'I honestly don't think you should, Uncle Roddy. You said yourself – just the one.'

There was a moment of wavering silence. Max was profoundly aware of his uncle fighting something within himself, making a desperate effort to rally his fragile strength of will and not destroy the good work of the past few weeks. But the second drink, such a slight thing, had wrecked his resolve. The grin that he threw Max as he got to his feet and went to the drinks trolley himself was truly piteous. He brought the bottle back and set it on the table next to him.

For the next half an hour Roddy sat regaling Max with wartime tales, his face growing more flushed, the stories more maundering. Just when Max had decided he could take no more, and was about to make his escape, he heard the sound of the front door opening and closing. A few seconds later his aunt came in. She took in the scene with a swift glance. Roddy turned his rheumy eyes to her.

'Jus' having a li'l chat and a drink with Max here.' He waggled his head absurdly.

'Max, can I speak to you, please?' asked Diana in clipped tones.

When they were out of the room, the door closed, his aunt hissed at him, 'How on earth have you allowed that to happen?'

Max was taken aback. 'What? It's not my fault – how can I stop him?'

'Every day for the past week he's managed to have just one drink and no more, and now you come home and everything falls apart.'

'That's not fair! If having a loaded drinks trolley within his reach is some kind of test of his will, it's a pretty daft idea. It's nothing to do with me whether he chooses to get himself plastered or not.'

'How long have you been in there with him?'

'An hour or so. But what's that got to do with anything?'

'Only an hour, and you let him drink himself into that state—'

'What was I meant to do? I did say something, but it's his house, in the end. He can do as he likes.'

Diana closed her eyes briefly and ran her fingers through her hair. Her face looked strained and tired. 'It's just that he was doing so well. I really thought he was coping.'

'I think you're being over-optimistic. He used my coming back from school as an excuse. He'd have found another if I hadn't been here.' Max paused. 'I'm sorry.'

'Well, we're both sorry, and there's nothing to be done about it.' She turned the handle on the morning room door and looked in again. Roddy was dozing now, the hand holding his glass slack on the armrest. Diana took the glass from his hand and the bottle from the table and put both on the trolley, then came out, leaving the door ajar. 'He'll have to sleep it off.' She glanced at her watch. 'We might as well have dinner.'

'I've booked the hotel in Torquay for a fortnight at the end of the month,' said Diana. There were only the three of them at the table; Roddy was still asleep in the morning room. 'I'm sure we could all do with the break.'

'I'm frightfully sorry, Aunt Di,' said Max quickly, 'but I've arranged a few things with Alec – cricket, that kind of thing. I think I'll have to bow out.'

'Oh – well, that's a pity. Still, you're quite grown up now. You must make your own arrangements.'

Morven put down her knife and fork. 'I don't see why Max gets to do what he wants when I don't.'

'That will be quite enough, Morven. As though I don't have enough to worry about without your constant complaints—'

There was a sudden thudding sound, and conversation ceased. Diana pushed her chair back and left the table.

Morven's eyes met Max's. 'Daddy's sozzled again, isn't he? I assumed it was why he's not at dinner.'

Before Max could reply, Diana shouted, 'Max, quickly! I need you here.'

Max hurried to the morning room, Morven following, to find Roddy on the floor. He seemed to have risen from his chair and collapsed. His face drooped strangely on one side and he was groaning.

'Help me get him into the chair,' said Diana. 'Morven, go and telephone for an ambulance.'

Morven fled to the phone in the hallway. Diana took Roddy's legs and Max his shoulders, and between them they lifted him into the chair.

'God, what's that smell?' exclaimed Max, then realised his uncle had soiled himself. Even in his worst bouts of drunkenness, he'd never done that.

'I think he's had a stroke,' said Diana, loosening his tie and unbuttoning his shirt. Roddy's breathing was hoarse and rasping.

'I'll get him some water,' said Max, and left the room.

Diana smoothed the thick red hair back from her husband's forehead, which was waxy pale. The stench was revolting, and she rose and unlatched the French windows, pushing them open to let in the fresh evening air, musky with the smell of the roses that bordered the terrace. As she turned to look at Roddy, prone in his chair, with his twisted face, she was suddenly visited by the memory of the first time she had met him. It had been at Hazelhurst, Meg and Paul's home in the country, on a summer's day. She and Meg had been chatting indoors, and Meg had left the room for some reason. She'd heard voices from the terrace and had stepped outside to find her brother sitting there, talking with two men. One of them was Roddy, dressed in oil-stained racing overalls. So frightfully well-mannered, springing to his feet at the sight of her, putting out his cigarette. How handsome and charming she'd thought him. That was their beginning. And now.

With tears in her eyes she knelt on the floor next to him and took one of his hands, stroking and kneading the puffy flesh. Whatever happened, she would not remember him this way. She would think of him as he had been, not as he was now.

Morven reappeared. 'The ambulance is coming.' She looked at her father and burst into tears.

Max came in with a glass of water and handed it to Diana. She tried to put it to Roddy's lips to help him drink, but he couldn't swallow properly and the water dribbled down his chin and on to his shirt. The three of them stayed there, waiting, helpless, while the birds sang in the garden outside.

Diana went in the ambulance to the hospital with Roddy. The evening passed without word, and Max and Morven eventually went to bed. Max was lying in the darkness with his random thoughts, trying to put the miserable events of the afternoon and evening behind him, when he heard the telephone bell jangle in the hall below, and then Morven's feet on the stair. He switched on his bedside light and waited. After a few moments the door opened and Morven came in. She crossed the floor in her nightdress and sat on the edge of his bed. When she spoke, her voice was hoarse with anguish. 'Mummy rang from the hospital. Daddy died.'

Max sat up and put his arms around her, and she fell against him, sobbing. He tried to hush her, to think of soothing things to say. At length she stopped crying, and muttered, 'I know everyone thought he was silly and drunk all the time, and that he wasted his life, but I loved him.'

'Of course you did,' Max reassured her. 'And he

didn't waste his life. Far from it. The things he did during the war – there weren't a lot of chaps as brave as that, I can tell you. When I was little my father used to say that if we ever won the war, it would be because of men like him.' He stroked her hair, feeling the rise and fall of her breathing as she lay against his chest. Not sure whether it was what she wanted to hear or not, he went on, 'It must have been hard for him after the war, you know. To find that same sense of purpose.'

Morven drew away from him. She wiped her eyes, and sat pleating the edge of her nightdress with her fingers. He regarded her in the half-darkness, noticing the curve of her budding breasts beneath the thin material of her nightdress. He'd always thought of her as a little squirt, but she was growing up.

She nodded, and let out a ragged sigh. 'I should let you get to sleep.'

'I don't think I'll be able to sleep. Stay and talk if you want.'

For half an hour they talked, their murmuring conversation moving from memories of Roddy in better times, to how they thought things would be now in the house. A couple of times Morven wept again, and Max did his best to comfort her. Then they heard the front door open and close.

'That's Mummy,' said Morven. 'I'd better go down.'

She regarded Max gravely, then suddenly kissed him lightly on the lips. She sat back, as if considering something, then kissed him again, the pressure of her mouth a little more insistent.

'Night night,' she murmured, and stood up.

'Night,' replied Max. She left, closing the door behind her.

14

IT WAS A summer of change for Max. In the aftermath of the funeral he thought a good deal about his uncle, trying to reconcile the dashing young man in RAF uniform he'd known as a child with the mildly embarrassing and useless middle-aged drunk he had become. He felt he understood for the first time the bafflement of older people, seeing the world they had fought a war for growing unrecognisable around them. He remembered what Philip had said to Edgar Lightfoot that rainy afternoon at Chalcombe, and saw that he had been pitilessly right. People like Roddy were remnants. Time moved relentlessly on. The future belonged to a new generation, and he was a part of it. In London there was a mood of unpredictability and excitement, and Max felt as though he and the times were evolving together, going through mystifying and rapid changes, with young people in particular carving out new identities for themselves. Teds with duck-tail quiffs, drape jackets and brothel-creepers had begun to eclipse beatniks with their beards and black clothes and Gauloises, and the music of Bill Haley and Gene Vincent came crashing on the scene like a tidal wave. Adults who had come through the war looked on, outraged or perplexed, as old-fashioned certainties gave way to this new and incomprehensible phenomenon.

Max lived his life in two worlds, one run by grown-ups in which he and his school friends put on black tie and attended countless debutante parties thrown by society mothers – mothers who, on behalf of their daughters, had a beady eye on the Latimer fortune – and the other, younger world of coffee bars and jazz clubs, where strict social status and decorum counted for absolutely nothing. In the former, he acted out a part written for him by previous generations; in the latter he was free to play his own role, expressed in a language those generations could not comprehend.

Now that they were free agents, he and Alec spent much of their time in jazz clubs. They listened to skiffle in The 2i's coffee bar in Old Compton Street, and jazz at a place in Oxford Street which operated as a restaurant by day and a music club by night, and where Humphrey Lyttelton regularly played – Max had never forgotten that magical afternoon in Chalcombe, sitting playing his first jazz records while Harry tapped at his typewriter

– and Cy Laurie's club in Great Windmill Street, where he and Alec jived with girls from St Martin's School of Art. Max was less keen than Alec on modern jazz, but he was happy to indulge his friend and go along with him occasionally to smoky basements where no one danced, and where the music, free-form, complex and elusive, was listened to reverentially. It was on one such Saturday evening that he walked into the Three Jays and saw Laura.

Even with her back to him, he recognised her straight away. She was sitting at a table, her blonde hair pinned up, wearing black slacks and a tight black sweater. His immediate instinct was to go and say hello, but he hesitated. She hadn't answered his letters. That should tell him something. Still, he couldn't sit there all evening and not talk to her. He waited until the band finished its number and the audience began to clap, then said to Alec, 'I've just seen someone I know. Be back in a tick.' He rose and went over to her table, and touched her lightly on the shoulder.

She turned, and her look of dismay at the sight of him made him feel instantly wounded. Had her feelings towards him really changed so much?

She made an effort to smile. 'Max – what are you doing here?'

He shrugged and returned the smile. 'I'm a jazz fan. I didn't know you were, too.' He noticed she was smoking, and that she was wearing lipstick and black eyeliner that flicked up in a catlike way at the outer corners of her eyes. He'd never seen her wearing make-up before. That, and her pinned-up hair, made her look much older than the last time he'd seen her. But then, it had been three years.

Max sat down. 'How have you been? You didn't answer my letters.'

Her glance flickered away from his face. 'I'm sorry, I didn't know you'd written. I didn't get them.'

'Really?'

'I'm not living in Mount Street any more. I haven't been for a while.' She fiddled with her cigarette and then stubbed it out. 'Avril and I had a falling-out. Evidently she doesn't forward my mail.'

She gazed at him, thinking how much he'd grown up. He was quite a man now, tall, broad-shouldered in his checked shirt, his face angular and handsome, nothing boyish about him, except for the way his curling dark hair fell over his eyes. She was glad to see him, but she knew inevitably how he was going to react when he found out about her situation, and that made her sad. Not ashamed – she was careful never to feel ashamed – just sad. She wished he hadn't come here tonight. He, along with Avril, and Mount Street, and Chalcombe, was part of a world she had left behind, and could not go back to. She glanced towards the stage, and Max followed her gaze. The band was pausing for a break and the saxophonist, a big black fellow, had stepped down from the stage and was heading in their direction. To Max's astonishment, he stopped behind Laura and rested a hand on her shoulder, caressing it lightly. She looked up with a smile, and he sat down.

'Ellis,' said Laura, 'this is Max Latimer, an old friend. Max, this is Ellis Candy. We live together.'

Ellis put out a hand and Max shook it, stunned. 'How d'you do?' he murmured with reflexive politeness.

'Pleasure,' said Ellis. 'I've heard a lot about you from Laura.' He kept his tone cordial, but he could tell exactly what Max was thinking. A part of him was angry with Laura. Why had she had to tell him they were living together? The guy looked shell-shocked, and who could blame him? She should stop being so righteous and give everyone a break. He was used to people's attitudes, and while the injustice of them made him angry, it was a long-smouldering, quiet anger. He accepted there was nothing he could do. Laura's anger, on the other hand, burnt fierce and confrontationally bright.

Max struggled for something to say. He couldn't take in the idea that Laura was actually living with this man. It ran contrary to every convention by which she'd been brought up. But his good manners prevailed, and he managed to say, 'Can I buy either of you a drink?'

'I'm OK, thanks,' replied Ellis.

Max turned to Laura. Her eyes seemed blank. 'Laura?'

She shook her head. 'No, thanks. I haven't finished

this one yet.' She could read his face. It was just as she'd anticipated.

Max nodded, still trying to absorb it all. Was she married to this man? He saw no wedding ring. Did that make it worse, or better?

'Well' – he glanced across at Alec – 'I'd better get back to my friend.' He stood up, nodding to Ellis. 'Nice to have met you.' He glanced awkwardly at Laura. 'Bye, Laura.'

'Bye,' murmured Laura, watching him go. Well, that was done, and at least he knew.

'You see?' said Ellis softly. 'This is taking every friend you ever had away from you. I told you how it would be.'

She shook her head. 'Then I can do without friends like that.' She gazed at Ellis for a moment, then kissed him. 'I have you.'

'Who was that?' asked Alec, as Max sat down. 'An old girlfriend?'

'We were kids together. I've known her ever since I can remember.'

Alec caught sight of the kiss. 'Whew! She doesn't care what people think, does she?'

'Listen,' said Max, 'I don't really want to stay here. I'm not that into the music.'

Alec shrugged and swallowed the remains of his drink. 'Fine by me. Let's head over to the Flamingo.'

Max didn't so much as glance in Laura's direction as they left.

*

A few days later Max went to the gallery in Alfred Place. It was empty. He was pacing the white-walled rooms, examining the paintings, when Avril came out of the office at the back. She didn't recognise him straight away, and when she did she was surprised, both by the change in him and the fact of his visit. There had never been any love lost between them, certainly not since that time by the reservoir, on the fateful day of the picnic in the woods.

'Max. What brings you here?'

'I think you can probably guess. It's about Laura. I want to know everything that's happened.'

Avril set a pile of catalogues down on a table. Max noticed her style had changed since he'd last seen her. She was dressed in cropped green trousers, black suede loafers, and a black and white striped tabard over a black top. Her dark hair was swept up, and she wore chunky silver jewellery. It was all in keeping, he realised, with the tone of the gallery and the works on display.

She glanced at her watch and sighed. 'It's lunchtime. I'm closing up anyway. Let's go and have something to eat.'

They went to a nearby ABC, and Avril recounted Laura's story over coffee and sandwiches.

'Does she have any idea how she's ruining her life?' asked Max.

'It isn't what I expected,' replied Avril, then added after a moment, 'Then again, maybe it is.'

'What do you mean?'

'Tendencies run in families. I mean, look at her mother. Getting herself pregnant at sixteen, running off and leaving my mother with the baby.' She met Max's gaze. 'It seems Laura's as feckless as her mother was.'

'Have you tried to… I don't know, talk her round? Make her see what a mistake she's making?'

She could hardly tell Max that she was glad Laura was gone, and that she didn't much care what happened to her. 'Of course I have. I want what's best for her. But she says she's in love, that she doesn't care what people think. You would imagine, after the upbringing my mother gave her, that she'd have some sense of decency. But clearly she hasn't.'

'Don't say that.'

Avril said nothing, merely raised her eyebrows expressively.

After a moment Max said firmly, 'I'm going to talk to her. Do you have an address for her?'

Avril gave Max the address. 'You can't do anything, you know.'

'Here's two bob for my share of lunch,' said Max, getting to his feet. He had always known how little Avril cared about Laura, and he didn't believe for a moment that Avril had done anything to make Laura see what a mistake she was making.

*

Max found out which nights Ellis played at the Three Jays and went round to Luscombe Street on one of them, hoping he would find Laura alone. An old man came to the door.

'Top floor,' he told Max. 'But I reckon they're both out.'

Max climbed the shabby staircase till he reached the attic floor. He knocked and waited. There was no reply. He glanced around, taking in the uncarpeted stair, the stubby gas and electricity meters, the grimy skylight. How could she live like this? He realised, with a mixture of anger and unhappiness, that no one had forced her into it. She had chosen this.

He went back downstairs and into the street, and as he turned the corner towards the Tube station he saw Laura coming towards him. She had her head down and hadn't seen him. He'd already rehearsed what he was going to say, but he'd imagined doing it in the privacy of her flat. An encounter in the street wasn't ideal.

As she came closer she looked up and saw him.

'Max,' she sighed, 'just go away.'

'You don't even know why I'm here.'

'Yes, I do. You've come to tell me what a mistake I'm making, not to throw my life away.' She gazed at him. 'Haven't you?'

'Yes, I have. Someone has to make you see sense. And I think I have the right.' He could feel the blood rush to his face with the force of his emotion. 'Because I love you. I've always loved you. I even hoped—'

'Oh, Max, please stop. I don't think you have the first idea what love is.' To this he had no reply. 'I do. If you love someone, if you want to be with them because they mean more to you than anything else in the world, it means sacrificing things. I've found out all that.'

'It doesn't mean sacrificing yourself, your entire future.'

'Maybe it does. Anyway, don't you worry about my future. Worry about your own. There's no point in talking to me any more about it.'

'Then maybe I should talk to Ellis,' said Max. 'If he's half the man you think he is, he'd realise he's wrecking your life. Or perhaps he doesn't really care about you.'

'Of course he cares!'

'Then he should know that the best thing he can do is get out of your life. And if he doesn't, someone should tell him!'

'Well, it's not going to be you, Max! You won't interfere in my life. Stop thinking you know what's best for me. You don't.'

She tried to move past him, but he grasped her arm gently, trying to calm his anger. 'Laura, exactly where in God's name do you think all of this is going?' It was a question she often asked herself, and to which she could find no answer. She hesitated, and Max went on, 'What would Aunt Sonia say?'

She shook his hand off. 'That's a cheap shot. I'm not answerable to her any more. Or to you. Or to anyone. Don't come looking for me ever again.'

She walked away, leaving him standing on the pavement.

15

FRUSTRATED, STILL CONVINCED he had to do something to rescue Laura, Max decided the best thing would be to talk to Harry. Harry would know what to do. He rang and asked if he could come to Chalcombe for a couple of days, and Harry readily agreed.

On the afternoon of Max's arrival they took a stroll through the woods, Hamlet trotting at their heels, and Max explained Laura's situation in bald terms, expressing none of his own feelings until he had heard what Harry had to say.

'That's a bad show,' mused Harry. 'But then, I always thought she might be that kind of a girl.'

'What kind of girl?' asked Max sharply.

Harry gave him a mild glance. 'One with more feeling than sense. A girl who lets her heart rule her head.'

'Oh.' They walked for a while in silence, then Max said, 'She's mad. She's throwing everything away.'

Harry shrugged. 'A pity, but what can you do?'

'Something. I have to do something.'

Harry made no reply. Poor Max. He evidently thought that he could undo Laura's mistake, and gain her love for himself. The whole business was certainly regrettable. No doubt Sonia's death had taken away Laura's sense of security, so that the girl had gone looking for love in the first place she could find it, which happened to be a black musician in a Soho club. There was no legislating for the human heart, or for the folly of a teenager who didn't fully appreciate the ways of the world and the long-term consequences of her actions.

'What would you do?' persisted Max. 'What would you do to make her see sense?'

Harry sauntered along, knocking the heads off dandelions with his cane as he deliberated, and said at last, 'Perhaps it's not Laura you should be focusing on.'

'What d'you mean?'

'I recall my mother telling me how my grandfather dealt with some unsuitable chap who was after her sister, my Aunt Dora. She was young and impressionable, and he was a nice enough fellow, but his family weren't quite the thing, and he had no prospects. My grandfather could see it, but Dora couldn't. She was adamant she wanted to marry him, convinced they would be happy.

Nothing could persuade her to give him up, so my grandfather did the only thing he could.'

'Which was?'

'He bought the fellow off. Paid him enough money, and my poor aunt never saw him again. I say "poor", but she got over it, of course, and married some quite wealthy chap and was perfectly happy. So far as one could tell.'

Max seized on the idea with interest. 'You think if he were offered enough money, he might go away?'

Harry shrugged. 'I have no idea. But he must know his relationship with Laura can't be anything but a disaster for her, in the long run. Put a bit of money his way and he might see sense, do the decent thing. As Walpole said, all men have their price.'

Max dwelt on this idea, and when he got back to London he formulated a plan. He would tell his aunt that he needed five hundred pounds from the trust to buy a car. It was his money, and she'd been generous enough in the matter of an allowance, so with any luck it wouldn't be a problem. And with that sum of money he would try to buy Ellis Candy off. It was a risky step, but as he saw it, this was a desperate situation calling for desperate measures.

'I suppose you can have an advance from the trust fund,' Diana said when he made his request. 'But five hundred pounds won't buy you much of a car. Don't you want something sporty?'

'I just want a runabout.' He paused. 'Well, maybe seven hundred, then.' He supposed that whatever happened with Ellis Candy, a car would have to manifest itself. He would buy something cheap with the extra two hundred.

'I'll speak to the lawyers and ask them to put the money over to your account.'

'Thanks, Aunt Di.' Max hadn't expected it to be quite so easy. It was a relief to know he wouldn't have to wait around for the money. He wanted to get this thing over and done with.

The prospect of carrying out his plan put Max into a state of feverish tension. Should he offer the money to Candy by way of cash or a cheque? Was it too little or too much? What was he going to say when he saw him? What if the whole thing was a ghastly failure? Ellis Candy might just laugh at him. Or even attack him. He felt entirely out of his depth and, much as he wanted to think of himself as no longer a schoolboy, he knew in this matter that was exactly what he was. That knowledge frustrated and enraged him. It wasn't that he was afraid – certainly the prospect of what he was about to do filled him with apprehension, but his real fear was that he would handle it badly and everything would backfire.

A week after the money came into his account he had

still done nothing. He came to the conclusion that this was going to take a wiser head than he possessed, and a considered, mature approach. Someone like Harry would be able to handle it far better than he could – but whether or not Harry would agree to be involved was another question.

He tried several times to reach Harry at Chalcombe, but there was no reply. Then he remembered that he had said he was coming back to town at the end of the month. He went round to the offices of the *Modern Critical Review* on the off-chance that he would find him there.

Harry was indeed there, together with Edgar Lightfoot, putting together articles for the next edition of the magazine, and debating, when Max arrived, whether or not to include a poem submitted by a new young poet, Ted Hughes.

'Too much like a poor man's D.H. Lawrence,' was Edgar's view. 'But without the psychological insight.'

'I disagree,' replied Harry. 'I like the brutality, the force of will. It's very honest writing. We need some energetic new poetry, and less of the genteel stuff. I very much want to include it.'

'As you like,' grumbled Edgar, glancing up as Max put his head round the door.

'Max,' said Harry in surprise. 'What brings you here?'

'I needed to talk to you about something,' said Max. 'Hello, Mr Lightfoot.' Edgar gave him a nod and a smile.

Harry could tell from Max's face that it was something personal. He glanced at his watch. 'It's pretty much lunchtime. Can I leave you to put the rest of the articles together, Edgar? I'll finish the editorial tomorrow.'

Harry took Max to the Wheatsheaf, where they ordered pies and a couple of beers. He let Max spin out lunch with nervous small talk, but when they had finished their food he said, 'Come on, spit it out – why are we here?'

Max pushed his plate aside and reached into his inside jacket pocket. He took out a brown envelope stuffed with banknotes, and laid it on the table between them. Harry gave Max a questioning look.

'It's five hundred pounds. I intend to use it to make Ellis Candy leave Laura.'

'I see.' Harry took a sip of his beer.

'The thing is,' Max went on anxiously, 'I have absolutely no idea how to do it. What to say, I mean. The things I think of saying sound ludicrous in my head.' He smoothed the bulge of the envelope with his hand.

There was a moment's silence, then Harry asked, 'Have you given any thought as to how you want this to end, exactly?'

'I just want him out of her life. I want her to come to her senses.'

Harry said nothing.

'The thing is, I don't think I'm the right person to

do it. I'll make a hash of it, I know I will.' Max had been staring at his drink, and now he lifted his eyes to Harry's. 'I need you to help me. Please.'

Harry sat back with a sigh. 'You want me to talk to him? Offer him the money?'

Max nodded. 'You'll know the right things to say to persuade him. You'd be helping not just me, but Laura, too—'

Harry raised a hand. 'You don't need to sell it to me, Max.' He picked up the envelope and put it into his pocket. 'I'm not sure I should be getting involved, but because I'm fond of you, and because I think Laura would be better off without this man, I'll do what I can.'

Relief flooded Max's eyes. 'Thank you.'

'Where does he play?'

'The Three Jays in Dean Street.'

Harry nodded. 'I know the place. I'll go one night next week.' There was a pause. 'You realise there is no guarantee this will work?'

Max nodded. 'Of course. But I'll never forgive myself if I don't try.'

Harry went to the Three Jays the following Thursday evening around ten. He stood at the back of the small room and scanned the audience for Laura. If she was there, he would have to come back another night. But there was no sign of her. He bought himself a drink and sat down at a corner table. Free-form jazz wasn't quite his thing, but he had to admit that the sextet Ellis Candy played with was excellent, and that Ellis himself played the saxophone like a dream. When the band took a break and Ellis went to get a drink, he studied the man with whom he had come to bargain, watching him cracking jokes with the barman. He seemed decent enough. If Laura had chosen to be with him, who was he to interfere? He had half a mind to walk away from it all. Then again, he agreed with Max that in the long run this would not end well, that it would be kindness to rescue Laura from her own folly. Yes, it was insulting to offer the man money, but if he took it... well, that would say everything about him, and Laura would be better off without him. He decided he would see it through. But he couldn't help thinking, as he watched Ellis return to the stage for the next set, that he was a big fellow, one who looked like he could land a hefty punch if he chose to.

It was almost midnight when the club closed, and the audience began to drift from the basement. Harry approached Ellis.

'Great set,' he remarked. 'I really enjoyed your playing.'

'Thanks.' Ellis gave Harry a curious look.

'I wonder – could we have a word in private somewhere?'

'Nowhere private around here,' Ellis replied, glancing at the tiny backstage area busy with musicians. 'Best step outside.'

They went through the back door of the club and up a short flight of metal steps to a cobbled alleyway, empty except for a row of dustbins and a solitary street lamp throwing off a dim glow.

'So,' said Ellis, 'what's this about?' He surveyed the burly, bearded man in his tweed jacket and tie, wondering if he might be a music promoter, or a scout of some kind. He was older than most of the people who came to the club.

'I'm a friend of Laura's.'

'Ah.' Ellis nodded slowly. He supposed he'd been expecting a visit like this, was even surprised it hadn't come months ago. 'So... what? You come to warn me off? A little late for that, I reckon.'

'People are concerned for her welfare. Laura's not' – he hesitated – 'she's not very worldly. You must know that.'

'She knows what she wants, I guess.'

'Does she? She's given up a lot be with you, so I suppose she must love you a great deal. But she's young. She doesn't see ahead.' Ellis shucked a cigarette from a packet and lit it without offering Harry one. 'But you do, I think.'

Ellis made no reply. He was trying to make sense of this strange feeling of relief, like some tension slackening inside him. He almost felt like telling this man not to bother saying any more. That he already knew the truth of it, that it was only Laura who couldn't see.

'Tell me,' Harry went on, 'how do you see the future for you and Laura?'

Ellis frowned, flexing his fingers. Harry braced himself for the angry onslaught he thought might be coming. But the reply, when it came, surprised him.

'I've asked myself that question a million times. There ain't a day goes by when I don't wonder how it's going to turn out. I know in your bigoted white world there's no room for what she and I have going on. You think I'm not good enough for her. That's what you think, right?'

'You're a man of the world, Mr Candy. You know it's an unforgiving place, and that just wanting it to be different won't make it so.'

'Well, that's one way of saying yes to my question.'

'So tell me the answer to mine. What does the future look like?'

Ellis let out a long breath. 'One thing you have to understand is that I love the girl. She's the best thing in my life. I don't know why she's with me, but I count myself lucky every day.' He paused. 'Thing is, I don't count her so lucky. Like you say, the world is the way it is, hateful and narrow-minded, and while I might not want it to be that way, I know it's not going to change in a hurry. Not in time for Laura and me.'

How apt these words were to his own situation, thought Harry, the shameful secrecy with which he had to live his life to avoid the social and criminal penalties of being homosexual. Change, if it ever came, would be a long time coming for him, as well as for Ellis. The insight moved him.

'I understand how you feel.'

'No, you don't,' replied Ellis contemptuously. 'You can't begin to understand what it's like to be treated like dirt because of the way you were born.'

'I understand better than you think. Every day people like me face the danger of being locked up, of losing our livelihoods, of being socially shunned because of our sexuality. So I know about prejudice and hatred. I have the luxury of being able to keep my truth secret, to live a lie so that the world will be kind to me. You don't have that privilege. You face every day the kind of intolerance that I only have to fear. In a way I feel sorrier for you than I do for myself.'

Ellis studied him, making sense of his words. The man was saying he was a queer. He was reminded of his own prejudices, and felt a flush of shame and confusion.

'We both know what it's like to suffer the injustices of this sorry world,' Harry went on. 'I also know that I wouldn't want anyone I love to share that suffering if they weren't born to it.' He let his words sink in. 'If you love Laura, you must want what's best for her.'

'You came here to tell me there's no happy ending for us, that she'd be better off without me. You think I didn't know all that already?'

'Then give her up.'

There was a long silence. 'It would break her heart. I'd have to lie to her, tell her I don't love her. I can't do that.'

'Maybe you don't have to tell her anything.' Harry thought of the money in his pocket. 'Maybe you could just go away. If you were prepared to do that, I could help you.'

'Help me how?'

Harry drew out the envelope. 'Five hundred pounds. You simply take it and leave.' He gazed at Ellis. If ever there was a moment when the man might knock him down, this was it. 'Will you?'

Ellis dropped the remains of his cigarette on the cobbles and ground it out with his foot, then took the envelope from Harry. 'It was always going to happen. Didn't you know that?'

He went back into the club, leaving Harry standing alone in the alleyway.

16

HARRY LEFT THE alleyway, unsure if he had achieved his aim, and if he had, whether he had done a good thing or a bad thing. Old Compton Street had a deserted feel. The pubs had shut and the only people around were punters seeking out late-night drinking holes and strip clubs. Despite the lateness of the hour the air still held vestiges of the day's warmth, and there was a welcoming vacancy in the dark streets that made his mind wander irresistibly to his younger, wilder days, and chance encounters in alleyways and public toilets. Oh, those days. He experienced a faint throb of excitement as he recalled the furtive, faceless meetings, the melting sense of anticipation, the thrill of succumbing to urgent sexual desires kept fearfully under wraps. Anonymous figures – boys, sailors, brutes of men with wives and children at home, and the 'flat-capped respectables', as he had called them, who wore cloth caps to disguise their social status – any number of fleeting couplings in various well-known haunts, lavatories, cinemas, bath-houses. Part of the allure had lain in the riskiness of such behaviour, tangled up with voyeurism, but these days the danger was of a less titillating kind, with police everywhere, vigilantly intent on stamping out the vice of homosexuality. It was the reason he stayed away from Soho late at night. Temptation could be fatal. It had been different before the war, when a quiet tolerance had, by and large, prevailed. But then, everything had been different before the war.

As he walked up Berwick Street in the direction of Oxford Street, hoping to find a cruising cab to take him home to Chelsea, he passed the public conveniences. *Don't be a fool*, he thought, and kept walking. A cab would turn the corner any minute, its light on, and he would be saved. But he had reached a place in his mind where he knew it was only a matter of time, a futile number of steps, before he turned around. His common sense, the inner voice of reason, was no match for the unquenchable urgency of his desire for contact, for the touch of a stranger. Sex, pure and simple, drove him. The memory of those dark enjoyments, the squalid pick-ups that began with a brushing glance and ended in an ecstasy of anonymous orgasm, seemed to fill his brain like ink clouding clear water. He gave the cab five seconds to appear, and when it didn't, he turned and walked back, and moments later he was descending the tile-echoing staircase, the faint whiff of urine rising to his nostrils. Two men passed him on the stairs on their way out. It was chillier down here, the light was dim, and the place was empty. A moment later he heard a man's tread on the steps. He waited, heart in mouth. The man who stepped into the urinal next to him lifted his eyes to Harry's and smiled. Harry returned the smile, and let his glance travel downwards from the young man's handsome face as he unzipped his trousers. Then the man moved out of the urinal, and overwhelmed by the force of his own desire, Harry stepped towards him. Even as he did so he sensed something fatally wrong. A moment later he was being forcefully bundled back up the stairs to the street, to be placed under arrest.

Ellis left the club and walked home. Harry's visit seemed to have crystallised some knowledge that had been building inside him for months. He and Laura might love each other now, but they had no future. He fingered the envelope of banknotes in his pocket. He didn't want it, didn't know why he'd taken it. The idea that he could use the money to take Laura back to the States, and start over, died as soon as it was born. They couldn't begin to build a life in Memphis, where blacks and whites couldn't drink from the same water-cooler or eat in the same restaurant. The guy was right. He had nothing to offer Laura. She'd be better off without him. He knew it, she knew it – she just wasn't facing up to it. One of them had to.

Laura was asleep when he got in. He shucked off his clothes and crept in next to her. This might be the last night they would lie together. He tried to imagine having the strength of will tomorrow to let her go. He kissed her shoulder, and suddenly found tears coming to his eyes. Fool, he thought. Fool ever to have let this begin, when he should have known it would end in pain for both of them.

He slept little that night, waking after short spells to go through everything in his mind. Every time he woke and thought, he knew he had taken one step further away from her.

She woke around seven, hazy with sleep, pushing back her tumbled blonde hair and nestling against him. Morning was her favourite time for making love, when the world was new and its cares still remote, and he brought to it all the tenderness and urgency he'd felt the first time, this being the last. If he said little, was more subdued than usual, she didn't notice. She got up at last to make their morning tea. The gas was out. He lay in bed with his eyes shut, one arm across his forehead, listening as she rustled in her purse for money for the meter. He heard her go out to the landing, then the click of the coins. When she came back in he opened his eyes and watched her make the tea. She looked so carelessly beautiful as she opened the window to take the milk bottle from the sill where she'd put it to keep cool; he tried to imagine her being with him, making him tea ten, twelve years from now, and failed. Failed utterly.

As usual, he drank his tea in bed while she got ready to go to work.

'Are you playing tonight?' she asked, slipping on her jacket.

He nodded. 'Uh-huh.' The lie made his heart feel like stone. As she picked up her keys and handbag he said softly, 'Come on over here.'

She smiled and sat down on the bed. 'What?'

He smoothed a hand over her hair and kissed her. 'Just saying goodbye.'

He closed his eyes as she left the room, listening to the sound of her feet on the stairs, the slam of the front door, and the silence that followed.

Later that morning he went to the club, when he knew Vince would be in his office totting up the previous night's takings, to tell him that he wouldn't be playing that night, or any other night.

'Right you are,' said Vince. Musicians came and went, he didn't much care. He shifted his cigarette to the other side of his mouth. 'Bit more notice wouldn't have come amiss. It being a Friday.'

'Give that guy Robbie a call, he'll fill my slot. He needs the work.'

Vince squinted at him through the smoke of his cigarette. 'Lester planning on leaving, too?'

'This is my own thing. I'll talk to Lester.' He took out a piece of paper with some figures scribbled on it. 'What I reckon you owe me up to last night.'

Vince sighed, examined the figures, then took out a key and opened the petty cash box. He took out a handful of ten shilling notes and thumbed through them, handing three to Ellis with some loose change.

'All the best, mate,' said Vince.

'You, too,' replied Ellis.

He went back to the room in Luscombe Street and packed his case. Then he sat down at the table and wrote a letter to Laura. He said all that was necessary, keeping it short. Saying everything that was in his heart would have taken pages. He folded it and propped it against the brown envelope containing the money. He picked up his case and cast a last glance round the room. On the bedside table he saw one of Laura's hair slides, a cheap little thing in iridescent blue plastic. He picked it up. It had a couple of strands of golden hair caught in the clasp. He put it in his pocket and went downstairs and into the street, and walked in the direction of the Tube station.

*

Laura's Friday consisted of the usual routine of filing and typing up columns of figures. Apart from the fact that the work bored and depressed her, she had also noticed in the last couple of days a waning of friendliness among the other staff. They were never a bundle of fun at the best of times, but Mr Matthew had become noticeably taciturn, Miss Birley's remarks were sharper than usual, and even Florence, who normally enjoyed reading salacious snippets aloud to Laura from *Tit-Bits* during their coffee break and taking the occasional stroll with her round the shops in their lunch hour, had become withdrawn and unsmiling. Today Florence turned the pages of her magazine wordlessly as she drank her coffee, and hurried off alone at lunchtime.

At the end of the afternoon Laura found out the reason. Miss Birley emerged from Mr Matthew's office, where she had been closeted for ten minutes, and said crisply to Laura, 'Mr Matthew wishes to speak to you.'

Laura rose and tapped on the door, went in, and sat down.

Mr Matthew was brisk and to the point.

'I don't normally listen to gossip, Miss Fenton, but when I learn that one of my employees is behaving in a manner incompatible with the values of the firm, I am forced to pay attention.'

'I don't understand what you mean, Mr Matthew,' replied Laura in dismay, though she thought she guessed what was coming.

'I'm referring to your domestic circumstances, the black you're living with.'

Laura swallowed, her heart beating hard. She didn't know how he had found out, but the fact was, he had. 'What has that to do with my work?'

'It has to do with the standards of Matthew & Son, Miss Fenton. The way our employees conduct themselves out of the workplace reflects on the firm. I'm going to have to let you go.' He raised a stubby, dismissive hand to ward off whatever protest Laura was about to make. 'There's nothing more to be said. Collect your belongings and leave. I'll have your wages made up to today and sent to you.' He picked up the telephone and said, 'Please put that call through to Mr Rowland now, would you, Miss Birley?'

Laura went back to her desk. Wordlessly, her face crimson, she pulled the paper and carbons from her typewriter and slipped on its cover. She gathered her few belongings from the desk drawer and put them in her handbag. The other typists clacked away, darting furtive glances, saying nothing as she left the office.

It was almost six by the time Laura got home from work. She had already decided she wouldn't tell Ellis exactly what had happened. She would pretend it had been her own decision to leave Matthew & Son, that she didn't like the place and the work was boring. She badly wanted his comfort and reassurance, but if she told him the truth it would only give him another reason to say, as he said so often these days, that she'd be better off without him. She didn't want to hear that. It frightened her.

She expected to find him stretched out on the bed as usual, reading the evening paper, or making some supper before going to the club, and was surprised to find the room empty. He must have gone out early. Then she realised that the emptiness of the room had an extra dimension. She saw the bare hangers on the rail, and the note on the table, and felt as if the blood in her veins had turned to ice. She picked up the folded piece of paper with her name written on it, and sank down on a chair to read it.

Dear Laura,

I think you knew this would happen sooner or later. I wish things could have been easier for us, but with the world the way it is, they are only bound to get harder. I am leaving like this because if I had to see you and tell you, I do not think I would be able to do it. If you are wondering where this money came from—

Money? What was he talking about? She had scarcely noticed the envelope on which the letter had been resting. Now she drew it towards her and saw the wad of banknotes inside.

—one of your friends gave it to me last night. He came to say what I already know, that I am no good for you, and that you will be a lot better off without me. I could have broken his neck for thinking he could buy me away from you, but it just goes to show the way people think about black people. They will always think like that. You have to know that no amount of money could ever make me leave you. The reason I am leaving is because I do not want you to have a hard life, which is what you will always have if you are with me. Please do not doubt I love you. You are the best thing ever happened to me. Take care of yourself, and have a good life.

Ellis

Numb, she lay down on the bed and wept for a long time. When eventually she got up, she reread the letter several times, then sat staring at the sky beyond the attic window, watching the lavender edge of dusk creep in. Her soul felt utterly empty. She wanted to die. She remained in this stupefied state of misery until, around nine o'clock, her mind began to recover. She didn't believe he wanted this. Whoever had come to see him last night – and that made no sense to her – had done this damage. He said in the letter he loved her, that she was the best thing that had ever happened to him. She would talk to him and make him change his mind.

She splashed water on her eyes, combed her hair, changed her clothes and went to the club. As it was Friday, it was packed and alive with music, but Ellis wasn't on stage. Some other saxophonist whom she vaguely recognised was playing. Fear clutched at her heart. He had to be here. She went through to the back and found Vince in the office, smoking and reading a copy of *Sporting Life*.

When Vince looked up and saw Laura standing there with a haunted look on her face, he registered immediately what had happened. 'Hello, doll,' he said. 'How's tricks?'

'I'm looking for Ellis. I thought he was playing tonight.' Her mouth felt dry.

Vince shook his head. 'I paid him off this morning.' He gazed at her with curiosity and a modicum of sympathy. He'd always thought it was bleeding mad for a girl like her to take up with a coloured, even a decent one like Ellis Candy, but he'd got to know Laura over the years, and he liked her. And now she looked like she was going to cry. 'Here, don't start all that. Come on, sit yourself down.'

'Did he say where he was going?'

'Afraid not.' He watched her try to compose herself. Poor kid. She really had it bad. 'Didn't think he would scarper without telling you.'

'He did tell me. He left me a letter.' She looked at Vince hopelessly. 'Didn't he say anything else?'

'Just that he was off and wouldn't be coming back.'

Laura stared at the floor with empty eyes. He had put himself beyond her reach. She would never find him now.

'Come on, now, it's not the end of the world.' Vince reached into his desk drawer and took out a bottle of whisky and a couple of grubby glasses. He splashed a little into each and handed one to Laura. 'Have a drink. Make you feel better.' He put the bottle back in the drawer. 'You two have a bust-up?'

Laura shook her head. 'He said in his letter that I'd be better off without him.'

Vince reflected on this. Sad but true. 'Mind if I speak frankly?' She shook her head. 'First time I saw you two together, I gave you a couple of months at the outside. You did well to last this long. People don't take kindly to a white girl going with a black fella. Don't ask me why.'

'You were always decent to us, Vince. Why couldn't everyone else be like you, and just accept us?'

'Way of the world, girl.'

'I don't know what I'm going to do.' She stared into her whisky. 'I lost my job today. They sacked me when they found out I was living with Ellis.'

'Bad luck.' He knocked his drink back and said, 'If you need a job, you could always come and work in one of my shops. Money's not much, mind, but it would tide you over till you find something else.' A stunning girl like Laura behind the counter would definitely sell more records.

'Thanks.' She put down the untasted whisky and rose to go. She felt exhausted, and longed for sleep to swallow up her unhappiness.

'Chin up, girl. These things happen, and the best thing is to move on. Like I say, I'm here to help if you need me.'

She gave Vince a wan smile. 'That's kind.'

She left the club and a feeling of unreality set in as she wandered back through the Soho streets. She would have to come to terms with the fact that she was on her own now. Whatever his reasons for going, Ellis had abandoned her. She climbed the stairs to the room slowly, and unlocked the door. The first thing she saw was the envelope of money lying on the table. She had forgotten about it till now. She sat down and emptied the bundle of five pound notes on to the table, and realised there must be several hundred pounds. She fingered them, wondering who she knew who would have access to so much money, and would go to these lengths to separate her from Ellis. Not Avril. She wouldn't waste the money. Realisation dawned on her. It had to be Max. Who else? That argument they'd had in the street, everything he'd said. He had used his money to do this clumsy, reckless thing, in the mistaken belief that he was acting in her interests. Just like Avril, he thought he knew what was good for her, never stopping to think that he was breaking her heart, ruining her life. She would never forgive him, ever. Her fingers tightened on the wad of notes in a blaze of hatred. She began to weep again. She gathered the notes together and stuffed them back in the envelope, then, kicking off her shoes but still in her clothes, she huddled under the bedclothes, waiting for sleep to eclipse it all.

17

Max waited all week to hear from Harry, desperate to know whether anything had been achieved with Ellis Candy. Had he taken the money and left, or rejected it? The possibility that he might have taken it and yet stayed with Laura had only recently occurred to him. His mind ran in circles. By Friday evening he couldn't wait any longer. On his way out to the hall to telephone Harry, he met Diana coming in from town. She dropped a copy of the evening paper on the hall table next to the phone.

'You might want to take a look at page five,' she remarked coolly. 'I always had my doubts about that man.' She hung up her coat and went upstairs to her room.

Max picked up the paper and took it with him to the study. He sank into an armchair and flipped through the pages. There on page five, above a brief paragraph headlined 'Literary Figure Fined', was a postage stamp-sized picture of Harry. The story was brief, and stated simply that Harry Denholm, editor of the topical magazine *Modern Critical Review* and a prominent figure in London's literary world, had last night been arrested and charged with importuning in the Broadwick Street men's urinals in Soho, and fined £10 that morning at Marlborough Street Magistrates Court. Max's heart tightened with shock and misery. He was aware of such sordid goings-on, but was young enough still to believe that only a certain kind of man engaged in them. That Harry, for whom he had felt such fondness and admiration since childhood, was one of them seemed shaming and grotesque. Charged and fined within twenty-four hours – obviously he had pleaded guilty.

Max put down the paper. The world seemed to be forcing itself on him, thrusting at him realities for which he wasn't prepared, challenging his maturity and mocking his concept of himself as a grown-up. First Laura, now this. He put aside his immediate selfish concern – whether or not this had happened before Harry had had a chance to speak to Ellis Candy – and concentrated his thoughts on Harry. It was his plight was that mattered most. He looked down again at the page. The story occupied no more than a couple of square inches, a handful of reported facts delivered in a throwaway fashion, tomorrow's chip paper, as the saying went. A little thing, yet capable of wreaking enormous damage to a man's reputation, revealing his squalid search for the gratification of desires that the whole world regarded as perverse and criminal. How low Harry must be feeling at this moment.

Diana was coming downstairs as Max emerged from the study. She could see from his face that he had read the story.

'Well, now you see the kind of man he is.' She glanced at her watch. 'Dinner's in ten minutes.'

'I won't be having any. I'm going round to see him.'

'You're not serious?'

'Friends don't turn their backs on people when dreadful things happen to them.'

'He's the one who's done the dreadful thing. You're utterly mad to have anything more to do with him. You have your own reputation to think of, you know.'

Max made no reply, and left the house.

He found Harry alone in his flat, wearing a short velvet dressing gown over his everyday clothes, and slippers on his feet. He had a subdued air of weariness and his big, bearded face looked aged and strained.

'I saw the paper,' said Max. 'I'm so sorry. I had to come and see how you were.'

'Kind of you, my boy,' said Harry, as he led the way through to his snug drawing room, 'but I'm not sure you should have. Not after this. Questionable associations, you know. People may talk.'

'That's absurd.' He took the glass of sherry that Harry poured for him, and sat down. 'I don't care, anyway.'

'Don't you, really? Then you're the exception. I don't expect a lively time of it, socially, for the foreseeable future.'

'People will forget. Most of them probably didn't even see the story. Your real friends are what count, anyway.'

Harry smiled. 'You are an unusually nice young man, Max. And your attempt to be enlightened does you credit.'

The choice of words wasn't lost on Max. Maybe he wasn't as good at dissembling as he'd hoped. It was his fondness for Harry that had brought him here, not open-mindedness. He shared the general public feeling of revulsion for homosexuals and the things they got up to, preferring not to think about them.

After a pause Harry said, 'You want to know what happened with Ellis Candy.'

'That's not why I'm here. Please don't think that.'

'I don't. I know you are genuinely concerned for me, and I'm touched. Anyway, I did go to see him – last night, as a matter of fact, just before my unfortunate apprehension.' He gave a wan smile. 'It was an interesting encounter. I think he had already made his mind up that it would be a kindness to Laura if he were to absent himself from her life. I hardly had to persuade him.' He sipped his sherry. 'That said, he took the money.'

Max felt his heart begin to beat hard. 'He agreed to go away?'

Harry nodded, and scratched his beard. 'What was it he said? Oh yes – "It was always going to happen." Those were his words. It was always going to happen. He didn't say it in a brutal way, you understand. More with a kind of sad acceptance. I think he's a pretty decent fellow. No question that he loves her, more's the pity.'

Max felt a tumult of emotions. His relief that Laura had been delivered from the worst mistake of her life was tempered with an unexpected sense of guilt. He had come between her and the man she said she loved. Or thought she loved. But Ellis Candy had said himself it was always bound to happen. Even so...

Harry regarded him pensively. 'What do you expect now?'

'I don't – I don't have any expectations.' Max twisted the stem of his sherry glass in his fingers. 'I simply wanted to help her.' Even as he said this he felt a sense of unease. It had been done for the best, of course it had. He would wait a little while, she would go back to Mount Street, and then... Well, things would return to the way they had been. But no matter how hard he tried, he couldn't quite see it unfolding in this way. He felt confused.

'Have you eaten?'

'No, I skipped dinner to come round here.'

'Then I'll make us some supper, and we can put the world to rights over a glass or two of wine.'

Max slept badly that night. He had anxious dreams in which he kept opening the doors of rooms in an endless corridor, in search of Laura, and finding them all empty. He woke in the early hours with a racing heart, which he put down to the three glasses of claret he'd had with Harry, and lay sweating in the darkness, trying to untangle his feelings about what he'd done, and what might happen next, having the sense that he might have made an unholy mess. Eventually he fell asleep again, and when he woke things seemed better by the light of day.

He rang Alec after breakfast and suggested going to watch the cricket at the Oval.

'You can come along on my membership. Should be a good day. I'll see you at the gate around eleven.'

As he put down the phone the doorbell chimed. He opened the front door and there, to his astonishment, stood Laura. The first thing he thought was how young she looked in her red cotton dress and sandals, with her fair hair tied back, a raw, wild look on her face that he'd never seen before.

'Hello,' he said uncertainly. 'I was—'

She spoke across him. 'You did this, didn't you?' She

held out the envelope, now frayed and battered, with its bulging wad of notes. 'You went to see Ellis.'

'No, it wasn't me—'

His words were a denial and admission all in one. 'Don't lie. I know you did it.' Her voice was cold, her grey eyes like steel. 'He's gone, thanks to you, but he didn't want your rotten money. You destroyed the best thing in my life, and I hate you for it. You have no idea how much. I'll never forgive you. Never.' She struggled against mounting tears, and failed. 'Why couldn't you just leave us alone, Max?' She dropped the envelope on the step and walked quickly away.

Appalled, he picked up the envelope and ran after her. 'Laura!' He caught up with her, standing in front of her on the pavement so that she had to stop. 'Listen to me, please! Maybe the money was a mistake. It was a stupid idea, but it wasn't me who went to see him. It was Harry—'

'Harry?' Her eyes glittered with angry tears.

'I asked him to do it. I thought it was for the best. Everyone could see what a disaster it was, everyone except you. Even Ellis knew it. He told Harry as much. Surely you can see that you're better off without—'

The stinging slap caught him off guard, and was hard enough to make him momentarily dizzy.

'How dare you decide what's good for me? Do you have any idea what you've done? Of course you don't. You're nothing more than an over-privileged, emotionally stunted little boy. Stay out of my life, Max. I never want to see you again. Ever!'

She pushed past him, breaking into a run, heading for the end of the street. Max watched her go in despair, her humiliating words ringing in his ears. He looked down at the envelope of money. How could he ever have thought this was a good idea? How could Harry have let him?

He went miserably back to the house, and put the money in his desk drawer. He hadn't expected it to turn out like this. The last thing he felt like doing now was watching cricket, but he couldn't let Alec down, and so he left the house and took the Underground to the Oval. He was preoccupied by what had happened and found it hard to pay attention to the morning's play, but gradually sunshine, cricket, beer and Alec's company produced a softening effect. By teatime he had persuaded himself that, despite everything, she'd get over it and see it was for her own good. She didn't mean it when she said she never wanted to see him again. In a year or two, when she was calmer and steadier, things would change. He loved her, and in the end everything would be fine.

He telephoned Harry a few days later and told him what had happened, omitting to mention either the slap or Laura's scathing words about his immaturity. He had already excised these from his mind.

'I suppose she had every right to be angry, but she'll

thank me in the long run. At least he's out of her life.'

The resilience of the young, thought Harry, moulding everything to their optimistic perspective. 'Well, you've achieved what you wanted to, at any rate.'

Max failed to catch the caustic note in Harry's voice. 'It's only a matter of time till she comes round. Anyway, how have things been with you?'

'Oh, better. Friends have been wonderfully supportive, though I'm worried the scandal will dent the magazine's prospects. Leftie liberal intellectuals are generally no more broad-minded than the average *Daily Mail* reader. I'm going to Chalcombe tomorrow for a couple of months to lie low. You're very welcome to come and visit for a few days, if you like.'

'Thanks. Anyway, listen, I have to go and get ready for some deathly deb party. I'm sick of the damn things, I can tell you. I'll speak to you soon.'

How blithely Max dealt with it all, thought Harry, as he put down the phone. Having taken it into his mind to destroy Laura's love affair because he thought it was the right thing to do, regardless of her feelings, he imagined he only needed to wait for everything to come right. The selfishness was cruel. Having gathered from Max the state Laura was in, Harry felt deeply sorry for her. He wished now he'd never had any part in it. How presumptuous of them all to think they knew what was best for her. If only he'd seen it that way at the time. Still, it was done now.

*

As the time approached for him to take up his place at Cambridge that autumn, Max badly wanted to make peace with Laura, if he could. It had been nearly two months. She would be back in Mount Street, the episode of Ellis Candy behind her, and perhaps in a better frame of mind. Very probably she would be working for Avril in the gallery. He'd go and see her, and try to set things right between them.

On a rainy late September afternoon he went to Alfred Place. When the little bell chimed above the door as he entered the gallery, Avril detached herself from a couple of customers and came towards him.

'Hello, Max,' said Avril. 'How can I help you? As you see, I'm rather busy.'

'I hoped Laura might be here.'

'Here? Why would she be here?'

'She's broken up with that man. I thought she'd have come home.'

Avril sighed. 'Interesting as that is, Max, I think we both have to accept that Laura has moved on with her life. I haven't seen or heard from her in almost three years.' She glanced impatiently towards the end of the gallery. 'I'm sorry, I have customers waiting. If you want to wait half an hour, I can talk to you then. Though I doubt if I can be of much help.' She walked back to the customers, the crepe soles of her shoes squeaking on the gallery floor.

With a keen sense of having woken up from some complacent sleep, Max left the gallery, turning his collar up against the rain, and walked towards Tottenham Court Road. On the corner he hesitated, then turned in the direction of Somers Town. There was nowhere else to look.

He knocked on the door of the house in Luscombe Street, hoping against hope, but knowing this was futile. The old man who came to the door confirmed it.

'She went off a week after he did. That's, what, over two months now. Nope, sorry, son, no idea where she went.'

Max made his way back through Soho to Leicester Square. He had no one to blame but himself. He had taken it upon himself to interfere in her life, believing that it was for her own good and that she would come back to the world she had left, and to him, but all he had achieved was utter estrangement. Feeling sad, and a good deal older, he stood for a few minutes in the rain, then walked towards the Underground.

A couple of streets away, in a record shop in Wardour Street, Laura was serving behind the counter at Fat Cat Records. It was the largest of Vince's record shops, and had ten soundproof listening booths, of which Vince was very proud. It was five twenty, and a rush of people leaving work had come in to browse the stacks of records and listen in the booths. A tinny cacophony of the latest hits seeped out from the turntables, the plaintive crooning of The Chordettes blending with Bill Haley and Johnnie Ray. Laura served one customer after another, bagging purchases and handing out change. She glanced through the window and saw that the rain was easing off. Ten minutes till closing, and she couldn't wait. She was conscious of a young man on the other side of the shop watching her. He was of medium build, wiry, his dark hair combed in a quiff, and was dressed in jeans and a leather jacket. He was ostensibly browsing the racks, a cigarette in the side of his mouth, but he kept casting glances in her direction. He was nice-looking, with dark eyes and a wry expression, but the last thing she needed was yet another man wanting to know if she could recommend anything in particular, the inevitable prelude to asking her out on a date. She had enough of those every day. And she didn't want to go out on a date with anyone.

Eventually he approached the counter.

'Can I help you, sir?' she asked with a mechanical smile.

'Maybe,' he replied, giving her a charming, lopsided smile. 'That is, if you'll let me take your photo.' His voice had a light cockney lilt.

'I don't think so, thank you,' murmured Laura, glancing away. The line was original, if nothing else. She could see a woman behind him, impatient to make her purchase before the shop closed. 'Now, sir, if you don't want to buy anything—'

The dark-haired man slipped his hand into his pocket and took out a card. 'I'm kosher, you know. The real deal. This isn't a chat-up. You're a stunning-looking girl, and I could help you make a bit of money, if you wanted.'

She took the card and put it on the counter without looking at it. 'As I said, I don't think so.' She glanced past him at the waiting customer, who was brandishing a copy of Tex Ritter's 'Wayward Wind'. 'Thank you, madam, that'll be four and six.' Laura slid the record into a bag and handed it over with the change. She turned to the man. 'We're closing in a couple of minutes, so unless there's anything you want to buy—'

He grinned and shrugged and left the shop. Laura watched him go. Fifteen minutes later, after she had cashed up and was slipping on her coat, about to leave, she noticed the card lying on the counter. She picked it up. On it were printed the words 'Sid Jennings, Photographer' with an address in N1 and a telephone number. She stared at it for a moment. The name was strangely familiar. She slipped the card in her pocket and left the shop.

He was waiting outside, leaning against the shop front, and smiled when he saw her.

'You didn't let me finish my pitch.'

She sighed. 'Look, I'll try to say this nicely, Mr Jennings. I'm tired, I just want to go home, and I don't want my photograph taken.' She walked away down the street.

He followed and caught up with her. 'At least you read my card. You know my name, so you might as well tell me yours. Only polite.'

'It's Laura Haddon – I mean Fenton.' Three years on, and she still occasionally forgot. 'But it won't get you anywhere, you know. Now, if you don't mind, I've got to catch my bus.'

He caught her arm. 'It's never,' he said. Then he laughed. 'Little Laura. I thought your face rang a bell.' She stared at him. 'Don't you remember me?' She looked blank. 'You lived at that place in the country, whatsit house, in the war. Me and my brother Colin were evacuated there. Twice, if I remember right. We used to play together. With the gardener's dog, Star – remember?'

Recollection dawned. Colin and Sidney. She could see them in her mind's eye, in shorts and sandals and grubby shirts. Together they had built a den in the woods with Dan. 'Of course I remember. Oh, how funny.'

'There was that other girl – I've forgotten her name. Your big sister.'

'Avril. She wasn't my sister.' All kinds of memories came tumbling back to her, of Woodbourne House, Aunt Sonia, her own childhood.

'No?' They stood together on the pavement in baffled silence. It was beginning to rain again. 'I think this calls for a drink, don't you? For old times' sake.'

Laura hesitated for a moment, then smiled. 'All right.'

18

1962

THE FLAT WAS cold. Laura opened the cupboard in the hall and fiddled with the central heating thermostat, then wandered into the kitchen, still in her coat, and picked up an ashtray. The trip from Paris had left her hollowed out, and this place didn't feel like home. She'd taken the lease on it six months ago, after moving out of the Ladbroke Grove flat that she and Sid had shared for eighteen stormy months – 1961 was to have been the year of big changes, new beginnings. Then the job in Paris had come up before she could properly unpack, with the result that, now she was back in London, it still felt as though her life was stuck on hold.

She took the ashtray into the empty living room and sat down on one of the unopened packing cases and lit a cigarette. As usually happened when she found herself alone with time to reflect, she thought about Ellis, wondering where he was, what he was doing, whether he was thinking of her right now. He had been, in that hackneyed phrase, the love of her life. She would never know anything like that again. The memories of him – his face, his laugh, the touch of his hands – were as constant and fresh as ever, even though the days spent in the wake of his departure, trawling the clubs and music venues of London in hopes of finding him, seemed distant now. Maybe it was an unrealistic dream, but she still imagined that one day, somehow, she would find him again. She remembered how fiercely determined she'd been to save money and travel to Memphis in search of him – before time and fate, in the form of Sid, had taken her in another direction altogether.

She tapped the ash from her cigarette. Sid. With all their history, he was still a friend. Their mistake had been to let sex creep into their professional relationship. After three years of working together in perfect harmony they'd moved in together, partly to save money and partly out of a misguided notion that they were compatible, when in fact they'd been nothing more than mutual dependants, their work and life together habit-forming, letting affection turn into something it was never meant to be. It was a wonder either of them had survived the eighteen months that followed. The rows and bickering, the benders he used to disappear on, the other girls he slept with and thought she didn't know about. She remembered in particular the pictures she'd found in his darkroom of a doe-eyed, dark-haired girl, naked, legs splayed, staring into the camera in a supplicating way. That was one thing you had to hand to Sid – in his hands the camera never lied.

She drew the curtains and put a hand on the radiator, but it was still stone cold. She sighed. It had been early September when she'd left, and she'd never checked whether the heating worked properly. She went to the kitchen and opened the cupboard. Half a bag of macaroni and a box of tea bags. She hadn't eaten since breakfast, but it was gone five thirty and all the shops would be shut. She couldn't remember if there was a chippy in the area, and the thought of wandering the streets in search of one was dispiriting. She closed the cupboard, and filled the kettle and put it on the gas, wondering if she should call Sid. The last time she'd seen him had been the day she moved all her stuff out of the Ladbroke Grove flat, when he had lain on the sofa pretending he couldn't care less. Face it, she told herself, you're going to ring him sooner or later. Sid wasn't someone she could simply turn her back on, even if she wanted to. He was part of who she was now. He had made her, given her success – of a moderate kind. Even if it was impossible for them to live together, she couldn't imagine not having him in her life. Right now, tired and hungry, demoralised by the past six months, she wanted to see him. She switched off the gas, left the flat, and went to the phone box at the end of the street.

'Where are you?' asked Sid, when he heard her voice.

'I'm in a telephone box on the corner of Beaufort Street. Near my flat.'

'You've not got a phone?'

'I meant to get on to the GPO when I moved in, but then I went away. I'll have to go on a waiting list.'

'Oh.' There was a silence. 'How was Paris?'

'So-so.' Another silence. 'Actually, I've just got back, I've got no food in the flat, and I wondered if you'd like to take me to dinner. Unless you're busy, of course.'

'No, that's all right. Where would you like to go?'

'The Ark?' The Ark in Notting Hill had been one of their favourite haunts as a couple, and she couldn't think of anywhere else.

'OK. I'll see you there in half an hour.'

She went back to the flat and changed into a purple skinny-rib polo-neck, a short skirt, a new pair of white PVC knee-length boots, and a Jean Varon black and white fur coat she'd been given on one of the Paris fashion shoots. She brushed out her thick blonde hair, backcombing it a little to fluff it out, and carefully redid her make-up. Whatever there was or wasn't between them, she still needed to look good for Sid. It was a professional thing as much as anything else, dressing for his critical eye. After a dab of lipstick and a last glance in the bathroom mirror, she put on her coat and walked to the King's Road in search of a taxi.

Sid was already there when she arrived, sitting at a corner table in his trademark leather jacket with the upturned collar, a checked shirt, close-fitting jeans and Chelsea boots. His dark hair was longer now. It suited him, made him look more like a boy than ever. He looked up, saw her, and smiled. The face of an angel, she thought. A dark-eyed, dark-hearted angel. She sensed the wariness between them as she sat down. He made no effort to kiss her hello, and she was glad. She felt no regret at having left him, no pang of loss. That part was over, and just as well. No girl could survive Sid for long. Their new relationship was going to be something totally different.

Sid glanced at her coat as she handed it to the waiter, and remarked, 'Very trendy.'

'Not heard that word before.'

'You know me. All the latest lingo.'

They smoked as they studied the menu.

'What you going to have?' asked Sid.

'Steak and chips.' She closed the menu. 'And grilled tomatoes and mushrooms. I'm ravenous.'

He grinned. 'You're the only model I know who can eat like a horse and still stay skinny. I like an appetite on a girl. I did a shoot for *Honey* the other day. Those birds live on air, so far as I can tell.' He caught the waiter's eye and ordered two steak and chips and a bottle of Valpolicella.

'So you're getting a lot of magazine work?' asked Laura.

'Not as much as I'd like. The teen mags are all well and good, but I want to be doing the grown-up ones, *Vogue* and *Queen* and the like.' The wine arrived, and the waiter poured it. Sid lifted his glass. 'So, cheers. Nice that you're back.'

Laura took a sip of her wine. 'Did you move her in after I left? That girl in the photos?'

Sid looked a little affronted. 'No. It wasn't that kind of relationship.'

She gave him a scornful look, then shrugged. 'Anyway, it's all ancient history.'

'What is?'

'You and me.'

'Right.' He took a drag of his cigarette. 'I thought maybe you might reconsider. Move back in. Digby misses you. Anyway, isn't that why you're here?'

'He's your cat. And no, it's not why I'm here. I just wanted to see a friendly face.'

Their food arrived, and nothing was said for a few minutes as they ate.

Laura put down her knife and fork and drank a mouthful of wine. 'God, I feel a bit more human. Food always helps.'

He eyed her critically. 'You're looking good. Paris must have agreed with you. How did you get on?'

'Like I said on the phone, so-so. French models are a snooty lot. But I enjoyed the work, met some interesting people. The St Laurent debut collection was fun, but the clothes were completely square. All those long gloves, and hats like lampshades.'

They talked for another hour, finished the wine, and Sid ordered brandies. Laura began to feel as though she'd never been away.

'You're trying to get me drunk.'

'And what if I am? You're lovely when you're squiffy.' He leaned across and kissed her. 'Come back to Denbigh Road. It misses you. I miss you.'

She thought of the cold flat in Beaufort Street, her unpacked suitcase, the boxes standing in the empty rooms. It wasn't an appealing prospect. She surveyed Sid with an attempt at detachment. Half a bottle of wine and a brandy made it difficult. He was smiling that dangerous smile that she'd always found so sexy.

'Just tonight, then. And only because my central heating's on the blink.'

She woke the next morning with a dry mouth and an aching head. With a sliding sense of disappointment she realised where she was. This was exactly what she'd promised herself she wouldn't do. Sid was fast

asleep on his back, one arm dangling over the side of
the bed. She studied him dispassionately for a moment,
the serenity of his features, the feathery dark hair and
stubble, thinking how innocent he looked asleep. Then
she got out of bed, picked up her petticoat and slipped
it on. In the kitchen she made coffee, while Digby slunk
around her ankles, miaowing, until she retrieved half a
tin of Whiskas from the fridge and fed him. While she
was pouring out the coffee, Sid came into the kitchen in
his underpants and put his arms around her, kissing her
neck. His breath smelt of stale cigarettes and brandy.
She shrugged him off.

'No, Sid. Last night was a mistake. Don't get ideas.'

'Uh-uh. Don't play that one. It doesn't suit you.' He
picked up one of the coffees and took a sip, then reached
into the cupboard above her head for a bag of sugar.

'I'm not playing anything. Don't for a moment think
we're getting back together. Because we're not.'

'No?' He tried to kiss her again, but she dodged him
and he dropped the bag of sugar, sending it scattering
everywhere. 'Christ – look what you've made me do!'

'It wasn't my fault. I'm not clearing it up.'

They bickered, and the bickering turned into a full-
blown argument, at the end of which Laura stormed
through the bedroom and into the bathroom, slamming
the door. He was bloody impossible. She caught sight
of her reflection in the mirror, her eyes smudgy with
mascara, her hair all over the place, and sighed. She

washed and dried her face, then opened the bathroom cabinet. The handful of cosmetics she'd left behind were still there, some make-up and a pot of moisturiser, as well as an old comb. She wasn't sure what she felt about the fact he hadn't thrown them out. Either it was a sign of his incorrigible laziness, or else he had been expecting her to come back. Either way, she was glad of them. She rubbed moisturiser into her face and combed out her tangled hair. It so badly needed a wash that there was no way she could tease it into its usual cloud of marshmallow blondeness, so she combed it over and over until it was as straight as possible. She gazed at herself in the mirror. When she looked at herself she still saw the warm-hearted, open girl she had always been, but she was aware that to cope with the experience of losing Ellis – to say nothing of living with Sid and finding her feet in the competitive world of modelling – she had gradually built a shell to conceal her real and more vulnerable self. In her reflection, with her hair like this, that hardness and softness seemed to have blended. It looked rather good. She brushed her hair again, parting it on one side this time, letting its natural wave curve against one cheek. Even better. With a tissue and some moisturiser she wiped the smudges of last night's mascara from around her eyes. They looked dull and tired, and somehow smaller in her face. There was no mascara in the cabinet, but she found some eyeliner and stroked it carefully along the line of both lids. The effect was unbalanced, so she drew a line below both eyes, something she'd never done before. She hunted around for eyeshadow, but when she couldn't find any she picked up the eyeliner and boldly stroked some into the crease line. The effect was startling, making her eyes look enormous, and she laughed at her reflection. Playing with make-up was a nice way to cheer herself up after the horrible argument. She found a lipstick so pale it was almost white, and dabbed it on her eyelids. The effect was bizarre, but somehow wonderful. In the absence of mascara she wet the eyeliner brush again, leaned into her reflection, and carefully painted little fake lash-lines beneath her eyes. It was clownlike, but pretty. She was admiring her reflection when Sid banged on the bathroom door demanding to know how long she was going to be in there.

Laura turned on the tap, about to wash everything off her face, then paused and glanced again in the mirror. She liked the way she looked. It made her feel reckless. She turned off the tap, put away the cosmetics, unlocked the bathroom door, and swept past him. His eyes followed her.

'Your face looks strange.' She gave him a haughty glance over her shoulder, and picked up her suspender belt from the floor. He followed her back into the bedroom. 'Let me look at you.'

She straightened up and let him inspect her face. 'You look mad,' he said. 'But good, in a funny sort of way.'

She made no reply, and sat down on the edge of the bed to put on her stockings, then the rest of her clothes, while Sid went into the bathroom. When he emerged she was putting on her coat.

'Stop acting so huffy,' he said. 'Why don't you stay for breakfast? It's Sunday, there's no shops open, and you said yourself you've got no food in.' He saw her hesitate. 'Come on, get your coat off. I'll make us some toast.'

Half an hour later, as she cleared up their plates and cups, Laura said, 'I mean it, though, Sid. I'm not staying. I've got my own life now, and I'm going to go back to the flat, unpack my things, and start getting on with it.'

'As you like.' He left her to finish the washing up.

She was on her way out when Sid emerged, putting on his jacket, his camera slung around his neck.

'I'll come a bit of the way with you. You know I like to do a bit of snapping on Sundays, when things are quiet.'

It was eleven twenty, everyone was either in church or having a lie-in, and the streets were dead.

They reached the bus stop. Laura glanced at her watch. 'I'll probably have to wait ages.'

'I'll wait with you.'

Laura stood at the bus stop and Sid began to take pictures of her. 'That make-up you've got on looks really good with the coat. Quite an effect. Go on, lean against the bus stop. Yeah, like that.' He started snapping.

When the bus came they went upstairs and found it empty. The conductor came up, took their fares, and disappeared.

'Come on, let's sit up the front,' said Sid. They moved up to the front seats and at Sid's bidding Laura sprawled the length of a seat with one knee up while he took pictures from the other seat. He persuaded her to stand at the other end at the top of the stairs, leaning against the pole with one arm up, her coat unbuttoned, and took more pictures. Laura was content to stand and sit wherever he told her to. Posing for Sid was something she'd been doing ever since she'd met him.

They got off the bus at World's End.

'Let's have a wander round,' said Sid. 'I like seedy areas.'

'*You're* seedy.' She shivered inside her fur coat. 'I want to get home.'

'Come on. Just for me.'

She gave in, and they wandered through the chilly streets. They found a corner shop open, and Laura bought some bread, milk and a tin of beans. They came across an abandoned car on a patch of waste ground, and Sid took photos of Laura in ungainly poses with the car as a prop.

'I'm fed up,' said Laura at last. 'Can we stop?'

Sid glanced at his watch. 'Pubs are open. Let's have a swift one.'

'Not after last night. I've still got a headache.'

'Hair of the dog's the best thing for it. Come on – have a drink with me and I'll come back and have a look at your central heating after.'

They went to the World's End pub and had beer and a bad Sunday lunch, then went back to Laura's flat, where Sid succeeded in lighting the pilot light on the boiler.

'Thanks,' said Laura, still in her coat. 'Do you want a cup of tea?'

Sid shook his head. 'What I want is for you to come back home.' He put his hands on the upturned collar of her coat, trying to draw her towards him. She resisted.

'Sid, I want to be on my own. I want a bit of peace in my life. You and I – we're not good for one another.' He shrugged and dropped his hands. She could tell from his nonchalant manner he still thought she'd come round in the end. 'But we can still be friends.'

'Sure, doll.' He grinned. 'Just good friends.' He zipped up his jacket, picked up his camera, and left.

One evening a few weeks later, Laura came home to find him sitting on the doorstep.

She sighed inwardly. 'Hello, Sid. What brings you here?' She hoped he wasn't going to start acting like a lost puppy. It wasn't the way she wanted to think of him.

'Thank God you're back,' he said, getting up. 'I've been freezing my bum off here. I've got some news.' He followed her inside and upstairs to her flat. 'I had to come round, 'cause I couldn't ring you. About time you got a phone.'

'They're putting one in next week,' said Laura, unlocking the front door.

Sid wandered into the living room while Laura went through to the kitchen to put the kettle on.

'I see you got some furniture, then,' called Sid, glancing at the three-piece suite and coffee table. He settled himself on the sofa, and a few minutes later Laura came through with mugs of tea. She handed one to Sid.

'What work are you doing at the moment?' he asked.

'The Littlewoods catalogue.' She caught his expression and added, 'It's work, you know. I have to pay the rent.'

'That's not why I'm smiling. Like I said, I've got some news. Remember those shots I did of you that Sunday? I got them in front of the creative director at *Vogue*. She liked them. Said they were gritty, different. They want me to do a fashion shoot for them, and they want you as the model.'

Laura set down her mug and stared at him. 'You're kidding.'

'Nope.' He lifted his mug, still grinning. 'Here's to the big time, baby.'

19

AVRIL SAT AT the end of the gallery, pretending to be absorbed in paperwork, and studied the new visitor discreetly. He was tall, expensively dressed, and arrestingly handsome, and somewhere in his late twenties, she guessed. If it hadn't been for the fact that his dark hair was worn a little too long, she might have taken him for a City type. He had been roaming the gallery for over half an hour, having warded off with a wordless shrug the enquiry from Avril's assistant, Flavia, as to whether he was looking for something in particular.

The work the gallery was showing that spring – a dozen or so figurative paintings by two young Australian artists – hadn't been selling particularly well. With any luck, thought Avril, the well-heeled visitor might buy something. He'd been there long enough.

Ten minutes later he strolled to the end of the gallery and said to Avril, 'I'll take them all.' He took a card from his pocket and handed it to her. 'I'll expect a discount, of course. Perhaps you could work out a price and telephone me?'

She took the card. 'Of course...' she glanced at the name, noting at the same time the Belgravia phone number, 'Mr Carteret.'

'Thanks awfully.' His light blue eyes gave his expression a certain chilly intensity, but when he smiled, as he did now, the effect was transformative. He turned and left the gallery without another word.

When she rang the number the next day, a brisk young man with a foreign accent answered and told her he was authorised to negotiate the transaction on Mr Carteret's behalf. It emerged from the ensuing discussion that the five per cent discount the Haddon Gallery was prepared to offer on the paintings was not as great as Mr Carteret expected. After a waspish debate, Avril was forced to agree a price rather lower than she had hoped for. Still, it was quite something to be able to clear her entire stock and the commission was healthy. No doubt the young antipodean artists would be thrilled. To have a new collector on the scene, especially one with such deep pockets, was very good news.

Avril gave her new customer scarcely another thought until a fortnight later, when she went to a party thrown by one of her neighbours. The room was already crowded when she arrived, the smoky air loud with chatter and laughter, Frankie Vaughan belting out from the record cabinet. As she made her way through the throng she caught sight of Harry Denholm, whom she hadn't seen in ages.

'Avril!' he exclaimed. 'How very good to see you. It's been... what? Seven years? Eight?'

'More than that. We last met at my mother's funeral, I think. So nine years.'

Harry nodded. His smiling surprise at meeting a long-lost acquaintance was settling into a recollection of Avril as a prickly, challenging girl, not the most restful company. But her looks and manner suggested she had grown rather more at ease with herself, and she seemed pleased to see him.

'How are you?' he asked.

'I'm well, thanks. I hear you've launched a new arts magazine.' Avril was quite astonished at how large Harry had become. He was positively Falstaffian.

'Yes, I closed down the *Modern Critical Review* last year. The market for worthy literary magazines became simply too crowded, and anyway, I sense that kind of thing has become a little passé. *Scope* is going to be entirely modern, and more than just an art magazine – we'll cover architecture, photography, music, film, all that kind of thing. I'm convinced a wider range of topics will attract a wider readership. Or do you think I'm being too ambitious?'

'Not at all. Fashion is changing so fast, we need publications that can keep up with new trends. I wish you luck.'

'Thank you. I hear your gallery is doing well. I've often meant to stop by, but, well, you know how life is.'

As the conversational momentum flagged, the unspoken topic of Laura loomed in both their minds. Each had a different idea of what the other knew or felt. For Harry, the matter rested with Laura's disappearance after the failed intervention on Max's behalf, and even though he didn't think Avril had been especially fond of Laura, he felt an uneasy guilt at his own involvement. The extent of Avril's knowledge, through the trickle of rumour that had come via Diana and her aunt Helen, was that Laura's ill-judged love affair had come to a predictable end and no one had seen her since. She wondered if Harry ever heard from her. But neither of them was prepared to broach the subject.

From the other side of the room Philip Carteret saw his godfather talking to the proprietor of the gallery where he had picked up those figurative paintings for such a good price. He'd thought her androgynously attractive then, in her unconventional get-up of cropped grey slacks and a white, high-collar blouse, with her hair up. Tonight she looked distinctly feminine, dressed in a tight-fitting black dress with a pencil skirt, cut low to show a pretty amount of cleavage, her dark hair loose about her shoulders. He made his way over.

Harry spotted Philip heading in their direction.

'Ah, here comes my godson, Philip Carteret. I should introduce you. He's a collector.' Harry dropped his voice. 'He only began collecting seriously after his father died a couple of years ago. Lionel Carteret, the banker, you know – enormously rich.'

'Mr Carteret and I have already met,' said Avril, as Philip approached and shook her hand.

'Miss Haddon sold me some rather wonderful paintings a few weeks ago.'

'Please – I'd rather you called me Avril.'

'Then you must call me Philip.'

'How splendid,' said Harry. 'I'll let you two get reacquainted while I find myself another drink.' He disappeared in the direction of the drinks table.

'I hope the paintings turn out to be a good investment,' said Avril. 'Quite a brave purchase.'

Philip smiled. 'You probably thought I was mad.'

'No madder than I for showing them. But I like taking risks with unusual new artists. They're not always guaranteed to make money, but my instincts have served me pretty well so far.'

'I'm sure your instincts rarely fail you, in any department.' They were eyeing one other with speculative sexual interest, both aware of a strong current of attraction.

'So, is modern art your main area of interest?'

'Oh, my taste is pretty eclectic,' murmured Philip. 'I just sleuth around salerooms, buying whatever turns me on. I trust my own taste. Then again, I'm not really a believer in taste. Bad taste is anything that's boring. I don't like to be bored.' He was trying to keep his gaze from travelling in the direction of her cleavage. She was a hell of a turn-on, and he sensed she felt the same way about him.

They continued to talk for another fifteen minutes, discovering new mutual acquaintances, consolidating the chemistry of their attraction with a satisfying number of shared interests and experiences. Eventually Philip said, 'Listen, I'm heading off to a club. Would you like to come along?'

They left the party and caught a taxi. Avril wasn't sure what kind of club to expect – from the look of Philip, a plush Mayfair gaming or drinking club, perhaps – but the taxi took them to a basement club in Soho. Philip paid the driver and they went downstairs into a low-ceilinged cellar heaving with young people dancing. On stage a young man in a corduroy jacket backed by three guitarists and a drummer was giving a raucous rendition of 'Johnny B. Goode'. Philip and Avril made their way to a table at the back of the room, and Philip bought drinks. The music was too loud for conversation.

When the song ended Philip turned and asked her, 'Do you like it?' He asked the question seriously, as though her answer mattered.

'They're very dynamic.' Which was a polite way of saying loud and aggressive. She glanced at the stage, where the singer had taken off his corduroy jacket and was throwing it aside. The blond guitarist in the paisley shirt was very good-looking, certainly. The group threw themselves into Chuck Berry's 'Come On', and Avril watched Philip surreptitiously. He seemed to be concentrating on the music, but she couldn't tell if he was enjoying it or not. When the song finished she asked, 'Do you?'

'Do I what?'

'Like it.'

'Oh.' He gave a laugh. 'I thought you were asking if I wanted to dance.' He glanced towards the stage, his smile fading, thinking about the question. 'I'm not sure.' He paused, then said intently, 'I'm interested. They're part of what's going to be important to people, you see. I want to understand it. Art, music, literature, fashion – everything shapes everything else. If I'm going to recognise the right paintings to buy, I need to understand what's going on.'

Avril thought she knew what he was getting at. She felt much the same thing. 'What are they called? The group, I mean.'

'I'm not sure. But the singer chappie is Mick Jagger. He sometimes sings with another blues band that plays here.'

Avril, studying the group as they got ready for another number, asked, 'If they were a painting, would you collect them?'

'What a very good way of looking at it.' He thought about this as he sipped his drink. 'You know, I think I just might. It's not just about what one likes, after all. It's about what one thinks is going to endure. They're not boring, at any rate.'

No, thought Avril, as the group launched itself into Buddy Holly's 'Not Fade Away', they weren't boring. But she wasn't sure she shared Philip's belief in their endurance.

When a break was announced Philip said, 'I think that's enough of that for one night. Care to come back to my place for a drink?'

Avril had already perceived that Philip's approach in life was to examine, judge, collect or discard depending on value or interest. She had no intention of being an easy acquisition. A drink, yes, but no more.

They took a taxi back to Philip's flat in Ebury Street. It was very large, and Avril was intrigued by its interior. The furniture in the living room was mostly antique with a few modern pieces, and the paintings on the walls were the same haphazard mix – a Paolozzi collage hung next to a small Degas pastel, a Jim Dine painting next to a charcoal sketch of Philip sitting cross-legged in a chair with a cigarette. On a marble-topped Regency cabinet stood a small Henry Moore bronze of a reclining figure. The impression was not so much of confusion as of eager enthusiasm backed by considerable wealth. One wall was entirely filled with books, which Avril studied as Philip prepared drinks. They were mainly art books, and well-thumbed runs of *Cahiers d'Art* and *Minotaure*. For someone self-taught, he had thrown himself into learning about art with singular commitment.

Philip, as he handed Avril her drink, made his intentions perfectly clear by kissing her. It was a gentle, persuasive kiss that required no particular kind of return. He took his mouth from hers as though some satisfactory prelude had been accomplished, and said, 'Come and take a look at my other pictures.

'I don't keep everything here,' he said, as he led her into the next room, whose walls were covered with pictures. 'A lot is in storage – those Pughs and Blackmans I bought from you, for instance. But I keep my favourites here.'

Avril, as she wandered the room, couldn't help wondering how much Philip paid to insure it all. Among the more established artists she recognised several up-and-coming names, and saw nothing she might not have bought herself. She had to admit he had a good eye. She stopped in front of a portrait. She recognised the subject, a dark-haired man with luminous eyes, wearing a jacket, with a scarf thrown round his neck, a notebook in his hand. He had come to stay a few times at Woodbourne House when she was a child, and had taken her kite-flying once. Philip came and stood close behind her as she examined the painting.

'This is by my father,' murmured Avril. 'I remember the man, but not his name.'

'You're Henry Haddon's daughter? I had no idea. I suppose I should have made the connection. How simply amazing. He's one of my favourite painters.' She could sense this revelation consolidating something for him. 'That's David Gascoyne, the poet. It's a marvellous portrait.'

'You must be one of the few people interested in my father's work. He's rather fallen out of fashion.'

'Fashion comes and goes. Genius endures. I think Henry Haddon was a genius.'

'Nice of you to say so.'

She was intensely aware of his close physical proximity. His fingers touched her collar, tracing a line across the bare skin of her neck, then his hand came to rest on her shoulder as he bent to kiss her. She shivered lightly, then turned to face him and let him kiss her for a long, intense moment, longing flooding every part of her body. She drew away.

'You'll stay?' he murmured.

'I don't think so.'

'Really?' He kissed her again, pulling her close against him.

After a moment she drew away. 'I have to go.'

He said nothing, but she knew he was annoyed and somewhat surprised. No doubt most women gave into him easily. He had an extraordinary magnetic sexuality that was hard to resist.

He fetched her coat. 'Shall I call you a taxi?'

'No, thanks. It's not far to walk.'

'I'll walk with you.'

'You really don't have to.'

'I insist.'

They walked the few blocks to Mount Street, talking about paintings and people they knew.

'Thank you for this evening,' said Avril.

'My pleasure.'

She could tell he wanted to ask if he would see her again, but was holding himself back. She reached her face up and kissed him lightly. 'Goodnight.'

'Goodnight.'

She went inside and pressed the button for the elevator. She wondered how long it would take him to ring her. A week? Two? Or he might play a longer game and leave it a month. But he would ring, of that she was certain.

20

PHILIP RANG FOUR days later. Avril agreed to meet him for a drink, then cancelled the day before on some pretext. After a fortnight he called again. This time he invited her to dinner and took her to the Savoy Grill, where they ate and talked for four hours – and could have gone on talking for another four had the restaurant not been closing. She said no to Philip's offer of a late-night coffee, and after a passionate kiss in the back of the taxi he dropped her off in Mount Street and went home alone. The next day he turned up at the gallery, persuaded Avril to close early, and took her to the Colony Room in Soho. Avril had never much cared for the Colony; she thought it dingy and squalid, and she didn't like Muriel Belcher, who ran the place, but she was impressed by the fact that Philip seemed to know everyone there who was worth talking to. They had only intended to go for a couple of drinks, but a friend of Avril's, a wiry, bearded Czech artist called Karel Jirasec, turned up as well, and the three of them drank the evening away, listening to Francis Bacon hold forth on some topic that neither of them could recall later. In the taxi home, after a lot of drunken kissing and fumbling, Philip almost talked her into coming back to his, but she knew that going to bed with him after drinking so much could turn out to be a disaster, and wisely declined.

Although she was playing a long game, Avril knew there were limits; Philip might become impatient and drop her. She didn't think he would, because they were already enmeshed in something more than mere sexual attraction. They were developing an empathy based on mutual admiration, they made one another laugh, and they cared about so many of the same things that they could happily talk for hours. She knew this was a relationship with the potential to be more than just a love affair, and she wanted it to develop in the right way. She recognised that Philip's egotism would have to be judiciously managed, and allowances made.

Then something happened which, even if she had managed to manufacture it, couldn't have worked out more perfectly. Karel the Czech artist began calling her up. Since nothing of any substance had yet been established with Philip, she felt free to go out with Karel for the odd drink or meal. He was a man of great energy and charm, and in other circumstances she might well have been happy to have an idle fling with him, but she kept things steadfastly platonic. Soon Karel was turning up at every party or gathering she went to, and it became obvious to everyone, including Philip, that he was smitten. When Philip telephoned Avril to invite her to the first night of a pop art exhibition in Chelsea and Avril told him that she'd already agreed to go with Karel, he made no attempt to disguise his irritation.

'If you ask me, you're seeing far too much of that bloody Czech.'

'I didn't ask you,' replied Avril mildly, who didn't like to be told by any man, even Philip, what she ought or ought not to be doing.

'And frankly, I don't think he has a bath above once a week.'

At this she burst out laughing, and Philip hung up. When she went to the pop art exhibition with Karel, Philip wasn't there. For three weeks she heard nothing from him, and began to feel a faint disquiet. Perhaps a combination of wounded vanity and impatience had made him decide she was no longer worth bothering with.

Then one Thursday evening, just as she was closing the gallery, a taxi drew up, and she saw Philip's long-legged figure stepping from the cab. He whipped off his sunglasses and folded them into the breast pocket of his jacket as he strode into the gallery.

'Hello.' She spoke calmly to hide her elation.

'Are you busy this weekend?' asked Philip abruptly.

'I—'

'Actually, I don't care if you are, because whatever you're doing you'll have to cancel it. I'm taking you away.'

'I'm sorry?'

From his pocket Philip produced two airline tickets. 'To the south of France, for a long weekend.'

'But I have to open the gallery tomorrow—'

'No, you don't. I'm sure Flavia would welcome a day off.' He glanced at Avril's assistant as she emerged from the back office. 'Wouldn't you just love to have tomorrow off, Flavia?'

Flavia was a tall, coltish brunette with an impeccable social pedigree and cut-glass vowels, very pretty and always dressed in up-to-the-minute fashions. She was good for business in the way that Laura had once been.

She gave Avril a startled glance. 'That would be nice,' she murmured uncertainly.

'There. Will you come?'

'It doesn't sound like I have a choice.'

'I'll pick you up around eleven. The flight's at two. Now, you'd better go home and pack.'

Avril was somewhat overawed by the magnificence of the hotel suite that Philip had booked in Cap d'Antibes. She stood on the balcony, luxuriating in the warmth of the late-afternoon sun, gazing at the Mediterranean glittering beyond the pine trees fringing the beach. No man had ever gone to so much trouble just to get her into bed.

Philip, who had been taking a shower, came barefoot onto the balcony, dressed in a white cotton shirt and dark blue linen trousers. He put his arms around her from behind and rested his chin on her shoulder.

'You like?'

'It's stunning.' She turned in his arms and kissed him. His newly washed hair was damp and fragrant. 'But why bring me here?'

'I was going to take you down to my place in Surrey, but somehow it didn't seem romantic enough.'

'I didn't know you had a place in Surrey.'

'It's in a village called Boxgrove. My mother bought it after she and my father divorced. It's very special to me. And I only take very special people there.' He stroked her face. 'The reason I brought you here is because you seem like the kind of woman who needs the right place to fall in love.'

'That's what you think I'm going to do?'

'I very much hope so. I love having people in love with me.'

'I'm not sure I've ever been in love.' The passions she'd had for the men she'd been involved with over the years had been real enough, but she doubted if she had ever felt the helpless, devoted intensity that she associated with being in love.

'You should try it. I fell in love with my mother when I was six, then with myself around the age of fourteen. Those feelings endure to this day.'

She laughed. 'I can't promise anything.' She slid from his embrace. 'I'm going to unpack and take a bath.'

As she idled in a deep, foaming bath, she dwelt on what he'd said. Was he in love with her? He had a romantic nature, certainly, but she suspected it was of the fickle variety, not one that fixed too long on any one object or person. This weekend was clearly the fruit of her delaying tactics, but she liked to think, too, that he'd developed an emotional attachment to her that had its own particular strength. As for love, well…

When she emerged in her bathrobe she found him lying flat out on the bed on his back, smoking and squinting up at the last pages of *The Garden of the Finzi-Continis*, which he'd been reading on the plane. She sat down next to him.

'Your cigarette smells peculiar. Is it Turkish?'

He said nothing for a moment, reading the final lines, then chucked the book across the room. 'It's cannabis.'

'Oh.'

'Have you ever had any?' She shook her head. He handed her the reefer. 'Have a little toke.'

She took a few puffs, holding in the smoke the way

he told her to. The light-headed sensation was pleasant, if strange. Philip took the reefer from her and inhaled a final drag before stubbing it out in a bedside ashtray. He eased the bathrobe from her shoulders and kissed them in turn, moving down to her breasts, parting her thighs with his hands. She lay back on the bed and surrendered herself to the bliss of his touch. The body-heat temperature of the air in the room, coupled with the marijuana, made her feel as though she were floating, her senses pooling wherever he caressed her. The feeling was so delicious that she laughed aloud. Philip moved his mouth from her breasts and kissed her, easing himself out of his trousers. She put out a hand and felt the warm hardness of him, and seconds later he was inside her. The gauze curtain at the long window rippled and lifted gently in the warm air, so that patches of sunlight shifted on the floor as they made love.

When it was over, Philip murmured, 'Tell me you love me. I need to hear it.' It was true. For the first time in his life he'd met a woman whose independence and intelligence set her apart from the usual vapid socialites and debutantes. She ran her own successful business, she was to his mind beautiful, and she didn't give in to him too easily. Securing her love was a need, a challenge.

'No,' she murmured in reply. 'It's not good for you to have whatever you want, whenever you want it.'

'So you've spent the last two months proving.' He propped himself on one elbow, his head on his hand.

'But it was wonderfully worth the wait.' He traced his fingers across her lips. 'I love your mouth.' After a pause he said, 'I think I love you.'

'I won't say it, you know.'

'Hmm.' He glanced at his watch. 'Cocktails in half an hour. What say we do that again?'

She would look back on those few days as among the most precious of her life. They spent the time idling in the sun, eating, making love and talking endlessly. In May of 1962 Juan les Pins was at its fashionable height, full of young people, wealthy yacht owners, and French rock-and-roll stars. They drank cocktails at Pam-Pam, watching the Ferraris and Lamborghinis cruising past in the street, then went to Juan Casino to see Johnny Halliday, and afterwards they played the tables, Philip losing a small fortune at baccarat. In bringing her here, he had achieved his aim of making her fall in love with him. It was the consolidation of everything she'd felt about him since the day they met. She had no intention, however, of telling him so – not yet. She was sure that Philip was one of those people whose interest could only be sustained by withholding. She would always need to keep something back, some reserve of affection or attention.

On the last night of their stay they were drinking cocktails on the terrace of the Belle Rive Hotel, when Philip noticed two men who had just arrived.

'I say, look who it is.'

Avril recognised Max Latimer strolling across the terrace with another young man.

Philip raised a hand in greeting. 'Latimer, how are you?' He hadn't seen Max since that summer when he and a very pretty girl – whose name he couldn't for the life of him remember – had stayed at Chalcombe.

Max glanced from Philip to Avril in surprise. He shook Philip's hand, saying, 'My God, it has to be… what? Ten years? And Avril' – he bent to kiss her cheek – 'how are you?'

'You two know one other?' said Philip.

'We're cousins,' replied Avril.

'Something like that,' said Max. He turned to his companion, a diminutive young man with curling sandy hair, dressed somewhat incongruously in a pinstripe suit and a close-fitting white shirt, his eyes hidden behind sunglasses. 'This is Alec Orr-Lowndes – Alec, Avril Haddon, Philip Carteret.'

Alec pushed his sunglasses to his forehead and shook hands, saying to Philip, 'I remember you from school.'

'Of course – you two were both in the same form. I thought I knew the name. Good God, Juan les Pins is positively awash with OEs.' He glanced at Max. 'Are you both down here on holiday?'

'I'm staying with my grandmother,' replied Max. 'She lives in Antibes. I took her to tea at Butler's yesterday, and that's where I met Alec.'

'I'm working there as a waiter,' said Alec. 'Bumming my way around the south of France.'

'How very amusing.'

Philip's facetious tone reminded Max of the last time they'd met, when he'd been forced to watch in pain as Philip effortlessly charmed Laura away from him.

Avril, who didn't want to spend any part of her last evening with Philip making small talk with Max and his friend, said, 'We'd ask you to join us, but Philip and I are just off to dinner. Why don't you have our table, though? The place is getting busy.'

Philip drained his martini glass and he and Avril got to their feet.

'Thanks,' said Max. 'Well, lovely surprise seeing you both.' He was still trying to come to terms with the fact that Philip and Avril seemed to be a couple. He asked Avril, 'Will you be dropping in to see Helen?'

'I don't think I'll have time, I'm afraid. We're flying back tomorrow. But do give her my love.' She extended her hand to Alec. 'So nice to meet you.'

Alec and Max settled into the chairs that Philip and Avril had vacated. Alec let his sunglasses drop back on to his nose and signalled to a nearby waiter. 'Did I detect a slight coolness between you and your cousin?'

'She's certainly not my favourite relative. God knows what she's doing with Carteret. They probably deserve one another.'

'I remember he was the most enormous swank at

school. Though he did have style. Still does. What will you have? A negroni?'

'Thanks.'

When the waiter had left, Alec fished in his pocket and furtively produced a couple of pills. 'Want one?' he asked Max.

'What are they?' asked Max, mystified.

'Preludin. Speed. They give you a nice buzz.'

'No thanks. It's not a good idea for a member of the criminal bar to take drugs.'

'Of course. You're a righteous inhabitant of squaresville. Bad luck.' He popped one of the pills into his mouth, and gave Max a sunny smile.

As Philip and Avril left the terrace he asked her, 'Why the sudden getaway?'

'It was either that or invite them to have a drink with us,' replied Avril. 'Which I frankly didn't want. Max and I never got on terribly well.' A series of recollections tumbled through her mind – the fly on Meg's face as she lay motionless by the water, scrambling up the bank of the quarry in panic, the bright flare of blood on her dress drying later to a brown, dead stain. And Max, raging, weeping, inconsolable. He would never forgive her for her own part in the events of that day.

'Fine by me,' said Philip. 'Looks like Latimer has turned into the solid, dull citizen he always threatened to become. His friend, on the other hand, was something of a naughty boy, as I recall.' They stepped out into the evening sunshine and he kissed her. 'Let's have an early dinner, then go back and make the most of our last Riviera night.'

The weekend in France had resolved aspects of their relationship, in that they were now lovers, but Avril believed it was important not to let Philip take her for granted, or to allow things to become predictable. She had an important exhibition coming up that autumn, and organising it was going to take up much of her time, which gave her an excuse not to see too much of Philip – even though she would happily have spent every day and night with him. She knew Philip liked the fact that she was successful and respected in a world about which he cared, and these strengths – her status and her independence – had to be maintained. It also meant that the times when they were together were highly charged, sexually and emotionally, so that the level of pleasure they took in one another never slipped. He began to leave certain belongings at her flat in Mount Street – a couple of shirts, socks, a toothbrush – but Avril took care to leave nothing at his place in Ebury Street.

Throughout the summer, while Avril worked, Philip continued to live the life of a wealthy dilettante, rising late, seeing friends for lunch, browsing salerooms and auction houses, spending his money instinctively and discerningly, and on the evenings when he wasn't seeing

Avril, going with friends to clubs and music venues, watching, listening, keen to understand a world which he knew was somehow becoming important. He felt as though he was on a quest for something, but was unsure what it was. Collecting art for collecting's sake was beginning to lose its meaning, and the more insight he gained into the work Avril did, the more he began to think he might like to open a gallery of his own.

It was when he was doing the rounds of the West End galleries that he bumped into Alec Orr-Lowndes. Alec was working in a small establishment in Cork Street, and on the day that Philip came in he was in the process of trying to persuade a couple to invest in a large figurative painting. Philip waited until the couple had completed their purchase, then went to say hello.

'So you've exhausted the pleasures of the Riviera,' he remarked.

'I like to think of it as the other way round,' smiled Alec.

'I didn't realise you were a connoisseur of modern art. That was an impressive piece of salesmanship. How much did they pay?'

'Three hundred guineas. For them it's not so much an investment in art as an investment in social standing. People are desperate to be fashionable.'

This amused Philip. 'Even so, you knew what you were talking about.'

'I'm self-taught, but I still have much to learn. I met

Michael and Orla, who own this place, when I was in Paris a month ago, and they were kind enough to give me a job.' Alec, an avid reader of gossip columns, knew a good deal about Philip, including that he was a collector. 'Are you looking to buy anything today?'

'There's a Dubuffet gouache over there that I rather like.' Together they wandered over to the other side of the gallery.

Ten minutes later, the purchase of the Dubuffet concluded – at a price Philip knew was over the odds – he invited Alec to lunch.

That lunch marked the beginning of an important new friendship. Philip found himself enjoying Alec's witty conversation, his loquacious enthusiasm, and his irrepressible desire to keep up with everything on the fast-changing London scene. With his collector's instinct, he decided to make Alec his protégé. Over the weeks that followed he invited him to dinner parties at his flat, and to informal gatherings, and soon Alec was involved in purchasing art for Philip, displacing the Italian agent to whom Philip had previously paid commission. Alec in turn introduced Philip to his own circle, which generally consisted of people whom he had identified as being interesting and potentially useful, including pop stars, actors and musicians.

One of Alec's other attractions was that he seemed to have access to an endless supply of drugs. Philip was already an enthusiastic cannabis smoker, and his questing curiosity made him the ideal candidate for anything new and mind-expanding. It wasn't long before Alec had introduced him to the pleasures of speed and purple hearts, most of which Alec sold to him at an absurd mark-up, creaming off a tidy profit for himself. Getting high became an article of faith for Philip, but beyond the odd joint of cannabis he couldn't get Avril interested. Unlike Philip, she had a business to run and she faintly despised Philip's drug-taking. Nor did she much like Alec.

'He's a little bugger on the make,' she told Philip one morning over breakfast. 'And I mean that literally. The stories about him.'

'I don't care if he's queer,' replied Philip. 'He can live as he pleases. He's fun to be around, and that's all I care about. Anyway, when did you get to be such a prude?'

'I'm not, you know that.' She stood up. 'I have to get going. It's not about whether he's queer or not – it's about the kind of person he is. Look at all the money he keeps borrowing from you. Has he ever paid any of it back?'

'I don't care if he never does. He's worth it for the amusement value alone.' Philip, clad only in a silk dressing-gown, grabbed Avril's hand as she was on her way to the door. 'Don't rush off. I was just thinking it would be nice to spend another half-hour in bed.' He drew her towards him and began to unfasten the buttons of her blouse.

She extricated herself gently from his embrace. 'I'd love to, but I have a gallery to run.'

'Will I see you this evening?'

'Darling, I'm busy all week. I'll call you.' She kissed him, then left.

Philip yawned, lit a cigarette and reflected on the day ahead. He had some business affairs to attend to, but once they were out of the way he'd find someone to lunch with, then pop in and see Alec and arrange some fun for this evening. Alec always knew where the fun was.

When Avril arrived at the gallery, Flavia was already there, fanning out a few of the latest art and fashion magazines on the counter at the front.

'Morning,' she said to Avril. 'Would you like a coffee?'

'Thank you,' murmured Avril absently. She picked up a copy of *Vogue* from the counter, and as she glanced at it her heart plunged wildly. The cover model was starkly photographed against a dark background, dressed in a simple white turtleneck and white jacket, throwing into relief her flawless skin and beautiful mouth, the dark grey eyes and winged dark brows contrasting with her blonde hair. She was provocative, beautiful, and unmistakably Laura.

Whatever she thought might have become of Laura, she had never imagined this. Success, however fleeting, in whatever sort of fragile world – for a model's life,

Avril knew, was precarious – had not been envisaged. How had she managed this?

Flavia returned with Avril's coffee. 'We're nearly out of instant. I'll pop out later and get some.' She glanced at the cover of the magazine. 'Oh, it's Laura Fenton. Isn't she super? I just adore her look. I wish I had eyes like that.'

'I know her.'

Flavia's eyes widened. 'Really? Do you know Sid Jennings, too?'

'Who?' The name rang a vague bell.

'The photographer. He's her boyfriend. He's not as big as David Bailey, but very nearly. His fashion shots are amazing – terrifically quirky.' She handed Avril her coffee. 'How do you know her?'

'It was when we were younger.' Avril dropped the magazine on the counter and went into her office.

She sat sipping her coffee, trying to reconcile her feelings. She should be pleased – relieved, really – that Laura was doing well, that she was making a success of her life. But the feelings of childhood weren't easy to alter. She tried to set them aside and concentrate on the name of the photographer Flavia had mentioned. Sid Jennings. Why was that familiar? She pondered for a while, then it came to her – Jennings had been the name of the evacuees her mother had housed during the war, Sidney and Colin, two obnoxious and extremely common boys. Some extraordinary coincidence seemed to have brought Sid and Laura together again. The ways of life were very strange.

Well, lucky Laura. She resolved to be glad for her, to count her own blessings – the gallery, her reputation, Philip – otherwise those childhood feelings of envy and rivalry would poison and consume her. How she wished Laura would just disappear from her life, so that she could feel like a better person.

21

Laura was having what seemed to her like the hundredth argument that week with Sid.

'I don't care how good it is for business! I'm tired of pretending that we're some kind of Jean Shrimpton–David Bailey couple when we're not!'

'Look,' said Sid, in what he thought was a reasonable, placatory way, 'all we have to do is show up together tonight, let the paparazzi snap a few photos, and it keeps our faces in the papers. People like seeing beautiful couples—'

'Oh, put a sock in it, Sid.' Laura, who had come round to Sid's studio-cum-flat to have a coffee and collect some paperwork, emptied her mug into the sink and picked up her handbag.

Sid shrugged. 'Fine. I'll find some other bird to take tonight. Maybe I'll find some other model for the next *Vogue* shoot, too.'

Laura gazed at him in exasperation. Nobody had a bigger opinion of Sid than Sid himself. This place he lived in was testament to that, all white brickwork and fancy artwork, geometric glass tables. And the way he dressed these days, those tight white jeans with the broad black leather belt, the black shirt open to the third button, his hair down to his collar. How he loved his success. And how he thought of himself as the creator of her success, instead of the other way around.

'You think it's all about you, don't you? Well, maybe I'll find another photographer. You're not the only one in London, you know.'

Sid smiled at her. 'Face it, baby, people want to think of us as a couple. Like I said, it's good for business.'

'And like *I* said, I don't care! You can take someone else to this junket tonight. I'm sick of people thinking I'm your property.'

She left before he could say anything else, hurrying to the end of the mews in search of a taxi. The fact was, for the last couple of months Sid had shadowed her like some relentless demon, riding on the back of the success that had given them both fame, intent on making the world believe they were an item. She could hardly call her life her own. Well, it had to end. Sid could find some other girl to take to his photography awards dinner tonight, and she would keep her own profile up by being visible somewhere else. It wasn't really her bag, and she hadn't intended to go, but the event that her friend Cassie had invited her to would provide the ideal opportunity to be seen without Sid.

'What do you mean, a "happening"?' asked Philip.

Alec was perched on the edge of a sofa in Philip's drawing room, making up a joint on the coffee table. 'It's art. Lots of different things going on at once. Poetry readings, people doing weird things, performing, that kind of thing. Making art out of themselves. The last one I went to this girl emptied a pot of red paint over herself and walked around this big canvas, making footprints and dripping all over the place. She was chanting at the same time.'

'Sounds most peculiar.'

'Quite fun, actually, if you've taken the right drugs. But we should go, we really should. Everyone, I mean bloody everyone, is going to be there.'

'All right, then.' Philip thought for a moment. 'What do you mean by the right drugs? Grass?'

'Better than that.' Alec gave Philip a roguish smile. 'Some top-notch acid. But it's best to take it just before we get there. In the meantime, by way of an appetiser, so to speak,' he twisted the cigarette paper at the end of the joint tight, and produced his gold Ronson cigarette lighter, 'let's be getting on with this.'

The event was taking place in a large warehouse in Limehouse that had been divided into a series of rooms, something different happening in each. In some of the rooms strobe lighting cast swirling beams of coloured light, in others the light was starkly fluorescent. Music from different areas overlapped, strident rhythm and blues washing over trippy, ethereal sounds. People milled around, watching with politely detached British awkwardness as the performers did their thing – in one room a bearded man stood on a ladder reading poems aloud, in another a girl sat in a swimming costume on an upturned bucket peeling oranges with a knife, littering the floor around her with coils of peel and filling the air with a sweet aroma, handing segments to the audience.

'I'm not sure I get this,' said Philip to Alec, as they wandered among the rooms.

'It relies on audience participation,' said Alec. 'Trouble is, we Brits aren't terribly good at participating. I believe the Americans do it rather better.'

Philip took a hefty slug from the drink he had picked up on the way in. He wasn't convinced that the drug that Alec had given him – a tiny, greyish-brown tab of acid – was going to have any effect. He felt very sober and mildly depressed by what was going on around him.

Laura was listening to her friend Cassie expounding to an intently listening Frenchman the purpose of tonight's goings-on. She was conscious of the glances she was getting. There were a few well-known faces present, pop stars and actors, plus two society gossip columnists, and a photographer was snapping away discreetly, so she would get something out of the evening. To be seen out and about without Sid was enough.

'It's when things go wrong that they go right,' Cassie was saying. 'Think of it as spontaneous theatre. The performers are trying to emphasise the organic connection between art and its environment through the audience.' The Frenchman nodded uncertainly.

As Laura glanced around, she noticed a tall, bored-looking man in a suit and tie leaning against the wall with a drink in his hand. He seemed familiar. She studied his languid, handsome features for a moment, then realised it was Philip Carteret. Her heart gave a little jump, and every emotion she had ever had about him came surging back. Funny, she thought, as she gazed at him, how teenage feelings never really died away; they just stayed banked down, ready to reignite at any moment.

Philip in turn glanced in her direction. All he saw at first was an incredibly beautiful blonde, then after a few seconds her features resolved themselves and he recognised her. She was the girl who had come to Harry's place with Max that summer. Her name suddenly came to him – Laura. She had been pretty then, but now she was extraordinary, tall and graceful, beauty poised on the brink of perfection.

He made his way over. They smiled at one another.

'Laura, isn't it? We met at Chalcombe.'

'Yes. I haven't seen you since the day you got your call-up papers. You were rather upset, and you disappeared before I could say goodbye.'

'Did I?'

'How was it? The army.'

'Purgatorial boredom. What are you doing these days?'

'I'm a model.'

He gave a faint smile. 'Of course you are.'

'And you?'

'Oh, I don't do a lot. I just wander about looking at things. Collecting stuff I like.' He was suddenly aware that when she lifted her hand to brush a few strands of hair from her eyes, it seemed to leave a glittering, slow-motion trail of colour. How amazing, he thought. He was suffused with a strange feeling of warmth.

'What do you think about tonight?' she asked.

'Tonight?' His gaze was fixed on her mouth, and on the fact that when she spoke the words seemed to bubble deliciously from her. He could almost see the sound. 'I'm not really sure what I'm meant to think.'

She laughed, and this time he definitely did see the sound, a series of little silver crescents forming and melting. 'I don't think you're meant to think anything. That's the point. You just let it happen.'

She took him by the sleeve and led him into a room he hadn't been in before. The light was low and diffuse, and there were paintings on the walls. Music pulsed softly. 'This is my favourite room,' she was saying, and her voice seemed to come from far away. When he looked at the paintings the colours appeared elastic. He was saying things to her, and she was replying, and it all seemed sensible, but he felt a kind of floating detachment. The acid had most definitely kicked in; Alec was right – this wasn't like anything he had ever experienced before.

'Last time we met you said in ten years' time things were going to be different in ways we couldn't imagine. Maybe this is what you meant,' said Laura. She watched Philip as he surveyed the paintings. He looked amused, a little dazed. Then he turned and gazed at her intently.

'Did I say that? I don't remember.' He was transfixed by her earrings, a series of dangling plastic hoops in different colours that seemed to shimmer and give off streams of light when she moved her head. 'But I remember kissing you in the woods.'

They were alone in the room, and when he closed his eyes and put his mouth to hers, she didn't resist. The kiss was the most astonishing sensation. Her mouth seemed to melt under his, and his inner vision was filled with a series of bursting circles of radiant light. Time seemed to melt and then expand.

Laura didn't think she had ever been kissed by anyone for such a length of time. She was happy to let it go on for ever. It brought back everything she had felt when she was fifteen, her first kiss, the aching loveliness of it.

What was happening was the last thing she had ever expected from this evening, and yet it seemed to make the most perfect sense.

The kiss lasted several minutes. No one came into the room. They were in their own world. Philip had lost all sense of time. At last he took his mouth from hers.

'I'm sorry I didn't say goodbye,' he murmured. 'I won't let it happen again.'

She had no idea what he meant. Neither did he.

Suddenly a chattering gaggle of people flooded into the room. The creator of the paintings was among them, and the photographer. One of the girls stopped next to Laura and said, 'Gosh, you're Laura Fenton!' The photographer swung round, attention switched from the peeved artist, and Philip felt as though he were in a kaleidoscope of people, a bizarre array of colours and impressions swarming across his vision. The volume of the music suddenly seemed to grow louder, unbearably so, vibrating inside him like the voice of God. Laura said something to him and he couldn't hear a word. He had to get out. He left, and went from room to room, searching for Alec. The walls seemed to be rippling, breathing. Everywhere he went trails of light shimmered from people's limbs and mouths. Unable to find Alec, he went back in search of Laura. But she was nowhere to be seen. He felt a sudden sense of panic, as though he no longer knew who he was. Then with relief he caught sight of Alec.

'Something unbelievable just happened. I went back in time. This girl. But she's not here now. I have to find her. Was she here? Do you know?'

Alec grinned. 'Man, you're really tripping.' He watched Philip for a moment and realised he seemed genuinely distressed, definitely not OK. 'Come on,' he said, 'let's get you home. I've had enough of all this, anyway.'

22

WHEN PHILIP WOKE it was early afternoon. It had taken almost eight hours for the effects of the acid to wear off and even then sleep had been difficult. Never again, he thought. Thank Christ Alec had come back to the flat and stayed with him. He wouldn't have wanted to be alone when snakes started coming out of the electric sockets and the corners of the room began to close in on him. Alec had no such problems. He sat playing John Coltrane records and giving ecstatic descriptions of the colours of the music, and seemed to find everything endlessly funny. But before things had got bad there had been the thing with that girl Laura. The memory was like a beautiful, multicoloured dream. They had met, talked, and kissed. Just like that. How long had it lasted? Minutes? An hour? He had no idea. But that kiss. If the snakes had been the downside of the acid trip, the kiss was definitely the upside. He buried his face in the pillow, trying to relive the sensation, the warm softness of her mouth. Why had he left her? Ah yes, the people, all the people.

He got out of bed, slipped on his dressing gown, and went to the kitchen. Alec was up and dressed, drinking tea and eating toast, the newspaper propped against the teapot. He glanced up at Philip.

'Afternoon. Cup of tea?'

'Thanks.' Philip sat down. 'You look remarkably perky after last night. Do you do that kind of thing often?'

Alec poured Philip some tea. 'I'm partial to the odd spot of LSD now and then. I find it blows the cobwebs away.' He finished his toast and drained his teacup. 'But only on Fridays and Saturdays. Otherwise it interferes with work. Now, I have to be off. I'll call you later. Thanks for letting me crash.'

Philip took his tea and the paper through to the living room and stretched himself out on the sofa. A few minutes later the phone rang.

'Philip?'

He didn't recognise the female voice at the other end.

'Yes. Who is this?'

'It's Laura.'

'Wow. Hello – how did you get my number?'

'Don't sound so appalled. Friends of friends of friends.'

'I'm not appalled. I'm very happy. Look, I'm sorry about last night. Disappearing like that. I was a little, well, out of it.'

'Don't apologise. It was a strange evening altogether.'

'It was rather weird.' There was a silence. 'Let me take you to dinner tonight to make up for my rudeness. If you're not busy?'

'I'm not busy.'

'I'll book Quaglino's for nine.'

'Lovely. I'll see you there. Bye.' He was left listening to the purr of the dialling tone. He replaced the receiver. Hearing her voice had been a little surreal. Maybe the acid hadn't entirely worn off. The invitation to dinner had been on impulse. He thought of Avril, and felt a momentary disquiet. But she was eternally busy. He never quite knew how he stood with her. When life offered up golden opportunities, it was madness not to take them. Alec would most certainly have agreed.

Laura arrived late. Her blonde hair was swept up, and she was wearing a sleeveless black Givenchy dress, pearls at her throat and ears. The look was simple but stunning. Every head in the restaurant turned. Philip stood up as she came to the table, and pulled out her chair. Laura liked that. Not something Sid would ever have thought of doing.

'You look as though you blew in on a golden cloud,' said Philip, as they sat down.

She laughed. 'Are you still tripping?'

'It feels that way.' He paused. 'How did you know?'

'I've been around people who've taken acid – I know the look.'

'I love drugs as much as the next person, but I don't think I'll be trying that one again.'

A silence fell between them as the waiter brought menus and poured the wine that Philip had already ordered.

'Last night was weird,' said Laura. 'I almost didn't go, but I'm glad I did.'

'So am I.'

They gazed at one another for a moment, then Laura said, 'Now, I want you to start with that last day I saw you at Chalcombe, and tell me everything that's happened in your life since.'

Over dinner Philip gave an account of all he had done, his years with the army in Africa, the death of his mother and father, the world of art collecting into which he had drifted.

'I suppose my average day makes me sound pretty much like an idler with too much money.'

'My own life isn't exactly honest toil. Modelling can be deadly boring, but it's not what you'd call hard work.'

'Now it's your turn. How did you get from there to here?'

Laura sketched out her life, secretarial college, jobs here and there, the chance meeting with Sid, the slow then sudden rise to the high echelons of the fashion world.

'And your parents?'

She shrugged. 'Not on the scene. My mother wasn't married. She disappeared when I was a baby. I was brought up by the woman she was working for. She was pretty well-off, Aunt Sonia. Well, she wasn't my aunt – I just called her that. She died around the time I met you. After that it was just me and Avril, her daughter. Avril was a bit older than me, so she ran my life. She took me out of school, sent me off to college, then had me working in her art gallery. We fell out a few years ago. I haven't seen her since.'

Pieces of jigsaw dropped into place. 'Would this be Avril Haddon, by any chance?'

'Yes. How did you know?'

'I know her, vaguely.' The bizarre coincidence amused him.

She pushed away her dessert plate. 'I say, d'you have a cigarette? It makes me anxious, talking about her. I hardly ever do.' She took a cigarette from his case. 'Not if I can help it.' He lit her cigarette, and she blew out a little smoke.

'And what about Max Latimer? Do you still see him?'

She shook her head. After a brief silence she smiled and said, 'Why don't we have coffee at my place?'

It was a bold invitation, but he wasn't about to turn it down. 'Fine.'

They left the restaurant and took a cab to Laura's flat.

'Why don't you put on some music?' said Laura, switching on the lights in the living room. 'I'll make coffee.'

Philip searched among the stack of LPs and put an Ella Fitzgerald record on the record player. The haunting sounds of 'Blues In The Night' filled the room. He strolled around, inspecting everything, looking for clues. Unlike Avril, Laura seemed to possess no paintings or artefacts, just framed posters and a few big green plants, and some not very interesting books. Copies of *Vogue*, *Harpers Bazaar*, *Queen* and *Tatler* littered the sofa and coffee table. The furnishings were chic and modern, and the place had a messy, carefree feel, very much the flat of a busy girl-about-town. Unlike Avril's home in Mount Street, this was not a place that took itself seriously, which seemed just about to reflect the personalities of the two women. He had no idea what to make of the discovery that Avril and Laura had grown up together. The whole thing seemed too extraordinary. By rights he should be faithful to Avril – but it was not in his nature to be truly faithful. Otherwise he wouldn't have come here tonight.

Laura came back with a tray bearing two small cups of coffee and two glasses of brandy. She set it on the table, kicked off her shoes, and curled up on the sofa. She smiled at him reflectively.

'What?' Philip sat down next to her and picked up one of the glasses of brandy, swirling its contents.

'I was just thinking how utterly in love with you I was when I left Chalcombe that summer. It broke my heart that I couldn't say goodbye to you. I was miserable for weeks.'

'Hmm. I suppose I should feel bad about that.' Philip sipped his brandy, and lifted a stray lock of blonde hair from her eyes with one finger. He gazed at her mouth. It was the most incredibly beautiful mouth he'd ever seen, without a doubt. He kissed her lightly. 'You could easily get your revenge, if you wanted.'

'I don't believe you're that susceptible. Not for a moment.'

'That's wildly unfair. I'm deeply romantic.'

'Not the same thing.'

The record shifted to the next track, and the haunting sounds of 'Let's Fall In Love' drifted across the room. He kissed her again, more intently, and the experience was, he believed, an even bigger trip than last night.

They spent most of Sunday in bed. Laura got up to make a late breakfast of scrambled eggs and coffee, but for the rest of it they lay around talking. Late in the afternoon she rolled a joint.

'This is exceptionally good grass,' remarked Philip, after he had taken a first puff. 'Where did you get it?'

'You should know.'

'Should I?'

'Alec – the chap you were with on Friday. I met him through my friend Cassie. Apparently he can get just about anything you want.'

'He's a very resourceful young man,' said Philip, 'as well as being my dear friend.'

'Well, he's my friend too, now.' Laura shook back her blonde hair and reached out for the joint, pulling the sheet up over her breasts. Philip lay back on the pillow and regarded her dispassionately. She looked ravishing, incredible.

'Do you do a lot of drugs?' he asked.

'God, no. Just a bit of pot. I've seen a few girls wreck themselves with pills, uppers and downers, stuff like that.'

'I'm glad to hear it.' He closed his eyes, feeling an exquisite lightness in his brain and limbs.

They lay in murmured conversation, until at last Philip stubbed out the remains of the joint in the ashtray, rolled over, and tugged the sheet down from her breasts. He kissed her warm skin, feeling the hardening of his own desire. He needn't feel guilty about Avril, he told himself. This was just a little trip, a surreal interlude.

Three days later he telephoned Avril, complaining of boredom and suggesting dinner.

'I can't, I'm afraid,' she told him. 'I'm working flat out on the September exhibition. I honestly don't think I'll be able to come up for air for the next week.'

'You're obsessed with work. I hardly get to see you these days.'

It was no bad thing, in Avril's view, to keep Philip on a long leash. 'Darling, I'm sorry, but I have a living to earn.' It wasn't the first time she had implied that what she did was serious, compared to his dilettantism, and it irked him. 'But you'll come to the opening a week on Monday, won't you? I do miss you.'

'I'll be there,' he sighed.

Since the day Sid had taken those gritty, unlikely photos of her in the streets of Chelsea, Laura had slipped into an increasingly unreal world. She had become a celebrity, a 'face', validated by the simple fact of her beauty, and her fragile sense of self-worth was now dependent on her work as a model. She had told herself she wouldn't get hung up on Philip Carteret, but somehow the teenage feelings she'd had about him couldn't be unlearned. She craved his love and acceptance, needing him to see her as the rest of the world saw her. Surely, after the Sunday they had spent together, he would call her. She waited, but the phone didn't ring.

She had to fly to Rome for a photo shoot, and while she was there she thought obsessively about him, just as she had in the days after leaving Chalcombe. When the shoot came to an end she put through a call to him in London and invited him to fly out and spend the weekend with her.

Philip had had no particular intention of seeing Laura again. But he was fed up being left dangling by Avril, and there was something about the invitation that appealed to his impetuous nature. Jetting off to Rome at the behest of a beautiful woman seemed a rather cool thing to do. Avril and Laura's strange history, and the fact that neither knew about the other, added a certain relish.

Laura was anxious for Philip to be impressed by her world. She planned their three days together carefully, filling them with amusement, with lunches and dinners, shopping, drinks with friends in chic bars. One evening they went to a party thrown by a well-known Italian fashionista, the next to a restaurant frequented by the rich and famous, where she was recognised and welcomed. Her tall, handsome companion drew speculative glances, people trying to place him in their roster of celebrity. Fellini was shooting a film in the city, and Laura and Philip found themselves in the Caffè dell'Epoca drinking with the great director himself, and ending up in a nightclub with Marcello Mastroianni and some other beautiful, nameless people.

'What a delightfully shallow world you do inhabit,' remarked Philip in the taxi on the way back to their hotel. He said it in an amused and not entirely serious way, but his words startled Laura into anxiety.

'I thought you were enjoying yourself.'

'I am. I'm having a delightful time. But have you noticed how beautiful people don't feel they have to try to be intelligent? They think the way they look is enough. I suppose it is, for a while, at any rate.'

Wounded by self-doubt, she ordered champagne in their suite, and did her best to make herself amusing and seductive, to take things back to the place they had been that Sunday two weeks ago. When they were in bed together her anxiety melted away. He couldn't seem to get enough of her. He made love to her several times, and the urgency of his desire reassured her that she must be important to him after all.

She had hoped to spend Monday, their last day in Rome, strolling around the city, just the two of them, stopping for lunch somewhere, then going back to the hotel to make love again before catching their flight home. But Philip had other plans.

'There's an artist I want to visit, to see if I can buy some of his paintings.'

Laura hid her disappointment. 'I don't mind coming along.'

'I'd rather go on my own, if you don't mind. He's not the easiest of men. You might find it something of a bore.'

'How long will you be?'

'It's about an hour on the train. I'll be back by mid-afternoon, I imagine.'

And off he went, leaving Laura to wonder how it was that last night she had felt so desired and cherished, yet today so utterly excluded. She lunched alone in the hotel, angry and hurt, rehearsing various reproachful scenarios for when he returned. But when he did, she realised that a fit of sulking would make no impression, and achieve nothing. He was either unaware that he had done anything selfish, or entirely indifferent to the fact. With a flash of insight she realised that he would never love her. He would always be beyond her reach.

Avril, an untasted glass of champagne in her hand, kept glancing towards the gallery door. She couldn't help it. Much as she was trying to concentrate on her conversation with Lawrence Alloway, the influential art critic whose presence tonight was something of a coup, all she could think about was Philip, and where he was. He had promised he'd be here. The private viewing had started at six thirty, and it was nearly eight now. She should be thrilled that so many people – so many important people – had flocked to the opening of her new op art exhibition, but her anxiety and desolation at Philip's absence seemed to blot out everything else. It frightened her to think that he mattered so much.

'Some people say op art is a mere successor to geometric abstraction, but to me it's far more than that,' she heard Alloway say. 'It's more about illusion and perception.' As she struggled for an adequate response she was rescued by the arrival of *The Times*'s art critic. Alloway turned to him. 'Ah, Gerald. I was just saying, there are definite elements of anamorphosis in some of these works, wouldn't you say?'

Avril slipped away to the office at the back of the gallery. With a sense of desperation she picked up the phone and dialled Philip's number. Then, before the phone could ring at the other end, she hurriedly replaced the receiver. She mustn't become weak – it was a sure way to lose him. Besides, in half an hour the guests would be drifting away, leaving just a deserted gallery and empty champagne glasses. Perhaps he had a good reason. Perhaps he'd simply forgotten. She mustn't let it matter so much – it was only one evening, after all. Stifling her feelings of rejection, she left the office and returned to her guests.

An hour later, when everyone had gone, she helped the caterers to tidy up, then locked up the gallery and went back to Mount Street. She thought about making herself some supper, but had no appetite, so she poured herself a drink and lay on the sofa. In her hopeful mind she could almost hear the buzz of the intercom, and imagine Philip arriving, kissing her, profusely apologetic. But silence stretched out. In the end she couldn't resist it. She went to the hall and rang Philip's number, having decided that she would keep it light and casual. '*You missed a good party,'* she would say. Or, *'Darling, I'm sorry you couldn't make it, but the evening was something of a triumph, even though I say so myself. Why don't you come over for a drink? It isn't too late.'* Something along those lines. But the phone simply rang and rang at the other end, and in the end there was nothing to do but go to bed, alone and unhappy. And a little bit afraid.

A few days later Philip and Alec were sitting in Philip's flat listening to Booker T, drinking Scotch and smoking dope.

'Where were you last weekend?' asked Alec. 'You missed a couple of good parties.'

'I was in Rome,' replied Philip, 'with a girl.'

'Oh.' Alec regarded him with interest. 'Not Avril?'

Philip shook his head. He felt mellow, and a little drunk. He was in the mood to be indiscreet. 'Someone you know, actually. Laura Fenton.'

'Oh, the model. Very dishy. So, does that mean you and Avril are yesterday's news? Or have you just been playing away?'

'The latter.'

Alec smiled. 'You dog.'

'Actually, shall I tell you something extraordinary?'

'What?'

'They grew up together. Avril and Laura Fenton.

Laura was illegitimate and Avril's mother took her in, adopted her or something. They fell out a few years ago, haven't spoken since.'

'How very peculiar.' Alec smoked reflectively for a moment. 'Sleeping with them both sounds vaguely incestuous, if you ask me.'

'What's interesting is how different they are – each has something to offer that the other doesn't.'

'Some people would call your behaviour a tad reprehensible,' observed Alec.

'I know.' Philip finished his drink, and got up to change the music. 'I've no intention of carrying it on. The weekend just happened. Avril was busy with her exhibition…' He paused. 'Oh God.'

'What?'

'It opened on Monday. I was meant to be there.' He gave a groan.

'Oh, dear. She won't be best pleased.' Alec inspected the end of the joint, which had gone out. 'Still, as long as she doesn't find out what you were doing.' He drained his Scotch. He'd had very little to eat all day and was feeling hungry. 'Come on, leave the music. Let's go out and get dinner.' Philip wouldn't mind paying. He never did.

As they left the flat it occurred to Alec, reflecting on what he'd just been told, that there might be some fun to be had out of all this. Philip really should learn not to behave like a cad.

'You know what?' he said as they walked to the corner in search of a cab. 'You should have a party.'

Philip thought of ringing Avril to apologise, but knew it would be better done in person. He went to the gallery the very next day. Her expression when she saw him was cold.

'Please, will you let me explain?' said Philip. 'Listen, I'm sorry I didn't make it on Monday. I can't tell you how sorry. I went to Rome for a few days. I forgot. It's as simple as that.' She said nothing. 'But I hear the show's a fantastic success. Well done.'

'What was in Rome that was so important?'

'I went to buy some paintings from an artist who lives there. Look, let me take you to dinner tonight.'

She looked away. 'I can't believe you forgot.'

'I know. I hate myself.'

'That's one thing you're incapable of.'

'You're right. You know me so well.' He pulled her gently towards him and kissed her. 'But I am truly sorry.' She sighed, and he could tell she was relenting. 'Shall I call for you at eight?'

Avril hadn't intended to let him know how badly let down she'd felt. She'd wanted to be able to shrug his non-appearance off with a careless smile, as though it hardly mattered. But she was incapable of dissembling. She loved him too much. She was so utterly in love with him that she had almost been shaking with relief when she saw him come into the gallery.

'If you like.'

After dinner that evening they went back to Ebury Street.

'Let's have a look at these paintings that meant more to you than coming to my opening,' said Avril.

Two canvases were propped against the table, their wrappings still scattered on the floor. She examined the pictures, then nodded in approval. 'Cy Twombly. I saw some of his paintings in New York a few years ago. Some people don't care for his work, but I think he's going to do well. What I wouldn't give to exhibit him.'

'In that case,' said Philip, 'they're yours.'

'Don't be silly.'

'Seriously. To make up for my thoughtlessness. I'll have them framed.' He turned her to face him, and kissed her. 'And this weekend we can go down to Boxgrove and be together, just the two of us. Yes?'

'Yes,' she murmured, entirely happy.

23

AT TWENTY-FOUR, MAX recognised that it was probably time to find a place of his own. He'd never seen the need to move out of his aunt's house in Kensington until now. Life was comfortable there, and unlike Alec, who lived in a shambolic flat in Markham Square, he didn't have a lifestyle that involved endless parties and staying out till four in the morning. While Alec was carving a hustling reputation for himself on the fringes of the art world, rubbing shoulders with fashionable people, befriending anyone who looked like they might become someone, Max was diligently building up his fledgling practice at the criminal bar. His life was humdrum compared to Alec's. But when his aunt pointed out to him that the trust would advance him money to buy a flat, the idea grew in attraction. He spent a couple of weeks going through estate agents' details and viewing properties, until he finally found a ground-floor flat in Pimlico that he liked. He told Diana over dinner one evening.

'Pimlico?' Diana raised an eyebrow. 'Rather scruffy. I hope it's the Sloane Square end.'

'It's sort of in the middle, actually. But I like it.'

'You're moving out?' Morven stared at her cousin in dismay. Now twenty-one, she was tall and slender, with long, silky red hair and milky skin dusted with freckles. She had her mother's arresting blue eyes and her father's remarkable bone structure. 'Why didn't you say something? We could have got a place together. Think how much fun that would be.'

Max privately disagreed. He knew the chaos in which Morven lived. She was presently at drama school, and her life seemed to be a mess of parties and pubs, mixed up with a variety of boyfriends who came and went. Acting was the only thing she took seriously, with all the wild intensity of her personality.

'I'll leave you two to clear up,' said Diana, rising from the table. 'I have things to do. You and I can talk to the lawyers tomorrow, Max.'

'Honestly,' said Morven, when her mother had left the room, 'you should have told me. I'd love to have shared a place with you. Anything to get away from here.'

She adored Max, probably because his nature was in such utter contrast to her own. He had a steady kind of uprightness to him, and he was so dependable and sweetly serious. And the way he looked. She wasn't sure what the position was about having such a huge crush on one's cousin.

'I don't think it would have worked,' said Max. 'Besides, it's only a one-bedroom place.'

'Hmm. Anyway, I'd probably just have got wildly jealous of all your girlfriends.'

'I don't have much time for girlfriends.' He wondered if Morven had touched this raw nerve on purpose.

She leaned her head on her hand and regarded him. 'I don't understand it. You must be the most attractive man in London. All my friends think so. Didn't you have a girlfriend at Cambridge?'

'One or two.' This wasn't strictly true. There had been Veronica, who had studied English at Girton, and with whom he'd gone out a few times. He'd thought her objectively very attractive, but there hadn't really been much of a spark. She'd been much keener than he was, but beyond a few kisses nothing had happened. Things had just petered out. He suspected she'd given up in disgust. He baffled himself sometimes – but with romantic conviction he put it all down to Laura, enshrined in his heart as his grand passion. It was reassuring, too, that Alec didn't seem to be bothered with having a girlfriend, though there were always plenty of women hanging around him. They were both just too busy. That was what he told himself.

'You just *have* to get a girlfriend, Max. It's a dreadful

waste, otherwise.' Morven picked at the remains of the apple pie crust on her plate. 'That reminds me, someone called Philip Carteret is having a party on Saturday night. Do you want to come? Apparently it's going to be very cool. Just about anyone who's anyone is going to be there. I heard that Marlon Brando's coming. It's invitation only.' She smiled sweetly. 'But I'm sure I can wangle you one.'

'Thanks, I've already got one from Alec. We were at school with Philip.' He got to his feet. 'Come on, help me clear this lot. I've got to go through notes for my case tomorrow.'

'What a serious life you do lead.' Morven began to pile their plates together. 'Maybe you can let your hair down a bit on Saturday.'

On Saturday night Alec and Philip were conducting a little business at Philip's flat, ahead of the party.

'There you go.' Alec handed Philip a small plastic pot of pills. 'Twenty-four Mandrax. How are you off for grass?'

'I've still got the rest of the stash you sold me a fortnight ago.'

'Right, in that case I'll split.' Alec got to his feet. 'All set for tonight?'

'Avril has everything under control.' Philip lay back on the sofa. 'She's got the booze all laid on and the caterers coming in an hour.'

'So it's all cool between you two?'

'Seems that way.' He gave Alec a quizzical look. 'Are you sure about Brando?'

'He's Michael and Orla's house guest. They said they'd bring him.' Alec glanced at his watch. 'Anyway, Terence Stamp and his girlfriend are definitely coming. I've signed up most of swinging London for this party, cock.'

An hour later Alec was sprawled on the sofa in Laura's living room, sharing a joint with two of Laura's girlfriends. Laura came in from the bedroom, barefoot, wearing a Pucci dress in clinging blue jersey silk, unzipped at the back. She picked up her drink from the coffee table and said to Alec, 'Zip me up, would you?'

Alec rose and zipped up the dress. 'Is this your homage to Marilyn, then?'

Laura swallowed the remains of her drink. 'What d'you mean?'

'They buried her in her favourite Pucci dress three months ago, darling – one just like this, but in green.'

Laura looked horrified. 'Oh, God.' She left the room and returned a few moments later, this time in a backless black lace Balenciaga shift dress.

'Better?'

'Oh, wow,' said one of the girls, 'it's so unfair that you get all these stunning clothes.'

'Perk of the job.' She turned to Alec. 'Not worn by any dead film stars?'

'None that I know of.' He stood up, handed the remains of the joint to Laura, and clapped his hands. 'Come on, girls, let's get going. The party should be well under way by now, and we're all nicely primed.'

The tone set for the party was, at Philip's insistence, essentially formal. He knew the evening had the potential to end up being wild, but in his view even decadence should have the underpinnings of taste and style. At one end of the vast living room the lights were low and people were lounging on the floor on large cushions, smoking grass, while at the other end copious amounts of alcohol fuelled noisy conversations and loud bursts of laughter. The sound of Etta James spilled from the hi-fi console. Alec had, almost in the role of Philip's manager, issued invitations to most of fashionable London. To his satisfaction just about everyone he'd invited was here: writers, pop stars, actors and actresses mingling with London's well-heeled upper crust. In these egalitarian times old money was rubbing shoulders with new, classless talent, and they all seemed to be enjoying themselves enormously.

Alec, in his trademark dark-tinted glasses, and wearing a new Huntsman suit and Mr Fish shirt, shouldered his way through the hubbub in search of a drink. When he'd secured himself a whisky and Coke he went over to join Max and Morven, who were chatting with friends. Morven clutched his sleeve in excitement.

'Is that really Marlon Brando? I honestly didn't believe it when I heard he was going to be here.'

'Yes,' replied Alec. 'He staying with the people I work for.'

'Oh my God... do you actually know him? Could you introduce me? I'd love to talk to him about Stanislavsky.'

'If you like.' Alec took a swig of his drink. 'He's quite boring, actually.'

Max gave a loud laugh. He'd had a few rum and Cokes and was feeling quite drunk, infected by the mood of the evening. 'Philip's got a hell of a crowd here tonight,' he said. 'I saw Peter Cook a moment ago.'

'All thanks to me,' murmured Alec, then said to Morven, 'If you want to meet Mr Brando, come on.'

Avril was worried about Philip. He looked serene enough, chatting to his friends from the new Clermont Club, but he was definitely high. Why tonight of all nights? She'd like to be able to blame that little shyster Alec, with his endless supply of pills and grass, but the problem was really Philip's. Too much money, too much time on his hands. She left the people she was talking to and made her way over to him.

Laura, mildly stoned and on her second glass of champagne, was in a determined frame of mind. She hadn't heard from Philip since their weekend in Rome three weeks ago. Not so much as a phone call. She'd resisted the urge to ring him herself, knowing it would be entirely the wrong move, and had instead confided in Alec, hoping, since he was close to Philip, that he might have some idea of what Philip was playing at. Alec, mischievously sympathetic, had suggested the best thing would be to come to the party tonight and take things from there. She was too infatuated with Philip to care that he hadn't invited her himself, so here she was, scanning the room in search of him, trying to ignore Sid very blatantly chatting up some woman a few feet away. It was then, with a shock of recognition, that she saw Avril crossing the room. She looked poised and confident as ever, and quite lovely now, in her dark, intimidating way. Laura felt a rush of mixed emotions. Leaving Mount Street six years ago had been an escape from many things, but she felt she had to speak to her, to try and put things right after all this time.

Philip was feeling more out of it than he wanted to. Maybe he should have listened to Alec about mixing the Mandies with alcohol. He put down his glass of wine and was about to go and get himself a soft drink, when he saw Laura. What was she doing here? Then he saw Avril heading towards him, Laura towards Avril. Their impending convergence had a horrible kind of slow motion quality.

Making her way through the press of people to Avril,

Laura didn't see Philip. She laid a hand on Avril's arm and spoke her name. Avril's first thought, as she turned round, was how heart-twistingly beautiful Laura looked. The second thought was how much she had always detested that smile of hers. But she returned Laura's kiss, suppressing the familiar feelings of antagonism. She had no reason now to resent Laura, or her beauty. She had her life, her own success, and Philip.

'I'd been hoping we might meet like this,' said Laura. 'It's been such a long time.'

'Hasn't it?' murmured Avril. She had no wish for a sentimental reunion. 'What a surprise to see you here tonight. Who did you come with?'

'Alec Orr-Lowndes. Do you know him?'

'Oh, yes, we all know Alec.' She saw Philip a few feet away. 'Ah, here's Philip.' She was keen to let Laura know she had acquired one of London's most eligible men. She stroked Philip's sleeve proprietorially. 'Do you know our host?'

Laura looked at Philip, hating him for standing there with that blank look on his face, as though there was nothing between them. He wasn't going to get away with it. 'Know him? We spent the most divine weekend together in Rome not so long ago, just the two of us.' She kissed him on the mouth. 'Didn't we, darling?'

Avril was aware of the heads of people nearby turning, of voices falling silent. She felt as though the room were pressing in on her. There was nothing to say. Nothing at all. She walked away, moving quickly through the crowd. Someone on the other side of the room accidentally turned up the volume on the hi-fi, and for a few seconds Sam Cooke's 'Twistin' The Night Away' blasted out, before it was turned down again.

'What did I say?' Laura asked Philip.

Philip gave her a dazed glance and set off after Avril. God, he wished he didn't feel so damned woozy. What a mess.

Laura watched him go. Through the dope and champagne haze the penny slowly dropped. The look in Avril's eyes, her hand on Philip's sleeve, the tone of her voice as she'd been about to introduce him. They way she'd reacted when she'd said that thing about spending the weekend in Rome with him. Was he seeing Avril? Had he truly, actually been sleeping with both of them? If she hadn't cared so much about him, it would have made her laugh. What a bastard.

Philip could see no sign of Avril in the crowded hallway. She must have left. He knew he should go after her, but he felt too spaced-out. He should feel ashamed of what he'd done to her, but he didn't. Things happened for a reason.

He wandered back into the drawing room and made his way to the end where people were sitting around, passing a joint. He loosened his bow tie and settled himself on the floor against one of the big cushions, and closed his eyes.

Max was on his way to fetch another drink when he saw Laura. She was standing somewhat forlornly, holding an empty champagne glass. He shouldered his way across the room and touched her arm, and she turned to look at him. He had always imagined that when they met again it would be heart-stopping, but to his surprise he felt nothing. She was still as lovely as she'd always been, but in a painful moment of insight he realised that for years he had been spinning a fantasy, one that had begun that summer afternoon on the train to Chalcombe, when he'd been so struck by her beauty. Being entranced by beauty wasn't anything to do with love, he realised. There was nothing real between them except some shared experience. Everything else had been made up.

Laura stared at him bleakly. 'God, my past really is haunting me tonight. First Avril, now you.'

'It's good to see you again,' Max said, wondering if it really was. 'How are you?'

'I thought you'd damaged my life beyond repair, Max. But as you see, I'm managing. What are you up to these days? Living the life of a little rich boy?'

'I don't come into my money till next year.' He felt the words sounded ridiculous. 'I'm a lawyer now, a barrister. What about you?'

She gave a wry smile. 'I don't suppose you look at women's magazines very often, do you? I'm a model.'

He nodded. 'That makes sense.'

There was a silence, and then she said, 'There, we've done the polite small talk. You remember the things I said to you last time I saw you? When I slapped your face?' He assumed she was about to make an attempt to bury the past, and smiled in readiness, but she went on, 'If it weren't for the fact we're in the middle of this party, I'd say them all again. And I'd slap you even harder.' She turned and walked away. Seeing him had made the years fall away, bringing memories of Ellis surging back, making the pain fresh again.

Max stood rooted to the spot. He was glad he was a little drunk, because it blunted the edge of his humiliation. She still hated him. That much hadn't changed. But everything else had. He knocked back his drink in one. He wanted to be even drunker, to dull the sense of emptiness, so he got himself another and wandered into the hallway in search of Alec. He had to talk to someone.

Alec caught sight of Max looking somewhat the worse for wear. He detached himself from the group of people he was talking to, and drew him into the doorway of the room that housed Philip's collection of paintings.

'You OK?' he asked. 'You look pie-eyed.'

'I just met this girl I used to know. Laura.'

Alec blinked behind his dark-tinted glasses. What a spectacularly weird evening of connections. 'Fenton?'

Max nodded. 'You know her?'

'Sort of.'

'The thing is, for years I've thought I was in love with her. But it's all been in my head. There's nothing there. I saw her just now, and all the things I've been waiting to feel didn't happen. I mean, I've always told myself she was the reason I couldn't make it with any girl, because it was all about her.'

Alec stared at his friend. Poor guy. He thought back to stuff that had gone on at school; for some boys it had just been a way of channelling sexual feelings, for those like himself it had been a recognition of their true natures. Clearly Max had failed to realise it about himself. Was it possible that he understood Max better than Max himself?

He put a hand on his friend's shoulder. He'd always envied Max his looks, his athletic physique. But in that moment he didn't, not at all. Max had so little self-awareness, there was almost nothing to him. On impulse he kicked the door shut, put a hand on Max's neck, and kissed him on the mouth. He felt Max's resistance, but he made the kiss as passionate as possible, forcing his tongue into Max's mouth, holding him hard. The tension in Max suddenly fell away, and he responded, returning the kiss with an intensity that told Alec he was doing it in spite of himself. Then he pulled away, breathing hard, staring angrily at Alec.

'What the hell was that?'

Alec shrugged. 'Work it out for yourself.' He opened the door and left the room. Max leaned against the wall, drunk, angry, and bewildered.

Alec went back to the drawing room. He saw Laura threading her way through the guests to where Philip lay sprawled against the cushions, and watched her sink down next to him and rest her head on his shoulder. Philip opened his eyes, smiled faintly, and closed them again.

Alec lit a cigarette and gazed at the pair. Well, well. It seemed Philip's bad deeds would go unpunished after all. Not quite the result he'd anticipated. He would have expected any woman who'd found out her lover had been cheating on her to react in quite a different fashion. The way Avril had, in fact. Women were strange creatures. Still, it had been an interesting piece of mischief. And he'd never liked that bitch Avril, anyway.

24

THE FALLOUT FROM the party was painful for Max, particularly the realisation that his feelings for Laura had been nothing more than a fiction he had created to shield himself from reality. But he wasn't sure what that reality was. The encounter with Alec confused him even more. He tried to write it off as drunken horseplay, but the memory of it, his feelings of arousal, burned in his mind. Alec, of all people. When he thought about him, he felt nothing beyond what he had always felt. Fondness, but certainly no desire. The notion of desiring another man was revolting. So what had happened?

He and Alec met for a drink a few days later. After ten minutes of inconsequential chat Alec went to put a record on the jukebox, and when he came back Max said, 'Listen, there's something I need to talk to you about.' Alec guessed what was coming. 'That thing you did at the party. I can't get it out of my head.'

'Yeah, well – worse things have happened. We were all a bit high, one way or another. Just forget about it.'

Alec had done a good deal of thinking himself since that night. He knew Max better than anyone else, but he couldn't honestly put his hand on his heart and say that he was queer. Not the way Alec knew himself to be. If he were to tell Max one tenth of what he got up to – about the Moroccan he was currently bedding, for instance – he would be appalled, disgusted. So what did that say about Max? Whatever he was – and Alec guessed he might very possibly be one of those asexual people who drifted through life without any particular desire for anyone of either sex – he knew that Max couldn't begin to survive in the homosexual milieu of London. In fact, it was imperative that he be kept well away from it. He himself skirted danger regularly in the queer world; the police turned a blind eye more often than not to what went on, but prosecutions were not unknown. Max could do without any of that, and if truth be told, Alec couldn't really imagine him in a relationship with another man. He was an enigma, but he needed to solve his own riddle.

'The thing is,' Max went on, 'I'm wondering if there might be something wrong with me.' It was hard for him to articulate this, even to a friend he had known intimately for years.

'In what way?' Alec regarded Max with bemusement.

'To be honest, when you did that, it made me feel something. And that rather disgusts me.'

Alec drew a deep breath. 'Look, I was drunk, I did something stupid, and I'm relieved you're still speaking to me. Just put it out of your mind. There's nothing wrong with you. You need to get yourself a girl. Plenty around, God knows.' Alec regarded him with detachment. 'OK?'

'OK.' Max shrugged, and gave his friend a smile. He was right. Alec had reassured him, as he'd hoped he would. It had been nothing. Not worth thinking about.

'Good. Now get another round in.'

Alec saw two girls giving Max blatantly admiring glances as he walked to the bar. He felt he'd said entirely the right thing. As he saw it, Max could be exactly the kind of person he wanted to be, and lead the blameless life he wanted to lead. It was just a question of effort.

Avril moved through the days that followed the party in a dark trance of misery and anger. She immersed herself in work, mechanically preparing for the next exhibition while feeling hollowed out inside. She had loved Philip, she had given herself to him in a way she never had to any other man, believing entirely in him and their future together. What a fool she'd been. That he had polluted everything by having an affair with Laura, of all people, was devastating to her. The thought of the two of them together, making love, laughing at her – as she believed they must have done – robbing her of everything she thought was hers, twisted itself like a blade in her heart.

And yet a part of her waited and hoped for him to call. All he had to do was tell her that Laura meant nothing, that he couldn't believe what an idiot he'd been and that he needed her forgiveness, and she would relent. She knew she would. In some ways, that was the worst of it. Being in love with Philip had left her entirely abject. But there was nothing she could do to retrieve him. She clung to the belief that if she showed any sign of weakness, she would lose the last possibility of his love, if she hadn't lost it already. He had to come to her.

But the phone call never came, and at Christmas time a few weeks later, drifting on the wind with the rest of London's gossip, came the news that Laura had moved in with Philip. Every feeling she had ever had about Laura, every childhood resentment and petty jealousy, now fused into hate. The poison that had infected her life, but which she hoped had dissipated when Laura left Mount Street, flooded her system once again. She reserved it all for Laura; she still loved Philip too much to hate him, whatever he might have done.

'Moving in was her idea, not mine,' Philip told Alec. 'Not that I mind.' He lit a cigarette. 'Much.'

Alec padded barefoot across the white shagpile carpet of his living room. Although it was early evening he still hadn't cleared up from the night before, and the place was the usual chaos of bottles, overflowing ashtrays and empty record sleeves. He managed to find a couple of clean glasses, poured out two hefty measures of Scotch, and handed one to Philip.

'Anyway, it's not as though she's hanging about the place all the time,' Philip went on. 'Most days she's up first thing, off to some godforsaken location to hang about waiting for people to take pictures of her in silly clothes, then back late.'

'Careful she doesn't marry you.'

'No chance of that.'

Alec settled himself in an armchair. 'She's good for your image, at any rate. Makes you look like less of a stuffed shirt to have the most glamorous model in London as your live-in girlfriend.'

'You have this vulgar propensity to see everything in PR terms.'

Alec smiled and shrugged. 'It's what you pay me for. Laura Fenton's going to be very good for publicity when the gallery opens. She gives you certain swinging credentials you otherwise lack.'

'True,' murmured Philip. Every time he thought about his gallery project it gave him a warm surge of pleasure. He hadn't felt enthusiasm like this in a long time. He had Alec to thank for nourishing the idea, making him believe he could actually make a commercial success of exhibiting and selling the works he had collected over the years. It was Alec, too, who had found the premises in South Audley Street and then worked tirelessly on image and detail, commissioning a radical young designer to plan the look of the place, the stark white interior lit by carefully angled spotlights. The result was going to be a complete departure from established Mayfair galleries. There had been a bit of an argument over the frontage, but he'd given in and had to concede that Alec was right – the black exterior with the word **carteret** in white letters over the door captured the spirit of the times perfectly. There were just five days to go till the opening evening.

'I want you to know I've sweated blood over that invitation list,' said Alec. 'Every art critic in London is going to be there.'

'I'm eternally grateful. You've worked very hard. We both have.' He glanced at his watch. He'd promised to take Laura out to dinner. But somehow he wasn't in the mood to trot dutifully back to Ebury Street. He drained his Scotch. 'Go and put your shoes on,' he told Alec. 'Let's go out and score, and then find a club. I feel like having some fun.'

When Laura went into the bedroom next morning just before noon, Philip was still fast asleep. She gazed at him in irritation. When she'd been vaguely aware of him coming back in the early hours, she'd had to resist the urge to put on the light and ask him where he'd been. Now she rattled back the curtains and began tidying clothes away, loudly opening and closing drawers to wake him up.

He groaned and rolled over. 'Jesus Christ, do you have to?'

She forced a smile. 'Sorry, darling, I thought you'd be awake by now.' She dropped a kiss on his forehead. 'I'll make you some tea.'

She went through to the kitchen. His selfishness in staying out last night when he'd promised to take her to dinner made her want to howl with rage, but there was no point in reproaching him. That wasn't the way things worked between them. He could wound her in a hundred small ways, but to try to retaliate was pointless. He simply didn't care enough. The balance in the relationship was all wrong, but there was nothing she could do about it, except try to remain cool and sexy and nonchalant, the way he liked. She had hoped that moving in with him, becoming a part of his existence, might create a better equilibrium between them, but the opposite seemed to have happened.

She put the kettle on and reached for the tea caddy. It was from Fortnum & Mason, exactly like the one Aunt Sonia had brought with her from Woodbourne House to Mount Street, the same shade of duck egg blue. She spooned tea into the pot, conjuring up memories, and was struck by the sad realisation that ever since Aunt Sonia's death she had been wandering around looking for love and acceptance. Finding it, then losing it. She thought of Ellis with a familiar wrench of sadness. How she had loved him. But was this neediness she felt around Philip really love? She had no idea. All she knew was that he was part of the habit, that her present happiness lay in gaining his attention and approval. She was weak, far weaker than Avril. When she'd found out on the night of the party the game Philip had been playing, she should have walked away, just as Avril had. But she hadn't. She wanted Philip too badly, in a way she didn't quite understand.

She heard the sound of the bath running, and took a mug of tea through to the bathroom, where Philip was shaving, a towel around his waist. He gave her a glance in the mirror, but didn't acknowledge the tea as she set it down. She caught sight of her reflection, and the way she looked reassured her, reminding her of what he saw, what everyone saw. Sometimes her beauty felt like her only strength. Sure enough, just as he was wiping the soap from his face, Philip grabbed her wrist and drew her against him. She let him kiss her for a long moment, feeling his arousal.

'Christ, you're sexy,' he murmured. 'Come back to bed.'

She drew away from him, enjoying this brief instant in which the balance was tipped in her favour. 'No. Have your bath. Then you're taking me to lunch to make up for last night.'

He picked up his razor and rinsed it. 'No can do, I'm afraid. I'm meeting Alec at the gallery in an hour.'

She felt a flare of anger. Not about lunch, but about the fact that his terms dictated everything, always.

'Oh, the bloody gallery! I'm sick of hearing about it!' She cast around for some hurtful truth to throw at him. 'I sometimes think you're only doing it to spite Avril.'

This was a mistake. On the one previous occasion when she had brought Avril's name up, a few weeks after the party, it had prompted a furious outburst from Philip in which he'd forbidden her to mention Avril again, ever. It was the only time he had shouted at her.

He turned to her now and said coldly, 'I told you – I don't want you to speak about her.' The nerve she had hit was a raw one. Complicated motives lay behind the fact that he was competing directly with Avril. He was unable to unravel them, aware only that in destroying his relationship with her by his affair with Laura, he had lost something valuable, more valuable than he had known at the time. Turning himself into a competitor, operating on her territory, was a weirdly hostile form of maintaining a bond with her.

'You still haven't got over her, have you? That's what the gallery's all about. I know it is.' Laura couldn't stop herself from articulating her deepest fear. In a way she hoped he would explode, then she would at least feel capable of arousing some passion in him beyond mere sexual desire. But he simply looked at her, his expression tight and closed.

'You know precisely nothing. Now, if you don't mind, I'd like to take my bath.' He steered her gently out of the bathroom and closed the door, locking it.

She stood there in the hall, excluded, helpless. He always managed to do this. Maybe she should leave. Just pack her stuff up and go, show him that not everything operated on his terms. But whether she left or stayed, she knew it would make no difference to his feelings about her. If she was there at the end of the day he would accept her presence with his usual insouciance, take her to bed, and think no more about it. If she wasn't there, it wouldn't bother him in the slightest. So she would stay, of course.

The following week, in late January, Philip's gallery opened to glowing reviews. Avril, deeply wounded and betrayed, hadn't intended to look at any of them, but she accidentally came across a piece in *The Times*, with a picture of Laura and Philip at the opening, and read the first few lines before she could help herself.

Mr Philip Carteret's new gallery at 60 South Audley Street opened with a flourish last night, exhibiting in its high, wide and well-lit rooms the work of some of the most exciting names in British and American modern art. The gallery's ground-breaking inventiveness looks set to reinvigorate the London art scene, and its fresh, contemporary style was reflected in the eclectic group that thronged its opening last night. All seemed enthralled by the spontaneity and diversity of the works on display...

Avril stopped reading. She felt sick with the thought that he'd invaded her world with such sudden success.

Two weeks later she sent Flavia to South Audley Street to bring back a catalogue. She studied it in her office, and saw that the two Cy Twombly paintings which Philip had promised her were included for sale. So much for his love. They had been purchased the weekend he had gone to Rome, the weekend she now knew he had spent with Laura. She couldn't bear to think about it. She must simply wait for time to lessen the pain. But with Philip encroaching on her own territory, with pictures of him and Laura everywhere, and pieces about them in every gossip column, looking like the perfect couple, it felt as though the wound would never heal.

25

1963

I꜀T ꜀ᴡᴀꜱ Aʟᴇᴄ who introduced Philip to heroin. After smoking it one weekend at the home of a musician friend, he was soon enthusiastically promoting its virtues to Philip.

'It's more than wonderful. It's the best high ever.'

'I'm not doing stuff I could get hooked on,' said Philip.

'What? You think you can't get hooked on all those bennies you drop? No one gets addicted to stuff unless they want to. I took it last Friday and I haven't exactly been roaming the streets in search of another fix. I can't wait to do it again, though. It's the most amazing rush. This friend of mine gets some Harley Street doctor to write prescriptions for him. BP, he calls it. British Pharmaceutical. Isn't that a great name?' With his usual enthusiasm, Alec had wasted no time in acquainting himself fully with his subject.

'I'm absolutely not sticking needles into myself,' said Philip.

'You don't have to. You can smoke it.' There was a pause; Alec could tell Philip wasn't convinced. 'Look, I'll bring some round tomorrow evening. You won't turn into a drug addict overnight, I promise.'

Philip, his curiosity fired by Alec's ecstatic descriptions of the drug, agreed. When he told Laura, she was horrified.

'Why? You do enough grass and pills without getting into hard drugs.'

'Because I have an eternally questing spirit. You don't need to be here if you don't want to be.'

'Fine, I'll go out. I can't believe Alec is so stupid. Or you.'

Alec duly came round the next evening, and Philip smoked his first pipe of heroin, and fell in love. He bought Alec's line that this was something he could take or leave, maybe indulge in as a blissful weekly treat. He liked the fact that, unlike too much alcohol or Benzedrine, there was no miserable, dirty hangover at the other side. Simply a mellow memory of how good it had been to feel that way, and, of course, wanting to feel that way again. He began to use it a few times a week, far more than Alec, whose survival instincts and careful financial habits kept him in check.

Philip and Laura were now finding their lives shaped by the frenetic pace of the social scene they so prominently inhabited. The frailty of their relationship was rarely tested in private, because they spent most of their time in the company of other people. London in the early sixties was an exciting place to be, buzzing and alive with change. Laura worked constantly. Her face shone from magazine covers and advertising hoardings, and every girl longed to look like her. She lived in the moment, never daring to ask herself if she was happy, soothing her insecurities about Philip by believing in the projected image of them as a cool and dazzling couple.

Philip, as the owner of London's trendiest art gallery, found himself in a disorienting social vortex, his upper-class circle distended to include the unlikeliest people. The scruffy band he used to go to see in Soho were now rich and famous, and had somehow become his friends. In fact, he seemed to have acquired any number of new friends, although half the time he had no idea where they came from. They bought paintings from him, they came to his parties, and they took drugs with him, drifting through the flat by day and night, soaking up his hospitality, joking about his patrician voice and manner, but impressed, too, by his wealth and style.

All that spring and summer Philip and Laura bathed in the glow of their own celebrity, careless of the future. Like all good things, it couldn't last.

Despite the gallery's success, there were conservative elements in the art world that regarded Philip's unorthodox exhibitions as dangerous and decadent. Philip responded to this criticism by becoming increasingly bold in his selections, but it backfired on him when he exhibited a series of collages by a German artist that were ostensibly innocuous but which, on minute examination, contained depictions of female genitalia. The sixties youth cult might be shaping the future, but public sensibilities were still deeply rooted in conservatism and more than capable of being outraged by any hint of sexual display. The police arrived at the gallery one morning and seized the greater part of the show, together with the catalogues, and Philip found himself the subject of a prosecution under the Obscene Publications Act.

A couple of months earlier he would have met the police actions with cool amusement, paid the twenty guinea fine, and translated the event into positive publicity. But drugs were rubbing raw the volatile side of his personality – by now he was using heroin on a daily basis – and when he informed the officer in charge of the raid that 'the last person who should decide what the British public sees in an art gallery is a fucking little oik copper like you', he did himself no favours. An old Etonian with a patrician manner and lofty contempt for honest constables only doing their job was exactly the kind of person the police would take great pleasure in bringing down.

A month later, when the court proceedings were over and the fine paid and forgotten, Philip and Laura and a few friends, including Alec, went to Philip's cottage in Boxgrove for the weekend. At around nine in the evening, when a few joints of marijuana had been consumed by some, acid by others, and a considerable amount of red wine by all, Alec took himself off to the loo for a pee. He was passing through the hallway when, through the window to the side of the front door, he saw headlights swing through the gates and up the short driveway, following by the headlights of yet another car. With his unerring instinct for self-preservation, Alec doubled back to the loo, took two tabs of acid from his pocket, and dropped them into the pan. The cistern, having been flushed only a moment ago, was still filling.

'Come on, come on,' he muttered, staring at the floating tabs, listening to the agonisingly slow trickling of the water in the tank, waiting for the moment when it would be safe to flush again. Just as he pulled the chain there came a hammering on the front door. As he emerged to see Philip crossing the hall to answer it, he realised he still had a small bag of marijuana remnants in his pocket. He did the only thing he could and slipped the bag into the pocket of one of the coats hanging in the hallway, just as Philip was opening the door to the chief inspector of Surrey CID and several uniformed policemen.

The chief inspector nodded politely to Philip.

'Good evening, sir. We have a warrant to search these premises for illegal drugs.' He held out the warrant. Philip took it wordlessly. 'So, if you wouldn't mind…?' The chief inspector gestured to the policemen and they filed in. Philip watched, stunned and aghast.

Over the next twenty minutes they conducted a thorough search of the cottage and everyone's belongings. They found some tabs of acid and a quantity of marijuana, including some in a small plastic bag in the pocket of Laura's raincoat hanging in the hall. One of the constables came downstairs with a container of pills that he'd found in Philip's bedside cabinet.

'Can you tell me what these are, sir?' the chief inspector asked Philip, indicating the container.

'They're prescribed by my doctor for a stomach complaint.'

The constable tipped a few of the pills into his hand and sniffed them. Alec, watching from a few feet away, recognised them as jacks of heroin.

'My dear fellow,' murmured Philip, 'I can assure you there's absolutely nothing to them.'

The chief inspector, hard-nosed, experienced copper that he was, had no intention of letting Philip charm his way out of this. His friends in London had worked hard to get this tip-off, and he was here to make sure this condescending git got his collar well and truly felt.

'I doubt it,' he said grimly. 'Take the whole lot for analysis.' He turned to the assembled company. 'Thank you for your cooperation, ladies and gentlemen. A few of you may be hearing from us once our lab has carried out its tests. Until then, I'll bid you a good evening.'

The policemen trooped out.

'Jesus, what a drag,' muttered someone. People disappeared to various parts of the house, some to bedrooms, others to the kitchen to make tea. Alec sat down in a chair and ran his fingers through his hair.

Laura, sitting at one end of the sofa, began to cry. 'I don't even know how that stuff got into my pocket. Someone must have put it there.' She looked up at Philip. 'Do you think the police did it? Why would they do that to me? Am I going to go to prison?'

'I have no fucking idea,' replied Philip. He was white-faced. 'And I don't frankly care. You do realise that they've taken my heroin? They took it all. Where am I going to find any more out here at this time of night?'

He stood up and left the room. Alec slopped the remains of a bottle of red wine into a glass and drank it off.

'My God,' said Laura, 'I had no idea it was that bad. Is he really so desperate?'

'You live with him. I thought you knew.' Alec got to his feet. 'He uses two or three times a day, stupid sod.'

Laura stared at him. 'You're the reason he started in the first place.'

'Don't try and blame me.'

'Don't you care?'

'About Philip? About as much as he cares about me, I suppose. Or about you.' Alec took off his glasses and rubbed his eyes. 'Don't you get it? Philip is all about Philip. Everyone else is on their own.'

He left the room and went upstairs to bed. Bad luck that it had been Laura's coat pocket, but the thing was done now. She would have to ride it out, just like Philip. People had to deal with the predicaments they found themselves in.

Laura sat on her own for a while, little waves of panic washing over her. Life felt suddenly bleak and real, all the shine and fun stripped away. She went upstairs to the bedroom. Philip was ending a phone call as she came in. She went up to him and put her arms around him, looking for comfort and reassurance.

'Tell me it's going to be all right.'

He disengaged himself from her embrace. 'I can't tell you that, can I? Because it probably isn't.'

'What's going to happen to us?'

'Frankly, the way things stand, I've got a hell of a sight more to worry about than you have.' He picked up his car keys and wallet from the bedside table.

'Where are you going?'

'Back to London.'

'What about me?'

He glanced at her indifferently. 'I don't know. Go back with Alec tomorrow. I don't want you coming back with me.'

He went downstairs, and she heard the front door open and close, the sound of his car starting, then the purr of the engine fading into the night.

26

'THIS ONE SHOULD be fun.' Hugh French tossed a brief onto Max's desk. 'Care to help out, if your caseload's not too heavy?' As Max untied the pink ribbon, Hugh went on, 'Can't say I have an ounce of sympathy for these druggy celebrities and their hangers-on. A spell in the army would do them all no end of good. Still, as the great Lord Brougham observed, to save one's client by all means and expedients and at all hazards and costs, is one's first and only duty.'

Max glanced through the papers with interest. He wasn't entirely surprised that Philip's defence had come Hugh's way. Hugh was, after all, one of the shining lights of the criminal bar, with an unparalleled record for getting his clients off, particularly the wealthy and famous ones. Max had read the newspaper accounts of the police raid earlier in the summer, and had felt contempt for Philip for being such a fool, and for Laura for associating herself with him. He felt sorry for her, too, but that was as far as it went.

'As a matter of fact,' said Max, 'this chap's already spent a few years in the army.'

'Then he should bloody well know better.' He gave Max a glance. 'Is he a friend of yours?'

'I was at school with him. He's a couple of years older than me. I've seen him at the odd social occasion in the last year or two, but that's about it.' He didn't want Hugh to perceive some kind of conflict of interest. At forty-four, Hugh was the youngest QC in the country, tall, fair and good-looking, with a charming personality and a wonderful way with juries. Max wanted nothing more than to be a junior on one of his cases.

'Certainly nothing that would compromise my independence,' he added for good measure. 'I don't feel much about the fellow one way or the other. So, yes, I would very much like to help.'

'Jolly good.' Hugh paused in the doorway, about to leave, and added, 'Pop up to my room around six, and we can talk about it over a glass of sherry.'

A few days later Max was sitting in his Pimlico flat going through the papers in Philip's case, when the doorbell rang. London was in the grip of an August heatwave, and he was wearing only shorts and an unbuttoned shirt, and had the window open wide to the evening air. He answered the door and found Morven standing there.

'Happy birthday for last week.' She kissed his cheek. 'Here's your present.'

'Thanks. Come in.' He unwrapped it. 'Oh, Bob Dylan, excellent – I've been meaning to buy this. Have a seat. I'll get you a cold drink.'

She dropped her bag next to a chair and sat down. Max went to the kitchen and came back with two glasses of lemonade.

'What have you been up to today?' he asked.

'I'm rehearsing a play in a basement in Islington with an experimental theatre group. It's positively sweltering down there.' She sipped her lemonade. 'I don't suppose you've got any gin to put in this? We should celebrate your birthday with a proper drink.'

Max, since he knew he wasn't going to get any more work done that evening, obliged by finding a bottle of Gordon's and pouring a hefty slug in both their glasses.

'So,' she asked, 'how does it feel to be filthy rich?'

'I don't think about it.' It was true. The transfer of all the trust funds to his name the previous week felt unreal. There was nothing he could think of to spend money on, though he imagined in time he would.

Morven, who was wearing only a thin cotton sundress and sandals, picked up one of the sheets of paper from the table and fanned herself with it. She eyed Max. Did he have any idea how good he looked, his chest bare like that, his dark hair all tousled? Presumably not. Imagine if she were to say she wanted to go to bed with him, right here and now. She felt a little ache of lust at the thought. But that would probably be something he'd neither expect nor want, not from his little cousin. Did he still look at her in that way? Did he never see her as other men did? Maybe that was what made him so desirable, the fact that he evinced not the slightest desire for her.

She stopped fanning herself and glanced at the sheet of paper. 'Is this some case you're working on?'

'It's Philip Carteret's defence, as a matter of fact. You know, the drugs possession charge.' He took it from her, gathered up the rest of the papers, and put them in his briefcase.

'Oh yes, I read about that. How funny that you're acting for him. Well, I hope you get him off.'

'I doubt that's going to happen. I don't know why he doesn't just plead guilty. It would save him a lot of bother and expense.'

'I imagine he doesn't want to go to jail.' She reached for the gin and splashed some more into their glasses. 'I'm famished. Shall I make us something to eat?'

'If you like. I haven't got much in.'

Max put the Bob Dylan LP on the record player while Morven made cheese on toast. They ate and listened to the music as dusk fell. Max, enjoying the feeling of getting drunk, topped up their glasses with more gin and lemonade.

'I've just remembered,' said Morven, dusting crumbs from her fingers and delving into her bag. 'Mummy's been doing some clearing out, and she found loads of old photographs. I brought some to show you.' She dragged her chair next to Max's, reached out and switched on a nearby lamp, and together they went through the handful of black and white photos from their childhood, most of them taken at Woodbourne House.

'Look at you with your toy planes,' murmured Morven. 'You took them everywhere.'

'What a fat baby you were.'

'I jolly well wasn't!' She eyed the photo. 'Well, maybe I was, a bit. Not now, though.'

'No. Now you're rather perfect.'

Max meant nothing by this; the compliment simply came automatically. When he turned to look at Morven, whose face was close to his, she smiled and said, 'Thank you.' She held his gaze for a long moment, caught up her long red hair in one hand, and leaned in and kissed him.

Max didn't withdraw. The kiss was soft and sensual, but he felt nothing of the arousal he had when Alec had forced his mouth against his. He responded because he felt drunk and it was enjoyable. Somewhere in his mind he knew it was peculiar to be kissing one's cousin, but that didn't seem to matter to her. If the kiss surprised him, what Morven did next astonished him. She put a hand on his groin and caressed him gently. Instantly he grew stiff, lust pooling at the base of his stomach. Not because it was her touch, but because it was anyone's touch, and not his own. He gave a little groan, and moved his mouth away.

'Don't do that.'

'Why not?' she asked softly.

Her mouth sought his again, and he was aware she had switched the lamp off. The last notes of 'A Hard Rain's A-Gonna Fall' faded away, and silence filled the room. It was almost dark outside, and he couldn't see her, was aware only of movements and sensation. He felt her unbuckle his belt, and clamped a hand on hers to stop her, but she resisted with a strength that surprised him, and within seconds she had deftly unzipped his flies. Before he knew what was happening, she was astride him, and he was inside her, the soft curtain of her hair brushing his face rhythmically as she moved down on him. She gave a small cry and he felt his own unstoppable orgasm rising to meet whatever it was she was feeling. He shouted out, arching his back involuntarily, and then she sank on to his chest.

It was over in seconds. She lifted herself from him and he heard her leave the room. He lay with his head back, eyes closed, stunned. Then he sat up, wiped himself clumsily with his underpants, and did up his shorts. What was uppermost in his mind was the realisation that he had just experienced what every man he knew spent most of their time trying to achieve with any and every member of the opposite sex, working from the prelude of hand-holding, through fumbling caresses to the ultimate objective. He had never been interested in any of those things – possibly why Veronica had given up on him – and yet he had just lost his virginity without even trying. To his own cousin.

He switched on the lamp. Morven came back into the room and stood before him.

'What are you thinking?' she asked.

He shook his head.

There was a silence, and she said with a shaky note of defiance, 'Women can want it too, you know.'

Two thoughts came immediately to his mind: one, that she felt ashamed and was trying to excuse herself, and two, that whatever she might have wanted, he hadn't. Not actively. Not really.

Morven regarded him anxiously, impatient for him to say something. She could hardly believe what she had done. She had only ever had sex twice before, with her last boyfriend, and it had been clumsy and cautious and she had been entirely passive. The desire that had driven her a few moments ago had almost frightened her.

'Don't look so upset,' he said at last. He tried to give her a reassuring smile, but it didn't quite work.

She bent and kissed him quickly on the mouth, then

picked up her bag. 'I'm not sorry,' she said, her tone still faintly defiant.

He nodded. She left.

A month later Philip appeared in court to answer the charges of possession of heroin. Despite Hugh's best attempts, he was convicted and sentenced to nine months in prison. Max was able to see him briefly after the sentence was handed out.

'I don't suppose prison can be much worse than Eton or the army,' said Philip. In his Savile Row suit and regimental tie, he looked an unlikely candidate for Wormwood Scrubs.

'I'm sorry we couldn't do more.'

'I brought it on myself. I've been rather a fool, I suppose.'

'I heard that Laura got a suspended sentence. Which must be a relief for you.'

Philip nodded. For reasons best known to Laura she had stuck around after the drugs bust, and helped him through those bloody awful weeks when he'd been weaning himself off heroin. He probably couldn't have done it without her, and for that he was grateful.

Two warders came in. 'On your feet,' snapped one of them to Philip. 'Time to go.'

Max watched Philip being led away. He supposed if anyone could cope with nine months in prison, it was Philip. He'd probably turn it to his advantage, in the long run.

On the way back to chambers, Hugh said to Max, 'How about a swim at the RAC this evening? We can have a couple of drinks afterwards. The wife's out of town.'

'Yes,' said Max, surprised and pleased. 'I'd like that.'

The pool was relatively empty, and the swim brought a welcome sense of freedom and coolness after the day spent in a stuffy courtroom. Max watched from the shallow end as Hugh carved through the water in a showy crawl. As he drew near, Max said, 'Race you three lengths.'

'You're on,' laughed Hugh.

He was a strong swimmer, but Max's youth gave him an edge, and he finished the race just ahead. Hugh slung a friendly arm across Max's shoulder as he recovered his breath. 'Well done. But I rather think that's finished me off for the day. Time for that drink.'

The slippery weight of Hugh's arm and the feeling of his bare skin against his own produced strange feelings in Max. He was aware of a sense of loss as Hugh took his arm away.

They went to the changing rooms and showered, and Hugh sat down on the wooden bench next to Max, towelling his hair. Max glanced up to see the only other occupant of the changing room leaving, and was suddenly acutely aware of the proximity of Hugh's body. He let his gaze wander from the tendrils of hair that clustered at the nape of Hugh's neck, across the muscles of his shoulders and down to the broad splay of his thighs, dusted with golden hairs. Dazed and appalled, he was aware of his insides dissolving with desire, and felt the stiffening of his erection beneath the folds of the towel. Never in his life had he so longed to touch someone. And more – he wanted something he couldn't name, something he wanted so unbearably badly he felt ashamed. Hugh dropped his towel on to his lap and as he did so he rested his hand on Max's thigh, giving it what felt like a playful pat. His touch was electrifying.

'Now, what about dinner? I could rustle up something at my place.' His gaze held Max's, and his smile held something intense. He moved his hand a little further up Max's thigh, beneath his towel. 'As I said, there's no one home.'

Max got to his feet, his mind blazing with shock. 'Actually, I think maybe I'll give dinner a miss. There's some work I have to do.' He made for the lockers and got dressed swiftly, aware of Hugh putting on his clothes at a more leisurely pace a few feet away.

As he was about to leave, Hugh said with a smile, 'If ever you change your mind, remember – my door is always open.'

Max made no reply. He left the club and went home. That night he woke in an anguished state of arousal, leaving behind a dream in which everything that happened with his cousin was happening again, but the figure astride him was not Morven.

After that Max avoided Hugh around chambers, and tried to rationalise what had so nearly happened. He blocked off the memory of his own feelings of desire and told himself that Hugh was just like those predatory masters at school that everyone had avoided being alone with. He had narrowly avoided a dangerous and unpleasant situation.

A few weeks later Morven telephoned him in chambers. He hadn't seen her since the night she had come to his flat, and that was fine with him. Like the Hugh incident, he just wanted to forget about it. He wanted to forget about everything, to cocoon himself within the masculine world of the Inns of Court and focus on his work to the exclusion of everything about himself that troubled him.

'I need to see you,' Morven told him. 'We have to talk.'

'What about?'

'Can you meet me this evening?' Her tone was impatient. She named a café near the British Museum, not far from her drama school. 'About six?'

'Yes, of course. I'll see you there.'

She was sitting at the back of the café when he arrived, hunched over a cup of tea. Max bought a coffee and sat down.

'What's up?'

She toyed with her teaspoon, then lifted her long red hair from her shoulders and looked at him. There was something almost angry in her expression as she said in a low voice, 'I'm pregnant.'

Max felt as though he'd been hit hard in the gut. It took a minute for the shock to wear off, and the implications to sink in, a minute in which he said nothing. He thought back to the events of that summer evening. How was this his fault?

'Are you sure?' he asked, needing to grasp whatever feeble hope there might be.

'Of course I am. It's been over two months. I mean, it's October now, and what we did was in August. So I'm sure.' Her tone was laced with irritation.

What we did? He wasn't sure he'd done anything. But suddenly here it was, this dreadful, unspeakable situation.

Someone got up and put a sixpence in the jukebox, and the reedy, racing sounds of 'Telstar' filled the café.

'There are things I can do,' she said quietly. 'I mean, I know a girl who got rid of a baby. She went to some woman. I could do that.'

'No,' said Max abruptly. 'Don't do that.' He stared at his coffee. 'For God's sake, don't do that.'

'What, then?'

'We'll have to get married.' They were, he knew, the same miserable, helpless words uttered by countless young men who found themselves in his predicament. But did he deserve to be in this predicament? There was something monstrously laughable about it. Except it wasn't funny at all.

'You don't want to marry me. You don't love me.'

'I do love you. Of course I do.'

'Being cousins doesn't count. I don't mean in that way.'

'It's good enough, isn't it? I mean, what else are you going to do?'

'I don't know.' She looked away, her expression vacant, scared. She'd known before they met today that he would make the offer, and had told herself it could be worse. He had money, she liked him as much as any man she knew, more even. But it shouldn't be like this. She should have a choice, but she didn't.

'Well, then,' said Max. 'It's what we have to do.' As he said this, he realised that the life he'd thought stretched ahead of him, hazy with possibilities, was now starkly mapped out. Every door had suddenly closed, and he could do nothing about it. He had to do the right thing, even if he didn't think he'd done any wrong thing to begin with.

27

1964

NINE MONTHS LATER Harry and Dan were sitting in the Wheatsheaf over pints of beer.

'So, are you home for good this time?' asked Harry.

'I'm honestly not sure. Fifteen years is a long time to be away. I'm not sure I recognise England any more. But I'm home for the foreseeable, at any rate.'

'Where are you living? Belgravia?'

Dan shook his head. 'Too many memories. Better to go on letting it out. The income's been useful. I've found a flat in South Kensington. It'll do for the time being.'

Harry fished in his pocket. 'I brought you this.' He handed Dan a photograph taken at Max and Morven's wedding.

'Thank you.' Dan studied it. 'I must say I couldn't believe it when I heard they were getting married.'

'She's delightful, quite the live wire. They came down to Chalcombe with their baby girl a few weeks ago.'

'Were Avril and Laura at the wedding?'

'No. There never was much love lost between Max and Avril, as you know. As for Laura... well, no one's seen much of her since that drugs business last year.' He'd never told Dan about how Laura and Max had fallen out. He was pretty ashamed now of his own part in it.

'Lord, yes, that was a bit of a shocker.'

'I blame my fool of a godson. I always had an idea he might end up in prison. She stuck by him, helped him get off drugs, but after he got out a couple of weeks ago, they suddenly split up. I'd say she's well shot of the blighter.'

'Poor Laura. I feel I should get in touch with her.'

'I don't have an address, I'm afraid.'

'Maybe Avril does.'

'Well, now – and this is just gossip, mind – the word is that Laura broke up an affair between Avril and Philip Carteret. She pinched Avril's chap, so to speak.'

'Good grief. The things that have happened while I've been away. I'll pay Avril a visit, anyhow. Maybe go round to her gallery. I hear she's made something of a name for herself.'

'She's doing very well. Of course, all this revival of interest in her father's work has helped. The National

Portrait Gallery are doing a retrospective early next year, I believe.'

'Interesting.' Dan thought back to that fateful summer house party all those years ago, and the secrets that he knew. He rarely dwelt on them. They didn't seem important now.

It gave Avril a little shock of pleasure when Dan walked into the gallery the following day. The years had aged him only a little; his features were leaner and sharper, the eyes and smile still boyish, his fair hair touched with only a few streaks of grey.

'Dan! Where did you spring from?'

'I got back from New York three weeks ago.'

'How nice to see you. Are you staying long?'

'No idea, really. I'm doing freelance work at the moment.' He glanced around. 'This is quite a place you've got. I hear you're a great success. And you're looking very well.' It was true. Success had given her poise and confidence, and she had matured, he thought, into a very attractive woman.

'Thank you. I haven't time to talk, I'm afraid – I'm just off to visit one of the artists we're showing next month. Like greenhouse plants, they need careful handling.' She paused. 'Why don't you come to supper tonight?'

'I'd like that.'

'Come around seven thirty. In the meantime, feel free to take a look around. I have to dash.'

*

Dan arrived that evening with a bottle of wine. 'Supper smells good,' he remarked.

'Coq au vin,' said Avril. 'Go through to the drawing room and I'll make us a drink. What would you like?'

'I'll have a whisky, thanks.'

As Dan wandered into the drawing room he caught sight of the painting of Madeleine hanging on the wall. It gave him a shock to see it after all these years. He walked over to take a closer look, transported back to that day in the barn, the day of Henry Haddon's death. He could still see the flash of Madeleine's yellow sundress as she fled, could hear again the awful sound of Haddon groaning out his last breath, and the wailing of five-year-old Avril as she looked down from the hayloft. In his mind's eye he saw himself bending down and picking up the canvas, the last thing the great man had ever painted, and setting it with its face to the wall, as if to keep from the eyes of the world the secrets it held.

Avril reappeared with a gin and tonic in one hand and a glass of Scotch in the other, and saw Dan examining the painting.

'Madeleine,' remarked Avril as she handed Dan his drink. 'You remember her? My mother and I found the picture in my father's studio when we were clearing it out.'

Dan realised she clearly remembered nothing of that afternoon in the barn. 'I'm surprised your mother didn't give it to Laura,' he remarked, without thinking.

Avril stiffened slightly. 'Why on earth should she? It's my father's work, and it belongs to me. Besides, she doesn't even remember her mother. I'm not sure I'd want a picture of someone who abandoned me when I was barely a few months old.'

Dan wondered if the painting had been hanging here while Laura was living at Mount Street, and if so, what she'd felt about it. This prompted him to remark, 'I heard all about the drugs raid from Harry Denholm. I was surprised at Laura, getting caught up in that kind of thing.'

'To be honest, Laura seems to have a talent for making a mess of her life. First her negro lover, then this drug business. Perhaps one shouldn't be surprised, all things considered.'

'Which lover? Harry didn't mention anything.'

'She took up with a black musician – it must have been, oh, seven or eight years ago. We had an argument about it and she walked out. Went to live with him in some place near King's Cross. Can you imagine? She wouldn't listen to anyone who told her what a mistake she was making. Anyway, it all came to a bad end, predictably. He ran off. Then a quite extraordinary thing happened. She met up with one of the evacuees that came to Woodbourne House during the war. You remember the two Jennings boys?'

Dan could see in his mind's eye two small boys

running out of the woods, flinging dead leaves into the air as they imitated the sound of bombs falling. 'Yes, I remember them.'

'Well, one of them, Sidney, has become quite a well-known photographer. He helped Laura become a model, which at least made use of such gifts as she had.'

'I've seen pictures of her in magazines. She's stunning. But then, she always was.'

'I imagine the drugs raid and her suspended sentence will have put paid to all that. Whatever she's been blessed with, it's certainly not good judgement.' Avril drained her glass. 'Shall we go and eat?'

Over dinner they talked about the recent resurgence of interest in her father's work.

'I've often thought someone should write a biography of him,' remarked Dan. 'He led an interesting life, knew a lot of famous people.'

'Well, I have his correspondence stashed away, boxes of it. There are letters from all kinds of people. Augustus John, Jacob Epstein, the Woolfs – my mother knew both the Bell sisters quite well.'

'It would make an interesting project.'

Avril refilled their wine glasses. 'Why don't you write it?'

'Me? I've never undertaken anything of that kind.' He mused. 'But I could, I suppose.'

'I'd give you access to everything, all my father's papers, and Sonia's. I can't think of anyone who would do it better justice than you, Dan. You knew him, and Sonia. You knew Woodbourne House.'

'Let me think about it.'

At the end of the evening, as he was putting on his coat, Dan said, 'I don't suppose you have an address for Laura? I'd like to look her up.'

'No,' replied Avril shortly. 'We aren't in touch.'

'Well, thanks for dinner. I'll let you know about the biography idea. We'd need to get a publisher interested first, but with the exhibition coming up, I don't think that'll be a problem. I'll call you.'

Dan looked up Sid Jennings and went round to his studio. Sid was in his darkroom when the doorbell rang, and when he went to answer it he found a middle-aged stranger standing on the doorstep.

'Hello, Sid,' said Dan. 'I don't suppose you remember me. Dan Ranscombe. I knew you when you were evacuated to Woodbourne House in the war.'

Recognition dawned. 'Blimey, you're the soldier who built me and Colin the den. Of course I remember. Come on in.'

Sid made coffee. 'The reason I looked you up,' said Dan, 'is that I'm trying to track down Laura. I've been in the States for the last ten years or so, and I only recently found out what happened to her. I hoped you might have an address.'

'She was living with that bloke who got busted, but

I heard they split up after he got out of prison. Maybe she's back at her place in Chelsea.' Sid dug in a desk drawer for his address book. 'Such a bloody shame, that drugs thing. She had the world at her feet. Course, the magazines won't touch her now. All this talk about permissiveness and the swinging sixties – some things never change. Here you go. Forty-nine Beaufort Street, second-floor flat.'

Dan made a note of the address and finished his coffee. 'Thanks. It's been good to see you again. I'm glad you've done so well.'

'Nice to see you, too. Tell Laura Sid sends his love.'

That evening Dan went to Laura's flat. He rang the bell, and a moment later the door opened. The last image he'd seen of Laura had been in an American copy of *Vogue*, barefoot on a beach in a long, floaty dress, her skin tanned, her blonde hair long and loose, her smile enticing. The Laura that stood before him now was still lovely, but far from that world. Her hair was pulled back in a ponytail, her face was bare of make-up, and she was wearing a black skirt that came below her knees, and a dark blue cardigan over a white blouse, very much office attire. When she saw Dan her eyes widened with genuine delight, and seconds later she was hugging him, asking no questions about when he had come back or why he was here – just hugging him. Her joy at seeing him touched him.

'Come in,' she said. He followed her upstairs to her flat. 'A drink or tea?'

'Whichever you're having.'

'Oh, hang it, let's have a drink.'

She made gin and tonics.

'Tell me how you are,' said Dan. 'Harry wrote and told me about your prosecution.'

She pulled the band from her ponytail and let her hair fall loose over her shoulders. 'It was stupid. I don't even know how the cannabis came to be in my pocket. It wasn't mine.' She shrugged. 'I thought I was immune, that I was some kind of gilded person to whom bad things couldn't happen. But they did, and everything changed.' She took a swallow of her drink. 'I can't get any modelling work. That's all over.'

'Give it a year or so. People forget.'

'I'm already twenty-seven, far too old.'

'Don't be ridiculous. You're... well, you're beautiful. Amazingly beautiful.' It was true. He found himself wishing he was twenty years younger.

'Dan, by the standards of the fashion world I was pretty old when I started. No, that's dead and gone. So now I have a respectable job as a PA in a tiling firm in Fulham. It doesn't pay a lot, but I've got a fair bit saved up.'

'What about this fellow Carteret?'

'I don't want to think about him. I don't even know why it happened.' She paused. 'Well, I suppose I do, actually. He was the first person I ever kissed. I was fifteen, and I thought I was in love. When we met again last year I felt like I was fifteen again. I tried to make the relationship into something it wasn't. I suppose I knew all along the kind of man he was, but I had this stupid idea that when he came out of prison things would be better. If anything, they were worse.'

'You stole him away from poor old Avril, I hear.'

'Not at all! I had no idea she was seeing him. Anyway, it turns out he was always keener on her than me. The last time we argued he told me she was worth a dozen of me, and that he'd sooner spend a month with her than ten minutes with me.' She sipped her drink. 'That was a couple of weeks ago. She's welcome to him. He's a bastard. Anyway, I'd rather not talk about him.'

'Do you ever see Max?'

She gave a short laugh. 'There's someone else I don't really want to talk about.' She glanced at him. 'I don't suppose you know what happened, do you?' She told him all about Ellis, and about Max's part in the destruction of their relationship.

'I suppose Max thought he was helping you,' said Dan. 'But then, the road to hell is paved with good intentions.'

'The thing is, I can see now he was right. Everyone was right. Even Avril was right. It would never have worked out for us. But I was in love with Ellis. Really and truly. A bit of me always will be. And that's why I can't forgive Max.'

'He's married now, you know.'

'Oh? Who to?'

'His cousin Morven, of all people.'

'Lordy.' She made a face. 'Oh well, it keeps the money in the family. Diana will be happy.'

Dan smiled. 'You know, I'm glad to find you so chipper. I was worried you might be rather down, with all that's happened.'

She was silent for a few seconds, playing with her hairband. Then she looked up at him. 'Chipper – is that what you think I am? I suppose I've become rather good at pretending. It's part of what models do. But no, Dan, I'm not chipper at all.' She shook her head, her eyes brightening with tears, her voice breaking a little. 'If you want to know the truth, I wake up in the night and wonder who I am. I feel as though I barely exist any more. My mother abandoned me, I've never known who my father was, and then everything that held me together as I was growing up, all the things that made me think I had a place in the world, got taken away. When Aunt Sonia died, I had no one. I thought I had Avril, but she took me out of school, where I was happy, and made sure I did what she wanted, instead of what I wanted. I was too young to realise why it was impossible for her to love me. Aunt Sonia didn't even remember me in her will – not the tiniest keepsake. There was no reason why she should, but it made me feel as though I'd hardly mattered.' She drew a deep breath. 'Then I met Ellis, and he loved me, he made me feel loved, but that got taken away, too. And now the little bit of self-worth I felt as a model – that's gone. So who am I? What am I? What is the point of me, Dan?' She suddenly broke down, leaned her head on her hands and wept, her body shaking.

'Don't,' said Dan, laying his hands gently on her shoulders. 'Laura, don't.'

She lifted her head. She looked, even through her tears, so blazingly beautiful and so wretchedly unhappy that he followed an impulse and kissed her. He felt the warmth of her mouth, and the wetness of her tears as his fingers touched her cheeks, and desire took over. He could feel her kissing him back, trembling a little, needy and helpless in her misery.

When the kiss ended, he murmured, 'This is the point of you. The point of all of us. To live, and be loved.'

She closed her eyes and put her mouth longingly to his again. 'Stay with me, Dan,' she whispered after a moment. 'Please stay.'

Dan woke the next morning to see Laura moving around the bedroom, putting her things together for the working day. She pulled on her jacket and gave him a smile.

'Get yourself breakfast. I'm late, I'll have to pick up something on the way to work. Call me whenever you want. The number's on the phone.' She was gone, slamming the front door behind her.

Dan lay in the rumpled bed, gazing at the sunshine filtering through the curtains. There was something bloody wonderful about still being able to pull off an effortless seduction at fifty-two in much the same way as he had at twenty-two. Though on reflection, perhaps this wasn't so much down to his personal skill as to the fact that young women were rather easier to bed than they had been thirty years ago. In his youth he had taken a certain pride in his technique, but back then sexual conquest had mostly been a laborious, protracted affair. Now... well, now the codes seemed to have changed.

He rubbed his face. God, that he should be thinking of Laura, of all girls, in these terms. He reached to the floor where his trousers lay, and groped for his cigarettes, conscious of the ache in his bones from sleeping in an unfamiliar bed. He lit a cigarette and lay back on the pillow. Where did it go from here? Her parting words had left everything free and open, without any sense of obligation. Perhaps that was the way with young women these days. He hadn't had an affair with anyone under thirty in years. He was in unfamiliar territory. Did he really want to embark on a relationship? Had it been any other girl he might simply have let things lie, not seen her again, but with Laura that didn't feel like an option. The past made things more complex, and he was aware she was emotionally fragile. It was probably that insecurity, that neediness, that had been responsible for last night – and not, as his vanity would have him believe, his own fatal powers of attraction. He reached out to the bedside table for an ashtray, and the effort made him wince. No point in kidding himself. Young and lovely as Laura was, probably the last thing she needed in her life was a middle-aged lover, beginning to creak at the seams.

He thought about it for a few days and decided he was investing everything with too much significance. The moral climate had altered since his day, and so far as he could tell, even for a girl, sleeping with someone was a less momentous event than it had once been. But he had no idea what Laura's expectations were, and he felt a certain responsibility towards her. So he rang her. When he heard the warmth in her voice he realised, with a certain sense of trepidation, that it all mattered very much to her.

They arranged to meet for dinner in a King's Road bistro. Dan had thought through what he would say. He had only been back in England for a few weeks, after all, his life was in disarray, and it hadn't been his intention to embark on a love affair, certainly not of the intense kind which he imagined someone of Laura's temperament would involve.

When the meal was over, and they were finishing the last of the wine, Dan said, 'Look, about the other night... Wonderful as it was, I think maybe it would be better if we were simply to be friends, and no more. I'm probably the last thing you need in your life.'

'Let me be the judge of that,' replied Laura. 'And yes, it was wonderful. I was hoping tonight could be a repeat.'

This was a more than tempting thought. He felt himself weakening. He took her hands in his. 'If it's reassurance that you're looking for, and strength, and a way to believe in yourself again, I can try to give you that. But you don't have to take me into your bed.'

'It's love I'm looking for.' She looked earnestly into his eyes. 'And yes, I do.'

He felt his heart sink a little. She was undeniably lovely and loving. In fact, she was undeniable in every way. It wasn't what he'd intended, but there were, he reflected, worse things that could happen to a chap his age.

28

DAN HAD NO trouble securing the interest of a publisher in a biography of Henry Haddon. He rang Avril and told her the good news, and arranged to come to Mount Street one morning to take a look at the papers she had unearthed. When he arrived he found five cardboard boxes of letters and documents stacked next to Sonia's desk.

'There's a lot to go through,' said Avril. 'Sonia never threw away any correspondence.'

Dan fished in one of the boxes and drew out a letter at random, and read it. 'Good grief. This is from Augustus John, telling Henry to keep his hands off his sister. I had no idea your father had a relationship with Gwen John.'

'Nor did I,' said Avril. 'That must have been well before he met my mother.'

He slipped the letter back into the box. 'This is going

to be quite a project. I'll arrange to have the boxes sent round to my place so that I can make a start.'

'Why don't you work here? I'm out all day. You said yourself you'll need to talk to me about the family and his early life. We can do that over supper some evenings. I'll find you some keys so that you can come and go as you please.'

She went out and came back moments later with a set of keys.

'Thanks,' said Dan. 'Are you sure you don't mind?'

'Of course not. You can even admire your younger self while you're working.' She indicated the photo of Dan in uniform that Sonia had always kept on the desk.

'That can go straight in a drawer.'

'Well, I have to get off to work. I'll leave you to it.'

That evening, when they were in bed together, Dan said to Laura, 'There's something you should know.'

'What?' Laura rolled away from him and picked up her half-finished glass of wine from the floor next to the bed.

'I saw Avril recently. She invited me to supper and suggested I should write a biography of Henry Haddon, and I agreed. I'm going to be doing the work at Mount Street.'

She gave a laugh of disbelief. 'You're working for Avril?'

'Nothing of the kind. She came up with the idea,

that's all. And the material I need for my research is there, boxes of it. I just thought you should know.' He wondered, not for the first time, whether he should tell her about her mother and Henry Haddon. But he couldn't see what purpose it would serve. Such a discovery might simply make things worse for her. And it certainly wouldn't help where Avril was concerned. Best to let it lie.

She drank some wine and handed the glass to Dan. 'Does she know about us?'

'God, no. And I don't intend that she should. It wouldn't go down very well.'

'Because she hates me.'

'It's just not something she needs to know. I want this book to work and he's the perfect subject.'

'You're so lucky,' she said, tracing a line across his chest with the tip of her finger, 'doing something you love. And look at me, working nine to five in an office. I envy you.'

'There must be something you want to do with your life. If modelling isn't the answer, find something else.'

'I used to like designing my own clothes – and making them. I still do it now and then.'

'Well, then – why not try doing it professionally?'

'I wouldn't know where to begin.'

'Are you telling me that after working in the fashion world for the last few years, you don't know people who could help you?'

'I suppose. I honestly hadn't thought about it.'

'Then it's time you did.'

For the next few weeks Dan worked his way steadily through the boxes of correspondence, accumulating material. Generally he would leave before Avril returned from work, because otherwise she would invariably invite him to stay for a drink or supper. He sensed her loneliness. It seemed tactful – not to say useful, since he needed to spend time talking to her to learn more about Haddon's childhood and family – to accept these invitations now and again, but the fact she knew nothing about his relationship with Laura made him uneasy. If she knew about that, he was pretty sure her enthusiasm for him to write the biography would vanish in an instant. And that was the last thing he wanted.

'What do you think?' Laura turned the sketchbook round and pushed it across the table to Dan. They were sitting in the living room in Dan's flat, Dan working at his typewriter on one side, Laura on the other. To his relief, the relationship had turned out to involve none of the drama and passion he had anticipated, and had in fact become quite restful and domestic.

He studied the designs, leafing through the pages. 'They're very good.' He looked up and smiled. 'So far as I can judge. I'm not exactly an expert on women's fashions.' He handed the sketchbook back.

'Jill says if I can give her half a dozen dresses, she'll have a go at selling them in her boutique. The trouble is, I can't afford to pay to have them made up. I'll have to do it myself, which is going to be a lot of work. Still, wouldn't it be smashing if I could actually make some money out of it?'

'Why didn't you study fashion or textile design when you left school?'

'I suggested it to Avril, but she said it was a waste of time. She said I'd be better off getting some secretarial qualifications till a husband came along.'

'I still don't understand why she took you out of school.'

'She said she couldn't afford the fees.' Dan, speculating on what Sonia must have left her daughter, thought this unlikely, but said nothing. 'I wasn't exactly Einstein, anyway. Not a complete dunce, but not what you would call academic. Still, I was miserable when it happened. First Sonia dying, then losing all my friends. I felt like a sad little balloon that someone had let go of.' She got up. 'Poor old Aunt Sonia. She always wanted Avril and me to be like sisters. I wonder what she'd think of the ways things are now.'

'Sadly, I don't think she'd be in the least bit surprised.'

It was in late August that Laura knew for certain that she was pregnant. She had tried to discount the vague nausea she'd felt for the past few weeks, and the ache in her breasts, and had even tried to persuade herself that one missed period didn't necessarily signify anything. But as the days went by she knew with a sinking heart that she couldn't pretend any longer. She and Dan thought they'd been careful, but clearly they hadn't been careful enough. The thought of having a baby filled her with panic. She was living out exactly what had happened to her mother, and her mother before her, like some ridiculous destiny. A child was probably the last thing in the world Dan wanted at his age. She didn't even know where their relationship was heading. One way or the other she would have to tell him.

She went round to Dan's flat a few nights later.

'Fix yourself a drink,' he said, giving her a brief kiss as he let her in. He sat back down at his typewriter. 'I just want to finish this. I won't be a tick.'

'I'll make some tea,' said Laura. 'I don't feel like a drink. How's the biography going?'

'Not bad. Henry has just survived the Third Battle of Ypres and is about to be appointed an official war artist. No tea for me. I'll have a Scotch.'

Laura made herself a mug of tea and poured Dan a whisky. She sat down on the other side of the table and watched him as he worked, her nerves jumping at the thought of what she had to tell him.

Dan pulled a sheet of paper from the typewriter and sat back. 'There. Done.' He picked up his whisky and regarded her. 'What's up?'

'I've got something to tell you.' She took a deep breath. 'I'm pregnant.'

There was a long silence. Dan had no idea how to react or respond. He felt numbed, appalled. This was the last thing in the world he had envisaged, particularly given how careful they'd been. Accidents happened – he just didn't expect them to happen to him.

'You're sure?'

She nodded, looking so piteously anxious that he hated himself for having thought first and foremost of himself. This was a shared predicament.

'I've been so scared about telling you.' Tears filled her eyes. She looked away.

He got up from the table and went round to where she sat, drawing her to her feet and putting his arms around her. She rested her head against him. He stroked her hair, trying to rationalise his feelings. Having a child was the last thing he'd envisaged at his age, but maybe it was Fate's way of grounding him, putting an end to his restless impulses. He hadn't believed, since the dreadful events that had wrenched Meg and Max from him, that he would ever have a family again.

'Maybe it's not such a bad thing,' he murmured, half to himself, half to her.

She lifted her head and gave him a questioning look. 'But it wasn't meant to happen.'

'Most things in life aren't mean to happen. They just do.' He might not be in love with Laura, but he loved her. He'd always loved her. The relationship was tranquil, comfortable. And she was going to have his child. There seemed only one answer.

'Maybe we should get married.'

She gazed at him, testing her heart. She simply wasn't brave enough to bring up a child on her own. She had no idea if marriage to Dan was what she wanted, but at least she would be safe, loved. 'We shouldn't rush into anything. I don't want you to feel you have to.'

'I wasn't thinking of charging off to the registry office first thing. And I'm not asking you because I feel I should. This is a joint responsibility. I'm asking if you think we can make it work.'

Laura hesitated. She'd already wearied herself with the possibilities. Like him, she saw no other answer. If she was to have the baby, staying together seemed inevitable.

'Yes,' she said. 'I think we can.'

'Good. Then we should start feeling happy about it.' He wiped a tear from her face and smiled. 'Don't you think?'

He'd often wondered what he would end up doing with the rest of his life, and now, like it or not, he seemed to have the answer.

29

IT WAS LATE September when Dan received a phone call from Edgar Lightfoot, Harry's business partner, telling him that Harry had had a heart attack and was in hospital. He went to see him straight away. He had been astonished, on his return from the States, to see how fat Harry had grown, and now his corpulent figure looked too large for the narrow hospital bed. He seemed cheerful enough, but his face was pallid and when he spoke he seemed weak and exhausted.

'Just as well Edgar was in the office with me when it happened. I went down like a ton of bricks, apparently.' Harry's gaze wandered around the ward. 'The bastards are keeping me on starvation rations to avoid putting strain on the old ticker. I told them it's a bit late for that.' He looked at Dan, silent for a moment, then said, 'There's a copy of my will in the filing cabinet in the office. The original's with my solicitors down in Kent.'

'Why are you telling me that?' Fear clutched at Dan. He didn't want to contemplate Harry dying. Not Harry.

'You need to know that I've left Chalcombe to you. That godson of mine has enough money and property of his own, so I want you to have the place. It would mean a lot to me to know you'll look after it.'

'Don't talk like this. You'll be up and around in no time.'

Harry's big barrel chest heaved in a sigh. 'Anyway, there's another thing. I've left Max a few things at Chalcombe that I know he values, and a letter. I've said in it that if he ever loved me, and if he's got any sense, he'll see you and talk to you. I think what I've said will persuade him to do that. I like the thought of brokering the peace between you from beyond the grave, so to speak.'

'Don't be so bloody maudlin. This has just been a bad fright. You're recovering, aren't you? You've got years in you.'

Harry gave his friend a sad smile. 'Do you think so, old fellow? It doesn't feel that way to me. It really doesn't.'

*

Two days later Harry had another heart attack, and died without ever leaving hospital. Dan couldn't believe that his old friend was gone; the sudden space left in his life was huge. Harry had been the nearest thing to family that he had known for much of his life, and he had somehow imagined that he would always be there, with his short temper and acerbic wit, his gravelly voice and his large heart, the heart that had done for him.

Max was among the mourners at the funeral. When Dan approached him to speak to him, Max walked away without a word. So much for Harry's hopes, thought Dan.

As executor, he was kept busy sorting out Harry's affairs. After the funeral he drove down to Chalcombe, intending to spend a few days there and work out what to do with this unexpected legacy. The silent house, full of all Harry's beloved books, paintings and possessions, was so freighted with memories of him that when he first stepped inside, Dan didn't think he could bear to spend one night there. He wandered through the rooms, and at last sat down in the conservatory, remembering evenings when he and Harry had sat drinking and smoking and talking. Then he realised that he didn't feel as melancholy as he had thought he would; the place held such happy shades of Harry that it was almost as though he might come rolling in at any moment with the whisky decanter in his hand, ready for conversation and laughter. Harry had wanted him to look after the house that he had loved, and so he would. He had brought his notes and typewriter with him, and he could work in Harry's study. He would feel near to him; it would be a good way of easing his grief, of coming to terms with the loss of his friend. He phoned Laura to tell her he would be away for a few days, and drove to the nearest village for groceries.

Two days later, around six in the evening, Dan was reading in the conservatory when the doorbell rang. He opened the door, and there stood Max.

'Harry's solicitor said I would find you here,' said Max. His expression was wooden.

'Come in,' replied Dan. Max followed him through to the conservatory. 'Have a seat.'

Max sat down, fiddling with his car keys, clearly uneasy. Dan sat down opposite.

'By the way, I haven't had a chance to congratulate you. I hear you have a daughter.'

Max's expression changed slightly. He nodded. 'Thanks.'

'What's her name?'

'Theodora.'

'That's unusual – but pretty. I like it.'

'Harry left me some things. I thought I should come down and fetch them, while someone was here.'

'Of course.'

'He also left me a letter.' Max paused. 'The thing is,

he said some things that made me realise I can't go on not talking to you. Harry was one of the kindest people in my life, and I'm here because of him.'

'I'm glad you came.'

'My feelings haven't changed, you know.'

'I wish you would let me explain to you about me and your mother.'

'I'm not sure I want to hear any of that.'

'Then perhaps Harry's letter was a waste of time.'

There was a silence, then Max said, 'Very well. Go on.'

Dan offered Max a cigarette from the box on the table, but Max shook his head. Dan took one for himself. 'Nothing I'm about to tell you is an attempt to excuse what happened. It's simply an explanation.' He lit his cigarette. 'Meg was barely more than a child when she married your father. She believed she loved him. She wanted to love him. He was everything she had been brought up to admire – handsome, honourable, kind, the perfect English gentleman. Rather like you.' Dan smiled, though Max didn't. 'She and I had had a bit of a romance before that. Nothing' – he searched for the right word – 'nothing untoward had happened, but I knew she was in love with me. I told her as much, because I was very much in love with her. But she didn't want to believe it. She had her heart set on marrying Paul, and I wasn't... well, I wasn't anything like as decent as your father. In some ways I don't think Meg thought much of me, not at the time. Looking back, I don't blame her. The thing about your father, though – he was a tremendous fellow in many ways, but he wasn't much cut out for loving women. By that I mean he didn't understand them. They weren't part of the world he identified with. He didn't understand Meg. I think throughout their marriage he loved her in his way, but he wasn't in love with her. He was just, well, doing what he always did. Doing his best.' Max was listening intently, but Dan couldn't read his expression. 'So really their marriage had failed long before anything happened between Meg and me.' He put down his cigarette. 'God, I think we both need a drink.' He went to the drinks tray and poured two whiskies. He handed one to Max, who took it without a word. 'Meg wanted to wait until the war was over before leaving your father. Maybe that was a mistake, but she had her reasons.'

'But he knew. He died knowing about the two of you.'

'Yes, and I wish with all my heart he hadn't. Meg and I were cowards. People in love are often cowardly. And selfish. Their love matters more to them than anything, or anyone else. Think about the way you love Morven. It was like that for us.'

Max's face was inscrutable. He took a swallow of his drink.

'You can go on hating me, Max, if it helps. But not your mother.'

Max shook his head. 'I don't. I forgave her a long time ago.'

'Good. Though by that I take it that you still haven't forgiven me. Maybe I don't blame you.'

Max was silent. What Dan had said about his father and women frightened him; the resonances were unmistakable. And the assumption that he was in love with Morven in the way Dan had been with his mother... Dear God, if only that were true. He took a deep breath and said, 'I began hating you when I was eleven. I've been trying to keep that feeling alive ever since. But I see now that it isn't any use. You were never anything other than a decent stepfather to me. I'm going to do as Harry asked and put it behind me. I have to.' He drank the remains of his Scotch.

Dan picked up the whisky decanter and refilled their glasses. They sat in silence for a while. Outside, dusk was falling.

At length Max said, 'I'm going to miss Harry like hell. He did his best for me after Mummy died. I always thought when I was younger, what a wonderful life he seemed to have. Then when I got older, I realised that in some ways it must have been a nightmare.'

'You mean, because he was a homosexual? No, it wasn't easy for him, or his friends.'

'It seems terrible that people have their lives ruined just because they love the wrong way.'

'Is it the wrong way?'

'Yes. It's beastly, that kind of thing.'

The firmness with which Max spoke reminded Dan forcibly of Paul; the same rectitude, the same certainty. He wondered in how many other ways, deep down, he was like his father.

'Well, where adults are concerned, I'm not so sure that any kind of love is wrong,' said Dan. 'Surely love is a force for good? Doesn't the Bible say, "love covers a multitude of sins"?'

'Well, that's it exactly – homosexuality is a sin. I'm not saying Harry wasn't a good man. He was one of the best. But still.'

Dan nodded. He remembered how, when they were young men, he had envied Paul his certainties about life, his clear and simple views on what was right and wrong. Now, years later, he had come to understand that such intractability usually masked complex emotional problems. He wondered what Max's were.

'Well,' he said, as he got to his feet, 'it seems that parliament and most of the country agrees with you, despite the Wolfenden Report. I was about to make supper. Would you like some?'

Max hesitated. 'Perhaps I should just collect the things Harry left me, and be getting back.'

'Probably not a good idea to get behind the wheel with a couple of whiskies inside you. Besides, we'll have to look the things out. I suggest you stay for supper, bed down here for the night, and we can do it in the morning.'

'All right. Thanks. I'll phone Morven and tell her.'

30

THE NEXT MORNING Dan opened his bedroom curtains and saw Max already up, strolling around the garden. He watched him for a moment. What a closed book the young man had become. At least they had taken the first steps to patching things up.

He washed and dressed, and went downstairs to make breakfast. Max came into the kitchen a few moments later.

'Toast will be ready in a jiffy,' said Dan. 'You can take the coffee through, if you like.'

Over breakfast he observed, 'I suppose you're looking for a house, now you have a family?'

'Yes. Well, Morven is. She wants a place in the country. Her ideas seem to be rather grandiose, but since money's no object, who can blame her?' He uncapped the marmalade jar. 'What will you do with this place?'

'I suppose I'll keep it. Harry loved it. I'll try to get down as often as possible.'

Max nodded. He watched Dan serenely buttering his toast, and suddenly wished with all his heart that the last fifteen years could be swept away, that he could unburden himself to his stepfather. But that possibility was well and truly gone. There was no one he could talk to. And what could anyone do, anyhow? He must simply soldier on.

After breakfast they went round the house, putting together the things that Harry had left to Max. In the study they boxed up the jazz records.

'You needn't take them if you don't want to,' said Dan. 'I mean, these old thirty-threes are damnably heavy. You could replace them with LPs.'

Max shook his head. 'They were Harry's. I had some good times listening to these when I was a kid. I know they're a bit scratchy when they're played, but I find that sound rather special.'

Dan smiled. 'I know what you mean.'

They loaded everything into Max's car.

'Well,' said Dan, as Max closed the boot, 'maybe we can meet in town some time.'

'Perhaps.'

They shook hands, and Max got into the car. Dan watched as he drove away. It was a start, at any rate.

*

It was almost midnight, and the large dinner party that Avril was attending was disintegrating – people were either leaving, or making their way into an adjoining room where music was playing and more drink being poured. She could either stay or go. She had just opted to do the latter when Alec Orr-Lowndes appeared out of nowhere and sat down in the empty chair next to her.

'Hi,' he said. 'I spotted you earlier on. Thought I'd come and have a chat.'

'Hi.' Avril often wondered how Alec managed to navigate his way indoors wearing those ridiculous dark-tinted glasses of his. They did give him an air of cool and mystery, but even so.

'Have you seen Philip since he got out of jail?' Alec tapped the ash from his cigarette into a dish of discarded dessert. It was such an Alec thing to do, thought Avril, and suddenly saw him as he would be in twenty years' time, still wheeling and dealing, always with an eye out for the next big thing, steadily enriching himself at the expense of others. He would be successful, of course. She'd heard he was currently the manager of two successful pop groups. The years would transform him from a skinny little queer in tight suits, skimming like a gadfly over the London scene, into a prosperous, middle-aged mogul of some kind, still flicking ash into half-finished puddings. It would be sensible to stay on his friendly side.

'Of course not. Why would I?' She felt an inevitable

pang when she thought of Philip. She had tried to hate him, and failed. She'd been too much in love with him. They had had such a good thing. The best she'd ever known. And that bitch had had to wreck it all.

'You know he and Laura have split up? Things went west a couple of weeks after he got out of jail.' Avril digested this, saying nothing. 'To be honest,' Alec went on, 'she wasn't good for him. Too flaky, too happy to let him do whatever he wanted. He needs someone to keep him in line, make sure his finger stays off the self-destruct button.'

'Someone like you?'

The sarcasm seemed to escape him. 'I was thinking more of you.' He paused. 'You were good for him. You made him his best self. It was a shame when Laura came on the scene. I think' – Alec fished out a Benson & Hedges and lit it from the end of his current one – 'that you should go and see him.'

'Are you joking?' After a pause she asked, 'How is he?'

Alec made a rocking motion with his hand. 'He's OK. He should be trying to get the gallery up and running again, but he needs someone to rev his engine a bit. Not that I don't try, but I think you might do better.'

'Why should I help him? He set himself up in rivalry to me, you know.'

'No, no. He doesn't see things that way. He wasn't thinking about you, or anyone else. Just about himself, and what he wanted to do. You rather inspired him.' He stood up. 'Anyway, I think he'd like to see you.'

'Then maybe that's an effort he should make himself.'

'Hm. Yes, that's possibly true. Anyway, I have to split. Somewhere else I need to be. I'll see you around.'

She watched Alec weave his way through the dining room stragglers, a word for everyone, a hand on a shoulder here and there. He did everything for a reason. Maybe he had said what he'd said tonight because Philip had asked him to. A little spark of hope kindled within her.

Dan, not having been at Mount Street for a while, rang Avril to tell her he would be coming round the following week.

'I told you – you can come and go as you please. You don't have to let me know every time.'

'Well, I thought I should, as I haven't been round lately. Anyway, I wanted to check that I could look at Sonia's correspondence.'

'Whatever isn't in those boxes will be in her desk. She kept everything. You're more than welcome to take a look.'

They said goodbye and hung up. Avril had been in an irritable mood since the evening she'd run into Alec. The news that Philip had broken up with Laura had thrown her. Did he want to see her, to try again? She thought of the damage he had done, the pain he had caused her, and admitted none of that mattered. She kept going over the conversation with Alec, looking for clues. Philip generally got Alec to do his donkey work for him; maybe brokering a reconciliation was part of that. 'I think he'd like to see you' – those had been Alec's words. That suggested Philip had said something to Alec. But if he wanted to see her, he should make the effort. It was his call to make. A week had passed since the dinner party, and now her nerves were constantly teetering on the edge of hope.

Dan spent the morning going through the boxes, sorting through correspondence from 1921, which was when Henry and Sonia had first met. Evidence began to emerge of an apparently scandalous row between Henry and another artist, Wyndham Lewis. Dan had never come across any mention of the incident – which seemed to involve Wyndham Lewis making a pass at Sonia, and had even come to blows – in any of the biographies and diaries of the period, and he was intrigued. This could be a nice little nugget for the book. But the jigsaw was incomplete, and he realised from the dates that letters from Sonia to Henry were missing. If they weren't in the boxes, perhaps they were in her desk.

He opened the desk drawers one by one, starting at the bottom. Each one was bulging with papers and letters. For some reason Sonia seemed not to have bothered cataloguing her own correspondence as she had Henry's, and Dan could tell the search was going to take a while.

An hour later, he still hadn't found what he was looking for. He'd also been distracted by discovering and re-reading his own letters to Sonia during the war years and beyond. More in despair than hope, he moved on to the final top drawer, and as he was sifting through its contents, a single piece of folded paper fell out from among the bundles of envelopes. Out of curiosity he opened and read it.

I, Sonia Elizabeth Haddon, of 85 Mount Street, London, declare this to be a first codicil to my will dated February 23rd 1938.

In addition to the legacies bequeathed in my said Will, I give the following items to Laura Fenton, who is presently under my care and protection, as tokens of my affection and regard: my Fabergé diamond bracelet and pendant, my two Vever brooches, my Buccellati gold necklace, and my Graff rose diamond necklace and earrings, all of which items are presently kept at Coutts Bank, Strand, London. I also wish her to have the portrait of a seated girl painted by my late husband, Henry Haddon, being a portrait of her mother.

In all other respects I confirm my said Will.

The codicil was signed by Sonia and witnessed by Sonia's sister Helen and one Muriel Cardew, and was dated July 29th 1953. He sat at the desk, digesting this revelation. Laura had always been hurt that Sonia had left her nothing, not even the smallest keepsake, yet this document told quite a different story. How had it been overlooked? Avril had administered her mother's estate, evidently unaware of its existence. Had Sonia done this because she had somehow guessed who Laura's father was? He struggled for a moment with feelings that told him this was none of his business. But it was his business, he realised. It had been since the day of Henry Haddon's death.

Avril came home from the gallery that evening to find Dan still in the flat, papers spread out on the table in the drawing room.

'You've evidently been working hard,' she remarked. 'I think we both deserve a drink. I've had an exhausting day. Sherry?'

'Just a small one, thanks.'

Avril poured two drinks and handed one to Dan, and sat down in an armchair. 'How's the biography coming along?'

Dan sat down opposite her. 'A bit of a jigsaw, but I'm getting there.' He hesitated. 'I found something today while I was going through your mother's letters. None of my business, obviously, but I thought you should see it.' He handed her the codicil.

Avril's soul froze as she unfolded it. Dear God, why had she not destroyed this thing years ago? A recollection of that day, the day before her mother's death, of hearing her aunt's voice in the hallway and then stuffing the document into a drawer, came back to her in a flash. How could she have been so stupid as to forget about it? That it should surface now, like this. She fought to calm herself. It didn't matter. It couldn't possibly matter. She set her drink on the coffee table, marshalling her thoughts, her eyes fastened on the document as if reading it carefully and for the first time. Her face gave nothing away.

'I had no idea about this.' Avril's glance rested on the codicil with an expression of regret. 'I'm afraid it's rather late in the day to revisit things. The estate was administered years ago.'

Dan hesitated. 'Well, yes, I appreciate that. I would have thought it makes a difference, though, knowing what Sonia's actual wishes were.'

'Not really. Otherwise she would have made sure this was left with her will, wouldn't she? Perhaps she had second thoughts.' She looked at him in apparent surprise. 'Why – were you thinking I should do something about this?'

He was a little taken aback. 'It's not for me to say.'

'I'm certainly not about to hand over my mother's jewels to Laura. I'm not sure my mother had any business trying to leave them outside the family, anyway. I'm afraid this means nothing. Neither legally, nor to me personally.'

The words came without difficulty. She had long ago persuaded herself that Laura had no entitlement to anything, regardless of what Sonia might have written, and especially not such precious personal items. It was simply a pity that Dan had found it, and that she herself had been so stupid as to leave it there, but since this wasn't his business he was hardly in a position to take it any further.

Dan realised that silence was no longer an option. 'Well, I have something to tell you that may make a difference. I think the reason your mother wanted Laura to have those things was because she had guessed that your father, Henry Haddon, was also Laura's father.' He paused. 'Your father was having an affair with Madeleine the summer she got pregnant. Laura is almost certainly your half-sister. Perhaps I should have spoken out long ago, but there were plenty of reasons why I didn't. Adding to Sonia's unhappiness was one of them. But I think in the end she worked it out for herself. And that's why she wrote this document. I'm sorry if it's a shock to you.'

Avril stared at him. The possibility had never occurred to her before, and she recoiled from it instinctively. The last thing in the world she wanted was for there to be any connection between herself and Laura – Laura, the interloper who had robbed her of attention and affection, and with whom she'd had to share things that by rights were hers alone. Her mind grew frantic, struggling to reject the idea. She mustn't let anything come of this. She forced herself to speak calmly.

'That's an absurd notion.'

'Is it?'

'Frankly, I think it's offensive.'

'Avril, I know it for a fact. I saw them together.' Should he remind her of what she'd seen as a child, but had clearly forgotten? It seemed unkind.

'I don't care what you think you know. I don't believe any of it. And I'm afraid this' – she folded the codicil and put it on the coffee table – 'doesn't change anything.'

She smiled, but the pretence at amicability between them was fading, and with Dan's next words it vanished completely.

'So you're just going to ignore it?'

Avril realised, too late, that this discussion was a mistake. She should simply have thanked him for finding the codicil, told him it would give her a lot to think about, and left it at that. She was furious at having to justify herself.

'The will was proved long ago. This is irrelevant. And I don't know why you care so much. I know you've always been fond of Laura—'

'We're seeing one another,' said Dan abruptly. 'I should have told you before. I had the feeling you might not be so keen on letting me write the biography if you knew.' He drew a deep breath. 'But it's best that things are out in the open. This resentment you have of her is unhealthy. I hoped that what I've just told you would make you feel differently towards her—'

'I've told you – I don't accept anything you've said. But I see now why you're so keen that I should. As for my feelings about her, I'll never forgive her for destroying my relationship with Philip.' Avril's temper spilled over. 'She's a slut, just like her mother. I would have thought you'd be more fastidious, Dan.'

Dan shook his head. 'You refuse to accept the truth when it's staring you in the face. Laura's your sister. I realise it's a shock, but I genuinely thought it would alter your feelings.'

'Really? You tell me what you think you know, and I'm supposed to accept it without question? You show me a piece of paper I've never seen before, and expect me to start giving my family's property to *her*? I don't even like her. I've never liked her. I'm behaving exactly as I'm entitled to. Your ridiculous theories don't change anything.' Dan picked up the codicil from the table, and she held out her hand. 'Give me that.'

'No. Laura has a right to see this, and to know what Sonia's wishes really were.'

Avril stood up, her eyes blazing with anger. 'You have incredible impertinence! This family's affairs are none of your business.'

'Laura is your family. And you should behave decently towards her.'

'What utter rubbish.' Avril's tone suddenly relaxed. 'Anyway, why should I care what you do? As I said, that document is irrelevant, it makes no difference to anything.'

'Laura always thought Sonia didn't care enough to leave her anything. At least she can see this and know that wasn't the case.'

Dan took his jacket from the back of the chair and left. His notes and papers still lay on the table where he had been working. Avril sat down, her heart thudding. That had been ghastly. But she must calm herself. The codicil was meaningless. Laura could read it and think what she liked, but she was entitled to precisely nothing. She buried her face in her hands. What if Laura really was her half-sister? How could Dan think that could possibly make things better? It would make everything ten times worse. But he was merely speculating. There was no proof. Nothing needed to be true if she didn't want it to be.

31

D AN REALISED HE had well and truly opened a can of worms. Avril knew now, so he was going to have to tell Laura. How she would react, he had no idea. Whichever way one looked at it, he could be accused of hiding from her – from everyone – a truth he should have revealed long ago. For years he'd said nothing, thinking it was for the best. How much good was it going to do anyone for it to be out in the open now? It evidently wasn't going to improve relations between Avril and Laura. But at least the codicil showed Sonia hadn't forgotten about Laura, and that would mean a lot to her.

The following evening Laura came to Dan's flat for supper. He waited till the meal was over, and took a glass of wine to the sofa while Laura fished through his record collection. She was in an upbeat mood. She'd finished six dresses over the weekend, and they were due to be delivered to Jill's boutique the next day.

'God, why don't you have anything decent?' she murmured, as she leafed through the albums.

'By which you mean that hideous pop you're so fond of. Forget about music and come over here. I need to talk to you.'

Laura went to join him on the sofa. She hoped this wasn't going to be about getting married. For some reason she couldn't quite bring herself to take that step, not yet. She'd even begun to think that maybe they could wait till after the baby was born. She had recently switched jobs, and at her new place she called herself 'Mrs' and wore a cheap ring, so that she wouldn't have to worry about what people said when her pregnancy became obvious. She hadn't told Dan. It was a silly little ruse, and she felt slightly ashamed of it.

She curled up next to him. 'Come on, then – what's it about?'

'It's about your mother.' He hesitated for a moment, then took the plunge. 'I happen to know that the year before you were born, she had an affair with Henry Haddon. I believe he's your father. In fact, I know he is.'

She drew away from him. 'What?'

'On the day he died, the day he had the heart attack in his studio, I came in and found him and your mother... Well, let's just say, in a compromising situation. I was pretty stunned, I can tell you. No one had had the least clue what was going on, except for me.' Laura stared at him, saying nothing, and he went on, 'When it turned out Madeleine was pregnant, she refused to say who the father was. Everyone assumed it was some young fellow who'd visited Woodbourne House that summer. I knew differently. A month or two after you were born, your mother and I had a conversation in which she effectively admitted to me that Henry Haddon was your father.'

There was a long silence, and then Laura said, 'You've known all this time?'

'If you're asking why I didn't say something before now…' he hesitated, 'at the time, it would have done no one any good to know. Sonia had just lost her husband. God knows how it would have affected her. After you were born, Madeleine intended to have you adopted. Not because she didn't love you – I'm sure she did, but it was even harder then that it is now for an unmarried mother, and she was only seventeen. And when Sonia offered to look after you, it seemed the ideal solution. I persuaded your mother to accept Sonia's offer. I said that that way, at least you would grow up where you really belonged.'

Laura absorbed this, then said, 'But if not then, why not later?'

'What, while you were growing up? Just think how that would have played out. Maybe I could have said something after Sonia died, but again – to what end?'

Her gaze wandered from his face, her expression stunned and lost. 'No, I understand that,' she said slowly. 'I'm not blaming you. It's just – why now? Why have you suddenly decided to tell me now?' Her eyes were filled with tears, and he understood what a huge emotional shock this all was.

'Because of this. I found it yesterday in Sonia's desk.' He took the codicil from his pocket and handed it to Laura. She read it, hunched over, her blonde hair around her face.

'Oh,' she murmured faintly. 'She left me jewellery. And a painting. Is it the one hanging in the drawing room in Mount Street? The girl in the yellow dress?' Dan nodded. 'I never knew it was of my mother. Avril didn't tell me.'

'It's too late to do anything. I've looked into it. Sonia didn't put it with her will, and this kind of thing hasn't any validity on its own. But it shows she didn't forget you. I think she knew you were Henry's daughter.'

Laura nodded, wiping away her tears. 'Perhaps,' she said slowly, 'if Avril knew about this – I mean, if I am who you say I am – she would at least give me the picture? I don't care about the other things. But I would like the painting of my mother.'

'Oh, Avril knows. After I found the codicil, I waited till she came home and showed it to her. I had to tell her about her father and Madeleine, of course. I said I thought Sonia had drawn it up because she had probably worked out that you and Avril were half-sisters. That wasn't something she wanted to hear.'

'No, she wouldn't.'

'I have to say I don't really understand that.'

Laura sat back on the sofa and closed her eyes. 'Oh, Dan, she's never liked me. All throughout our childhoods she saw me as some sort of interloper, taking things that belonged to her. The business with Philip must have felt like the same thing all over again.' She sighed, opening her eyes. 'I have to talk to her. I can't let things stay like this between us. If she's my sister, we have to try to find a better relationship.'

'You won't find her very receptive.'

'But you said you're certain.'

'I am. But she refuses to believe it. As for what's in that codicil, she made it pretty clear that she doesn't intend to give you anything, including the painting.'

'I'll go and see her.' She looked down at the paper in her hand. 'She should give me the picture of my mother. She must know she owes me that much.' She got up from the sofa. 'Dan, all this has been a shock. I have to go.'

'Stay here tonight.'

She shook her head. 'I just want to be on my own. I've got a lot to think about.' She held up the codicil. 'I want to hold on to this.' She bent and kissed him. 'I'll call you.'

*

When she got home Laura went into the living room without switching on the light, and sat in the darkness for a long time, thinking. Dan wouldn't have told her about Henry Haddon being her father unless he was entirely sure. Piecing the evidence together, it all made sense. No wonder her mother had left Woodbourne House. Had Sonia guessed the truth? Maybe, maybe not. She was sure Aunt Sonia would have shown her the same love and kindness, no matter what. She thought back to her childhood, recalling Avril's treatment of her, the constant reminders of her second-class status in the Haddon household. Then the bleak days after Sonia's death, when Avril had taken her out of school, away from her friends, turning her into a secretary, employing her in the gallery. It had been Avril's way of controlling her, a kind of subconscious revenge. And the painting of her mother. She remembered Avril bringing it home from the framers, hanging it in the drawing room in Mount Street, saying nothing. Of all the wrongs Avril had done her, she deserved the chance to put that one right.

The next day Laura went round to Mount Street after work on the off-chance that Avril would be in. She pressed the bell, and when she heard Avril's voice on the intercom, said, 'It's me, Laura.'

After a moment's silence the buzzer sounded. She

opened the front door and crossed the hallway. It was almost ten years since she'd left, and as she closed the expanding metal gate of the lift, all the associations of the past came flooding back, making her feel like a child again, threatening her confidence. But she reminded herself that the past no longer had a part to play, and that there were new truths now, truths that overrode everything.

Avril was waiting for her in the doorway of the flat.

'I thought it was only a matter of time,' she remarked, and led the way into the drawing room. She was wearing her customary gallery attire of white blouse and black slacks, expensive shoes and jewellery. Laura had come straight from work, and looked what she was – an underpaid secretary.

'I assume you're here because you've spoken to Dan,' said Avril.

'Yes.'

Avril gestured towards a chair, and they both sat down. Avril regarded Laura critically, noticing the cheap suit and shoes, the lack of make-up, the simple way she wore her hair. Quite a change from the glamorous fashion icon of a year ago. That was gratifying. But she could see, too, that Laura's looks were as luminous and lovely as ever, and that her expression was purposeful.

Laura came straight to the point. 'Avril, you and I have never exactly been close. But from what Dan has told me, we share more than either of us imagined. And that has to be important.'

'We don't share anything. You choose to believe his rubbish. I don't.'

'Dan knows what happened that summer. He even talked to my mother about it. He wouldn't have told either of us if he wasn't entirely certain.'

'You can believe what you like, but you have no proof. I'm sure you'd like to think you're a member of the Haddon family, but as far as I'm concerned, you're no one.'

'Why are you so determined not to believe it? Would it be so awful if I were your sister?'

After a moment's silence Avril said, 'Laura, I'm not entirely sure what it is you want from me.'

'Acceptance. Maybe this means we can start again.'

'After what you've done?' Avril stared at her contemptuously. 'Start again. You always were ridiculously sentimental. Which is probably why you want to believe whatever Dan says. Now, is that all you came for?' Laura opened her handbag and took out the codicil. 'Ah,' said Avril, 'I wondered when that would put in an appearance. I hope you realise it means precisely nothing.'

'Perhaps not legally, but the fact that she ever wrote it means everything to me.'

'You think I should feel some moral compunction to

honour it? I'm afraid things don't work that way.'

'All I want is the painting of my mother.'

'You can want all you like. I'm not going to give it to you.'

'Avril, all my life you've begrudged me things. Affection, education, a sense of security. You've always resented me. And now you're keeping from me something Sonia wanted me to have because it was of my mother, and she knew I had nothing, not even a photograph.'

'The fact that it's your mother is neither here nor there. My father painted it. I'm not about to hand it over to you.'

'Even though you know he's my father, too?'

'I know no such thing.'

'Well, that's something you're going to have to acknowledge sooner or later.' She paused. 'I feel sorry for you, Avril. You're a cold, heartless person.'

Avril's reply took her by surprise. 'No, Laura, I'm not cold. I'm simply not like you. I don't go around with my heart on my sleeve, expecting the world to adore me. But I truly loved Philip, and then you came waltzing along, in your silly, brainless way, and ruined it. You didn't really want him, and evidently he didn't want you much either. You destroyed the best thing in my life. You're the heartless one.'

Laura was momentarily lost for words. She felt a sudden rush of compunction, a childlike need to put things right. 'Avril, I didn't even know there was anything going on between you and Philip when I met him. If I had, I wouldn't have—' She stopped. 'Oh, this is pointless. It's done now. You're right. He never cared for me. But he cares about you. Probably not so much as he does about himself, but that's the man he is. Anyway, you can think what you like. You may hate me, but you're going to have to accept who I am eventually.'

She left without another word. Avril sat listening to the front door close. Nothing Laura had said – not about who she thought she was, or the picture, or anything – mattered except those words, 'he cares about you'. There was something almost unbearable in taking comfort from Laura, of all people. But she had to take it where she could find it, and keep hoping that Philip would get in touch. At least he and Laura were done with one another, that much was clear.

Laura told Dan what had happened. 'It's just as you said. She doesn't want to believe any of it.'

'Maybe you should just let it go.'

'No,' said Laura angrily. 'I want her to acknowledge who I am. I want her to recognise that she never had any right to look down on me, to treat me the way she did all my life. But how can I? Beyond what you know, I can't prove anything. She can go on denying me for ever, if she wants.'

Dan placed a mug of tea in front of her. 'There is one

person who could establish the truth. Your mother.'

'Well, yes. But she disappeared years ago. She may not even be alive.'

'I somehow doubt she's dead. She'd only be – what? – forty-four?'

'How would I begin to find her?' She sipped her tea, then after a moment said, 'You know, when I was modelling, when my face was on the cover of *Vogue*, I used to think, maybe she'll see my name and know it's me, and get in touch.' She gave a wan smile. 'I really got my hopes up.'

'I could have a shot at finding her. When she left Woodbourne House she went to work for a family in Yorkshire. One of Sonia's friends found her the job. She might be able to help. Damn – what was her name?' He frowned. 'I can see her now. Big woman, very hearty, always organising people. She had a daughter, Constance, who went on to become a doctor... No, it's no use. I'll never remember it.' He pondered. 'But I know where I might find it.'

'Where?'

'Among Sonia's correspondence. They must have written, and she never threw letters away. I'll know the name when I see it.'

'Well, Avril's not going to let you start poking about, is she? Not after what's happened.'

'I still have the keys to Mount Street. Perhaps one more visit is in order.'

32

D AN WENT ROUND to Avril's flat late the next
morning and let himself in, feeling distinctly
like a trespasser. He searched through the drawers of
Sonia's desk until he found correspondence from the
war years and, at last, a letter with the name he wanted.
Daphne Davenport. The letter heading had an address
and a telephone number, which Dan noted down. Not
only had she been Sonia's friend, she'd also been the
local billeting officer, and the letter concerned the two
evacuees who had been billeted at Woodbourne House,
Sidney and Colin Jennings. How things came around,
thought Dan, as he returned the letter to its drawer. He
left the keys on the hall table, and let himself out.

When he rang the Surrey telephone number, he
discovered that Daphne Davenport had been dead
for ten years, and no, the new occupant of her former
home couldn't help regarding the whereabouts of the

daughter. This was discouraging, but finding Constance turned out to be far easier than he had expected. He'd had visions of combing through the General Medical Register, but it occurred to him that he might as well try the London telephone directory first. He didn't hold out much hope – she had very probably married and changed her name. But there in the directory was a Wimpole Street listing for a Dr C. Davenport, and a surgery number. It could be her. He hoped to God it was. He dialled the number, and a receptionist answered. He asked if the practice belonged to a Dr Constance Davenport, and when he was told it did, he made an appointment. It would be amusing to see old Constance again. The last time had been during the war, when he and Constance and Meg had, for some reason, gone to the pictures together. She'd had a bit of a crush on him, as he recalled.

The Constance of his memories had been a pretty, plump girl, with large eyes. The well-upholstered, handsome woman behind the consulting desk held glimmers of her younger self. When she saw Dan her courteous professional expression changed to one of delighted recognition.

'Dan Ranscombe, isn't it? What a surprise!'

She rose and shook his hand. She was dressed in a dark suit, her dark hair tied back in a bun, and she had half-moon spectacles on a chain around her neck. He noticed she wore no wedding ring.

'I'm afraid I've come on false pretences,' said Dan, taking a seat. 'I'm not here as a patient, so I apologise for taking up your surgery time.'

'Don't be silly. I'm delighted to see you. How are you and Meg? I quite lost touch with her after the war.' Dan told her about Meg's death. 'Oh, how dreadful. I had no idea. I am so sorry. She was a good friend to me when I was in London and knew nobody.'

'I'll tell you why I'm here.' He explained his mission, how Laura wanted to trace her mother. 'I remember Sonia telling me that you found Madeleine a place with a family in Yorkshire. If you can give me their name and some more information, I thought that would be a good place to start.'

'Yes, I do remember that. The Witham family. They were neighbours of my aunt. I don't know their exact address, but they lived in the same road as my aunt, so I imagine you won't have much difficulty in finding them. If they're still there, of course. They were a young family, but it was a long time ago, wasn't it?' She produced her address book from a drawer, and gave Dan her aunt's address in Helmsley.

'Thanks,' said Dan. 'I don't know how far it's likely to take me, but it's the best lead I've got.'

'I'll give my aunt a call and let her know you're coming. Good luck. Let me know how you get on.'

*

Constance's aunt was a small, wiry woman in her early nineties, loquacious, and blessed with a very good memory. She welcomed Dan with afternoon tea and a lengthy account of all she knew of Madeleine's time as a nanny with the Withams, who, it turned out, had left Helmsley a few years after the war. Dan listened patiently, consuming two pieces of cake and two cups of tea, as she recounted significant events – an outbreak of chicken pox and whooping cough combined, the family's brief evacuation from their home following the dropping of a bomb, Madeleine's rescue of the youngest Witham from drowning in a nearby river, and similar domestic excitements – until he was at last able to interject a question.

'Do you know what happened to Madeleine after she left the family?'

'Oh, she married while she was still with them. The last year of the war, it was. A very nice young man from one of the county families, the Lockwoods. I don't think his parents were too taken with the match – she having no family to speak of, you know – but they married, anyway. Then he died just six months later. He was a fighter pilot, you see.'

'Might she have gone to live with the Lockwoods?'

'I couldn't say. I didn't know the family – they lived over in the West Riding. Some big house, but I don't know the name. Once she got married and left the

Withams, that was the last I heard of her.' She refilled his cup and proffered the cake plate. 'Some more parkin?'

'No, thank you.' He glanced at his watch. 'I'd like to try and find the Lockwoods' place, if I can, though I probably don't have enough time left today.'

'I know it was outside Pontefract, if that's any help. Though a lot of those big places went to rack and ruin after the war, didn't they? The families just couldn't keep them up.'

He put away his notebook and pen. 'Thank you for the tea, and for the delicious cake. And for your time.'

'Well,' she rose to see him to the door, 'I wish you good luck, Mr Ranscombe. And if you need a place to stay the night, I believe the beds at the Royal Oak are very comfortable.'

The following morning Dan drove to Pontefract and went to the public library, where he explained to the helpful librarian that he was trying to find the Lockwood family home. After consulting a number of books and records, the young man managed to identify a manor house, Oldcross Hall, which had been built by the Lockwoods and occupied by them for several generations.

'The Lockwoods may not live there now. So many of the big family houses hereabouts have been sold. But you might be lucky.'

'I might,' agreed Dan, though he doubted it. 'Thanks for your help.'

With an ordnance survey map spread out on the passenger seat, he set off through the countryside, along winding roads, until at last he found Oldcross Hall. It was a handsome old manor house, not as grand as he had imagined, built of grey Yorkshire stone and set at the top of a long driveway. A raw October wind whipped up a scattering of dead leaves as he rang the bell. Dogs began to bark deep in the house, and at length a woman came to the door, four red setters nosing around her. She was in her mid-forties, tall and ruddy-faced, with a look of the outdoors.

'Good morning,' said Dan. 'I wonder if you can help me. I'm looking for the Lockwood family.'

One of the setters reared up, barking, and she gripped its collar. 'I'm afraid the Lockwoods haven't lived here since fifty-seven. We bought the place from them. Old Mrs Lockwood went into a nursing home in Pontefract, but she died three years ago.'

Dan's heart dropped. This was surely the end of the trail. 'Ah. That's a pity. I'm trying to track down her daughter-in-law.'

The dogs began to rear and bark again, and the woman spent several seconds quietening them. Then she said casually, 'If you mean young Mrs Lockwood, she lives over in Little Mitton House, on the edge of the estate. Or what used to be the estate.'

'Madeleine Lockwood?'

'I believe that's her name. I don't know her terribly well.'

Despair shifted to elation. 'Can you give me directions?' asked Dan.

With the dogs surging around her, she told him which roads to take, and Dan set off.

Little Mitton House, which sat on the outskirts of a hamlet, was neat, old and modestly sized, surrounded by a pretty garden. As Dan drew up, a woman was coming down the road on the other side, wearing an overcoat and carrying a basket of groceries. She stopped at the gate of the house and turned to look at Dan as he got out of the car.

Dan could see that it was Madeleine as he walked towards her. The blonde hair was a little darker now, tied back in a loose ponytail, and the grave, pretty face that he remembered from years ago was thinner, but still lovely, with ghostly echoes of Laura's features. She looked younger than her forty-four years. She watched him as he approached. He stopped a few feet away from her.

'Dan Ranscombe,' she said in a murmur.

He smiled. 'How are you, Madeleine? It's been an awfully long time.'

'Why are you here?'

'I needed to find you.' She gazed at him with that fathomless look he remembered so well. 'May I come in?'

Without a word she unlatched the gate, and he followed her down the path and into the house. She led him into a low-beamed living room with a large stone fireplace, in which was set a gas fire. The furniture was well-worn, cosy, a bowl of roses from the garden sat on a polished dining table, and there were large rugs on the wooden floorboards. The house had a settled, comfortable feeling. She took off her coat, put her basket of groceries on the table and bent to light the gas fire.

'Please, have a seat,' she said to Dan.

He sat on a sofa next to the fire, glancing around. 'How long have you lived here?'

'Since the war.' Madeleine settled herself in an armchair opposite. 'The estate belonged to my husband's family. They gave me this house to live in after he died.'

'That was kind.'

'Yes. But it was largely to make sure they could see their grandson.' She nodded towards a photograph on the mantel of a tall, fair-haired young man. 'That's Charlie.'

'He looks like you.'

She smiled. 'He's at university in London, studying to become a doctor.'

There was a nervous silence, broken only by the ticking of a clock in the hallway and the rasp of the gas fire. 'Why did you need to find me?' asked Madeleine at last.

'Because of Laura.'

She nodded. 'I thought so.'

'Do you know anything about her?'

'Of course. I see magazines when I go to the hairdresser's. I only recognised her by her name, of course. I'm happy for her, I'm glad that she's found success. But when I left Woodbourne House, it was for good, you know. For her good, and mine. I can't see any point in bringing us together – if that's why you're here.'

To this he said nothing, and at last she asked, 'How is Mrs Haddon? And Avril?'

'Sonia died some years ago,' said Dan. Then he proceeded to tell her all that had happened following Sonia's death, about the relationship between Avril and Laura, and how things stood between them now. 'It was a shock for Laura, finding out who her father was. It made me think I should have said something sooner, but that would probably have created more problems than it solved. At the time, at least. The point is, after all that's happened between them, Laura simply wants Avril to recognise who she is, to accept her as her half-sister. Avril point-blank refuses to believe any of it. She doesn't remember anything about what she saw in the barn the day her father died.'

Madeleine said nothing. Dan wondered if she was remembering that day. She turned her gaze back to him. 'Can I offer you some tea?'

'That would be nice, thanks.'

They sat talking over the events of their respective lives for an hour or so. Eventually Madeleine said, 'Whatever it is you want me to do, I can't help you, you know. That part of my life – it's not something I ever want to go back to. I'm settled here. I have a life here, and friends. I have Charlie.'

'I wish you'd reconsider. If you spoke to Avril, she would have to accept the truth. It would help Laura.' Madeleine said nothing, and in a moment of sudden perspicacity Dan asked, 'What is it you're afraid of?'

She smiled. 'You still think you can read women well, don't you? I remember that summer house party – you had every girl eating out of your hand. What a charmer. You had a fine conceit on you.'

'I'm afraid I did. Don't most young men?'

'You had a higher opinion of yourself than most.' She was silent for a moment. 'But you're right – I suppose I am afraid. I'm afraid of Laura reproaching me, hating me for what I did. I can do without that.'

'I don't think she feels either of those things. She knows how young you were, how trapped you were by the situation. She's a very generous, compassionate girl. I don't think she blames you for anything.' He paused. 'Given what you said about me a few moments ago, I'm not sure how you'll take this, but Laura and I are... well, we're something of a couple.'

'I did wonder. The way you talk about her. You obviously care.'

'Anyway, I thought you should know. So, would you be prepared to meet her? Help her?'

She shook her head. 'I'd rather leave the past as it is.'

'Here's my address and phone number. In case you change your mind. It would mean the world to Laura.'

She took the piece of paper from him. 'I'll think about it.'

Ten minutes later Dan was back in his car, beginning the long drive south, feeling he had accomplished something.

String, thought Avril. *String. I must be mad.* She stared at the pieces of art littering the gallery, yet to be hung. Some of them were 3D, others were large creations stretched over brightly coloured canvases, and all of them were made entirely out of string held taut between points, straight lines blending into curves. What title could she give the exhibition? Not 'String', at any rate.

As though answering her thoughts, a voice behind her said, 'Tangents. Perhaps that's what you should call it.'

She turned and saw Philip standing there, smiling and assured, impeccably dressed as always. He certainly didn't look as though his spell in prison had done him any harm. She was breath-catchingly glad to see him, but she wasn't about to show it.

'I'm such a fan of conceptual art,' he went on. 'Very brave of you to show it. When do you open?'

'What's it to you?' she asked coldly. 'I honestly don't know what you think you're doing here.'

'Oh, Avril – be my friend. Forgive me.'

How was it, she wondered, that he could make the words sound touching and beseeching, and at the same time faintly mocking? He really was the limit. She folded her arms, trying to resist his smile and the look in his eyes. 'Tell me a single reason why I should.'

'Because it would be an absurd waste, otherwise. All I did in prison was think about you, and regret everything I did to hurt you. Truly.'

'I simply don't believe you.'

'It's true. Let me take you out to dinner and convince you.' He sensed her hesitation. 'Come on, what harm can it do? Didn't we always have fun? Let's go out and have fun.'

'Philip,' she said helplessly, 'you take so much for granted.'

'I won't ever do that again, I promise. I'll pick you up at seven.' As he turned to go, he added, 'Tangents, I think.'

She watched him stroll out of the gallery, glad in her heart, but fearful. She didn't think she could bear to be hurt so badly again.

When Dan got back to London that evening he went straight round to see Laura.

'I found her,' he said as he took off his coat. 'I found

Madeleine. She's living in Yorkshire. It took a couple of days to track her down.' Dan recounted the events of the past week, culminating in his visit to Little Mitton House, and the conversation with Madeleine. Laura absorbed it all.

'What's she like?'

'She hasn't changed much. Still beautiful, but she always had a sort of detached quality about her. She doesn't give much away.'

'You said she saw me in magazines. Why didn't she contact me?'

'When she left you with Sonia, she was doing what she thought was best for everyone. And she admitted that she's afraid that you might not forgive her.'

'Of course I do.'

'I told her that. She said she'd think about what I've asked her to do.' He paused. 'Oh – there's another thing. You have a half-brother. I suppose he must be about nineteen, twenty. Charlie.'

'Charlie. That's nice to know. Maybe I'll get to meet him.'

'Maybe you will. All we can do is wait and see.'

She brooded for a moment, and then her face brightened. 'Guess what happened while you were away?'

'Tell me.'

'Jill sold all of my dresses. I've actually made some money. She reckons she could have sold twice as many.'

He smiled at her enthusiasm. 'That's pretty marvellous.'

'I'm so excited that my designs are a success.'

'So you'd better get working on some more.'

'I already have. But I really need someone to make up the clothes for me. I can't produce enough sitting at my sewing machine. And I want this to be more than a hobby. Jill said that if we could find the capital we could start our own business. Think how great that would be.'

'You could try to get a bank loan.'

'I'm not sure a bank would lend me money on the back of selling half a dozen dresses. It's so frustrating, knowing I could do it, and not being able to find a way.'

Dan gazed at her. Her energy and ambition made him feel old, left behind, the way so much of the world of the young did. He didn't doubt for a moment she could make a success of running her own business. But would it be the right thing to do if she had a baby to look after? To his mind, a woman couldn't bring up a child and run a business. One or other would suffer. Somehow he had the feeling it wasn't something Laura wanted to hear.

At dinner that evening Avril was in no mood to let Philip assume he could be easily forgiven, and he had to employ all his charm to bring her round. She tried to tell herself that he couldn't just wipe out the pain he had caused her with a meal and a couple of glasses of champagne, when his affair with Laura was scarcely cold – but the fact was, he could. By the end of the meal he had effectively succeeded. Still, she needed him to acknowledge how badly he'd behaved.

'A part of me still hates you, you know. I don't think you have any idea how much you hurt me.'

'I am truly, truly sorry. I was a rat and a louse, and I can't simply blame the drugs. Though they didn't help.'

'I hope that's all over.'

'God, yes.'

'You need to keep people like Alec at arm's length.'

He nodded. 'I know. I'm going to be thirty soon. Time I grew up and out of all that.'

There was a long silence, then Avril said quietly, 'There's something I need to know. And you have to tell me the truth. Did you love Laura?'

'No.' He said it with such blunt conviction that she believed him. 'That whole thing was insane. You left me, and the next thing I knew she'd moved in. I didn't much want her there, but I was strung out half the time, things were a bit mad… It wasn't a good time.'

'Not so strung out you couldn't open your own gallery. I didn't entirely appreciate the competition.'

He shook his head. 'It was only while I was in prison that I managed to work that one out.' He spoke seriously. 'I think I did it as a way of connecting with you. It was my way of trying to get back part of what

I'd lost.' He met her gaze. 'I'd like to get the other part back, if I can. I was stupid to lose you. I didn't know how much you meant to me till you left me. We were good together. A good partnership. I think we should try that again.'

'You sound like you want to go into business with me.'

'Actually,' he smiled, 'that had crossed my mind. I was all right at certain aspects of the gallery thing, but you have better business acumen than I do. But no, that isn't exactly what I was talking about.' He paused. 'I was thinking of asking you to marry me.'

She stared at him wordlessly, assuming he must be joking.

'You were the best thing that ever happened to me,' he went on, 'and I was too stupid to recognise it. I don't want to lose you a second time. Seriously, what do you think?'

'Seriously?' She tried not to smile. 'I think it's time you got the bill.'

33

A WEEK LATER Dan had a call from Madeleine.
'I'm coming to London at the end of November
to visit Charlie. I'll be there for the weekend. I'd like to
meet Laura. I'm prepared to talk to Avril, too, if you
want.'

'What changed your mind?'

'I've thought about everything you told me. About
the way Avril has behaved. It's unfair to Laura. My son
always knew who his father was. I'm sorry it's taken so
long for Laura to know who she is. But that was just
the way it was at the time. It couldn't be helped. But it
can be now.'

'Yes. A lot can be put right. I'm glad you see that.'

They made an arrangement to meet on the Saturday
of Madeleine's visit at Dan's flat, and as soon as the
conversation had ended, Dan telephoned Laura at work
to tell her.

'I didn't expect it to happen,' she said.

'You sound a bit doubtful.'

'No, no, I'm happy.' She hesitated. 'But I'm a bit frightened, too, if I'm honest.'

'What's to be frightened of?'

'I don't know...' She couldn't articulate her deepest fear, that her mother had left her because she didn't like her then, and might not like her now. She was afraid of having nothing to say, nothing to offer, nothing to make her mother glad at being reunited. 'But it's good news. Thank you, Dan.'

The call ended and she put the phone down. Soon Avril was going to have to accept her as her half-sister, whether she liked it or not.

Dan was slowly rebuilding his relationship with Max. Since Harry's death they'd met up a few times, each encounter easier than the last. A couple of weeks after his trip to Yorkshire he rang Max and they arranged to meet for a drink in a pub near Max's chambers. At six o'clock it was filled with lawyers and journalists, smoking and drinking. Dan found a table while Max went to the bar.

'I haven't been in this place since my Fleet Street days,' said Dan, when Max returned with the drinks. 'Cheers.' He took a sip of his beer. 'How's your practice coming along?'

'Work's pretty steady. The bigger cases can be quite a grind, but I shouldn't complain.'

'And Morven and the baby?'

'Both well, thanks. Teddy's a marvel.' Max took a photograph from his wallet and showed Dan, adding apologetically, 'I'm sorry. We should have had you round before now to meet her, but life's rather chaotic. We need a larger place, but it's not easy to go house-hunting with the baby in tow.' He returned the photo to his wallet. 'Do you get down to Chalcombe much these days?'

'I'm ashamed to say I've only been once since that time you came down. I had this idea that I'd live there a lot of the time and get work done, but the fact is, I'm too much of a city-dweller. I get restless in the countryside after a day or two. It's all very pretty, but it just... well, it just sits there. I need people and bustle. I'm honestly not sure what I'm going to do with the place. I feel I owe it to Harry to keep it on, but the house needs to be lived in.'

There was a silence, and then Max said, 'I don't suppose you would consider selling it to me?' Dan looked at him in surprise, and Max went on hastily, 'Morven has her heart set on being out of town, but she hasn't seen anything she likes enough. The fact is, she compares every house we look at to Chalcombe. She fell in love with it when we visited, when Harry was alive.

The place means a lot to me, too – you know, because Mummy helped Harry to make it what it is. I like the idea of living where she once was. Where she was happy.'

It could be, Dan realised, the perfect solution. He had been plagued with a sense of guilt about the place, but if Max and Morven took it over he would retain a connection. It should be a family home. Harry would have approved.

'Are you sure? It's a bit of a commute.'

'No more so than most chaps do each day. We can keep my flat in town as a bolt-hole.'

Dan weighed it up for a moment, then said, 'Very well. If you really want to buy it, I'm happy to sell. I'll have to have a word with an estate agent, find out what the place is worth.'

Max's face cleared, and Dan realised this was something he'd been thinking about for a while. 'I'm good for the money, at least you know that.'

Dan grinned. 'Yes, at least I know that.'

They discussed it for a while, then Dan went to buy more drinks. So far he had said nothing to Max about Laura. It was about time he did. People were going to have to know sooner or later, and Max should be among the first.

When he returned to the table he said, 'By the way, there's something you should know.' He paused and lit a cigarette. 'I got in touch with Laura when I came back to London, and we've been seeing quite a bit of one another. In fact, we're getting married.'

'Good God!' exclaimed Max. Then he added, 'No, I'm sorry, that sounded terribly rude. It's just... well, it's something of a surprise.'

'She's having a baby.' Dan gazed at the glowing tip of his cigarette. 'Not exactly planned, but we're very happy about it, of course.'

'Of course.' Max was amazed to think that Dan had ended up in the same boat that he'd found himself in. It probably happened to countless couples every day. Marriages built on necessity. Like himself and Morven, he doubted whether Dan and Laura would have been getting married had it not been for the baby. Dan must be over fifty, and Laura had always struck him as a girl who'd never quite worked out what she wanted from life. 'Well, that's – that's marvellous. Congratulations. Does Avril know?'

'Not yet. Relations between Avril and Laura have never been good, as you know. And something happened lately which hasn't exactly improved them.' He'd told Max about the baby. He might as well tell him everything else.

Fifteen minutes later Dan finished telling Max about Madeleine and Henry Haddon, and his discovery of the codicil and the subsequent conversation with Avril. 'Maybe it would have been a lot better for everyone if I'd said something years ago.'

'I can see why you didn't. If Sonia had known, she'd never have taken Laura in.'

'I wonder. I'm pretty sure she wrote that codicil because at some point along the way she guessed the truth. It's just a pity it didn't come to light with the will. I've even asked myself if Avril had anything to do with that. But that doesn't make sense, because if she knew about it and wanted to scupper it, she'd simply have destroyed it.'

'I don't know about that. Not easy to make a document like that disappear when there are witnesses who know it exists.'

'I hadn't thought of that.'

'It's an interesting area of law. A codicil isn't valid unless it's found with the will, so it's a pity this one went astray. But, you know...' Max paused.

'What?'

'Well, let's just say for the sake of argument that Avril did know about it. She was the executor of her mother's will. It would be fraud on her part not to reveal its existence. And, as Lord Denning has observed, fraud unravels everything.'

'By which you mean...?'

'It's not my area, but I imagine you would have some kind of remedy. And the person who committed the fraud would probably end up in jail. You'd have to prove it, though. And the standard of proof would be extremely high. Who were the witnesses, out of interest?'

'Sonia's sister Helen, and some other woman, probably Sonia's nurse.'

'My grandmother was a witness? That's interesting. She must have gone back to France before the will was proved. Probably had no idea that the codicil never surfaced.' He thought for a moment. 'I could speak to her. Tell her about the codicil, and ask her.'

'Ask her what?'

'Whether Avril knew about it. Of course, she might not know.'

'But she might.'

'It's always worth asking.'

When Max got home he told Morven about Chalcombe.

Her eyes lit up. 'Are you sure he means it?'

'As sure as I can be. From what he said, it'll be a weight off his shoulders. He reckons we should be able to complete the conveyance pretty quickly and be in by Christmas.'

'How perfect! We'll have enough rooms to have people down to stay, and we can employ a nanny, and I'll be able to start acting again...' She talked happily on, constructing her new world. Max listened, reflecting. His marriage wasn't such a bad thing, in many ways. He had an adored and adorable daughter, Morven seemed happy enough – though lately she had begun to fret about getting back to acting, fulfilling what she saw as her unrealised potential – they had more than enough money, and he liked his work. He had a hazy sense of building up a fortress: his marriage, Morven and the baby were one wall; his legal practice and life in chambers formed another; the security of his inheritance a third; and now Chalcombe would consolidate it all. He could close himself in, and never turn an inward eye on the dark and troubling aspects of his soul.

He was roused from his thoughts by Morven sliding her arms around his neck and kissing him. It was a long, lingering kiss, and he knew where it was leading. Whenever she was ecstatically happy, or lacking some outlet for her emotional energy, she came to him for sex. He had schooled himself to oblige without any difficulty. He had discovered that arousal didn't depend on desire, and that familiar stimuli did the work. Morven never seemed to notice or care that it was always she who initiated their lovemaking. He suspected she enjoyed her role as a passionate, impulsive creature, the one she wanted to project to the world.

She suddenly got to her feet. 'Oh, I forgot. This came today.' She fetched a card from the mantelpiece and handed it to him. 'Avril's getting married.'

Max inspected the invitation. 'Hmm. Very jolly. January the twenty-sixth at St James's Church, Piccadilly, afterwards at the Carteret Gallery, South Audley Street. They make a pair, at any rate.'

She plucked the card from his hand and put it aside, and her mouth sought his again.

'Let's go to bed,' she murmured, 'before Teddy wakes up from her nap.'

'I met Max for a drink this evening,' Dan said to Laura. 'I told him about us.'

Laura got up from the table and began clearing away plates. She was happy for Dan that he'd repaired his relationship with Max, but for her he was just a reminder of that terrible time when Ellis had walked out of her life. He'd been entirely to blame for that.

'I'm not sure he needed to know.'

Dan followed her to the kitchen and took the dishes from her hands. He kissed her, running a hand over her stomach. 'We can't keep all of this under wraps indefinitely. We have to start making changes. Don't you think it's time you gave up the place in Beaufort Street and moved in here?'

'Yes, I suppose so.'

'And we should get married before the baby becomes too obvious. When does the doctor say it's due?'

'I haven't actually been to the doctor. I keep meaning to.'

'Laura, I don't know much about these things, but surely you need check-ups, and so on? You should make an appointment.'

She nodded. 'I'll do it first thing tomorrow.'

*

The doctor's voice was critical. 'You should have been to see me before now.' He pressed on Laura's stomach. She felt uncomfortable, and vaguely humiliated by his manner and questions. 'How far along did you say you thought you were?'

'Three months.'

His fingers pressed further down. 'When was your last period?'

'I'm not terribly sure. Sometime in July, I think.'

'I can't believe you women are so scatterbrained.' He shook his head. 'You're at least four months pregnant.'

Laura stared at him. 'No, that can't be right.'

He raised his eyebrows. 'My dear young lady, I'm not generally wrong about these things. I can tell by how full the uterus is. Now, pop your clothes back on and come round when you're ready. I'll make you an appointment to register yourself at the local hospital.' He disappeared behind the curtain.

Laura sat up, straightening her clothes, trying to make sense of this. She and Dan had first slept together in mid-August. It was November now. The timing didn't tally. With a cold clutch of fear she suddenly remembered the last time she and Philip had had sex, the night before she'd walked out on him. It had been the culmination of yet another row, their way of resolving it, the habitual outlet for their exhausted passions. She hadn't meant for it to happen, but it had.

She sat down opposite the doctor, who was writing, and said tentatively, 'I don't suppose...' He glanced up with a frown. 'I mean, there's definitely no chance that it could be three months?'

He gave her an exasperated look. 'I can assure you your pregnancy is more advanced than that. I'd estimate your due date as sometime next April.' He handed her a piece of paper. 'Take that to reception and they'll make the hospital appointment for you. Please tell the next patient to come in.'

Laura left the surgery and walked to the bus stop in a daze. She hadn't even considered the possibility that Philip could be the father. But the doctor seemed utterly certain, and the more she weighed the dates, the more probable it seemed that it wasn't Dan's baby. No use in pretending. And yet she could so easily do that. Put Philip out of the picture and carry on as though that had never happened. After all, if she hadn't gone to the doctor, if she'd just carried on for the next however many months until the baby was born, would she herself have ever known? But she did know. The question was whether she could in all conscience deceive Dan. She fought down her anxiety, trying to look at it coolly, rationally. He'd brought up Max, another man's child. He'd love this baby and be a wonderful father to it. Perhaps that was all that mattered.

The bus came and she got on. She stared unseeingly out of the window. If she told him, one of two things would happen. Either it would put an end to things between them, and she would be left on her own. Or he would accept the situation, and they would carry on – but in a relationship that would be fraught with emotional difficulties. If they were to get married, and have a life together, wouldn't it be better for him never to know? Wouldn't that be easier? But there was the child to think about. The dishonesty would go further than Dan. Her son or daughter would grow up never knowing who they really were. She knew all too well the pain and confusion that could result from that kind of deception. Which brought her to the question of whether Philip should be told. No, she didn't want him to have any part in this. Her thoughts zigzagged desperately back and forth, and by the time she got off the bus and went to work, she was no closer to deciding what to do.

34

THE MEETING BETWEEN Laura and Madeleine had been arranged for eleven, and Laura got to Dan's flat at quarter to. She sat down to wait. Dan was talking, but she barely responded to anything he said. She had spent a fortnight trying to work out whether or not to tell him about the baby, her conscience pulling one way, then the other. She tried to close down the conflict in her mind. Today she had to deal with meeting her mother.

The minutes ticked by. At five past eleven she got up, pacing the room and said to Dan, 'She's not coming.'

'She'll come,' replied Dan. 'Try and calm your nerves.'

A few minutes later the doorbell buzzed, and Dan went to answer it. Laura sank into a chair, then stood up an instant later as a blonde woman and a tall, fair-haired young man came into the room. Laura took them in in one glance. The woman was dressed in a dark red suit with a thin fur collar, her hair swept behind her ears and falling to her shoulders. The only jewellery she wore was a wedding ring and simple gold earrings. The young man had a handsome, narrow face, and was wearing elephant-cord jeans and a polo-neck sweater beneath a duffel jacket, and his hair was long, curling to the collar of his jacket.

The woman smiled tentatively, and Laura smiled back, recognising elements of herself, the shape of her face, the mouth. It was an odd moment.

'Hello, Laura,' said Madeleine, and put out her hand.

Laura put out her own, and for some reason, as their hands touched, tears came to her eyes. She hated that about herself, the way she cried so easily.

'Sorry,' she murmured, and wiped her eyes.

The young man smiled at her and said, 'Hello... sister.'

'This is Charlie,' said Madeleine. 'Your half-brother. He knows all about you.'

'That's not strictly true,' said Charlie. 'I only found out about you a week ago.' He smiled and Laura was grateful to him, for the fact of him. It meant something to have a brother, far more than she had imagined.

'I'll make us all some coffee,' said Dan.

Laura had expected the meeting to be strained and difficult, but there was no tension. It was like encountering two pleasant strangers with whom one had a lot in common. There were no apologies, no questions asked or reasons given. Maybe, thought

Laura, that would come later. They talked about the here and now, the stuff of their lives. They talked about Sonia, too, but apart from that the only concession made to the past was when Madeleine said to Laura, 'I wish I'd found you sooner. But here we are.'

'Yes,' said Laura. 'Here we are.' She gazed at her mother, wondering if she would ever truly get to know her.

They talked eventually about Avril. 'I'm happy to see her and explain things to her,' said Madeleine, 'if it'll help.'

'She has a gallery in Bloomsbury,' said Laura. 'We could go and see her there. I'd rather do that than go to Mount Street.'

'No time like the present,' said Madeleine briskly. 'Let's go and find a taxi.'

'I'll come with you part of the way,' said Charlie.

They left Dan at the flat and caught a cab, dropping Charlie off en route. The first thing Laura noticed when they arrived at the gallery was the 'To Let' sign on the window. Inside, workmen were moving about, hammering at partitions and taking down lights. She opened the door to the familiar tinkle of the bell, and they walked to the office at the end.

'Wait here a moment,' said Laura. She knocked on the door and opened it.

Avril, alone in the office sorting through papers, glanced up. She gave Laura a cold look. 'What do you want? I'm rather busy.'

'I've brought someone to see you.' Laura opened the door wider.

Avril frowned for a second at the unknown woman standing in the doorway, then recognition dawned. 'Madeleine.'

'Hello, Avril.'

Avril was lost for words. The sight of Madeleine's face brought childhood memories rushing back. Kneeling on the nursery floor, playing with the dolls' house while the summer rain pattered on the window. Sitting on Madeleine's lap, listening to fairy stories and fingering the long, flaxen plait of Madeleine's hair. Running giggling through the orchard past the barn where her father had his studio, Madeleine calling after her.

Laura's voice broke the spell.

'The last time we met,' said Laura, 'you told me I couldn't prove I was Henry Haddon's daughter. Well, I've brought you proof.'

Still Avril said nothing.

'I'm sorry to have to come here and rake over the past,' said Madeleine, 'but I gather some things need to be set right. May I sit down?'

Avril, recovering herself, nodded.

Madeleine regarded Avril. 'The last time I saw you, you were just a little girl. How—'

'Please,' Avril interrupted her. 'No sentimental pleasantries. I'd rather you just said what you've come to say.'

There was an awkward silence.

'Very well. When I left Laura with your mother twenty-six years ago, it was because I thought it was best for both of us. I didn't think I'd ever see her again. But, as you see, she found me. I'm glad she did. She's asked me to come here and tell you that everything Dan Ranscombe has told you is true. Henry Haddon is her father, as well as yours. I was a virgin when I came to Woodbourne House that summer. Your father made love to me in his studio. You probably don't remember, but you saw us. You hid in the hayloft.'

Images rose in Avril's mind, dark, disturbing memories washing on top of the others. Looking down and seeing Madeleine and her father against the wall of the barn. Dan coming in, and the ladder falling away. The sound of her own crying, the feeling of the straw sharp against her knees. Her father shouting.

'So you see,' went on Madeleine, 'there's no doubt that Laura is your half-sister.'

Avril said nothing for a long moment. The shock of recollection died away. She looked at Laura. 'Even if you are—'

Laura let out a long breath. 'So you accept it?'

'It makes no difference to the way I feel about you.'

'Oh, Avril, it wasn't always so bad between us, was it? Why do you dislike me so much?'

'Why? Well, I disliked you when we were children because you took things that should have been mine,

447

things you didn't deserve. Everyone doted on you. I was shut out. You robbed me of my mother's time and affection—'

'No,' said Madeleine sharply. 'That's not true. Your mother loved you, she tried her best, but you were a difficult child, Avril. You pushed people away. You were hard to love. Don't blame Laura for that.'

Avril flinched visibly, and her expression darkened. 'Then last year you tried to take Philip from me—'

Laura shook her head. 'You know it wasn't like that.'

'It doesn't matter. Whatever you were trying to do, you failed. He and I are getting married in January.'

Avril's small gleam of triumph as she uttered these words was lost on Laura. She was too shocked by the revelation that Avril was marrying the man whose child she was carrying. The terrible irony of it. She fought to make sense of her feelings. For a moment everything seemed quite pitiful, beyond comedy or tragedy. If Avril only knew.

She searched for something sensible to say. 'Congratulations.' She paused. 'Is that why you're closing the gallery?'

'Yes. I'm moving the stock to the Carteret Gallery in South Audley Street. Philip and I are going into partnership. So, now we've established how I feel about you, and why those feelings are never going to change, I don't think there's anything more to be said.' She got to her feet. 'As you see, I'm very busy.' She put out a hand. 'Madeleine, I doubt if I'll be seeing you again.'

'Avril.' Madeleine shook her hand.

They left the gallery. On the pavement outside Laura glanced around, suddenly recalling Ellis pacing up and down here every lunchtime, shoulders hunched in his raincoat, waiting for her. The pain never dulled.

'Well,' she said with a sigh, 'that was something of an anticlimax.'

'She accepts who you are,' said Madeleine. 'Isn't that what you wanted?'

'I'm not sure what I wanted.' Laura reflected for a moment. 'Actually, what I really want is for her to stop being so unhappy about everything. To stop resenting me.'

'You can't wipe out the feelings of a lifetime. I'm sorry for her, in a way.'

'Why?'

'I felt sorry for her when she was a child. She was always such a sullen, solitary little thing, hungry for love and attention. Especially her father's. No wonder finding out that you're her half-sister doesn't give her a warm glow. Freud would have a lot to say about it.' A taxi swung through Alfred Place with its light on, and Madeleine raised a hand. 'Let's go back to the hotel and have something to eat.'

They talked intimately over lunch. Madeleine tried to explain to Laura the events of twenty-seven years ago.

'I was so young when you were born. Just seventeen. I can't begin to tell you how alone and frightened I felt. Ashamed. And horribly guilty. It was just the most awful thing to be an unmarried mother in those days.'

'It still is.'

'It's hard, but I like to think the world is growing kinder.'

Laura laid her napkin on the table, folding it into nervous creases. 'If you were young and unmarried now, and you were pregnant, what would you do?'

Madeleine mused. 'Well, it would depend on the circumstances. Marry the father, possibly, if I loved him. That was hardly an option in my case. If you don't have a supportive family, I suppose the alternatives aren't easy. Backstreet abortion. One of those homes for unmarried mothers, then adoption. I know some girls nowadays choose to keep their babies. I think they're very brave.' She met Laura's gaze. 'I'd like to think that if I had my chance again, I would try to keep my baby and be a good mother. But that's easy to say when you're not seventeen.'

Laura wanted so badly to talk about her situation, and here was someone who wouldn't judge her. Or would she? She hesitated for a moment, then said quietly, 'I'm pregnant. I thought it was Dan's. But it turns out that it can't be.' She let it all spill out, the story of Philip, the drugs bust, his spell in prison, and the stormy fortnight after his release. 'We were never right for one another. But when he got sent to prison things became weird, and I had this romantic notion that when he got out we'd be better and stronger. It was an insane idea. Things went straight back to the way they'd been. Two weeks later I left. But not before I'd slept with him a couple of times. So…'

'So it's his baby. And I take it Dan doesn't know?'

'I only found out a fortnight ago. That was the first time I'd been to the doctor's.' Laura gazed down at her plate. 'You probably think that I deserve the mess I've made for being promiscuous.'

'Laura, I don't think anything of the kind. Things are more confusing for girls nowadays. No one's sure what the rules are.' She put her hand over Laura's. 'And that's not the point.'

'Do you want to know the worst part? If it wasn't so awful it would be laughable. Philip – the baby's father – he's the man Avril's going to marry.'

Madeleine's eyes widened. 'Oh dear.'

'So what do I do? I don't ever, ever intend to tell Philip. By the time I left him we could hardly bear to be in the same room with one another. If I say nothing to Dan, he'll be none the wiser – but that's not fair to him, is it? I know it isn't. I can't believe I'm even thinking of not telling him. But the alternative is I'm left on my own. I'm not sure I can face that.'

There was a silence, then Madeleine said at last, 'I don't think I have an answer. Except that the truth has a way of catching up with all of us, eventually. You know, if you tell Dan, he might decide to support you anyway.'

'Or he might end things. I wouldn't blame him.'

'If what you're really frightened of is being on your own, don't be. I'm here, you know. This is my grandchild we're talking about.'

Laura gave her a sad smile. 'Thank you.'

'You should only marry Dan if you really want to. It's one thing to put your faith in other people. The most important thing is to have faith in yourself.'

Laura left Madeleine and went back to Beaufort Street. The phone rang almost as soon as she'd taken her coat off.

'How did it go?' asked Dan.

Laura told him about the meeting with Avril. 'She accepts who I am – she has no choice. But it doesn't seem to have changed things between us.'

'Maybe it was unrealistic to expect it to change anything.' He paused. 'You sound a bit down. Do you want to come round this evening? We could see a film, have dinner.'

'No thanks. Things have been a bit strange lately. To be honest, I need some time to myself, if you don't mind.'

'I understand.'

'I'll call you in a few days.' And then she would have to tell him. She couldn't go on avoiding the truth.

She had intended to spend the afternoon working on some new designs, but the weight of her worries made it difficult to concentrate. After a couple of unproductive hours she put on her coat and went for a walk. A raw November wind sent drifts of golden leaves from the plane trees gusting along the pavement. Dusk was beginning to fall, but the King's Road was still bursting with life, lights spilling from boutiques, young people milling around in search of the latest thing, the next piece of fun. To Laura everyone looked beautiful, their clothes extraordinary. It felt like the sexiest and grooviest place on earth. For a moment every anxiety seemed to float away, and she found herself smiling. She wandered past the boutiques, weighing up everything she saw, turning over her own ideas in her mind, alive with the sense of possibility. If only she could get some money together. This was her world, she knew it and understood it. She was gazing at Mary Quant dresses in the window of Bazaar when someone spoke her name, and she turned to see Sid. He was wearing a military greatcoat over jeans and black boots, and his hair was even longer than when she'd last seen him, almost to his shoulders. She felt strangely grateful to see him.

'Wotcher,' he said. 'Doing a bit of shopping?'

'Don't have the money these days, Sid.'

'No? You're still looking good.'

'Thanks. You're not looking so bad yourself.'

He turned up the collar of his coat. 'Shops'll be closing in a few minutes. Fancy a drink?'

They went to a pub in a side street, and over gin and tonics Sid told her everything he had been up to. His success seemed undiminished, and he was busy and in constant demand.

'What about you? You working?' he asked.

'The modelling agencies won't touch me, not since the publicity from the drugs bust. I'm doing office work. But I've been working on the side, designing dresses. I even sold some in a friend's shop.'

'Far out. You were always good at making your own clobber.' Sid finished his drink. 'Listen, what you up to for the rest of the evening?'

'Not much. Why?'

'I was thinking we could have a bite to eat, then maybe go to a club – for old times' sake.' He held up his hands. 'No funny business. Just pals having a night out.'

Laura didn't hesitate. The alternative was an evening alone in front of the television.

They went to the Chelsea Kitchen for dinner, then wandered along to the Six Bells pub. The club upstairs was packed and smoky. Sid found a table, shouldered his way to the bar and came back with a couple of ciders. As she sat surrounded by music and people, Laura was filled with a sense of elation. For a few hours she could feel free, and forget about everything. Being out with Sid felt like the old days. She thought sentimentally about their beginnings together, the things they had shared. The scruffy flat, the lack of money and food, the endless bickering, the good times and the fun – and the simple belief that they would make it. It hadn't been a perfect relationship, and it had certainly never been love, more a partnership of convenience, each seeking what the other had to offer, but sure enough, in the end they had made it. Though she had lost it and Sid still had it. Her heart tightened at the thought of what was gone, and what lay ahead.

From the stage came a ripple of piano notes and the brushing hiss of a snare drum, signalling the start of the next set. A jazz quintet launched into a gutsy number, then slowed into a rendition of 'Autumn Leaves'. The music wove wistfully beneath the hum and chatter of the club. As the first notes of the tenor sax slid in, Laura glanced towards the stage – and the world seemed to stop. She gazed at the tall profile in the dim light, the long fingers stroking the saxophone keys. Her heart began to thud. The voices of the people around her seemed to recede on the waves of her heartbeat. She held her breath as she watched and listened. When the sweet, troubled notes drifted to a close, a ripple of applause broke out. Ellis glanced up with a half-smile, then stepped back into the shadows.

Laura sat motionless. The quintet played five more numbers, and every time Ellis stepped a little way out of the shadows to play, she was flooded with a sense of connection. How near he was. Only a few yards of grubby floor and a scattering of chairs and tables separated them. All she had to do was stand up and go to him. But she stayed where she was, trying to untangle her thoughts. Had he been here in London all this time? In the years since the terrible night of his leaving, had he been just a bus or a taxi ride away, perhaps round the corner, eating in some restaurant or playing in some club she happened not to go to? The thought was almost unbearable.

The final number drew to a close and the quintet prepared to take a break. She watched him step down from the side of the stage, his big, rangy figure heading towards the bar. A moment later the crowd sealed him off. But she could go to him if she wanted to. She imagined getting to her feet and pushing her way through the people, and his face as he turned and saw her. It would be heartbreakingly easy. And heartbreakingly pointless. They were a million miles away from the possibility of ever being together again. She was pregnant, mired in the consequences of her own choices and bad luck, with nothing to offer.

Sid's voice broke into her thoughts, and she turned to him. 'What?'

'I said, are you OK?'

'I'm fine.'

'You don't look fine. You want another drink?'

She shook her head. 'Actually, Sid, I'm not feeling so good. I think I'm going to head home. I've had a long day.'

'I'll walk you back.'

She shook her head. 'It's only round the corner. You stay here and enjoy yourself.' She kissed his cheek. 'It was good to see you.'

She got up and left. It felt unreal to be walking away from the only man she'd ever really loved, the man she'd never thought she would find again, when every instinct was pulling her in the opposite direction.

35

THE DOORBELL RANG a little after ten the next morning. Laura padded to the door in her dressing gown to answer it, and found Sid standing there.

'Morning. Thought I'd come and see how you are.' He held up a paper bag. 'Brought some croissants.'

'That's nice. Come in.'

She took the croissants through to the kitchen, put them into the oven to warm, and filled the kettle. Sid followed her through and sat down at the kitchen table.

'How you feeling?' he asked. 'I was a bit worried about you last night.'

'I'm fine. I've just got a lot on my mind.' She made a pot of coffee and brought it to the table with the croissants and a pot of jam.

'So what was all that last night, then?'

'How do you mean?'

'You were fine at dinner, then when we got to the Six Bells and that jazz band came on you had a face on you like a smacked arse.'

'So poetic.' She poured the coffee. 'Maybe I just don't like jazz.'

Sid helped himself to a croissant and a liberal spoonful of jam. 'Was he that bloke you used to live with?' Laura put down the coffee pot and stared at him. 'When I first got to know you when you were working in the record shop, you used to bang on about him non-stop, the lost love of your life. The tears I used to mop up.'

It was true. She remembered going out drinking with Sid and baring her soul, telling him all about Ellis, probably boring him senseless. The wounds had been very fresh then, and Sid had been a perfect shoulder to cry on.

'Ellis Candy's not a name you forget in a hurry,' Sid went on. 'You sat there last night like a rabbit in the headlights while they were playing, and then you shot off. I had a look at the names on the line-up after, and there he was. I'm right, aren't I?'

'You're right.'

'Well then, what are you waiting for?' She looked at him blankly. 'Go and see him. I could see from your face last night that you've still got a thing about him.'

'It was years ago, Sid. We're not the same people. Anyhow, there's no point.'

'You don't know that.'

'I do.' How could she tell him that she was pregnant, her life was messed up, and that in just a few months she might very possibly be on her own with no money and a baby to look after? So she told him the least of it. 'I'm with someone.'

'Oh.' Sid shrugged. 'Fair enough.'

'But thank you for your concern. You're very sweet.'

Sid helped himself to another croissant. 'I was thinking,' he said, 'about your dressmaking business. I could chip in a bit, if you wanted a financial leg-up. And I could maybe help organise a fashion show, try to get your clothes in the magazines.'

Few things now seemed more remote than that possibility. The little flame kindled yesterday on the King's Road had sputtered out. But she gave his arm a squeeze. 'Sid, that's very kind. Thank you.'

'What friends are for. Pass us the jam.'

On Sunday evening Max rang Dan.

'I called my grandmother in France. I asked her if she remembered signing a codicil to Sonia's will. She said yes, quite distinctly. She remembered it was just the day before Sonia died.'

'That's right,' said Dan. 'The twenty-ninth of July. The date didn't register with me till the other day. It was when I flew back from Korea. I've been asking myself how it could possibly have gone astray in such a short space of time.'

'But here's the thing. Avril knew about it. Grandma said she was there when Sonia gave the codicil to her.'

'She hid it?' said Dan. 'That doesn't make sense. Why didn't she just destroy it?'

'As I said, that's a dangerous thing to do when there are witnesses who know about it. Safer just to put it away somewhere and wait. The chances of anyone else knowing about it were very slim. She was the sole executor, and she knew Sonia's nurse would be off the scene after Sonia died, and that Helen would be safely back in France when the will was proved.'

'What do we do?'

'I suppose that's up to Laura. She's the one who's lost out. Grandma still has all her marbles, and if it came to it, she would testify as to what she knows. We have the codicil. Bang – case over. She didn't ask me why I was asking her all those questions. But she must be wondering.'

'No, a court case is the last thing anyone wants. The last thing Laura would want.'

'But she's been defrauded. What about the jewellery Sonia left her?'

'She's already told me the only thing she wants is the painting of her mother. But you're right, she's owed more than that.' Dan deliberated for a moment. 'The idea of taking this to law, dragging your grandmother over here... we can avoid that. We have enough evidence, surely, to put pressure on Avril privately.'

'You mean, speak to her?'

'Just a quiet word. Maybe that will do the trick. I think we should go and see her together.'

Dan rang Avril the following day and suggested they should meet.

'I have something to discuss with you,' he told her.

'You can say anything you have to over the phone.'

'I think this is better done in person. You may not much like what I have to tell you.'

His tone made her uneasy. 'You can at least tell me what it's about.'

'It's to do with Laura.'

'I've said all I want to on that score.'

'When would be convenient?'

She hesitated. Laura was like a canker she wanted cut out of her life. Best to get whatever it was dealt with, finished. 'I can spare you twenty minutes tomorrow after the gallery closes.'

'I'll be there at half five.'

Avril was alone in the gallery at the end of the day. The assistants had gone home, and she was putting the finishing touches to what would be her first joint exhibition with Philip, due to open in two days' time. When the bell rang she went to the door and was surprised to find Max standing there with Dan.

'A delegation?'

'Just a little legal back-up,' replied Dan.

The words gave her a faint chill. She let them in, then locked the door and led the way to Philip's office. The room was redolent of Philip's eclectic taste, the walls painted white, the ceiling purple, with a papier-mâché model of James Dean propped in one corner. In the middle of the room stood a chrome and glass table surrounded by four red fibreglass chairs.

'I hope this isn't going to take long,' said Avril, taking a seat. Dan and Max sat opposite her on the other side of the table.

'I hope not, too,' said Dan. 'It's about the codicil that turned up among Sonia's letters.'

'I told you – that was as much a surprise to me as to you. And if you've come here to harp on about the injustice done to Laura—'

Max interrupted her. 'I spoke to my grandmother two nights ago. I asked her about it. She remembers you were there when she witnessed it. She also remembers Sonia giving it to you.'

Avril's heart went cold. There was a silence, and then she said, 'Max, I don't really see what business this is of yours. Anyway, that's simply not true. Helen's memory is at fault. But then, she's getting on a bit.'

'Her memory is sharp as a tack,' replied Max. 'She may be over seventy, but she's still perfectly capable of coming over here and giving evidence in court.'

Avril maintained her composure. 'Don't be so ridiculous. A piece of paper turns up after all this time, and you really think you can come here and threaten me about it?'

Dan was grudgingly impressed by Avril's determination to brazen it out. 'It's your word against hers. You were Sonia's executor, and it makes no sense for her not to tell you about it. If Helen can testify that she saw Sonia give it to you, and a jury believes her, you'd be found guilty of fraud.'

'And that carries a prison sentence,' added Max.

Avril stared from one to the other. She felt her heart beating hard. It was only Helen's word against hers. Helen was old, she might make a feeble witness. Her mind froze. What in God's name was she thinking? She couldn't possibly let this go to court. That gamble could prove fatal. She could lose everything, including Philip. Whatever his flaws, he was generous to a fault, and he despised selfishness in others; people who behaved dishonourably were beneath his contempt. She could never begin to explain to him how Laura was like poison in her life, why the idea of her having her mother's things was too much to bear. He would never understand. Nobody would ever understand. Giving in was detestable, but the situation had her trapped; the best she could do was to emerge from it with her dignity intact. It was only a painting, after all, and instinct told her that there was a deal to be done for the rest. For Dan and Max to take the matter to law involved a high degree of risk on their side, too.

She was silent for a moment, and then said coolly, 'It so happens that I've lately been giving the matter a lot of thought. And I had already decided to honour my mother's wishes by giving Laura the painting, and whatever the jewellery is worth. So you could have spared yourself this visit, and the intimidation. Of course, I'm not legally obliged to do any of this, but it's in my nature to be generous.'

Nicely done, thought Dan. No admission of wrong-doing, and complete saving of face. He exchanged a glance with Max, then replied, 'Well, that's good to hear. It saves everyone a great deal of trouble. I think I can safely say on Laura's behalf that she's grateful for your magnanimous gesture. Between us we can arrange for an independent valuation of the jewellery.' He had already calculated that their worth would provide Laura with more than enough to make her clothing project a realistic venture. 'And you can transfer the painting as soon as you like. Perhaps it would be nice if you were to write to Laura and tell her what you're doing.'

He didn't intend to tell Laura what Avril had done, or about this evening's meeting. Better that she should think Avril was doing this of her own volition.

'I'd already intended to.' She got to her feet. 'I'm sorry your visit was so unnecessary.'

They left the gallery, and Avril locked the door behind them.

465

'You have to hand it to her,' said Max, as they stood on the pavement.

'Indeed you do,' agreed Dan. 'Let's go and find a drink. I need one.'

Philip wasn't expecting to see Avril that evening. He was waiting for Alec, who had promised to call round at half seven with some 'merchandise'. Although Philip had promised Avril he was finished with drugs, and with Alec, the fact was that both were indispensable to his life. He had persuaded himself that if he were discreet, no harm would come of it and she need never find out. So when he heard her key in the lock at half six, he was mildly perturbed.

'Hello,' he said, 'I thought you were spending the evening packing up?'

'The removal people do all that. I only have a few things left to attend to.' She kissed him. 'I just wanted to see you.'

'Sweet,' he murmured, returning her kiss.

She pressed her face against his chest and held him. 'I need to feel loved.'

'You are, my angel.' He glanced surreptitiously at his watch. 'Do you want a drink?'

'Please. A nice stiff one.'

He mixed two generous gin and tonics and they sat together on the sofa, talking about business. Avril wanted to clear her mind of Max and Dan's visit.

'I'm going to have to sue Robert Fraser for the money he owes me on that Warhol picture,' remarked Philip. 'Two bounced cheques and a lot of promises. I absolutely can't stand that way of doing business. I certainly won't be doing any more deals with him.'

'I thought you adored Robert?'

'I adore a lot of people, but when they try to cheat me out of money, I draw the line. I simply cannot bear people who cheat others. It's the lowest form of behaviour.'

She flinched inwardly. 'I don't think he means to. You know Bob – he's always strapped for cash. Not a natural businessman.'

'Maybe. But I don't like having to threaten to sue people. They should behave decently in the first place.'

His words struck too close to home. She swallowed the remains of her drink. 'I should be going.'

'Why don't you come back later and I'll cook us dinner?' suggested Philip. He was already wondering what gear Alec would turn up with.

'That's a lovely idea,' said Avril, and kissed him goodbye.

When she got back to Mount Street she took the painting of Madeleine from the wall, found packing material and brown paper and wrapped it up. Tomorrow she would have it sent to Laura. Then it would be out of her life once and for all, and Laura with it. She would have to pay her a fair sum for the jewellery, too, but it was only money; she and Philip had more than enough between them. Philip – he was what mattered most, and if by doing this she could avoid threats of a scandal and a court case, the money would be more than worth it. She consoled herself with the thought that if she had put the codicil with the will in the first place, Laura would have inherited Sonia's jewellery, which would have been far less bearable than giving her money now. So in one way she was coming out of this on top.

She went to Sonia's desk and took out pen and paper and wrote a brief letter to Laura. It sickened her to have to write it, but she managed to make it sound as though what she was doing was out of the goodness of her own heart. She put on her coat and left the flat, and posted the letter in the pillar box at the end of the street before catching a taxi to Philip's.

Three hours later she and Philip were lying in bed, Philip drowsing, Avril with her head propped on one hand, fingering a lock of his hair and studying his features in repose. She leaned in and sniffed his hair.

'Have you been smoking grass?' she asked.

'Just a little toke. You know, to stave off boredom.'

'Philip,' she sighed, 'you know you really shouldn't. Not after everything that's happened.'

'It's only a bit of grass.' He thought of the heroin that he'd bought from Alec a few hours earlier. Knowing it was sitting there in a drawer in his dressing room gave him a secret thrill of excitement. This time he wasn't going to let things get out of hand. Just a little now and again. It wouldn't rule his life, the way it had before.

'So long as you're not buying from that creep Alec.' Avril lay back against the pillow.

'As if I would.' He pulled her close and she nestled against him.

'Tell me you love me,' she murmured. 'I need to hear it.'

He smiled, his eyes still closed. 'What a needy thing you are these days. Of course I love you. We're getting married.' After a while he said, 'You know, we haven't talked about having children.'

She hadn't expected this. 'No, we haven't,' she said cautiously. She'd never imagined herself as a mother. But if it was what Philip wanted, then she wouldn't argue.

'I like babies,' Philip went on. 'Having one might help me stay steady. I'm sure as a parent I'd be an improvement on my own father. Couldn't be worse, at any rate.' He opened his eyes to look at Avril. 'What do you think? Shall we get working on that?'

36

ON WEDNESDAY DAN drove to Chalcombe. Max was due to join him the next day, and on Thursday morning Dan began making an inventory of the house contents. He started at the top of the house and worked his way down. It was a laborious task; Harry had accumulated a fair amount over the years. The last room he inspected was the cloakroom in the hall. It contained hats and mackintoshes and a muddle of old galoshes and wellingtons, and in the corner stood a wicker hamper and Hamlet's old dog basket. The sight of them brought back memories of the picnic, Max and Laura lugging the hamper through the woods, Hamlet scampering behind them. The swing, Laura screaming with laughter. Max coming along the path, his eleven-year-old face tear-stained and bleak with fury. Meg lying deathly pale and motionless by the water's edge, the dark blood on the stones, the hum of the insects in the grass.

He slipped into a reverie, one familiar from the dark weeks after Meg's death, in which he went back in time to undo the events of that day. Any little twist of fate could have stopped it all from happening. If only Avril hadn't gone for a walk with Max and Laura. If only it had rained that morning and there had been no picnic at all. If only... It was a long time since he'd tormented himself with such thoughts, and it took an effort of will to bring his mind back to the here and now. The same fate that had ended his happiness with Meg had brought him to his present situation. He had a new future to face. But if it hadn't been for Laura's pregnancy, would they even be contemplating getting married? Each of them was subject to forces tugging them in different directions. She was young, she belonged to a world he didn't really comprehend, and she had ambitions that didn't seem compatible with his ideas of what it meant to be a wife and mother. As for himself, he knew in his restless heart that without ties he would be thinking of travelling again, letting the journalism take him where it led. At his time of life it was going to be hard to settle down to being a father. But things were as they were, and they could only try to be happy.

A car horn sounded. He went outside and saw Max getting out of his car. He shook off his thoughts and went to greet him.

Together they made a tour of the house.

'I've done the inventory,' said Dan. 'All you have to do is decide what pieces of furniture you want to keep. You're welcome to whatever you like. Your mother chose most of it, and it suits the house. Though Morven may have other ideas. You don't want to live in a mausoleum.'

'She'll be happy to keep everything as it is for the moment,' said Max. 'No doubt she'll make her own changes in time.'

They went from room to room, labelling various items for removal, and when they were finished Max helped Dan load a number of books and paintings into his car. Dan locked up and dropped the keys into Max's palm. 'You might as well have them now. I won't be coming back.'

Max closed his fingers on the keys and looked around. In the chill of autumn the garden looked bleak and overgrown, the lawn ragged and carpeted with dead leaves from the mulberry trees, but he would make sure that six months from now it would be as beautiful as the summer when he'd first come here with his mother. His last summer with her. Dan's last summer with her, too. As a boy, he'd been fiercely possessive of the loss, feeling it was his alone. He knew better now.

*

Laura had never felt more confused and emotionally adrift in her life. She thought constantly about Ellis. He was no longer just a memory. He was playing in a club round the corner, just a few hundred yards from her. Yet how far away. The distance created by the years, and the past few months in particular, was unbridgeable now. If only she'd walked into that club six months ago and seen him playing, how different things might have been. They might be together now. It tore at her heart to think of it. She struggled through the routine of work in a numbed state of mind, trying to solve the problem of her future, defeated by the inertia that seemed to have settled on her soul.

When she came home from work on Wednesday she found a letter in Avril's handwriting among the evening post. Without bothering to take off her coat, she sank into a chair to read it. The contents astonished her. She couldn't imagine why Avril had had such a change of heart. *I'm having the jewellery valued, and will let you know its exact worth in due course.* It would be worth a great deal, that much Laura knew. And the picture would be hers, too. The tone of the letter wasn't exactly warm, but it could only mean that Avril cared more than she'd thought. Laura was filled with a faint sense of guilt, and even though she knew it was absurd, she couldn't help it. She was carrying Philip's child. It was as though, yet again, she was taking something away from Avril. Ridiculous, she thought. No one would ever know, least of all Avril.

She folded up the letter. It was just as well Avril wasn't actually giving her Sonia's jewellery – if she had, she wouldn't have been able to bring herself to sell it. As it was, the money would be of far more use. It might even be enough to provide sufficient capital for her to start her business. She felt a momentary flicker of excitement, but it died in an instant. How could she run a business and bring up a child at the same time? She simply wasn't brave or capable enough. There had been a time, when she'd been with Ellis, when she'd had more belief in herself. But that time was gone. She almost wished now she hadn't gone to the Six Bells and seen him. It made the pain fresh, the recollection of their time together too vivid. She closed her eyes, remembering the shabby attic room in Luscombe Street, sweltering in summer, freezing in winter, and the sagging bed that had been their haven and retreat. She could almost hear his feet on the stair, the sound of him whistling as he shaved, imagine again his big arms grabbing her from behind, his laughter as he pressed his lips to her skin. With every memory she could feel herself edging closer and closer to the temptation – just one meeting, one brief hello. It would be worth everything simply to look at him again, hear his voice, see his smile. There might be no future for them, but it could do no harm. She pictured herself years from now, looking back and asking herself why she hadn't gone to see him one last time. She couldn't let the chance slip away.

It was after nine when she walked up the scruffy stairs to the club above the pub. The place was packed and smoky. A blare of jazz spilled from the stage, but she couldn't see Ellis. Her plan had been to sit and have a Coke and watch him play for a while, settle her nerves and work out what to say to him. Probably not much more than hello, goodbye, a little bit of how-have-you-been and what-are-you-up-to in between, but better than nothing. She couldn't see a table anywhere. Maybe he wouldn't be on till late, and she'd have to stand for ages, on her own. She didn't want to do that. She tried to calm her jumping thoughts. This was no good. She'd come here to see him. If he was backstage, this was her best opportunity to speak to him, before he started playing. Her imagination leapt ahead. They would talk, and afterwards he would play while she sat listening, the way she used to in the Three Jays, and he would look up and catch her eye, and make some music just for her.

No, it couldn't be like that ever again.

The music came to an end. Trembling with nerves, Laura made her way through the crowded room to the edge of the stage. The band were coming off for a break, and she touched the arm of one of the musicians.

'Excuse me, is Ellis Candy playing tonight?'

'Not sure. Hold on.' He put his head round the side of the stage. 'Here, Wally, can you help this young lady? Wants to know if the Shade Quintet are on tonight.'

A middle-aged, avuncular-looking man in a bow tie appeared, shrugging on his jacket. 'Afraid not.'

Laura's heart plunged. 'Will they be on tomorrow?'

The man shook his head. 'Far as I know they're finished here. I think they've gone back home. They were on a three month tour, something like that. Here, Al,' he accosted another passing musician, 'Ellis Candy and his friends still in London?'

Al shook his head. 'Saturday was their last gig. Then they were going back to the States.'

Fingers of ice seemed to creep around her heart. The night she'd seen him had been her one and only chance. And now it would never come again. He was already thousands of miles away, and she had let the moment, the one moment when she could have been with him again for just a little time, slip through her fingers.

'Thank you,' she said, and edged back through the milling people to the exit. She went slowly downstairs, out of the smoky warmth and into the cold night air, stepping aside as a group of people crowded up the stairs, talking and laughing. She walked along the street, past the shuttered shops, past strolling couples. She turned the corner into Beaufort Street, but when she reached her flat she couldn't face the thought of its empty silence. She carried on walking until she reached the Embankment, and the glimmering lights of Battersea Bridge. She crossed the road and leaned on the stone wall.

The dream she had nursed all week was gone, just like that, blown away. Life lay before her, stark and real as the chilly pavement on which she stood. No use pretending she had lost Ellis again. He had never been hers to find. The future seemed to close around her. She looked up at the bridge. People drowned themselves, they threw themselves off walls and bridges to put an end to their misery, letting the river close over them. How cold it must feel. She tried to imagine wanting that kind of oblivion. She stared down into the black water lapping against the stone piers and wasn't remotely tempted.

At that realisation something close to hope lifted her heart. She imagined walking the length of the river till morning, watching the grey light pearl the water and the winter sky whiten into day. There might even be sunshine. Another day, another chance. She thought about Dan, and wondered why she had ever been afraid. She would tell him the truth about the baby. She would tell him, too, that she wasn't going to marry him. The memories of Ellis, the feelings that had taken her to the club tonight in search of him, had reminded her what real love was. She would live her own life, and work as hard as she could, look after her child, and if another chance ever came to find Ellis, she would take it. Take it or make it. Nothing ended here. She suddenly recalled what he'd said to her that day in the café, after she'd left Mount Street to be with him. *Baby, what happens now is up to you.* She remembered the look in his eyes and the strength she'd felt in her own heart when he said it.

She pulled her coat tighter around her, and turned and headed home.

About the author

Caro Fraser is the author of *The Summer House Party* and of the bestselling *Caper Court* novels, based on her own experiences as a lawyer. She is the daughter of George MacDonald Fraser, author of the bestselling *Flashman* novels, and lives in London.